Stepping close to the car he peered in the rear window. What he saw not only took him completely by surprise but caused him to back away from the window in amazement. Moving back to the window, he looked inside again hoping that what he had previously seen was nothing more than his imagination. It wasn't his imagination, it was real! *A baby wrapped in an old blanket laying on the backseat.* Checking the front and backseats there was no one else in the car. Next, he checked the parking lot to see if anyone was close by—no one!

Looking back in the window it appeared the baby was sleeping. Then, he had a horrible thought. *What if the baby is dead?* He had heard the news on numerous occasions where people had left a child in a car while they were shopping and the child had died from lack of air or heat exhaustion. Thank God it wasn't that hot out. He tried the door but it was locked. The front passenger door was missing its handle so he couldn't open that door either. He tried both doors on the opposite side. Same thing—locked! Looking around the parking lot once again he wasn't quite sure what he should do. This was one of those things you heard about, but never experienced. But, *this was real!* It was actually happening right before his eyes. He had to do something—but what?

Running around to the side the baby was on, he tried to calm himself as he thought, *Calm down...use your head...do the right thing...call the police. No! That might be too late. Check and see if the baby is alive first, then call the police.* He shoved the car, but the baby remained perfectly still. Shoving the car more violently he spoke to himself, "Please let the baby be alive."

.

SHADOWS OF DEATH

MARLENE MITCHELL
GARY YEAGLE

Davis Studio Publishing
Louisville, Kentucky

SHADOWS OF DEATH: THE SMOKY MOUNTAINS MURDERS

A Davis Studio Publication
P.O. Box 4714
Louisville, KY 40204

Printed in the United States of America.

ISBN: 978-1505866797

First edition: June 2013
Second edition: October 2013
Third edition: January 2015

CHAPTER ONE

HE HEARD VOICES; VOICES COMING FROM BELOW AND above him. Voices interrupted by the clapping sound of helicopter blades as the noisy machines zigzagged back and forth across the canyon ridge. Trying to focus his eyes, he stared straight ahead not sure where he was. His mind was full of cobwebs; he was confused. He scanned his surroundings and discovered that he was trapped in a web of brownish-green vines. The stinging pain in his right shoulder reminded him of the last gunshot wound he had taken, but he remembered little about the fall. His mind was starting to clear as he closely examined the vines. He was tangled in a cluster of gnarled branches and thick stems woven around a large tree limb growing out of the rock cliff. Realizing his fall had been broken by the dense web of greenery, he looked at the river below. Through the branches he could occasionally see the men who were searching for him.

Russell rubbed his eyes and wiped away the drops of warm blood streaming down his face. Reaching up, his fingers ran across the deep gash in his forehead. Once again, he looked through the branches and saw a group of five men walking up the river bank. One of the men yelled to the group, "We found his bloody boot!"

Another yelled, "We found his shattered rifle on a rock near the water."

As the men grouped together, Russell wondered why he wasn't dead. He had been shot three times, had a serious wound on his forehead and figured he probably suffered a number of broken bones. The fall alone should have killed him, but the thick vegetation on the cliff wall had prevented him from falling to the bottom. The forest he loved so much had saved him from certain death. In an attempt to calm himself, he took a deep, long breath. If he was going to die, it would be on his own terms.

His left arm was wrapped tightly in the tangle of vines, but he pulled his right arm free. Two of the fingers on his right hand were swollen and he found it difficult to bend them. His right foot was planted solidly onto the main branch of the tree and his left foot held in place by the ledge of rock. Russell realized he was hidden high above those who were looking for him. He wondered how long he could remain where he was. He was safe for now, but at any moment he could be discovered.

The blinding lights from one of the helicopters circling overhead swept back and forth across the side of the steep ridge, each time creeping closer. On the opposite side of the canyon, the sun was just beginning to dip below the tree line. *Soon, it will be dark,* he thought. *If I can free myself from the vines and I'm not careful, I could drop the rest of the way down to the river. If the fall doesn't kill me I could be shot to death on the river bank, or worse, put in a cage like the bear I rescued.*

He laid his head against the tree and closed his eyes for a few seconds. If he was to survive he was going to have to regain some of his strength. He was thirsty and weak from the loss of blood. Taking deep breaths, he tried to clear his head. To get out of the situation he found himself in, he couldn't panic.

His body was shaking as he slowly turned and faced the rock wall. Removing his knife from his belt, he cut a long strip of cloth from the bottom of his shirt. With unsteady hands he slowly raised his knee and tied the cloth around his bleeding lower leg. He cut another piece and wrapped it around his throbbing head.

A helicopter passed directly overhead. He remained perfectly still as he heard the crackle of a speaker and then the amplified voice of the pilot, "We're heading back to base to fill up. Be back in a few!" With that, all three copters swung northeast, the sound of their blades slowly fading. The men down below gathered in a circle next to a huge rock as one of the voices echoed up the cliff wall: "We've searched every inch of the immediate area with no luck. We need to split into two groups and search further up and downstream. It'll be too dark soon to get much more done tonight. We can bring in the dogs tomorrow."

Good! Russell thought. *That'll give me time. Which way should I go? Up or down? If I go down to the river bank my scent will be on the ground. Tomorrow morning, when they bring in the dogs they'll pick up my trail. They could track me down. In a few minutes it'll be dark. I'll climb as far across the rock face as I can, then I'll make my way to the top.*

Just as the moon was beginning to shed its pale light across the canyon, Russell carefully stepped sideways, holding onto the face of the ridge. It was easy at first, the cliff wall provided a number of limbs, stems and vines which offered him foot and handholds, but the further he crept along the rocky edifice, the less overgrowth there was. His progress was slow. He thought carefully about each and every move he made, loose rocks at times crumbling beneath the weight of his body. Stopping every few minutes, he rested.

After an hour of laborious climbing, he needed a longer break. His fingers were bleeding from holding onto the sharp, jagged rocks and his knees were rubbed raw from leaning inward and banging against the cliff. As he ran his tongue over his lips he tasted the clotted blood that had formed around his mouth. Despite his numerous injuries, he felt no pain. His will to live had taken over any sensations he was feeling.

Once again on the move, he wondered how long it would be before he reached a place of safety. Reaching out for yet another vine for support, he realized he had come to a section of the cliff that was minus vegetation. Now he had to start the difficult climb up the cliff wall.

He reached up and located a protruding rock. Wrapping his bloody fingers around the rock, he painfully hoisted himself upwards, placing his foot on another rock. On and on the process went: hand then foot, hand then foot. The effort it took to drag his body up the side of the cliff caused his body to shake uncontrollably. The sweat mixed with his blood was impairing his vision. He had to constantly wipe his eyes. The agony of pulling his heavy body up a few inches at a time caused him to bite into his lip, the blood running down the side of his mouth.

When he thought he could go no further, his right hand touched something soft: either dead leaves or grass. With every ounce of strength he could muster, he pulled himself upward, his feet slipping from below him sending a shower of loose rocks and dirt back down the cliff wall. He pulled himself over the top of the precipice and heaved his body up onto the flat surface as he let out a low groan of pain. He quietly lay on his back and tried to regain a normal pattern of breathing. Russell listened for the voices, but the only sounds he could hear were the night sounds of the forest:

the hoot of a distant horned owl, birds settling in the tree tops, the buzzing of insects and the flapping of bat wings.

The moonlight revealed the thicket of the forest just ten feet in front of him. He began to slowly roll over, again and again until he was up against the base of a tree. Painfully, he crawled into the safety of the tree line. Twenty feet into the covering of the forest he was prevented from going further by a moss covered log. Exhausted, he knew his journey had come to an end. He edged himself as close to the log as possible and tried to cover up with dead leaves and moss. Now that he had met his goal of reaching the top of the precipice his thoughts returned to the excruciating pain that wracked his body. He could feel his life slipping away. He relaxed and closed his eyes. It was okay. He would die in peace right here in the forest, amongst the trees and his friends, the animals.

Just as the sun was breaking over the ridge, Dwayne Stroud leaned out the window of the pickup truck and shouted at his brother. "Push...dammit...push! Put yer ass into it!"

"Screw you," Arliss yelled back. "When I git back in the truck I'm gonna push yer head in!" Leaning forward, he dug his boots into the soft mud and let out a grunt as he pushed against the dented tailgate of the truck. A volley of tiny rocks and watery mud shot out from beneath the well-worn tires as the wheels gained traction and the truck began to move.

"Son of a bitch!" hollered Arliss as the filthy spray hit him square in the face and ran down the front of his shirt. Backing up, he spit on the ground, wiping the muddy water from his eyes. He walked around to the passenger side of the beat up truck and yanked the door open. He slammed his fist on the dashboard and pointed at his older brother. "I tol' ya not to git too close ta the edge of the road...didn't I? If ya weren't so damn fat and lazy we could a walked up here and I wouldn't be covered in mud!"

Dwayne clenched his jaw and tried his best to keep from laughing at his brother. "Aw, go on Arliss. You know how heavy them traps are. I sure as hell ain't gonna cart 'em back down the mountain. Quit yer bitchin.' Now, here's what we're gonna do. We're gonna git them traps as fast as we can and then git the hell out of here. This place is gonna be crawlin' with the law in another hour or so."

"Ya see, that's what I mean about you, Dwayne. You and yer harebrained ideas. Ya drag me over here last night, make me stay in some flea bag motel, muck around settin' them traps and now I'm supposed ta be real giddy when the game warden puts a load of buckshot in my ass or them lawmen shootin' us thinkin' we're the killer they's lookin' fer."

"Don't see no gun pressed against the side of yer head," said Dwayne. "Ya was as eager ta git up here as me when ya found out about all the fox and coon in this here part of the state."

Letting the truck roll to a stop in a small gully, Dwayne lifted his hefty body out of the truck and stuck a wad of chewing tobacco in the side of his mouth. With the chaw next to his cheek, he ordered, "Okay, let's go!" Dwayne slowly made his way across the patch of rocks separating the ridge from the trees as he looked for the markers they had hammered into the ground. At the first marker, he placed a heavy stick into the empty trap and stood back as the clawed, jagged teeth slammed shut with an ugly thud. He called out to Arliss, "This one's empty. Ya got anythin'?"

"Nope, not a damn thing! I tol' ya this mornin' when we was eatin' breakfast at that hash house that all them helicopters and men in the area yesterday would scare off any critter within ten miles of the river. Remember what that waitress said? They's lookin' fer some man who kilt a bunch of folks."

Steadily, they worked their way along the ridge, collecting the traps. Finally, back at the truck they tossed the empty traps into the bed, making sure they were all accounted for. Dwayne stopped and looked back into the trees a few feet away. "Ya hear that?"

Arliss, counting the traps answered, "Hear what?"

"Sounds like somebody moanin.'"

"Yer nuts. C'mon let's git out of here."

Dwayne held up his hand for silence. "There it is again!" Picking up a fair sized rock, he walked to the tree line and entered the forest. He stopped and listened intently until he heard the strange sound again. Cautiously, he approached a downed tree and peered over the back side. Turning, he yelled, "Got damn, there's a man layin' over here! Arliss, take a look at this."

The two brothers stared down at the body half-wedged under the trunk of the tree. Dwayne leaned over and examined the man's face. I betcha anythin' that's the guy they's lookin' fer. He's all bloody and beat ta hell!"

"Ya jest might be right, brother," agreed Arliss. "Don't even look like he's alive. Let's git down the mountain." He turned to leave.

"Hold on a damn minute!" snapped Dwayne. "We need ta at least see if he's still alive." Dwayne, going down on one knee, cocked his head and placed his ear on the man's chest. After a few seconds he smiled. "Ticker's still beatin'." Getting up, he pointed. "This guy, he might jest be the one they's after. Might jest have a big price on his head. Hell, I bet we could take him back ta town and git a big reward. What'd ya say about that?"

"I say yer nuts. How we gonna explain what we was doin' up here? Besides, I got a warrant out on me in Campbell County. I ain't takin' this man nowheres. I say we go home."

"Now jest wait," said Dwayne. "I got me a plan. Why don't we put him in the back of the truck, take him with us and let Effy decide what ta do with him."

Arliss shook his head. "Naw. If he ain't already dead, he sure as hell will be by the time we git back ta Townsend. It's a two hour trip and then some. Makes no good sense ta me. Jest let him be, I say."

"Look, if he dies on the way home, we'll jest pitch the body out of the truck on some back road. But, I gotta tell ya, a big fat reward sounds good ta me, since we ain't got no pelts ta take back home." Bending down, Dwayne began to drag the body away from the log.

Arliss let out a long line of cursing, then added, "Ya jest remember ta tell Effy, not ta mention Maude, this was yer idea." Grabbing Russell's legs he helped Dwayne carry him to the truck. After dumping him into the bed, Dwayne wrapped Russell in an old tarp they had brought along to conceal their illegal catch and then tied it to the inside of the truck. Back in the truck they headed down the mountain road and on to Townsend, stopping every half hour to check and see if the wounded man was still breathing.

Pulling through the gate at the farm, Dwayne shook his head. "Mebbe ya was right, Arliss. I bet Effy is gonna be surprised when she sees what we done brought home instead of a passel of fox and coon pelts."

Arliss laughed and commented sarcastically, "If yer havin' second thoughts, I reckon it's yer problem. This was yer plan, not mine. I had no part on this one."

"Okay, dumb ass, but you jest remember that when I collect that reward."

Effy was in a foul mood when her two great grandsons walked up onto the porch of the main house. Before they could utter a word she started in on them as she threw her mending into a basket and sat forward in her rocking chair. "I can tell by the look on yer faces that you've been up ta no good. Ain't got no time fer no nonsense today. I've been fightin' with them stupid ass cousins of yers. I jest run 'em off the porch with a broom." Getting up slowly, she opened the door and ordered them inside. "Git in the house and make sure ya close the door unless ya want a bunch of damn flies sharin' supper with ya. Now, what'd ya catch up north?"

Dwayne looked down at the floor, realizing that the fact he had come home empty-handed might not go down well with his ninety-two-year-old grandmother. He glanced sideways at Arliss, looking for support. Arliss rolled his eyes and shrugged his skinny shoulders. Effy, growing impatient ordered, "Well, out with it boy!"

Finally, Dwayne spoke, "We didn't git no critters, but we did git somethin' else." He started talking faster so his grandmother didn't hit him before he was finished. "We found a man up on the mountain. We think he might be a killer the law is lookin' fer. Anyways, we put him in the truck and hauled him down here. He was alive. The last we checked he still was. That was back about an hour ago. He might be dead now, but still, I betcha we can git a whole lot of money fer a reward."

Effy put her hands on her hips as she stared at Dwayne. "Got dammit boy! Yer so stupid ya got ta look in a mirror ta see if yer eyes are open. What'd ya go and bring him home fer? Oh, what the hell. Let's have a look at this man."

Wiping her hands on her soiled apron, she followed the two boys out to the truck where she found Maude, her daughter-in-law, staring down into the back. She tapped the tailgate with her cane and asked, "What ya got inside that tarp?"

Dwayne, who was more afraid of the wrath of his aunt Maude than his demanding grandmother reluctantly unwrapped the body and let it roll across the bed of the pickup. "Damn fire!" said Effy. "If he ain't one hell of a mess. Looks like he's still breathin'. Did ya check ta see if he's got a wallet or any money?"

Arliss shook his head no and then jumped up in the truck and reached into Russell's back pocket. Pulling out a blood-stained wallet, he extracted some bills which he quickly counted. "Looks like twenty-one dollars, a license and an ol' picture."

"Lemme see those," said Maude as she held out her hand. Running the dirty picture over her wrinkled dress, she held it up and squinted her eyes. She turned the yellowed and bent photograph sideways and then looked at the back which had some faded writing that was barely readable. Flipping the picture back over, she stared at it for a few seconds then commented, "Lord have mercy! This here is a picture of my younger sister, Etta, and her family." Pointing her dirty finger at the individuals in the picture, she identified each one. "This man here is Millard Pender, her husband. Them two boys is Conrad and Russell, Etta's sons. Gimme that license, Arliss. What's the name on it?"

Arliss held up the license as he read, "Says here...Russell Pearl."

"Well, I'll be dipped. This here man ya found is my nephew, Russell. Don't cotton to the name Pearl, but I know this man is Etta's youngest boy. Haven't laid eyes on him or Conrad since they was youngins. Ya said somethin' about how the law was lookin' fer him. Ya said they say he's a killer? If he is, he must of had a good reason. The Russell Pender I remember was slow. You boys carry him out ta the barn. We'll have a gander and see what needs fixin.' After that, we'll talk about what we're gonna do with him."

Ten minutes later, Effy and Maude inspected Russell who was lying on an old horse blanket in the corner of the barn. "This man is in a heap of hurt," said Effy. "Three bullet wounds, cuts, mebbe some broken bones and who knows what else. Might take months fer him ta heal."

Dwayne stepped forward. "Ya mean we ain't gonna git no reward."

"Ya shut yer mouth," ordered Effy, "or I'll give ya a reward up the side of yer damn head!" Looking at her daughter-in-law, Effy addressed the woman, "Ya ain't never talked about yer sister, Maude. How come?"

Maude sat on a bale of hay as she braced herself with her cane. "When I was growin' up in Southwest Virginia, we was dirt poor. When I turned sixteen I got the hell out of that place. I went up around Nashville. I was workin' on a sharecroppin' farm when I met up with yer son, Otis. Etta, was only fourteen when I left. She stayed on the farm in Virginia and married up with a nasty ol' moonshiner by the name of Millard Pender. After a few years they moved to Tennessee. I visited her once over in Johnson County when her two sons were jest babies. Me and Otis moved up into Kentucky fer a few years and by the time I got around to payin' Etta another visit she and Millard had been murdered and them boys was gone. Never knowed where they'd went. We asked some questions, but nobody up in them mountains knew nothin'. I didn't have no means ta track 'em down so I jest let it be." Pointing her cane at Russell she explained, "So ya see, I gotta do right by this man and help him ta git back on his feet."

"Damn, Maude," interrupted Dwayne, "he's a killer! They say he done kilt a bunch of folks. Ya sure ya want to take him in and patch him up?"

"Don't go gittin' so all high and mighty on me, Dwayne. It ain't like we never kilt nobody before. This here man is kin. Now, go on up ta the house and git my medicine box and a pint of shine."

CHAPTER TWO

CRYSTAL ANN ROCKED BACK AND FORTH IN HER baby swing as she tossed her yellow teething ring across the room. It bounced off the front of the sink and landed on the floor for the fifth time in the last fifteen minutes. It was an unending game that she and her mother, Dana Beth played. Greta, Grant's mother, opened a can of baked beans and dumped the store-bought concoction into a pan next to the sink. "I don't know where you get the patience. In my day we would have picked the toy up after the second or third time and that would have been the end of it."

Ruth, Dana Beth's mother, chimed in as she grabbed a mixing bowl out of a utensil drawer. "It's a different world today, Greta, but I agree with you. The modern day mother has more patience than I could have ever mustered."

Dana Beth placed the teething ring back on the plastic tray of the swing as Crystal Ann stuffed three Cheerios in her mouth and giggled. At the kitchen table, Dana Beth emptied a can of blueberry pie filling into a molded pie shell and asked, "How many pies are we baking?"

Mixing the special potato salad recipe in a large bowl, Ruth answered the question, "Well, besides blueberry, we're making a cherry, apple and Dalton's favorite: rhubarb."

Dana Beth made a gagging motion with her index finger, placing it into her open mouth, exclaiming, "I'm sorry, but I just don't get it! Rhubarb isn't even a fruit, is it? If it's all the same, I'll stick to my favorite; cherry."

Opening a bottle of barbeque sauce, the first ingredient for her doctored up baked beans, Greta added, "I don't care much for rhubarb pie myself."

Dana Beth spread the pie filling evenly across the pie shell. "Despite rhubarb pie I still think family cookouts are one of the best times of the year; the family getting together, the food, the wonderful smells." Looking at Ruth, she went on, "It's hard to believe it's already Labor Day weekend. Why, in just a little over two months from now it'll be Thanksgiving...a year since dad passed away."

Ruth stopped mixing for a brief moment and stared out the kitchen window. Dana Beth apologized, "I'm sorry, Mother. I shouldn't have brought father's death up."

Ruth smiled as she graciously responded, "It's alright. We all have to move on. It would have been nice if Conrad were here to see his grandchild, but God doesn't always guarantee us things will work out the way we plan." Returning to her mixing, she smiled to herself and explained, "After Conrad passed away I didn't think I'd ever get back to a normal way of life, but time has a way of curing things. The Good Lord may have taken my husband from me but now I'm blessed with Crystal Ann. To tell you the truth, moving back in with Grant and Dana Beth and taking care of the baby has been very healing for me."

Changing the subject, Greta turned to the window and commented, "It's starting to rain. We might have to eat on the back porch instead of in the yard. I figured as much. The weatherman said we might get some light rain this morning with a slight chance of thunderstorms in the afternoon." Dumping a measuring cup full of brown sugar and onions into the beans, she added, "I don't think a little rain will put a damper on our day. It's really been a dry summer. We're way behind on rain this year. They say it's going to be an early Fall."

The yellow pretzel careened off the front of the cabinets and rolled into the middle of the kitchen floor, Crystal Ann giggling once again. Dana Beth picked up the pretzel, placed it back on the swing and walked to the coffeemaker and poured herself a second cup. "You're right, I do believe it's going to be an early Fall," she remarked, setting the cup on the table, "and I hope this coming year is nothing like the last year and a half. If someone would have told me we were going to have all these murders around here, I wouldn't have believed them. It's been hard on everyone."

Ruth tossed a handful of chopped celery in the potato salad mixture. "From what I understand that's all over with, well except for Luke Pardee being shot to death in his own home."

"Ya know, it's strange," said Greta. "There hasn't been all that much said about Luke's murder."

"I know," commented Ruth. "It's almost as if we as a community have become accustomed to hearing about local murders. That seems rather odd to me, kind of out of place for a small town like Townsend. I remember when Asa Pittman was killed up on Thunderhead Trail. Everyone was shocked! As the murders continued over the months it's like we all became callous to bad news, acting like people who live in big cities. Murders there are a way of life. That's just the way it is. Here in Townsend, we survive for over a century without a single murder, then bam! Nine murders in the surrounding area in a year and a half. It's unbelievable!"

"Enough talk of murders!" said Dana Beth. "That's all behind us now. We've got pies to bake; a family cookout to put together." Picking up the teething pretzel, she remarked, "We've got a lot to be thankful for. I'm going to take a break. Watch the baby for me, Mom."

Dana Beth picked up her coffee and walked out onto the back porch. Looking out across the open expanse of fields behind the house she thought, *Maybe it's just me, but I can't believe how those two can talk about the murders in such a nonchalant way. Don't they remember everything we all had to go through? All those reporters coming to our house after they found out who Russell really was and then the news conference. Having to stand in front of that microphone and answer their questions was so embarrassing. It was as though they didn't believe Ruth and me when we told them we didn't even know Russell Pearl existed, let alone that we were actually related to the man. Mom acts like it doesn't even bother her that it was Conrad's brother who killed all those people. Deep inside, it has to bother her. It bothers me. Maybe Dalton is right. Maybe we should both consider going to counseling and let a professional make some sense of this. Mom says she doesn't want to go, but I think I will.*

Ruth opened the back door. "Are you alright, Dear?"

Dana Beth downed the last of her coffee as she answered, "Yes, Mom, I'm fine."

Looking at the clock on the kitchen wall, Ruth asked, "What are the boys up to?"

Greta, finished with the baked beans, opened the refrigerator. "Dalton and Grant are out in the barn. They're doing a little early Fall cleaning. Dalton just can't seem to get around like he used to so Grant is giving him a hand."

Ruth began to slice some cheese that she placed on a relish tray. "If we get the burgers on in the next hour, we'll be ready to eat around one o'clock."

Dalton sat on an old, empty drywall bucket as he worked on an ancient generator that stopped working years ago. Removing the plastic protective cover from the Briggs and Stratton engine, he examined the interior.

Grant, on the opposite side of the barn was sorting through a crate of tools that Dalton had picked up at yard sales over the years. Holding up a rust-covered handsaw, he asked, "You really don't want to keep this ol' thing around, do you?"

Dalton looked up and squinted in Grant's direction. "Naw, that thing was rusted out when I bought it years ago. I don't know why I purchased the damn thing...yeah, I do remember. It only run me fifty cents."

Two jet black cats chased one another across the dirt floor and disappeared into one of the three stalls that were no longer used. Grant laughed as he pointed at the swift moving animals. "How many cats do you have out here now?"

Dalton shrugged. "Last time I counted there were five. Over the years I reckon I've had hundreds. They just come and go. Every time I get one spayed or neutered they run off and a new bunch shows up. Whenever there's a litter I run the kittens up the road to Mrs. Casey. She always finds good homes for them. God bless her...she's a good woman." Pointing at a large black and white female that walked casually out from behind a pile of boxes, Dalton smiled. "That big one right there is about to have kittens. Probably in the next week or so. Maybe you and Dana Beth would like one."

Pitching the old saw in a throw away box, Grant answered, "I'll talk with her about it. We need a pet around the house."

Dalton loosened a small bolt from the top of the engine and without looking in Grant's direction asked his next question, "How long has it been now since Russell Pearl took a nosedive over that mountain up near Jellico?"

Grant picked up a set of heavy-duty pliers as he estimated, "Ah, let's see...I guess it's been a little over two months now."

"That's hard to believe," said Dalton. "All this time and they still haven't found his body or any remains. Are they still searching?"

"No, well, not as far as the Cumberland River Gorge is concerned. They've searched up and down the river for miles. The only thing they're still doing is once a week the Jacksboro Police stop by Russell's cabin to see if anything has been disturbed, which to date it hasn't. Russell Pearl simply disappeared."

Dalton frowned. "I just can't accept that. Call it my old police instinct from being in law enforcement for over twenty years. Didn't they find his bloody boot, his broken rifle and his hat at the bottom of the cliff?"

"That they did. I was just ten yards away from Pearl when Chief Blue shot him. Within seconds, I was standing at the spot where he went over the side. We saw a number of areas near the top where there were traces of blood where he had bounced off the cliff wall, but when we got down there...no sign of Russell Pearl."

Pointing a screwdriver at Grant, Dalton motioned, "He couldn't have just disappeared into thin air. He had to go somewhere. The body has to be down there someplace."

"There are a number of scenarios as to what may have happened," said Grant. "He could have been washed downstream below where we searched or sucked beneath the water under a large rock at the bottom. In the past they've lost a lot of people on the river who have never been found, so it's possible we may never find the body."

Unfastening another bolt, Dalton smirked. "Ya know, there are quite a few people around town that claim ol' Russell Pearl is still running around up there in the Jellico Mountains."

Grant objected, "That's a bunch of hogwash! Just another opportunity for people to sit around a campfire years from now and tell the ghost story of Russell Pearl; the Smoky Mountain Killer. The truth is, he's dead. Probably got washed downstream like I said and either drowned or washed up on the river bank and got hauled off by wolves. It's just one of those unexplainable things."

"Maybe...maybe so," said Dalton. "So how is your schooling going?"

Grant inspected an old roofing hammer as he answered, "I've got about three months of study before I can take my final exam.

After that I have to drive up to Connecticut for a final interview with two different professors, then I get the certificate for my degree."

"Then what? Are you going to stay on with Brody?"

"I'm not sure, probably not. I received job offers from Chief Blue over in Cherokee and the FBI. I'd probably learn more working for Blue, however, there is no doubt more opportunity for advancement working with the Feds."

"You could have run for the Chief of Police here in Townsend. A lot of folks thought you were going to take a shot at it. Didn't you tell me Brody said he was going to quit, that he wasn't going to run for office again, especially with Luke Pardee getting murdered?"

"Yeah, he did say he was done being the Chief of Police. I never considered running for the position to begin with. When I didn't run, neither did anyone else. Brody was a shoe-in, ran unopposed and got reelected."

"Do you think this will be his last term?"

"Probably. He's getting up there in years. Next term we'll have a new local lawman in Townsend, but it won't be me."

Dalton fiddled with the inside of the small engine as he backtracked, "A minute ago you said the main reason Brody decided to hang up his spurs was due to Luke's death. The folks in town I told you about who believe Russell Pearl is well and alive are also of the opinion that he came back to town and that *he killed* Pardee. It makes all the sense in the world when you take the time to think about it. Out of the five men who hung out at the Parkway Grocery, according to the Feds, Russell killed Asa and Charley. Now Luke is dead. That puts three of the five in the grave."

"Look, I'll admit it is a bit strange, but that being said, there's no way Russell Pearl could have survived that fall; at least for very long. He was shot three times. He lost a lot of blood and then fell over two hundred feet, straight down. Even if he did manage to survive the fall, he couldn't have possibly had the needed energy or the means to get back to Townsend and kill Luke Pardee six days later."

Their conversation was interrupted by the loud beating of rain on the metal barn roof. Dalton looked up at the rafters and commented, "That's one of the best sounds I think I've ever heard. I can't tell you how many times I've come out here to the barn during rainstorms just to sit and listen to the rain."

Standing, Grant walked over and opened the barn door and stared out at the pelting rain. Thinking for a moment, he turned back and leaned up against the side of a stall and continued where he had left off. "Like I said, Russell didn't kill Luke. As a matter of fact, he didn't even kill all of the people the Feds said he did."

Dalton, confused, gave Grant a strange look but remained silent.

Grant could see his grandfather hadn't understood his last statement. Walking toward Dalton, he sat on an old bench a few feet from him. Taking a deep breath, Grant spoke softly, "I'm going to share something with you, Dalton. You can't tell anyone about what I'm going to say. Not mom, Dana Beth...anyone!"

Dalton, seeing his grandson was quite serious, laid down the engine and focused on Grant.

Grant pushed some dirt around with his shoe, remained quiet for a few seconds and then started, "Russell didn't kill Luke and as far as the other eight murders we've had over the past year and a half, he only killed four of those people." He hesitated for a moment, then emphasized, "Conrad was responsible for the first four murders."

Dalton couldn't believe what he was hearing as he asked halfheartedly, "What are you saying, Grant?"

"I'm telling you the truth...the gospel truth! Conrad, not Russell Pearl killed Asa Pittman, Mildred Henks, Butch Miller and Charley Droxler."

Dalton sat quietly, at a loss for words, but then asked as he shook his head in wonder, "What on earth brought you to that conclusion?"

"It's not a conclusion," uttered Grant. "It's a fact. A fact based on what Conrad told me nearly a year ago."

"Wait a minute! You're saying that Conrad...Conrad Pearl, told you he killed Asa and the others you mentioned?"

"Yes, he did. Remember last year when we had Thanksgiving at Conrad and Ruth's house? After dinner, later that evening, you fell asleep in their living room watching football. I went out onto the porch. Conrad happened to be out there and told me to have a seat; there was something he wanted to talk to me about. The long and short of it is he explained to me that he was responsible for the four killings we had during the year."

Dalton held up his right hand signaling for Grant to stop for a moment. "Why would Conrad kill those people? Why would he kill anyone? What you're telling me doesn't make any sense."

"That's what I thought too. But then, after he shared his reason for killing those people with me, his motive became very clear. By now, everyone has heard the story that was circulating after Russell was killed; about how Russell and Conrad were the sons of the Pender family that was killed over forty years ago by four drunken hunters over in the Iron Mountains. Story has it Conrad and Russell as young boys witnessed the killings of not only their parents but the animals on their farm. The two boys vowed that someday they would get even with people who mistreat animals. The two brothers were adopted by a family by the name of Pearl from Knoxville and eventually, forty years later, Conrad decides to get his long awaited revenge, so he starts out by killing Asa Pittman, a man who we all know was no friend to the local animal population. Mildred Henks was next, what with her mistreatment of the dogs she had at her place. Butch Miller was the third victim and then finally, Charley Droxler. They were all unkind to animals."

Dalton, acting as if he truly wanted to believe Grant's story, made an odd face. "If what you're telling me is actually true, why would Conrad wait all those years; four decades to take his revenge?"

"According to Conrad," answered Grant, "he was waiting for the right time. The part of the story that no one knows, aside from me is that Conrad had cancer and did a great job of shielding that fact from everyone, including his wife and daughter. When it got to the point where he was informed he only had a year or two left, he decided the time had arrived for his revenge."

Dalton stood and walked to the open barn door and looked out at the rain. "I can only assume since you told me I cannot share this information with anyone, that you've kept this to yourself?"

"You're right in your assumption. I did *and have* kept it to myself. But it's just not that cut and dried. There's more to this. Conrad gave me a choice that day on his porch. He told me as an officer of the law I could turn him over to the police, the murders would be solved and I'd wind up being a hero, or I could just let things go, since he was soon going to die anyway. He pointed out that if I did turn him in, I could ruin Ruth and Dana Beth's lives when the truth came out. I mean, think about it? Ruth would have to live the rest of her life knowing her husband was a serial killer and Dana Beth would have to live with the fact that her very own father was a brutal killer. Dana Beth was pregnant at the time and I had to consider not only Crystal Ann, but any other children we might bring into the world. I couldn't fathom the idea of our children eventually finding out their grandfather was the Smoky Mountain Killer. Either way, Conrad told me, it was my decision."

Dalton walked back further into the barn as he shook his head. "Conrad really put you in an awkward position. What a decision to be faced with: doing your job as an officer of the law or being the dutiful husband and son-in law and protecting the integrity of your own family."

"I can tell you one thing, Dalton. That night I didn't get much sleep. I read my Bible like always and asked the Lord to give me direction, because at that point I was torn between the two different options I had. I knew I had to report for work early the next morning and I still didn't know what I was going to do. This was going to be one of the toughest decisions I ever had to make. The next morning, I drove to work still undecided about my decision. I sat in front of the police station and finally came to the conclusion that I had to honor the oath I had taken as a police officer despite the fact I was going to be hurting my family. I walked down the street to where the Feds had set up their temporary headquarters prepared to spill the beans, so to speak. I had my hand on the doorknob when my cell phone rang. It was Dana Beth. She told me to come home immediately. Her father, Conrad, had died overnight in his sleep. That one phone call changed everything. Conrad, the Smoky Mountain Killer was dead. There didn't seem to be any point in turning him in. The murders would stop, remain unsolved and eventually everything would return to normal and Ruth and Dana Beth would never have to know the truth about Conrad. So, I never told anyone. Well, I stand corrected. I did tell Chief Blue. I had to. It was the only way I could get him to help me solve the Russell Pearl murders. So, besides you, me and Chief Blue, no one else knows the truth. Each week, each month that I keep the truth from Ruth and Dana Beth, it gets harder for me to believe they will believe me. I feel this is something they should know but I don't know if they'll ever forgive me for not telling them the truth. They, along with everyone else think Russell Pearl killed all those people. It's not fair for me to let them go on believing a lie."

Dalton held up his index finger, signaling for Grant to wait a second. Crossing the barn floor, he stopped in front of some old kitchen cabinets he had hung in the barn. Opening one of the doors, he extracted a bottle of Jack Daniels. Holding up the bottle of brown colored bourbon, he unscrewed the top and took a short swallow. "Normally, I don't drink, but once in a great while I see or hear something that requires me to take a nip. This, my dear grandson, is one of those moments." Taking another swallow, he offered the bottle to Grant.

Grant stood and crossed the barn and took the bottle to his lips. Handing the bottle back to Dalton, he raised his eyebrows. "Whew! Been quite some time since I've had anything other than plain old beer."

Dalton took another sip, then closed the top, wiped his mouth with the back of his shirt sleeve and replaced the bottle back inside the cabinet. Sitting once again on the drywall bucket, he looked directly at Grant and pursed his lips. "Grant, I served here in Townsend for two decades as the police chief, so I understand what you said about standing by the oath you took as an officer. In all my years I prided myself in always doing what was right and always being honest with my dealings in handling my authority as a lawman. It's always been important to me, not only as a former police officer, but in everyday life, to tell the truth. That being said, I feel there are those times when the truth is better left unknown, because to be honest with you, which is what I'm trying to do here, sometimes the truth can do more harm than good. I don't know what I would have done if faced with the decision Conrad put on you. I didn't have to make that choice...you did! It must have been hell carrying around that burden all this time. But, here's the thing. If you want my advice, I say leave it be. Don't ever tell Ruth or Dana Beth the truth about Conrad. Besides that, your children, my great grandchildren, don't need to have the horrible truth about Conrad hanging over their heads for the rest of their lives."

Suddenly, their conversation was interrupted as Dana Beth,

wearing an old raincoat entered the barn. Noticing the look of surprise by Grant and Dalton, she stated, "Looks like I walked in at the wrong time." Jokingly, she added, "You weren't talking about me...were you?"

Dalton hesitated in answering but Grant responded, "No, you just took us by surprise."

Smiling, Dana Beth angled her thumb back over her shoulder in the direction of the house. "Greta said you fellas need to finish out here and get washed up. Burgers will be on the table out on the back porch in about thirty minutes." Turning to head back to the house, she snapped her fingers, remembering, "Oh yeah, she also said you need to bring in two extra chairs."

Later that evening, Grant looked at his watch: just after ten o'clock. He had to work tomorrow so he'd hit the hay in about an hour. He always enjoyed sitting on the front porch just before turning in for the night. Sipping on a cup of coffee, he thought about the day at Dalton's farm: the cookout, sitting on the back porch enjoying dessert, taking endless pictures of Crystal Ann's first cookout. And then there was the conversation he had with Dalton. Maybe Dalton was right about not ever revealing the truth about Conrad to Ruth or Dana Beth. In two months it would be Thanksgiving and a year since he sat on the very porch where he was now seated when Conrad had confided in him. He appreciated Dalton's support but he wasn't sure if he could go on much longer without revealing what he knew to his wife and mother-in-law.

CHAPTER THREE

AMELIA WHEAT INSPECTED HERSELF, BRAND NEW bright orange apron, nametag, new shoes and a great smile. She was ready for whatever the day ahead might bring. Her week of training finally over, this was her first day alone at the customer service desk. The assistant manager looked at his watch: 6:00 a.m. Time to crack open the front doors. The first two customers of the day passed through the sliding glass double entrance.

The two large men reminded Amelia of one of the many tag team wrestlers her father had a habit of watching on television every Friday night. The first man through the door had to be at least six foot, four inches in height, his massive body weight close to two hundred eighty pounds. His oversized head was covered in long, stringy black hair that fell to his muscular shoulders and fronted by an unfriendly face that hadn't seen a razor in quite some time. The piercing eyes, topped by bushy unkempt eyebrows stared directly at Amelia. The man's clothing was simplistic: long johns under filthy denim coveralls, his large feet encased in marred, well used steel-toed work boots.

The second man was a good three inches taller than the first and was closer to three hundred pounds. His head was completely shaved except for two mutton chop sideburns framing a grayish-black goatee. A black sweatshirt worn inside out could be seen underneath the unbuttoned, ripped black and white flannel shirt. The man's dirty brown cargo pants were tucked into high top hunting boots, the left boot untied near the top.

The two, who appeared to be good ol' boys, walked up to the counter, the shorter of the two reaching down and picking up a small wastebasket. Holding the container a few inches below his mouth, he spit out a wet, dark brown chaw of chewing tobacco then wiped his mouth with his hand while the baldheaded man gave Amelia a blank stare.

Amelia, well trained in her job as a customer service representative, welcomed the two customers to the store as she spewed out her canned greeting, "Good morning, how can we at Home Depot serve you today?"

Neither of the men answered, which made Amelia slightly uncomfortable as she looked from her right to the left, looking for assistance from someone in management. Assistance for what she wasn't quite sure. There was something very odd and frightening about the two large men.

The coverall wearing man finally spoke in a deep voice, "Ya must be new around here." He looked Amelia up and down as if he were thinking, then continued, "We be the Stroud's. I'm Ambrose." Nodding at the taller man, he explained, "This here be Cletus, my little brother."

Not quite sure what to say, Amelia decided to answer the man's question. "I am new. This is my first day at the customer service desk."

Bumping his older brother on the arm, Cletus half grunted as he suggested, "C'mon Ambrose, quit pussy footin' around. We gotta git them hoses then we gotta drive over ta Cherokee fer them skids."

Ambrose flashed a yellow-stained tooth smile, stating, "We're here ta see the manager, Mr. Wilcox. He's expectin' us. Call him up here."

Amelia had been trained when asked by a customer to see the manager to inquire as to what the request was about, but she wasn't about to ask the two rough looking characters less than two feet from her why they wanted to see the manager. She smiled at Ambrose as she picked up the desk phone. "Just let me call Mr. Wilcox."

A few seconds passed when she politely spoke into the phone, "Mr. Wilcox, you have *two gentlemen* at the customer service desk who would like to speak with you." She placed extra emphasis on the words 'two gentlemen' in hope of giving her boss a warning as to what to expect when he came out of his office. Hanging up the phone, she turned to Ambrose and stated calmly, "Mr. Wilcox said he would be right out." Ambrose remained silent as he gave Amelia a slight nod of thanks. Cletus just stood there wearing a deadpan stare.

It seemed like an eternity to Amelia as she stood face to face with the two towering brothers, but in all actually it wasn't even a minute until Wilcox approached the desk. She was amazed at the smile on Wilcox's face and his friendly manner as he reached for Cletus' hand. "Cletus...Ambrose! Maude told me to expect you early this morning. I gave her a call yesterday about some water hoses we overbought. Got seventy-three pulled and waiting for you at the back loading dock. Mostly fifty-footers, with a few seventy-five-footers mixed in. Brand new, not even out of the package. I told your Ma I'd let her have them for two dollars each. You should be able to realize a good profit. The fifty-footers retail for $29.99 and the larger hoses go for $39.99. I bet you can get ten bucks a piece."

Ambrose reached into his coveralls dragging out a wad of folded money. "How much that come ta?"

"Got the bill right here for you," responded Wilcox. "One hundred forty-six dollars."

Taking the bill in his large calloused hand, Ambrose didn't even look at the paper. Stuffing it into his coveralls, he handed Wilcox two fifties, two twenties, a five and a one. Looking toward the back of the store, Ambrose asked, "Ya say the back loadin' dock?"

Wilcox gave the brothers a half-assed salute as he confirmed, "Yep, I'll have one of my employees from receiving help you load up." As the two men turned to leave, Wilcox added, "I also told Maude to have you boys drop by in two months. We'll be discontinuing all of our ceiling fans and two of our lighting vendor inventories. She said she'd take the whole lot. Guess I'll see you then."

Once at home, Ambrose pulled the old pickup into a small dirt parking area next to a ten by twelve pop-up tent. Beneath the faded green canopy there were four dilapidated picnic tables displaying canned tomatoes, peaches and pears, baked pies and cookies, a few quilts and cardboard boxes filled with an assortment of hand tools. Next to the tent, Otis and Maude Stroud sat on two old lawn chairs, a cooler of beer separating the seventy-three-year-old couple. To Otis' left there was a rusted metal bucket filled with cigarette butts and to the right of Maude a metal trash container overflowing with empty beer cans. As Ambrose and Cletus climbed out of the truck, Maude greeted her two sons as she raised her cane in the air speaking to Otis at the same time. "They's back!"

Ambrose grabbed two packages of hoses from the back of the truck and walked past the tent, Cletus close behind. Standing in front of Maude, Ambrose held the hoses out for her inspection and explained, "Got seventy-three of these here hoses. Wilcox said we might git ten bucks each."

Otis reached out and took one of the hoses. "They looks like good hoses."

Maude removed a handheld calculator from a frayed burlap bag at her feet. Punching some numbers into the small device she spoke, "Ya say they's seventy-three? At ten bucks a pop, we'll haul in seven hundred thirty dollars." Looking at her son, she asked, "Ya got the bill?"

Ambrose handed her the crumpled paper. Doing some quick math on the calculator, Maude smiled, "One hundred-forty-six fer the hoses. We sell 'em fer ten bucks a crack. Leaves us with a tidy sum of five hundred eighty four dollars."

Cletus, seeing that his mother was pleased, chimed in, "Manager said we was ta come back later ta git some fans and lights."

"Ya boys did right good," said Maude as she pointed at a twenty by thirty foot storage shed on the opposite side of the dirt clearing. "Put them hoses in the shed. We'll call it a day."

As her sons drove across the clearing to the shed, Maude poked Otis in the side with her trusty cane. "Git off yer lazy ass Otis and git the trailer loaded up so we can head up fer supper."

Minutes later, she watched Ambrose carry the last of the hoses into the shed. Cletus lifted the cattle gate that blocked the road leading back into the dense trees surrounding the property. Finishing her ninth beer of the day, Maude let out a huge belch, flicked her unfinished cigarette toward the trash container and yelled at her husband, "Dammit Otis! Ya gonna take all damn day ta load that crap?"

Otis looked past the tent at his wife and swore beneath his breath. "Bitch at me will ya! I might jest take my good ol' time!"

With that, he carried a crate of canned peaches to the back of the tent and loaded them into a rusted dump trailer that was hitched to an old, nasty looking golf cart. Looking toward the dirt road, he watched as Ambrose's truck disappeared in a cloud of dust.

The short drive through the towering Tennessee pines that flanked both sides of the dirt road leading to the Stroud's place, as it was referred to in the county, was not one of the typical picturesque tree lined roads that crisscrossed Blount County. The football-field-length drive was unsightly to say the least, the beauty of the stately pines and maples marred with piles of old tires and rusted appliances. There were discarded cans and bottles and a number of old cars, most of which were elevated on cinderblocks. They were rusted shells minus windows, doors, engines and tires.

Exiting the trees into the clearing, Ambrose honked the horn, startling three of his youngest children who were playing inside an old delivery truck. He beat on the steering wheel, stopped the truck, got out and yelled at the children, "Got dammit, I tol' ya ta stay away from that truck. Go on...git." His seven-year-old twin daughters ran off into the trees to escape their father's wrath. His oldest son, Raymond, who was nine, stuck out his tongue, gave his father the finger, picked up a rock and tossed it at the truck, then disappeared in the trees. Ambrose, pissed, picked up a rock and threw it in the direction his son had fled. "Got damn that boy. I'm gonna whip his ass good when he comes fer supper!"

Back inside the truck, Ambrose reached into a cooler next to him and withdrew a cold beer, downed it in five large swallows then tossed the can to the side of the road. "That kid ain't nothin' but trouble. I swear, the Devil's got him by the sleeve."

Cletus, opening a beer, laughed as he remarked, "Aw, c'mon, brother. Ya know Ray's not all there. Why, ya could beat him senseless and it wouldn't make no difference. Maude's the only one that can handle that boy."

Putting the truck in gear, Ambrose turned to the left to avoid a large dip in the road. They passed the main house that sat back thirty some yards next to the eastern border of the one hundred forty-three acre property. Effy, their grandmother, and matriarch of the family, as usual, was perched in her rocking chair on the front porch crocheting one of her latest quilt creations. The old woman looked up as her two grandsons drove by, but could have cared less as she swatted at a pesky fly. Twenty yards further up the road, Arliss and Dwayne, twenty and twenty-two years of age, Maude's oldest son's boys, were involved in changing a tire on an older mustang they had recently purchased. Aside from the main house where Maude, Otis and Effy lived, there were three mobile homes where Maude's three son's families lived. Cletus' family lived at the first of the trailers which was situated in front of a large fenced in pasture that held a small herd of cattle and two swayback horses, some Billy goats and a few sheep. Ambrose's trailer was on the right and surrounded by a number of old cars and out buildings. Maude's oldest son, Harmon and his family lived near the back of the property next to the large barn and utility shed. The only animals that were not fenced in aside from a few dogs and cats were numerous pigs and chickens that had the run of the place.

Coming to a stop in front of Cletus' trailer, Ambrose opened another beer as he slapped his younger brother on the shoulder. "After supper mebbe we'll git drunk and play some poker tonight."

Cletus, stepping out of the truck, shook his head, indicating no, as he answered, "Reckon not. Me and Ruby Jean might have a good' ol roll in the hay this evenin.' Haven't fooled around with the ol' lady fer goin' on a week now. Guess I'll see ya in the mornin'."

Ambrose honked the truck horn, causing a mother pig and her five piglets to run from the middle of the road and into an adjacent field. Cletus stood and watched the truck make its way up the road. Crossing the front yard which was nothing more than a patch of dirt dotted with occasional weeds, Cletus looked at his home; a two-tone blue double-wide trailer that was covered with streaks of brown rust and corrosion. All the windows were open except for the front kitchen window that was covered with clear plastic attached with duct tape. The trailer skirting for the most part was missing, revealing a conglomeration of old tires and lumber stacked beneath it. An old discarded washing machine sat next to a well-used gas grill. Approaching the front door, he saw his six-year-old daughter, Violet, playing in a pile of dirt by the front steps. The freckle-faced, pigtailed little girl wore a dirty pink dress and was shoeless. She smiled at her father as he approached, but the smile on her face quickly disappeared when he ordered her, "Git yer butt in the house Vi and git washed up fer supper. Momma 'ill have it on the table soon."

Violet, Cletus' only child and the most obedient and quietest child of the Stroud's clan, answered her father, "Yes sir." She stood and climbed the three cinderblocks that led up to the dented aluminum storm door. Cletus looked off into the distant sky. Storm clouds were forming and within the hour it would be raining. Removing a rumpled pack of cigarettes from his shirt pocket, he took one of his last three smokes to his lips, flicked his lighter and took a long drag. Knocking some caked mud from one of his boots on the first cinderblock he reached for the storm door and yanked it open, the flimsy door falling from its hinges. Tossing the door to the ground, he kicked at the metal frame, "Piece of crap trailer!" An old hound lying beneath the corner of the trailer whined and retreated back underneath.

Stepping up into the trailer, Cletus entered the cluttered living room. The coffee table was overflowing with newspapers and magazines. There was a pile of dirty dishes on the floor next to the couch. Three sets of hanging antlers were draped with clothing and the filthy green shag carpet was dotted with cigarette burns. Ruby Jean, Cletus' wife, was sitting on the end of the ripped, green-striped couch, a cigarette in one hand, a cold beer in the other. Cletus blew a stream of smoke toward the ceiling as he gave his wife a disgusted look. There she sat; her dyed red hair was put up in curlers. She wore a yellow food-stained tank top, pink peddle pushers and dirty white slippers on her feet which were propped up on the marred coffee table. Sarcastically, Cletus pointed at the television as he spoke, "See yer busy as usual watchin' more of that damn soap opera crap. Ya oughta try gittin' off yer ass and gittin' a life fer a change."

Ruby stubbed out her cigarette in a broken glass ashtray and shot her husband a nasty look. "Well, look who's talkin'. Ya ain't nothin' more than a glorified junkman runnin' around the county collectin' crap nobody else wants."

Cletus was tired and hungry and at the moment, wasn't about to listen to his lazy ass wife spout off. "That so! Well, here's a news flash fer ya. Jest so happens that my runnin' around the county collectin' crap nobody else wants has not only put a damn roof over yer head, bought those clothes yer wearin', the cigarettes ya smoke, the beer ya swill down all day long, the couch yer sittin' on and that damn TV yer ass is always glued ta." Walking past her, he kicked over an end table, a pile of magazines and an ashtray full of cigarette butts falling to the carpet. "Why in the hell I married up with you, I'll never figure out!" Flinging open the refrigerator door in the small kitchen, he slammed the door shut so hard that a canister of sugar was jarred from the top and fell to the tile floor, the container shattering. "Dammit it woman, we're out of beer again. How hard can it be to git in the car and drive inta town and pick up a case of beer? And why in the hell would ya drink the last damn beer, when ya knowed I'd be comin' home thirsty."

Ruby tossed the half full can of beer she had been drinking at Cletus who stepped to the right just in time, the can smashing up against the wall, beer running down the ripped wallpaper. "Ya want a beer. There's one fer ya. Drink that!"

Cletus clenched his fists and took a step toward Ruby, then backed off as he realized he was letting his temper get the best of him. Calmly, he stated, "It's supper time and I don't see no pots cookin' on the stove or any dishes set at the table, so git off yer ass and make me and Violet somethin' ta eat."

A sad look came across Ruby Jean's face as she sat on the edge of the couch. "Gimme a break, Cletus. I'm tired. I don't have the energy ta make you and Violet supper tonight."

"Tired! Tired from what?" barked Cletus. "Sittin' on yer ass all day watchin' soap operas!"

Ruby Jean stood and stomped her foot. "Ya jest don't understand, Cletus. Ya know I jest had me a miscarriage two days back. Takes a lot out of a woman. I need some time ta rest up, ta git back ta normal."

"Normal! What the hell's normal? You sure as hell ain't! That makes what…five, six miscarriages ya've had over the past ten years and it ain't my fault. I keep plantin' the seed and you keep losin' babies. If I know'd that ya was a piece of crap when it come ta child bearin' I wouldn't of married ya. Ya must be some kind of freak. Why can't ya be like Harmon and Ambrose's wives? They've given their husbands a bunch of kids. All we have is Violet…jest the one child. The truth is, ya jest ain't a good wife. Now, quit bitchin' about how tired ya are, git in the kitchen and make us up some supper before I whup yer ass!"

Biting her lower lip, Ruby Jean looked down at the floor as she began to cry. Cletus didn't feel the slightest bit of compassion for his wife as he remarked sharply, "Yeah that's right, go on and cry. That don't cut no ice with me and it ain't gonna git supper on the table either. Now, move yer skinny ass over ta the kitchen and git some vittles cookin'."

Ruby Jean wiped her eyes, glared at her husband, turned and marched to the refrigerator. She opened the freezer door and removed a bright red and black package which she held up and read aloud, "Meatloaf, mashed potatoes and corn!" Turning, she flung the small container at Cletus as she yelled, "There's yer dinner! Make it yerself!"

The TV dinner glanced off the side of Cletus' forehead. Reaching up, he felt the small cut, his hand coming away with blood on his fingertips. "Ya shouldn't done that, Ruby Jean. Now, I'm gonna have ta kick yer ass!"

Ruby Jean bolted for the door, but was blocked by Cletus, who for a big man was surprisingly quick. He blocked the doorway, grabbed Ruby Jean by her hair and flung her to the carpet. Getting to her feet, she ran into the kitchen, grabbed a cast iron skillet and held it out in front of her as a weapon. Cletus laughed, "Ya really think ya can hold me off with a fryin' pan?"

"Yer not gonna hit me again," warned Ruby Jean. "I'm tired of bein' pushed around and ordered like I was yer slave."

Cletus started across the floor toward the kitchen as Ruby Jean opened a cabinet drawer and took out a long steak knife. "Ya come any closer and I'll cut ya."

Picking up a small imitation green leather hassock, Cletus threw it violently at Ruby Jean. As she stepped to the side to avoid the flying piece of furniture, Cletus made his move as he lunged at her, his foot catching on the edge of the couch, causing him to stumble forward. Ruby Jean, seeing her opportunity to defend herself, brought the frying pan down on the right side of his head. Falling to the carpet on one knee, he held his head and struggled back to his feet. The blow to his head made him dizzy, his eyes not completely focused. As he retreated back across the room, Ruby Jean, now with the upper hand, advanced toward him, wielding the knife in her hand. She yelled at her husband, "If anybody around here's gittin' an ass kickin' it ain't gonna be me!"

Holding his hands up in front of himself in a defensive manner,

Cletus shook his head while backing further into the living room. The knife slashed at his right hand cutting three of his outstretched fingers. Ruby Jean was now screaming, "Ya ain't never gonna beat me ever again!" She slashed again with the knife, but missed the mark. Cletus stumbled to the side at the same time grabbing Ruby Jean and flinging her across the room where she collided with a china cabinet, her head hitting the sharp wooden corner. Collapsing to the floor, the knife fell from her hand. A small stream of blood ran across the carpet.

Backing up, Cletus leaned against the wall, trying to regain his bearings. His breath coming in short pants, he looked down at Ruby Jean who wasn't moving. The small pool of blood on the carpet was growing larger and suddenly his anger turned to concern. He knelt down and rolled her over, noticing the wide gash on her forehead gushing blood. Her eyes were closed and her body was lifeless. "Good God, what have I done? Ruby...wake up, c'mon ...wake up!"

As she stood at the end of the hallway, Violet, who was used to seeing her parents battle it out on many occasions had witnessed the entire fight. Her soft, tear-filled voice interrupted Cletus' attention on his wife. "Ya hurt Momma real bad, Pa."

Shaking his wife, Cletus spoke into her motionless face, "Com'n Ruby Jean, snap out of it! I'm sorry. Didn't mean ta push ya like that, but ya jest wouldn't listen ta me." Sensing that something was wrong, Cletus ordered Violet, "Go git Maude or Effy. Tell 'em ta git down here right quick. Tell 'em they's been an accident!"

Violet remained frozen in place as she stared at her mother. Cletus ordered his daughter again, "I said ta go git Maude or Effy. Now, go on...git!"

Running out the front door and down the cinderblock steps, Violet saw Otis guiding the old golf cart and attached trailer up the dirt road. Maude, sitting in the passenger seat had just lit up a cigarette. Signaling them to stop, Violet could hardly get the words out. "Papa hurt...Momma...real bad. She's layin' on the floor. They's blood...on the carpet. Papa said ta tell ya, they's been...an accident!"

Otis, not all that fond of children, stopped the cart as he questioned Violet, "Whadda ya mean, hurt real bad? Ya say they's blood? Is Cletus inside?"

Maude thumped her husband on the arm with her cane as she cursed, "Dammit, Otis, ya heard the child. Ruby Jean's hurt."

"Well hell!" answered Otis. "Ain't like this is nothin' new. They's always fightin'. Ruby Jean probably sassed Cletus and he gave her the what fer. I say we move on and git our supper."

"I swear ta God, Otis Stroud, if ya don't pull this cart over, I'm gonna be givin' you the what fer!"

Otis, realizing that getting into a spitting match with his wife would only result in his coming out on the losing end, pulled the cart over in front of the trailer as he complained, "Guess supper can wait fer a spell."

Getting out of the cart, Maude tapped the side of the small vehicle with her cane as she ordered her husband, "I'll go in and see what the hell's goin' on. You drive up ta the house and git Effy."

Taking Violet's hand she led her granddaughter across the yard to the trailer as Otis sped up the dirt road. Passing the next trailer, he yelled at Ambrose, "Git on down ta Cletus' place. He and Ruby Jean been at it again."

Using the cane as a brace, Maude made her way slowly up the cinderblock steps and entered the trailer. The first thing she noticed was Ruby Jean sprawled out on the floor, the deep cut in her forehead oozed blood down the side of her face and onto the stained carpet. Cletus, slouched in a broken recliner lit up a cigarette. Maude began to take charge as she spoke calmly, "Violet, you go and sit over there on the couch. Cletus, ya need ta fetch a pan of cool water and a washcloth."

Cletus inhaled a deep, long drag of nicotine and wiped tears away from his eyes as he answered, "Won't do no good, Ma. Ruby Jean's dead. I checked and she ain't breathin. She ain't got no pulse."

Poking her daughter-in-law with her foot to make sure she was dead, Maude walked over to the recliner and smacked Cletus across the face with her cane, leaving a cut on his left cheek. "I tol' ya ta back off on all the fightin'…didn't I?"

Cletus stood in objection to being hit. "Hell, Ma, what'd ya do that fer? It ain't my fault. She jest wouldn't listen ta me! Ya know how lazy assed she was. She wouldn't git up and make me and Vi no supper. I tried ta reason with her, but she went off the deep end. She come after me with a damn fryin' pan and look!" Holding up his right hand he displayed the three cut fingers and the blood running down his arm. "She come at me with a knife. She cut me! She wouldn't back off. I jest shoved her back...that's all. She was actin' all crazy!"

Maude looked at Violet and gently asked, "Is that what happened Vi? Did ya see the whole thing?"

Violet sat quietly and stared back at Maude then to Cletus, then back to Maude.

Maude pointed her cane at Cletus as she addressed Violet. "Now listen ta me child. I want the truth. Cletus ain't gonna hurt ya none. I'll see ta that. Did yer Momma attack yer Pa?"

Violet hesitated, but then spoke softly, "Yes, Ma'am. Momma attacked Pa but not 'til after he shoved her. She was afraid of Pa."

Turning back to Cletus, Maude placed her cane squarely on his chest and pushed him back in the chair as she scolded her youngest son. "If you ain't one dumb ass sum bitch!"

Pushing the cane to the side, Cletus started to get up as he objected, "What the hell was I gonna do? Let her kill me? I tell ya...she was actin' nuts!"

"Shut the hell up, Cletus," ordered Maude. "I brought ya inta this world and I sure as hell can take ya out! Now...sit down!"

Just then Effy and Otis walked into the trailer. Bending down, Effy looked at Ruby Jean. "Looks like the end of the road fer Ruby. I can tell she's dead. Ain't no life in her eyes. What happened?"

Following a brief rundown from Maude, Effy turned to Otis as she gave her orders, "Go round up the entire family and have 'em come on down here, but make sure they stay outside fer now."

As Otis exited the trailer he mumbled to himself, "Looks like it's gonna be a late supper. Damn!"

Looking around the trailer, Effy motioned with her right hand, "Ruby Jean sure wasn't much on house cleanin' but then again I never liked her much. Harmon and Ambrose, now they's got good wives...the pick of the litter I say. Ruby Jean jest never measured up."

Ambrose entered the trailer and stared down at Ruby Jean's lifeless body. "Otis said they was an accident down here."

"Accident my ass!" bellowed Effy. "Yer idiot brother went and kilt his wife."

Getting out of the chair, Cletus lit his last cigarette as he walked to a window and looked out. "I tell ya, it was self defense. She threatened ta kill me. She was comin' at me with that knife!" Turning back to Maude and Effy, his hands were shaking as he suggested, "That's what we got ta tell the police when they git here. It was self defense!"

Effy motioned with her hands, "We ain't tellin' the police nothin' of the sort. We ain't tellin' 'em nothin' cause we ain't callin' no police. This is a family matter and we'll take care of it ourselves."

Ambrose opened the refrigerator and searched for a beer. "Do ya think that's the best thing ta do...I mean not tellin' the police? We could git in a heap of trouble."

Maude spoke up as she looked disgustedly at Ambrose. "Ambrose, yer as stupid as yer younger brother. Think about it. How many times has Sheriff Brody been up here cause Cletus and Ruby Jean was fightin'. The last time he was here he tol' us the next time he had ta come back up here over this fightin' business he was goin' to haul Cletus off ta jail. If he finds out he kilt his wife, he'll send him ta prison. Now, listen up! None of my boys is goin' ta no prison. Not if I can help it."

Effy chimed in, "Maude's right, we've got ta take care of this ourselves."

Cletus held out his hands as if he were confused. "What are we gonna do with Ruby Jean? Sooner or later folks are gonna wonder where the hell she is."

Effy looked at Maude then at Cletus. "We're gonna bury her right here on our property. We'll take her back out behind the garden near the back of the big shed and that'll be the end of this."

Ambrose closed the refrigerator door and walked over to where Ruby Jean lay. Looking down at her he stated, "I agree...makes sense ta bury her. But what do we tell folks when she shows up missin' over the next few weeks?"

"That's easy," said Effy. "What we do, is we have a family meetin'. We tell everyone ta start spreadin' the word that Ruby Jean up and left Cletus cause she was tired gittin' beat on."

Maude agreed as she spoke up, "And everyone will believe that, because everyone knows Cletus and Ruby Jean don't git along all that well."

Violet curled up on the couch in a ball and began to sob. Effy went to the couch, placed her arm around her great granddaughter and spoke softly to her. "Everythin' is goin' ta be alright child. Now, listen ta me. Ya can't tell anyone, I mean no one that yer Pa kilt yer Momma. Ya have ta tell 'em that yer Momma run off. If anyone finds out what really happened then the police will find out, come and take yer Pa off ta jail. If that happens then they'll come git ya and take ya away. Ya don't want ta live with strangers, now do ya?"

With a tear stained face, Violet answered, "No, Ma'am."

"Then ya understand what ya need ta tell folks?"

"Yes, Ma'am."

Using the arm rest for support, Effy got up from the couch as she ordered, "Ambrose, I want ya ta git yer wife, Harmon and Loretty down here ta git this bloody mess cleaned up. Maude, ya need to head on up ta the house and git some vittles on the stove fer a family meetin' later tonight. Ambrose, before ya leave help Cletus load Ruby Jean up in the back of the cart so he can put his wife in the ground."

Cletus took a careful step toward Effy as he questioned her orders. "Ya mean Ambrose or nobody's gonna help me ta bury Ruby Jean?"

Effy stopped Cletus in his tracks as she stated boldly, "Ya kilt yer wife...you bury her! Plant her next ta that tractor salesman that screwed us over back three years ago. Vi, ya go with yer Pa while he buries yer Momma. And fer Lord's sake, don't none of ya let Russell know about this. He don't need ta be involved."

Violet sat quietly by the barbed wire fence that bordered the north end of the property as she watched Cletus use a backhoe to dig her mother's grave. It was always so peaceful back by the large garden that was surrounded by the tall pine trees. She fought back the tears as she watched Cletus drag her mother from the back of the cart and lower her down into the grave. As Cletus shoved the dirt back over the face of his wife, Violet sat in the tire swing that hung from the large oak and sadly looked out across the distant fields.

CHAPTER FOUR

GRANT ANSWERED HIS CELL PHONE ON THE SECOND ring. "Yes dear, I know. I forgot the bag with the paper plates and napkins. I just pulled up at the Parkway Grocery. I'm going to run in and buy some. Gotta run. Love you!" Getting out of the Jeep he thought to himself, *The last thing Dana Beth told me was not to forget the bag sitting next to the white cake box.*

Hurrying into the store, Grant picked up what he needed and took his purchases to the counter where he poured himself a cup of morning coffee. He dumped some sweetener into a styrofoam cup. Glancing to his left, he noticed Zeb Gilling sitting at his usual table by the front window. Dunking a donut into a cup of coffee, Zeb was busy reading the paper. After paying for the plates, napkins and his coffee, Grant walked over to the table. "Mornin' Zeb. How goes it?"

Startled, Zeb looked up and answered, "Oh, sorry Grant. Didn't see you walk in. Just reading the morning news. Not much going on in town these days. Fall festival will be coming up soon along with the hordes of tourists wanting to take a gander at the leaves."

Grant took a drink as he spoke, "I just thought that maybe you were waiting for Buddie. I haven't seen him around much lately and that's strange. You guys always have coffee here in the morning. You fellas having a tiff or something?"

"No, nothing like that, but come to think of it ol' Buddie's been acting on the strange side ever since Luke's funeral. Well that, plus he's been pretty busy. In case you haven't heard he and his wife, Mary are selling their place and moving down to Foley, Alabama. Earlier this year he told me Mary wants to move down closer to her children and grandchildren." Zeb laughed. "Buddie always claimed he'd never leave Townsend despite what his wife said. But, it looks like that's all changed now. I never thought I'd see the day when Buddie would up and leave town. I guess maybe he's had enough. There used to be the five of us that met here at the Parkway for coffee and local gossip. When Asa got murdered that left four of us and then when Charley bit the bullet we were down to three. This recent murder of Luke has put our number at two, but as you can see it looks like I'm the Last of the Mohicans."

"Yeah, Luke's murder was a shock. We're not any closer now to solving his murder than the day we found him. So, how are you Zeb? Are you doing alright?"

Fingering the rim of his cup, Zeb responded in a negative tone, "As good as one can expect, I guess." Holding out both of his arms he gestured. "Here I sit...all alone! Maybe I should just pack up and move too. Truth is, I don't know where in the world I'd go. Besides that, the wife would never leave Townsend."

Grant glanced at his watch. "Well, I better get going. Take care of yourself."

Zeb held up his cup in a toasting fashion as he nodded and smiled.

Back in the Jeep, Grant put the bag on top of the cake box then removed the white envelope from his pocket and placed it on the seat. Placing his hand on the box, he double checked himself as he spoke, "Okay, I've got the cupcakes, plates and napkins and birthday card. Good to go!"

As he pulled out of the parking lot he could see Zeb sitting next to the window. On the Parkway, he wondered, *Why wouldn't Buddie at least come and have a cup of coffee with his old friend Zeb, just like he had done for years in the past?* Thinking back, it seemed odd to Grant; *Even during Luke's funeral, Buddie and Zeb had seemed distant from one another, standing on opposite sides of the casket. They never even talked, not one time. And then after the service, Buddie opted not to attend the luncheon at the church.* It also seemed rather strange that neither Buddie or Zeb had dropped by to see Brody. *They had to be curious about how the investigation was going. Following the previous murders, Luke, Zeb and Buddie had raised ten kinds of hell with Axel because they didn't think he was doing nearly enough to solve the murders. They felt their very lives were in danger and now, Zeb and Buddie were going on with their lives with no apparent concern over Luke's death. Both had been questioned following Luke's murder and their alibis were solid. Besides that, Brody knew neither one of them had any remote reason to kill their long time friend.*

Someone honked at Grant bringing him out of his daydreaming. It was one of his neighbors driving in the opposite direction. Slowing down, he made a left hand turn into the police department. Balancing the cake box in his hand he locked the Jeep and walked to the main entrance, pushed open the door and entered the office. Marge was sitting at her desk wearing a silver crown on her head as she held a bouquet of fresh flowers. Grant laughed and remarked comically, "Well, happy birthday, *Queen Marge!*"

Marge touched the crown and responded, "The crown's from Kenny and the flowers from Lee. Kenny told me that I have to wear it all day. You just missed both of them. Kenny just got off the night shift and Lee stopped by to wish me happy birthday."

Grant sat the box on the corner of the desk and handed her the card. "Dana Beth made you some cupcakes."

Laying the flowers on the desk, Marge beamed, "How sweet of her and thank you for the card." She pushed herself away from the desk, rolled out into the hallway and spoke loud enough so Axel could hear her voice. "At least some people remembered my birthday!"

Brody stuck his head out his office door and yelled back, "Aw, come on Marge. I was gonna get you a cake but I figured with all those candles on top of the damn thing they'd have to call the fire department to put it out."

"Very funny, Axel! Don't you be coming out here looking for one of these cupcakes Grant brought in. I'm going to give some to *my friends* and eat the rest myself." Rolling back to the desk, Marge flipped open the box and offered one of the baked treats to Grant. "Sit down with me for a minute and have a cupcake."

Moving a small cardboard box out of the way to make room for the cake box, Grant asked, "What's in the box?"

"Oh that," said Marge. "Apparently, a lawyer from over in Pigeon Forge by the name of Jason Abrams called Brody earlier this week and said that Luke Pardee had, according to his will, left his house and everything in it to the church. The pastor and his wife took in Luke's cat and today some people from the church are cleaning out the house. Mr. Abrams said if the police wanted to take a last look around before they cleared everything out then it would be best if they got over there. Axel, as usual, put it off and by the time he got around to going over to the house most of the stuff had been moved out. One of the men from the church gave

Axel that box he said he found back in the corner of a closet. It wasn't anything the church was interested in so the man gave it to Axel just in case he wanted to look at the contents. When he brought it back here to the office we went through it. The box was crammed with old photographs, cards and recipes. Nothing that seemed very important."

Grant removed a wrapper from one of the cupcakes and set it on a plate. "Mind if I have a look?"

Marge smiled as she reached for a cupcake. "Knock yourself out."

Grant opened the box and removed a framed picture from the top of the numerous papers. The picture displayed five young hunters kneeling down in front of a large deer. All five were dressed in camouflaged hunting outfits with their rifles held proudly at their sides, the man in the middle holding up the head of a twelve point buck.

Biting into the cupcake, Marge asked, "Recognize those fellas? The names are on the back of the picture."

Flipping the frame over, Grant scanned the written names from the right to the left. He turned the frame back around and exclaimed, "I'll be darned! Let's see, the one in the middle is Asa. On his left we have Luke and Zeb and on the right, Buddie and Charley. Boy, they sure look young in this photo. They must have been in their mid-twenties when this was taken."

Marge nodded. "Probably. Did I ever tell you my dad went to school with those boys? They were a couple of years behind him, but still to this day, he remembers them well. He said they called themselves the Five Caballeros. Those five boys went all through school together from kindergarten through high school. My father played football with them when they were in high school. He told me the school had a horrible winning record, that is, until the Five Caballeros showed up as freshman. That year my dad was a senior and we won the state championship. The five of them were a team by themselves. If you saw one of them on the street the others were close by. If you so much as tangled with one of them, eventually you'd have to deal with the other four. I guess they were all pretty good kids, well except for Asa. He was a hellion. The other four had to keep him under control most of the time. After high school, Zeb, Asa and Buddie joined the army. Charley didn't pass the physical and Luke was his mother's only son so he received an exemption. When Zeb, Asa and Buddie returned from the service, the Five Caballeros were back together. They went hunting whenever they had a chance, even after Zeb and Buddie got married."

Marge was interrupted by the phone. Grant pulled a brown folder out of the box and leafed through it. There were receipts for a number of items Luke had bought for his house, some dating back as far as fifty years. Another folder contained birthday and Christmas cards from years past. Pulling out a third envelope, Grant removed a thick rubber band and looked inside where he discovered a stack of hunting licenses all in order by year. He noticed the date on the last license: forty-two years ago. Luke would still have been in his twenties. Since there were no more licenses in the folder Grant assumed there was a possibility that Luke had stopped hunting. That struck him as odd.

As Marge hung up the phone, Grant asked, "Your dad ever go hunting with any of these men?"

"No," she answered. "My father never liked hunting. He thought it was crazy to go out and sit in a tree in the cold for hours on end just to shoot some poor animal he wouldn't eat anyway. Besides that, he says there are just way too many crazy fools running around the woods with guns. Come to think of it, I guess Luke found that out the hard way."

Grant confused, asked, "What do you mean?"

Taking another bite of her cupcake, Marge explained, "Luke got shot in his leg one year when he was climbing down from a tree stand. That put a damper on his days of hunting. I remember it because there was a small article in the paper about it."

Grant suddenly seemed very interested in her story. "Do you remember how far back that happened?"

"Well, let's see. Probably forty some years back, I guess. Why the sudden interest in Luke's hunting career?"

Not wanting to divulge what he was thinking, he politely blew her off, "Oh, it was just something I was wondering. It's not that big of a deal. Listen, do you think it would be alright if I took this picture?"

"Sure, I don't think we have any use for it. By the way, before you leave I want to tell you about the strange phone call I just received. It was Carol, my hairdresser. There's a rumor floating around that Ruby Jean Stroud up and left town. I guess she must have gotten tired of her husband, Cletus, beating on her. Funny thing is; I can't believe Ruby Jean wouldn't take Violet with her. I've never seen the woman without that child at her side. I know how she loves that little girl. Personally, I think there's more to the story than meets the eye." Snapping her fingers as if she had remembered something she yelled down the hall toward Brody's office, "Axel! Ruby Jean Stroud has run off. Do you think we need to put out an APB on her?"

Axel's voice echoed back down the hall, "Are you kiddin'? Hell if we put an APB out on every wife or husband that runs off, I wouldn't have room on my wall for all the photos. She'll no doubt turn up in a week or so. She's probably tryin' to teach that dumb ass husband of hers a lesson."

Grant got up as he finished his cupcake and started down the hall toward Axel's office. Marge gave him a thumbs up as she spoke softly, "If by chance you see Ruby Jean make sure she's alright. I don't trust none of those Stroud's any further than I can throw them."

Sticking his head in Brody's open door, Grant spoke, "I'm getting ready to head out on patrol. Anything I should know about?"

Axel grunted, "Hmmm, looks like Marge filled you in on what we've got goin' on...which at the moment isn't much. I do have somethin' I want you to handle today. Otis Stroud is supposed to fill out his county vendor's license application. I gave it to him last week and I told him someone would be droppin' by to pick it up. I told him he can't keep sellin' junk near the road every day without the license. I also told him to move that crap he sells back from the shoulder of the road. Without that license he's squattin' on county property and he's gonna cause an accident. Folks pull over to the side to see what he's sellin' and block the road. So, besides pickin' up that license, tell Otis to get that junk moved back. Got it?"

"Got it, Chief." Leaning in the doorway, Grant asked, "Why is it that the Stroud's seem to be giving us fits as of late?"

Axel frowned. "Lately! They've always been a big pain in the ass for me. Wasn't so bad when they all had their own places, but since they moved all those trailers onto Effy's place they've been actin' like a pack of wild dogs. When Effy was younger she used to keep those boys in check. Anymore, they just seem to do whatever they please. Now, Harmon ain't so bad. He keeps to himself most of the time, except when he gets drunk and runs down the road buck naked hootin' and a hollerin'. Ambrose is the toughest of the bunch. You have to be right careful when you're dealin' with that one. His younger brother, Cletus is the meanest of the lot. He reminds me of a stick of dynamite on a short fuse. But, I'm just waitin'. One of these days the Stroud's are goin' to cross the line and I'm gonna toss the whole damn bunch in jail or run them out of the county."

Grant smiled as he backed out of the doorway. "I'm on it, Chief. I'll pay the Stroud's a visit later on today."

Just as Grant was walking out the main office door to the parking lot, a delivery man from the local florist was carrying a large fruit basket tied with a pink bow in the door. Walking up to the desk, he announced, "I have a delivery here for a Marge. It looks like it's from Chief Brody." He placed the basket on the desk, smiled and walked back out the door as he winked at Grant.

"Well, I'll be!" blurted out Marge.

Grant grinned and pointed his finger at Marge. "Better watch out Marge. I think ol' Axel might be sweet on you."

He closed the door quickly as he heard Marge's response on the other side of the door. "Grant Denlinger, I've a mind to give you a good whuppin'."

Once on the Parkway, Grant found himself in the ever-present parade of cars, RVs and buses, tourists hailing from states to the north, south, east and west, even Canada. Fall was his favorite part of the year and for late September there was a nip in the air; perfect weather for those who chose to come to the Smokies in the Fall: not too cold, not too hot. Soon, Mother Nature would work her magic and the leaves would change from various shades of green to bright red, golden yellow and brilliant orange. Passing a number of shops along the Parkway he noticed that many of the businesses in town were already preparing for the upcoming fall; display windows crammed with pumpkins, corn stalks and scattered leaves. It was a good time of the year. First there was Halloween, then Thanksgiving and Christmas. His thoughts were interrupted as Marge called him on his radio explaining that there was a fender bender out on the outskirts of town that had the already heavy traffic in a snarl.

When Grant arrived at the accident scene, the two sets of vacationing families had swapped IDs and insurance information and were simply waiting for the arrival of the local police. After checking to make sure everyone was okay and satisfied that the proper information had been shared, Grant told them they could be on their way. It took Grant nearly thirty minutes to get the backed up traffic on the move once again.

Following a quick lunch of a hot dog and an orange soda at the Parkway Grocery, Grant found himself driving down Chapel Hill Drive; and not by accident. Buddie's strange behavior was still on his mind so he decided to drive by his house. Two blocks down the street he saw the FOR SALE sign in front of the brick ranch. Buddie had two sawhorses set up in the front yard and he was busy painting shutters. Pulling into the paved driveway, Grant rolled down the window. "House looks good, Buddie. Sorry to hear you're moving."

Buddie put the paintbrush down and wiped his hands on an old shop towel as he walked to the car. "Yep, it was a big decision, but I think we're doing the right thing. Hey, you looking for a house?"

"No thanks. I've got my hands full with the house I have. I've got some basement leaks and I have to get new gutters put up." Reaching for the framed photograph, Grant held it out the window. "You remember any of these guys, Buddie?"

Taking the picture, Buddie smiled, but then frowned. "God! Where in the world did you get this?"

Grant thought it seemed odd that Buddie's smile had instantly changed to one of concern, but Grant went right on talking, "It was in a box we retrieved from Luke's place. Says on the back that picture was taken over on Iron Mountain."

Buddie studied the picture for a few seconds and then spoke, "I remember that day like it was yesterday. It was freezing cold and I grumbled all the way over to Mountain City. I never liked hunting over in that neck off the woods because of all the snakes they have over there, but Asa said it was less crowded with hunters and more deer for us to hunt. If I recall, I think we only went over there twice." Tapping the picture with his finger, he explained, "I remember this day. Asa shot a buck not even ten minutes after we stepped into the woods. There were some other hunters nearby so we had this picture taken. After that, Asa gutted the deer and we headed on home. He gave us the business all the way back over here saying we were losers because none of us wanted to stay and hunt longer."

Handing the picture back to Grant, Buddie continued, "Years later we stopped hunting, well except for Asa. He wasn't happy unless he had his sights on some poor animal. Charley bought his farm and that kept him pretty busy. Luke was taking care of his invalid mother and me and Zeb got married. Seems like life has a way of changing things even if you don't want them to."

Grant looked at the picture and asked, "I thought Luke quit hunting because he got shot in the leg. I heard it happened over in the Iron Mountains."

Buddie stepped back away from the car as he answered nervously, "You know…I…don't recall where that happened. I can tell you this, that wouldn't have stopped Luke from hunting. If I remember that was a bad wound, but Luke, he got over it. It was sometime after that his mother took to a wheelchair and he had to stay with her most of the time." Buddie backed further away from the car as if he were politely asking Grant to leave. "Look, I better get back to those shutters. They ain't gonna paint themselves. 'Sides that, the realtor told me somebody's coming by tomorrow to have a look at the place. Gotta get those shutters painted and hung." He waved halfheartedly and spoke with a tone of sadness in his voice, "I'll see ya around, Grant."

Grant watched as Buddie walked back to the sawhorses, looked up at his house and slightly shook his head as if something were bothering him. Backing out of the driveway, Grant honked the horn and headed up the street. Buddie didn't even look up. *Something really odd is going on,* thought Grant. Turning left at the next street, Grant continued to contemplate Buddie's strange behavior. *He didn't seem nervous until he saw that photograph. It was almost as if the picture jogged his memory back to a time that he didn't want to think about. It seemed like he was hiding something.*

Two more turns and he was back on the Parkway heading for Wears Valley Road and the Stroud's place. The more he thought about Buddie the more he was convinced that he might just be on to something. What was Buddie hiding? He remembered over a year ago when Marge had told him that Buddie had dropped by the office to see Chief Brody, but then at the last moment left the office in a hurry as if he were upset. Then, there was that time a few months back when he had run into Buddie at the IGA and Buddie said that he had to get over to the office and talk with Brody about something. Buddie was definitely hiding something, but what was it? *How could Buddie remember every single detail about Asa shooting a buck over on Iron Mountain but he couldn't recall when one of his best friends had been shot in the leg?* Turning onto Wears Valley Road he smiled as he thought about something Dalton was always saying: *Ya can't go rolling manure in confectionary sugar and expect to come out with a jelly donut.* The fact that Luke Pardee had been murdered was bad enough, but the who and why still remained. Something just wasn't right and he was determined to find out what it was.

As usual, Maude and Otis were seated in their lawn chairs by the roadside next to their ragged green tent. Puffing on a cigarette, Maude gave Grant a leer as he passed slowly by, turned around and parked on the shoulder of the road.

Getting out of the cruiser, Grant approached the tent and asked, "I see you have tomatoes for sale. Are they homegrown?"

Maude stubbed out her cigarette. "Sure the hell are! Jest picked 'em this mornin.' They's fifty cents each. I ain't got no scale ta weigh 'em so's I got ta sell 'em by the piece."

"Sounds good," said Grant. "I'll take four."

Otis handed him a bag and Grant picked out four that looked good. The last one had a half torn off sticker that read: Grown in California. Grant smiled to himself. *So much for homegrown!* Extracting two dollars from his wallet, he handed the two bills to Otis. "My grandfather had a great garden this year, but his tomatoes are all gone. You folks must have the magic touch." Grant had to be careful how he talked to the Stroud's. He certainly didn't want to get them all riled up. He was looking for information. "I heard Ruby Jean left town. That true?"

"Ya betcha it's true," answered Maude defiantly as she raised her cane in the air. "Damn bitch up and left without so much as leavin' a note. Worst part is she left me ta tend ta her youngin while Cletus is off workin'. But I say good riddance ta bad rubbish. She weren't no wife or mother ta speak of. If ya happen up on her, tell her lazy ass I got a few things ta tell her. Don't think that'll likely happen though. Heard she hitched a ride out of town with some trucker." Changing the subject, she pointed her cane at one of the picnic tables. "Got some of Effy's hand crocheted dishcloths over there on that table. Dollar a piece. Want a few fer the misses?"

"No thanks," said Grant. "My mother-in-law crochets and she keeps us well supplied." Maude spit on the ground and lit up another smoke.

Not wanting to appear too forward, Grant turned to leave but then stopped and snapped his fingers, "Oh, by the way. I don't suppose you filled out that paperwork Chief Brody gave you?"

"The hell ya say," bellowed Otis. "I ain't filled out no papers and I ain't never gonna! This here be my property and I don't need no damn license ta sit here in my own front yard, so if yer a tellin' me that I got ta move from this here spot ya jest might go on and git that dumb ass Brody up here ta see if he can git me out of this here chair." Shaking his fist, Otis added, "And ya can tell 'em I says so!"

Grant stopped at the cruiser as he answered Otis, "I'll tell Axel what you said. He won't be very happy I'm not bringing that paper to him, so I reckon he'll be out to pay you folks a visit." Tipping his hat, he smiled. "Have a nice day." He was no sooner in the cruiser when a car whizzed by. Leaning out the open window, Grant started the engine and pointed at Otis. "See there...how close that car was. Ya know, it might just be one of those cars that knocks your ass out of that chair."

After pulling out, he looked in the rearview mirror and saw Otis standing by the side of the road, yelling and shaking his fist at Grant. Grant drew in a deep breath. He didn't like dealing with people like the Stroud's. They had no respect for the law and because of that very fact he was never sure what they would do. Reaching up he rubbed his right shoulder. For some reason it was sore; probably the after effects of the weight lifting and swimming he had been doing recently at the YMCA. He had told Dana Beth that he needed to get into better physical condition; especially after chasing Russell up the side of the mountain up near Jellico. He wasn't even thirty years of age and yet, he felt like a much older man. After going to the doctor and getting his yearly physical, he was told that a better diet and more exercise would eventually have him feeling his age. Looking down at his watch he noticed the time at 2:17 in the afternoon. His shift would be over at four, then he'd drive over to the Y, swim, lift weights, and then drive home for a relaxing evening with his family.

His shift over, he drove back to the station and the expected wrath from Brody. Grant knew he was in for a tongue lashing when Axel found out he didn't get the signed papers from Otis Stroud. Hesitating at the door, Grant wasn't in the mood for any of Axel's crap. Shoving the door open, he figured he might just as well get it over with. Marge was in the process of gathering up her birthday presents and cards when Grant walked in. "Here, let me help you," offered Grant as he picked up the flowers and the cake box.

"Thanks sweetie," said Marge. "Did you get that license Axel wanted?"

"No, I didn't and I'm not in the mood to listen to Axel go on and on about it."

Marge smiled. "It's not only my birthday, but your *lucky day* as well. The Chief isn't in at the moment. He got a call from an angry gift shop owner up town about people parking in his lot and then walking next door to the restaurant. If I were you, I'd sign out and hightail it out of here before the old fart gets back."

Grant pushed open the door, "Good idea."

Deciding to skip his workout, he headed home, showered and changed clothes. Something smelled really good when he walked in the kitchen. Ruth had made a salad and a big bowl of spaghetti; his favorite. He sat next to Dana Beth and gave Crystal Ann, who was sitting in her highchair, a kiss on her rosy cheek.

Just as Grant finished saying the blessing, he was about to fill his plate, when the front door opened and someone called out, "Smells like an Italian restaurant in here. You got enough for one more?" Dalton sauntered into the dining room and slipped into an empty chair at the opposite end of the table.

Ruth, always the gracious host, stood instantly and gestured toward the kitchen. "Here, let me get you a plate."

Dalton held up his hand and laughed. "Sit, Ruth. Enjoy your dinner. I was only kidding. Greta and I just finished up a big meal and I'm stuffed. That being said, I think I will get myself a cup of coffee."

Minutes later, Dana Beth shoved the spaghetti around on her plate and ran her hand across her forehead. "If you would all kindly excuse me, I need to lay down. I have a terrible headache." Looking across the table she asked, "Grant, would you mind keeping an eye on the baby for about an hour or so?"

Grant, with a mouthful of pasta and sauce answered as best he could as he placed his hand over his mouth. "Sure, you go ahead and lay down for awhile. I'll check on you later. Take a couple of aspirins."

Ruth waited until Dana Beth had climbed the stairs before she commented, "She's been getting a lot of headaches lately, but I can't get her to go see the doctor. And grouchy, whew! It's really hard to talk with her these days." Finished with her meal, Ruth stood and suggested, "I'll take care of Crystal Ann. Why don't you two go out on the porch and have your coffee."

Grant filled his cup as he addressed Dalton. "Actually, I do have something I want to talk over with you. Let's go outside." Without waiting for an answer, Grant picked up his coffee and headed for the front door, Dalton trailing right behind him.

They were hardly settled in the rockers on the porch when Dalton spoke, "Okay, what's up now? I'm still reeling from what you told me on Labor Day about Conrad. Does this have anything to do with that?"

"Not directly," said Grant, "but it could have a bearing on how this whole thing got started. It's about the murder of Luke Pardee. It's just a hunch I have and to be honest, I might be way out in right field on this but I just want to run something by you. You know I value your opinion and I might need some advice."

Dalton looked back into the picture window as if they were being overheard and seeing no one, leaned back in the rocker. Looking down at his cup he suggested, "Something tells me I may need a shot of whiskey in this coffee. So, what's on your mind?"

"Everyone seems to have given up on Luke's murder," said Grant. "Nobody is asking any more questions, there's nothing in the paper about how the investigation is still ongoing. It's like it's come to a dead end or something. Brody told me since it seems to have cooled down, he is assigning anymore investigating of Luke's murder to me. It's like he's given up. He knows it's a cold trail and I have little time to work on it. With Lee, Kenny and I rotating shifts, I'm pressed for time. But, just recently a series of strange events that happened strictly by accident, are starting to add up. So, just hear me out and keep an open mind."

Dalton grinned. "After what you told me in the barn a couple of weeks back, I think I'd just about believe anything at this point."

Grant stood up and started to pace back and forth across the porch. "Okay, you've got five friends that have known each other since childhood: Asa, Charley, Luke, Buddie and Zeb. Now, you and I know that Conrad killed Asa and Charley, but everyone is of the firm opinion that Russell committed those two murders. The remaining three men continue to go for morning coffee to the Parkway Grocery just like they always have, until one day they show up in the afternoon. Cora, who works at the Parkway reported when interviewed that the afternoon prior to Luke's murder she remembered Zeb, Buddie and Luke talking very loud, almost as if they were having an argument. All of a sudden, Luke gets up and storms out of the place and speeds off up the street. The other two leave a little later and are not seen for the rest of the day. The coroner's report says that Luke was killed around two in the morning. Luke must have known the killer since there was no evidence of forced entry. Both Buddie and Zeb along with their wives were questioned. Turns out, according to their wives that Zeb and Buddie were asleep at the time of the murder. But, I distinctly remember Mary, Buddie's wife, saying that her husband was in *his bed*. From that statement I think we can assume they have separate beds which means Mary wouldn't have known if Buddie was home at that late hour or not. If their beds were in different rooms or if Buddie's wife was a deep sleeper, she wouldn't have known if he slipped out of the house. Another thing, you would think that after their friend had been murdered Zeb and Buddie would have leaned on one another for moral support. They never talked with each other at the funeral and Buddie didn't even hang around for the church luncheon. Earlier today, I ran into Zeb over at the Parkway. He never mentioned one word about Buddie until I brought up his name. I guess you heard Buddie and his wife are moving down to Alabama as soon as they sell their house. That seems odd to me." Grant stopped by the porch steps and took a drink of coffee.

Dalton put his cup down on the porch floor. "Sit down Grant. You're making me dizzy watching you pace back and forth."

"Sorry," apologized Grant as he plopped down in the rocker. "Another thing, Buddie tried to see Brody on two different occasions during the past year or so. One time he left the office without even talking with Axel and the other time he never even showed up. It was like he has something on his mind, but is afraid to talk about it. I think that one or either both of them know a lot more about Luke's murder than they're letting on."

Dalton looked out across the front yard as if he were thinking, then asked in amazement, "Are you saying you think one of them killed Luke?"

"Possibly...I don't know...I hope not!"

"Look, Grant. Just because they're not talking with one another plus the fact that Buddie is moving out of state doesn't mean they're hiding something. I mean, they could still be in a state of shock from their best friend just being killed."

Grant disagreed. "If the murder was just last week I'd agree with you, but Luke's murder was what, nearly eight weeks ago. Nah, there's something else going on here."

"Well, speaking for myself I can't say as I blame Buddie for moving away from here. How would you feel if three of your four best friends were killed in less than two years. Kind of a scary thought. Wouldn't you say? Anyway, what possible motive could either one of them have for killing Luke?"

Grant stood up again and started pacing. "I've got a hunch as to their motive. I have the strangest feeling that Buddie, Luke, Zeb and either Charley or Asa were four of the five hunters that killed the Pender's back forty some years ago. I also think that for some unknown reason Luke cracked and had intentions of going to Brody. He was going to tell him the whole sordid story...a secret they had kept for over forty years. Either one or the other, or maybe both wanted him stopped. So they killed him!"

"Good Lord, Grant. Where in the hell did you come up with that? I've known these men for years, since they were little kids.

The only one that was ever a problem around these parts was Asa. The rest of them are good, church going citizens of Townsend. Why, a few years back, Zeb even sat on the city council."

"I know my theory must be hard to swallow, but hear me out. The five of them used to go hunting all the time. Suddenly, they stop! Why? Could it be because of what happened over there on Iron Mountain at the Pender farm? I know for sure that Luke never renewed his hunting license the year after the Pender's were murdered. I also found out that was the year he got shot in the leg and that it happened over in the Iron Mountains. Conrad told me ol' man Pender managed to shoot two of the hunters before they took him out. He shot one in the shoulder and the other in the leg. How much more obvious could it be? If you were wearing a heavy coat and hunting vest, getting shot in the shoulder might not cause that much damage. Getting shot in the calf of your leg is much more serious. It seems odd to me that Buddie was with Luke when he was shot and yet, he can't recall exactly where it happened. Buddie said he stopped hunting because he got married. What a crock! Women who marry men that hunt know what they're getting into and for the most part men will keep right on hunting despite the fact that they get married."

Dalton stood and placed his hand on Grant's shoulder. "What you're saying could be plausible. The thing is...it's something you would never be able to prove. All you have are a bunch of theories with no hard evidence: no gun that killed Luke, no eye witness, in short...no proof whatsoever. Now, I will say this. If what you say is true, the gun that was used to kill Luke Pardee is long gone. And as far as those men killing the Pender's is concerned, I have no earthly idea how you would go about proving it after all these years. Despite the fact that there is no statute of limitations on murder, I'm not so sure you could even acquire a warrant to go after either Zeb or Buddie. If I were you, I think I'd just sit on this for awhile. Grant, you can't take the weight of the world on your shoulders and not expect to get a backache. Zeb and Buddie have been pillars of the community for years. They have always been willing to help folks out and have been active in the church. First of all, I just can't believe they would have shot down the Pender's let alone keep it under wraps for over four decades."

Grant put his hands on his head. "I know and I hate to even

think I might be right. I've known these men for years, not as long as you, but for quite some time now. Even when I was a kid and I'd go to the Parkway Grocery. They would always give me change so I could buy a soda and some chips. They were always kidding with me. Buddie was the one who threw a party for me when I got on the Townsend Police and Luke, Buddie and Zeb all sent wedding gifts to me and Dana Beth."

Dalton walked to the porch steps as he spoke, "Let's face it, Grant. These past two years have taken their toll on most everyone around these parts. It's bad enough to have murders, but having them linked to your own family and friends is more than tough. I can see how it's affecting Dana Beth. Ever since it was revealed that Russell was Conrad's brother, making him her uncle, I can see a change in her."

"I know, Dalton. I just want this to all be over soon. I have a hard time thinking about the idea that the Pender's were Dana Beth's grandparents and that her father and uncle were both brutal killers. I just want Russell's body to be found and Luke's murder to be solved." Slamming his fist down on the porch railing he pitched the rest of his coffee out into the front yard. "Dammit! I just want this to be over!"

"Take it easy son," said Dalton. "You're doing the best you can. Give yourself some time and see how things play out. The answers are out there. It's just going to take some more digging before they surface."

CHAPTER FIVE

GRANT FINISHED HIS LAST THREE SWALLOWS OF cold milk and the last bite of meatloaf then walked to the sink to rinse off his dish. Looking out the window at the garage, he remarked with a mood of satisfaction, "That was one great meal, Ruth. I'm stuffed."

Ruth, walked over to the kitchen counter where she picked up a freshly baked pie. "I hope you saved enough room for apple pie. We also have vanilla ice cream. Conrad always said the best part of a meal is dessert. Surely, you'll have a slice of pie?"

"I'm sorry, maybe later while I'm watching the news. Right now, I'm just too full. Besides that, I've got to go out to the garage and get the rest of Conrad's stuff sorted out. There are still a few boxes in the overhead storage area I need to go through." He looked at the kitchen clock and explained, "It's just after five. If I get out there now I can work until ten-thirty and be back inside before the eleven o'clock news." Giving his daughter a peck on the cheek, he headed for the backdoor. "Save me a slice of pie. I'm not gonna miss out on that, I'm just putting it off for a few hours."

Crossing the driveway, Grant had no intentions of cleaning out the overhead storage area. His main objective was to get the incriminating evidence out of the van and hide it in the overhead area, like he and Chief Blue had discussed. Now that Russell Pearl was thought to be dead and he was believed to be the Smoky Mountain Killer, the idea of Conrad being implicated seemed impossible. But still, he didn't want to take any chances. He'd hide the evidence in the second level of the garage until at some point in the future he would destroy the gym bag and its contents.

He flipped the garage light on, slipped on a pair of old work gloves and ducked beneath the black tarp that concealed the van. The oil stain was still on the floor near the back of the van. He thought about cleaning the spot up, but since the murders had been solved there didn't seem to be any urgency in doing so.

As he climbed in the passenger side door, he noticed the ever present aroma of peach brandy pipe tobacco. Reaching around the seat, he grabbed the old gym bag from behind the console and placed it on his lap. Unzipping the bag, he removed each item as an eerie feeling came over him. He was touching the duct tape that had bound Conrad's victims: a hypodermic needle and a small bottle of chloroform utilized to drug those he had killed; a pair of old gloves, a pocket knife, a number of large plastic bags and last but not least, the heavy-duty lopping shears. He examined the shears closely. There didn't appear to be any blood stains on the razor sharp blades, but there were traces of faded blood on the wooden handles. He opened the blades and snapped them closed, the sharp snapping sound sent a shiver through his body. He reached down and picked up the pipe and bag of tobacco and placed them inside the bag. Withdrawing his hand, Mildred Henk's blood-stained business card fell down in between the console and the seat. He replaced the items from the bag back inside and just when he was about to put the shears back he was startled as Dana Beth opened the driver's side door and climbed in. Sitting in the seat holding the lopping shears, he was taken completely by surprise.

Dana Beth, noticing the strange look on his face apologized, "I'm sorry, I didn't mean to scare you." Looking at the shears in his hand, she asked, "What are you doing with those?"

Grant tried to compose himself as he stammered, "Ah, oh yeah, these." Lying, he explained, "I was just putting a few things in this bag I might keep." Changing the subject instantly, he asked, "What brings you out here?"

Dana Beth took a deep whiff of the scent of tobacco and commented, "Peach brandy tobacco. My father loved to smoke his pipe." Holding up her index finger to make a point, she went on, "Mother never allowed him to smoke in the house or if we were in the car with him. He did his smoking out here in the garage and on the front porch." Smiling sadly, she remarked, "I guess there will always be traces of my father around here somewhere."

Just then, Grant noticed the bloody edge of the business card sticking up in plain sight. Trying to distract her, he pointed at the pull down stairs that led up to the storage area, explaining, "I'm going to put some things I want to keep up there and also clean out the rest of the garage." When Dana Beth leaned forward to peer out the front windshield at the stairs, Grant pushed the card down further so it could not be seen. Dana Beth looked back at him just as he was withdrawing his hand.

"You seem so jittery," she said. "Are you alright?"

"I'm fine," answered Grant. "I guess you just scared me. I wasn't expecting anyone out here in the garage."

Accepting his explanation, she turned in the seat so she was facing him. "The reason I came out here was to tell you I just got a very interesting phone call from a man by the name of Marshall Case. He's an attorney from Knoxville. He wants to meet me and you as soon as possible at his office. He said it was quite important but he couldn't discuss the matter over the phone. However, he did reassure me he had some good news. I thought since you have tomorrow off, maybe we could take a run up there to see him. I told him I'd talk things over with you and then I'd give him a call back."

Grant, still trying to recover from the close call he had just experienced agreed without thinking too much about what his wife said. "Sure, tomorrow will be fine."

Dana Beth leaned over and gave Grant a kiss on the cheek. "Great, I'm going in and call him back." Climbing out of the van, she reminded her husband, "Don't forget, you have pie waiting for you when you come back in." She ducked under the tarp and Grant sat back in the seat. He took a long breath of relief. Looking down at the shears in his hand he thought, *God that was close. If she only knew the truth!*

Early the next morning, Dana Beth ran across the front yard, opened the fence gate and hopped into the open passenger door of the Jeep. In her hands she held a paper sack and a thermos. She smiled and spoke, "Made us each an egg sandwich for the road. Got some coffee too. Let's go!"

Five minutes later, Grant turned onto the Alexander Parkway and headed northeast toward Knoxville. Handing Grant one of the sandwiches, Dana Beth took a bite out of the second and spoke, "Crystal Ann was crawling around the living room when I left. She'll be fine with Ruth keeping an eye on her. I'm so glad mom decided to move in with us. She's really been a big help and I think she's enjoying being back home. We shouldn't be gone all that long. Our appointment with Mr. Case is at nine. It's just seven thirty now. That should give us plenty of time to locate his office. He told me it was downtown on Cherry Street. I've got the address in my purse." Taking a second bite of egg and bread she asked, "I wonder what this is all about?"

Grant, sipping his coffee answered, "Lawyers always remind me of politicians and used car salesmen: smooth talking, slick individuals that you can never completely trust. But then again, he did tell you it was good news?"

"That's what he said. And another thing, he said he couldn't discuss the matter over the phone. It must be important and it must involve both of us or he wouldn't have told us to come to his office." Pointing her sandwich at Grant, she probed, "You don't think this has anything to do with what went on up there in Jellico, do you?"

Grant waved off her question and remarked, "I don't see how it could. What good news could possibly come from that? Officer Devers was killed, Agent Gephart was wounded, I got nicked in the earlobe and Russell Pearl went ass over tea kettle over that cliff down into the Cumberland River Gorge."

"Maybe they finally found Russell's body. They've been looking for it for months."

"No, I don't think so. If they found the body why would some lawyer from Knoxville call us? And besides that, why would he call you? You had no part in tracking Russell Pearl down. No, if that were the case, they would have called Brody or Chief Blue. There would have also been a write up in the paper about the discovery of the body. I don't have any idea what this lawyer wants to talk with us about, but I'm sure it doesn't have anything to do with what happened up there in those mountains. I wish he would have given you more information."

Looking out the passenger window at the passing countryside, Dana Beth elaborated, "Maybe, I guess we'll know soon enough."

Entering the busy city streets, Dana Beth held the sheet of paper with Case's address written on it, scanning the various office buildings as Grant drove slowly down Cherry Street. She pointed at the metal addresses affixed to the front of the buildings and spoke as they passed by, "Four seventeen, nineteen, twenty-one, twenty-three...there it is, four twenty-five Cherry. Pull in, there's a side parking lot."

Getting out of the Jeep, Grant stretched and looked at the three story brick building, the front of the structure practically covered with crawling vines. They climbed the concrete steps that were flanked on either side with statues of miniature lions. Grant pointed at the gold metal lettering indicating the street address, located next to an imbedded plaque which read: MARSHALL CASE ATTORNEY AT LAW.

Inside the front door there was a spacious foyer complete with a bench, umbrella holder and two large banana plants. Passing through double-wide pocket doors they found themselves in a walnut paneled reception area. The walls were adorned with various pictures of some of Knoxville's finest architecture. A black leather couch and two matching chairs were tastefully positioned around the room along with a cherry, glass-topped coffee table on which were displayed copies of the New Yorker magazine. A large crystal chandelier hung from the twelve foot ceiling and the focal point of the room was an oversized cherry desk toward the back of the room. Behind the desk sat a sophisticated older lady. Looking over the top of her chain suspended eye-glasses, the woman politely spoke, "How may I be of help to you this morning?"

Dana Beth approached the desk as she responded, "My name is Dana Beth Denlinger and this is my husband, Grant. We have a nine o'clock appointment with a Mr. Marshall Case." Glancing at a grandfather clock situated in the right corner of the room, she further explained, "I believe we're twenty minutes early. We weren't exactly sure where your office was located."

Looking down at an appointment pad, the woman answered professionally, "Yes. Mr. Case is expecting you. I believe at the moment he is on the line with a client. If you'll please have a seat, I'll check."

When the woman disappeared through a doorway on the left, Grant lowered himself down onto the couch, the black leather crinkling beneath his weight. Looking around the expensively decorated room, he remarked, "This Marshall Case, whoever he is, is in the twenty percent bracket."

Dana Beth, making herself comfortable in one of the chairs asked, "What are you talking about?"

"When it comes to lawyers people are always saying that twenty percent of the lawyers make eighty-percent of the money and the remaining eighty percent struggle for the remaining twenty percent. If his office furnishings are any indication, Mr. Case is most definitely making money."

The secretary returned as she announced, "Mr. Case will be finishing his call momentarily. He will be right out to see you. Would either of you care for a water, maybe a soda or coffee?"

Dana Beth was the first to speak as she declined, "No thanks, just had breakfast."

Grant nodded, "No thank you."

Grant no sooner picked up one of the magazines when a tall, distinguished looking man with graying hair and matching well-trimmed mustache entered the room. Adjusting the vest of his three-piece, black pin-striped suit he approached Dana Beth with an outstretched hand, exposing the gold cuff link on his custom white shirtsleeve. "You must be Dana Beth Denlinger. My name is Marshall Case." He then turned to Grant, offering his hand. "And this must be your husband, Grant."

Dana Beth, a tad bit intimidated by the apparent success of the man standing before her, answered humbly, "Yes, we're the Denlingers. I spoke with you on the phone yesterday."

Folding his hands, he nodded toward his office door. "I'm sorry you had to wait. If you would please step into my office we can discuss my reason for asking you to come today." He gestured graciously with his right hand and guided Dana Beth and Grant past the desk, down a short hallway and into an office that proclaimed the same level of success as the reception area.

Seated in one of two leather padded wooden chairs in front of a spacious, neat as a pin desk, Grant noticed a number of framed plaques centered on the left side paneled wall: Bachelor of Arts Degree from the University of Tennessee, Tennessee Alumni Award, Knoxville Man of the Year Award, Honorary Knights of Columbus Membership and a host of photographs depicting Mr. Case appearing with what Grant surmised were no doubt important individuals.

Taking a seat, Case opened a manila folder, looked across the desk and smiled pleasantly. "I'm sure you're interested in your reason for being in my office this morning, so let's begin. First off, Dana Beth, your father, Conrad and I were very good friends." Motioning at a photograph on the opposite wall he explained the picture of he and Conrad holding up two large fish. "Your father was quite the fisherman. That picture was taken up at Itasca Lake one year when he invited me up during the Fall." Pointing to a framed white sweater with a large bright orange T on the front, he expounded, "I played tennis for the university and graduated more years ago than I care to admit. My son also graduated from the University of Tennessee. He attended a number of classes taught by your father. My son claimed that Professor Conrad Pearl was the best teacher he ever had, bar none. I met your father at a number of school functions. He was very active in university activities. We hit it off and became the best of friends. We not only fished, but we played some golf and occasional tennis as well. He always talked about you, Dana Beth. I'm sure I don't have to tell you how much your father loved you. A little over three years ago, Conrad came to me in confidence, explaining that he had stage three pancreatic cancer, and the disease was getting worse. He didn't want anyone other than his doctor and me to know of his illness. At that time, he informed me that he had possibly a year or a little longer to live."

He opened the folder and placed his hands over the documents inside. "What I have before me is one of your father's two wills."

Dana Beth gave Grant a strange look, then nodded toward the folder. "You said one of two wills. I guess I'm not that familiar with most legal procedures, but isn't it unusual to have more than one will, Mr. Case?"

Case smiled as he answered, "You can call me Marshall. It just seems less formal. And yes, a person can have more than one will. It's unusual to have more than one, but it certainly is within the limits of the law. Conrad's other will, which I believe was read to your mother, Ruth, by another legal firm here in Knoxville was rather standard. I only know this because your father told me what was included in the will he left your mother. Your parents shared in the assets they had, so most of the things they owned automatically fell to your mother; things like insurance policies, checking and savings accounts, and investments that your mother was aware of."

Grant raised his hand. "You just said something that doesn't make any sense. You mentioned investments Ruth was aware of as if to say there are investments she was not aware of."

"Very perceptive, Grant. Normally, a wife would be aware of everything her husband owned. Conrad had a second life, so to speak. A better way to put it would be to say that he had a secondary financial life which is the reason for the second will." Looking at Dana Beth, Marshall explained, "The truth is, your father owned far more than your mother could have imagined and it's all explained right here in these documents."

Dana Beth looked at Case as she raised her hands in confusion and remarked, "I'm sorry, but I'm lost here. How could my father possibly have investments that my mother wasn't aware of. They shared everything and made family decisions together. Why would my father do something without my mother's knowledge or approval?"

"I realize it may be difficult for you to believe your father did some things your mother had no knowledge of. Let me explain to you what your father said when he told me about his terminal cancer. Now, rather than read to you from the will which contains a lot of legal jargon, I'm just going to lay out the highlights."

Leaning back in his swivel chair, Marshall crossed his legs and began, "Your father told me he had a brother that no one in his immediate family knew about. As you now are aware, that would be Russell. Conrad told me Russell was slow and didn't function all that well around most people. So over the years, even when they were youngsters growing up, he had to look out for his younger brother. Some time after they were adopted by the Pearls, who happened to live right here in Knoxville, the two boys were informed that their father's farm over in the Iron Mountains had been sold for close to four million dollars. Conrad and Russell were to be the recipients. Since they were too young to actually receive the money, a trust was set up stipulating when the boys turned eighteen they would be entitled to the money. A few years later, Conrad turned eighteen and graduated from high school. He received his potion of the funds which was approximately two million. At that time, Conrad made the decision to take his younger brother out of school and purchased a cabin from Mrs. Pearl which is up near Jellico. From that point on Conrad looked out for Russell making sure he had what he needed to live comfortably. When Russell turned eighteen, Conrad arranged to have the two million Russell had coming placed in a special account that Conrad was the executor of."

Case tapped the folder on his lap as he continued, "Conrad was intelligent enough to realize that after his upcoming death Russell would be lost with no one to look out for his best interest, despite the fact everything Conrad owned would fall to his brother. That's where I come in. Your father, Dana Beth, asked me to become the executor-custodian of the will in order to ensure his brother would be taken care of the rest of his life. The will also stated that in the event of Russell's death, everything would then fall to you, Dana Beth, his daughter."

Pitching the folder onto the desk, Case raised his eyebrows and pursed his lips as he explained, "This is where the entire situation gets a little bit tricky. Russell Pearl, at this time is only thought to be deceased since the body has never been found. So, at this juncture, there is no physical proof the state will accept that actually proves Russell Pearl is dead."

Placing the palm of his right hand over the folder, Case stated, "Until we have an official death warrant signed by a bona fide coroner all of the investments and monies in the will are frozen and will remain so until either the body is found or a reasonable timeframe has passed where the person in question cannot be located. The timeframe is generally about seven years. So, for now, we have three choices: First, we can only hope the body is located at which point the death certificate will be signed and you, Dana Beth, the beneficiary are entitled to all monies and property therein. Second, if the body is never found, when the seven year period finally rolls around, we file a petition, Russell Pearl is officially pronounced dead and the will goes into effect. The third option we have is that we can actually go to court and make a concerted effort to prove that Russell Pearl is in fact dead by means of eye witness reports, professional opinions and police documentation. If we choose to go that route, still with the way the court systems are run, it could take a couple of years."

Dana Beth, with a look of concern, asked, "You said originally my father and Russell got around four million dollars for the sale of their father's property. That had to be somewhere around thirty or so years ago. How much of that money could there possibly be left."

"I figured that question would come up," said Case, "so I took the liberty to get a ballpark figure." Opening the folder he removed a sheet of paper. Holding up the paper, he went on, "Now, this is not an exact figure but it's close enough to give you a good idea. Let's start off with the savings and checking account Conrad had at a local bank here in town. Both accounts are interest bearing with a current total of $45,700.00. Conrad also has the maximum amount insured by the FDIC, which happened to be $250,000.00 in five different banking institutions. These five accounts have grown, through interest, over the years to approximately $375,000.00 in each account. So, right there, that puts you at about 1.9 million. Conrad also invested in a number of stocks and mutual funds which as close as I can estimate equal around 3.1 million. That brings the current total to about five million. But that's not the end of it. There is also the cabin up near Jellico which sits on ten acres of prime timberland. I have no idea what that's worth. We can find out if you prefer but at this point I really don't think that makes much of a difference."

Pulling open the desk drawer, he withdrew a set of keys which he laid next to the folder. "Speaking of the cabin, these are the keys to the property. It's the only part of the will that you can actually place your hands on, at least for now. Understand, if you decide to spend some time at the cabin, clean the place up or in general just keep an eye on the place, you won't be breaking any laws. I wouldn't suggest living there as you do not officially own the property. That will not take place until one of the three options we discussed is fulfilled. Are there any questions?"

Dana Beth and Grant stared at each other, both seemingly frozen in amazement. Dana Beth acted as if she wanted to say something but she just couldn't seem to get the words out. Grant, sensing she was experiencing a moment of awkwardness, spoke up, "Mr. Case. In the meantime, whether it be months or years until this matter is resolved, what happens to all of this money."

"Good question," answered the attorney. "All of the accounts whether they be at the banks or from investment brokers will be frozen by the State of Tennessee. As future beneficiaries, you need not have any great concern over losing any monies currently held. For instance, even though the money in the bank will be frozen, the bank is still required by law to continue paying whatever the current interest rate is, even if it takes seven years to release the funds. So, as far as the banks are concerned, the longer the money is left untouched, the more money there will be when you eventually take over the accounts. The stocks and mutual funds are a different story. Depending on how the stock market pans out over the period of time between now and when the will kicks in, you may make money or possibly lose money. It's been my experience in dabbling in the market that over the long haul an investor will always make money despite the fluctuations in the market."

Dana Beth cleared her throat as she smiled oddly. "When you told me over the phone that what you wanted to share with me was good news I never expected to be driving back to Townsend this morning realizing that in the future Grant and I would be wealthy people...millionaires!"

"Yes indeed, life can be very strange," remarked Case. He slid the cabin keys across the desk toward Dana Beth. Closing the folder, he placed it back in the desk drawer and stood, looking at his watch. "I have another appointment at ten o'clock so if there are no other questions I guess that's it for now."

Grant, realizing the meeting had come to an end stood, while Dana Beth remained seated staring at the keys in her hand. Grant gently pulled her to her feet as he looked across the table at Case. "We'll keep in touch, Marshall. I guess the next time we talk will be when Russell's body is discovered."

"I imagine so," stated Case. "More than likely with you being a member of law enforcement you'll be contacted long before me. I'll wait for your call and I hope it will be soon. In the meantime, if you have any questions, feel free to give me a call."

Outside in the parking lot, Grant started the Jeep, and turned on the windshield wipers as it was starting to rain. Looking across the seat at his wife, he remarked, "The mystery of what Mr. Case wanted to speak with us about has been solved. Who would have thought not even an hour after we meet the man that we are sitting here as potential millionaires." Backing out of the lot, Grant corrected himself, "I'm sorry. What I meant to say is that *you* are a potential millionaire. I just happen to be lucky enough to be married to you."

As Grant pulled out onto Cherry Street, Dana Beth looked back at Case's office in astonishment. "Grant. When we took our wedding vows we agreed to share everything, so therefore *we* are potential millionaires. Actually, potential is not the right word to describe what has just happened. You heard what Case said. It's just a matter of time until Russell's body is located or seven years pass. We *are* millionaires. Of course, right now, we're just millionaires on paper. When you think about it, it's a frightening thought."

Grant made a right hand turn from Cherry when he noticed the directional sign that read: 75 SOUTH. With a look of confusion, he inquired, "How could being the recipient of five million dollars be frightening? I might be wrong here, but I think it's safe to say that ninety-nine percent of the world's population would consider this good, no, great news! I mean this could be life changing."

"That's exactly what I'm talking about. Yesterday we were normal, I guess middle-class people. The fact that we will eventually have five million dollars at our disposal is hard to comprehend. I know what I'm about to say might sound utterly crazy, but I'm not so sure I want this money. The thought keeps crossing my mind that this is blood money!"

Increasing the speed of the Jeep to fifty miles per hour, Grant cruised onto Route 75 as he looked in the rearview mirror. "How could this money be considered blood money? Maybe I've seen too many movies, but blood money always comes from financial gain because someone else looses their life; sort of like ill-gotten gain. Conrad and Russell were simply the recipients of the proceeds that came from the sale of their parent's farm. I don't see where that makes it blood money."

Dana Beth tried to explain herself, "Maybe blood money is the wrong way to put it. It's just that I feel guilty coming out on the upside of all the tragedy we've experienced the last two years. Think about it: eight people have been murdered, no, ten. We can't forget about Officer Devers and then more recently Luke Pardee. That's a lot of bloodshed!"

"I understand how you feel," said Grant, "but the fact the money came from the sale of a farm has absolutely nothing to do with all the murders."

Looking out the passenger window, Dana Beth shook her head and commented, "This whole thing is just so amazing, not to mention tragic."

Passing a tour bus, Grant changed the subject. "So when we get back home how do we handle this as far as Ruth is concerned? Do we tell her what Case told us...about the money, or do we keep this to ourselves?"

"I think it would be for the best, at least for now," said Dana Beth, "not to mention it to her. I have no doubt she would be happy for us, but on the other hand I'm not sure how this would make her feel."

"Why would you say that?" asked Grant.

"Ever since it has been revealed Conrad had a brother, a brother that I might add, none of us in the family ever knew of, her attitude about Conrad seems to have changed. The other night while we were folding baby clothes, she made the comment that Conrad may not have been the man she thought she knew. All those years, he had a brother and didn't share that with her, not to mention he kept the fact he had cancer from her as well. She made a comment about what else had Conrad kept from her that she was unaware of. If we tell her he had millions of dollars he didn't tell her about that might be something else for her to stress over."

"Alright, agreed then." said Grant. "We say nothing to Ruth. Of course, you realize this is just temporary. Whether we receive the money a month from now or seven years down the road, eventually we're going to have to say something to her."

Dana Beth reached over and placed her hand over Grant's. "We'll cross that bridge when we come to it."

Grant, just about to pass another tour bus, looked across the seat at his wife, "Listen, I've got an idea. Let's go to Lily's when we get back to Townsend. We can have lunch and chill out. You know Ruth can read you like a book. With the look of amazement that you still seem to be wearing she'll pick right up on the fact that something's up. So, let's just enjoy a good lunch and try to return to some state of normalcy before we go home. Besides that, we have to decide what we're going to tell your mother about what the lawyer wanted."

Dana Beth leaned over and kissed her husband on the cheek. "I've got an idea We simply tell her that dad left the cabin and some land to the family. How's that sound?"

"Sounds good," answered Grant. Paying attention to the road ahead once again, he commented, "The colder than normal temperature and the rain reminds me of a soup day. I hope they have their broccoli cheese soup today."

Lily's was bustling with locals and tourists when Grant opened the door and they entered. The hostess told them it would be twenty minutes before they were seated but was then interrupted by a waitress who told them a table by the front window had just opened up and for Grant and Dana Beth to follow her.

They no sooner ordered drinks, two iced teas, when Grant looked toward the front door. He couldn't believe his eyes. "I can't believe it. I'm pretty sure that's Doug Eland who just walked in."

Dana Beth looked toward the door as she asked, "Where have I heard that name before?"

"Doug. Doug Eland! He was the photographer who first stumbled on Asa Pittman's body up on Thunderhead Trail and then after that he was part of the investigative team. Remember, he's the photographer I told you about, the one from Louisville. Be right back. I'm going to go talk with him." He took two steps when he stopped and asked, "Would you mind if I invited him to sit with us?"

Taking a sip of her tea, Dana Beth smiled. "Of course not."

As Grant approached, he noticed that Doug was talking with a young woman who appeared to be with him.

"Doug Eland!"

Upon hearing his name mentioned, Doug turned and smiled at his friend. "Grant, of all the people to run into." Reaching for Grant's hand he kept right on talking, "Listen, you're not going to believe this, but Max and I were just talking about you on our way over here. I was telling her since I was in town that I needed to give you a jingle."

Grant stared at Max, not quite sure what to say. Suddenly, Doug blurted out, "How rude of me. Grant Denlinger, I'd like you to meet Maxine Turner, or as she prefers to be called, Max." Holding up Max's hand, he displayed a diamond ring as he proudly announced, "Max and I are engaged to be married. As a matter of fact, we're flying up to upstate New York to her hometown to be married next week."

"Congratulations," said Grant as he motioned toward the crowded restaurant. "Are you guys eating?"

"That was the plan," answered Doug, "but we've been told it's about a twenty minute wait."

"Nonsense, you can join us. My wife and I have a table for four and there's only two of us." Turning to the hostess, Grant spoke, "You can cross them off the waiting list. They'll be joining us."

As they approached the table, Dana Beth stood. Doug reached for her hand as he interjected, "And this must be the woman I've heard so much about."

Dana Beth smiled and before she could say anything, Grant made the introductions, "Dana Beth, this is Doug Eland and his fiancée, Maxine, or I guess I should say, Max. Max, Doug, I'd like you to meet my wife, Dana Beth."

After everyone shook hands all around, they were seated as the waitress approached and took Doug and Maxine's drink orders. Grant was the first to speak as he gestured at Dana Beth. "Doug and Max are engaged and to be wed next week." Once again, before Dana Beth could speak, Grant looked at Doug, asking, "How could this possibly happen? If I remember correctly on one of your trips down here you told me you were too obsessed with your work to be married." Motioning at Maxine, Grant emphasized, "So, what changed?"

"Well believe it or not we met in the woods," explained Doug. "I was on a photo shoot in the Catskill Mountains in New York State. Finished for the day, I'm hiking back down this mountain trail when Max running up the trail comes around a large boulder and knocked me square on my backside. She helped me up, bandaged a rather bad cut on my leg and it just kind of went from there. That was six months ago."

"So I guess you're down here on business; on one of your Smoky Mountain photo shoots?"

"I am, or I mean, we're down here on business. You know how much I love it here. We talked things over and since she was raised in the Catskills and loves the mountains, we decided to move to Townsend. We're going to open a combination gift and wildlife photo shop. Max makes handmade jewelry and custom walking sticks and picture frames from branches she finds in the forest.

She also makes handmade furniture from tree limbs and old logs, perfect for all of the log cabins in the area. Of course, I'll still do some occasional traveling around the country, creating my wildlife pictures which I can sell at the shop as well."

Dana Beth, finally able to get a word in, asked, "You said you were going to live here in Townsend. Have you put any thought into where your shop will be located?"

"To tell you the truth we came down here two days ago blind, not really having much of an idea where the shop would be. The first day we arrived we were on our way to meet one of the local realtors. We had some time to blow so we just kind of drove around Townsend. We stopped in a gift shop on the north end of town called the Black Bear. We met the owner and his wife, Mr. and Mrs. Callibrizzi. Nice folks. Well, we got to talking with them and found out they were retiring and moving to Boca Raton, Florida. When they found out Max and I were looking for a gift shop location, they said if we were interested they'd give us a great deal on their place."

"And that's not all!" said Max. "They just happen to have a log house on the outskirts of town they are also selling. They offered us a package deal; the shop *and* the house."

"We just got back from the bank," said Doug. "We've been approved for a loan and we'll be closing the week after we get back from the wedding."

Max took a drink of her tea. "I'm excited! I've always wanted to live in a log house. Everything is happening so fast." Changing the subject, Max asked Grant, "So how did you and Doug meet?"

Grant laughed at how ironic his answer was. "Actually the same as you and Doug met; the woods, up in the mountains."

Doug touched Max on the arm as he explained, "I'll never forget that day. It was the first time since my father had passed away that I had been down here to the Smokies. I started the day right here at Lily's. I had a good breakfast, then drove up to the park, got a horse and reported into the ranger station, then proceeded up to Thunderhead Trail. Like I said, I'll never forget that day. I discovered the mangled body of Asa Pitman just off the trail. Later on, when the police came, that's when I met Grant. We sat on an old log and talked while we waited for the county sheriff and the coroner; Asa, dead as a doornail not ten feet away. Little did we know at the time, but that was just the beginning of a series of brutal murders. Later on, I was part of the investigative team."

Max looked at Doug. "You never told me about any murders."

Dana Beth, not having any desire to relive the horror of the past two years, spoke up, "That's all over with now. The individual who was responsible was shot."

For the next hour, over good food and pleasant conversation Doug and Grant discussed the plans for the gift shop while Dana Beth told Max about the best places to shop for groceries and about the wonderful shops over in Pigeon Forge and Gatlinburg. Lunch finally came to an end as Dana Beth gave Max her phone number and told her to call when she had a chance so she could show her around the area.

Outside in the parking lot, Grant hung back as he grabbed Doug's arm at the same time checking to see if the girls were watching them. "Doug, since you were part of the investigative team, we need to get together so I can catch you up or how everything finally went down."

"Yeah that sounds good. I couldn't help but notice how your wife put the kibosh on talking about the murders."

"Around here you'll soon find out everyone would just as soon put that whole mess to bed. Give me a call when you get some free time and I'll fill you in."

"Sounds good. Look, it's great to see you again."

That evening Grant sat on the front porch steps and took a swig of his bottled beer. Looking down at his wristwatch he noticed the time: 12:30 at night. The rain had stopped, the trees and bushes scattered around the yard dripping from the all day drizzle. A sudden snapping sound came from the glowing bug zapper that hung at the far end of the porch as another local bug's life had come to an abrupt end. *What a day!* thought Grant. Despite the fact that Conrad was a serial killer, he still had looked out for his daughter, Dana Beth. Grant knew one thing for sure and that was with this new set of circumstances that had popped into his life that now he would never be able to tell Ruth and his wife the truth. Sooner or later they'd have to tell Ruth about the money; another mystery about her husband she had been unaware of all those years. The fact that their husband and father was a brutal killer would just be too much for them to handle. Dalton was right. Sometimes the truth could hurt. It was just better to let it be.

CHAPTER SIX

RUSSELL LAY ON HIS COT WATCHING A PRAYING mantis on the windowsill devour a spider. Suddenly, a flapping of wings announced the arrival of a blackbird. As the mantis flew off, Russell frowned. He liked praying mantis. Conrad always wanted to kill them, but Russell wouldn't let him.

He had been thinking a lot about Conrad the last week. He wished his older brother were here to take him home. Conrad always made sure he had money to spend and he took care of any repairs that needed done around the cabin. He played cards with him and brought good things to eat. Even though he liked being alone, he always enjoyed his visits with his brother. It was different living here with people who paid him so much attention.

He turned over in the bed that was too small to accommodate his large frame. The bed made a loud squeaking noise and the old springs beneath him groaned. Lately, he was getting used to a lot of new sounds; the roosters crowing in the early morning, an occasional squeal from the pigs roaming around the front yard, the laughter and squabbling from the noisy children and Effy's boisterous voice cursing everyone who ventured into her house.

He preferred the sounds that surrounded his cabin in Jellico: the babbling, peaceful sound of the water running over the moss-covered rocks in the creek and the wind blowing through the tall pines. He knew all the birds by their calls and could detect a deer or a raccoon by the sounds they made in the dry leaves. At night the cicadas and the owls lulled him to sleep. Even the sound of the coyotes baying at the moon was familiar to him. Now, the grating of creaking brakes on the old trucks and the men shooting at empty bottles disturbed him. He wanted so desperately to go home, but Effy said he wasn't well enough yet.

Russell remembered very little about the first few days after he had been rescued by Dwayne and Arliss. He couldn't recall the trip in the back of the pickup and he couldn't remember staying in the barn. He did remember the pain he felt as someone had removed the bullet from his leg and when the gash on his forehead was stitched up. He remembered someone saying, "Hold him down, boys! He ain't gonna like this one bit." After that, he must have passed out. When he awoke he was lying on a bed in one of Effy's bedrooms. Drifting in and out of consciousness for the next few days, someone had spooned a clear liquid into his mouth and two men carried him to the bathroom. Counting the nights, Russell figured it must have been at least ten days since he arrived at the farm. He recalled the first time he opened his eyes and stared into the faces of two older women who were hovering over him. He had tried his best to get up, but almost passed out from the pain that ravaged his body. The older lady of the two, who he now knew as Effy, had put a glass to his lips and he sipped on the acrid water. Later, he learned that she had crushed up some pain pills and placed them in the water. They were pills that were left over from an accident last year when Cletus had fallen off the tractor. It was the first time in twenty years Cletus had gone to the doctor. He had gotten pain pills for his back. Those pills kept Russell asleep for three straight days.

There were vivid memories of the first time he was fully conscious. He was lying in a stinking bed, naked and covered by a thin wool blanket. When he realized the repulsive smell surrounding him was coming from his own body, he had mumbled his first words since being rescued. "I need to take a shower...I stink!"

Effy had replied, "Yer damn right ya do! I'll fetch the boys an' they'll git ya ta the bathroom." He had protested and tried to rise from the bed, but his legs were too weak to support him. After Effy removed his bandages, Cletus and Arliss dragged his naked body down a hallway and helped him into a shower. Holding onto a wall covered in mold, his hand shook as he turned on the water. The first blast of warm water felt like a hundred bees attacking his body. All of the open sores and wounds on his body were caked with dirt and grime and he watched as the muddy water slowly ran down the rusted drain. Picking up a misshapen bar of soap, he leaned against the wall and with his good hand forced himself to cleanse his body. Effy opened the soap stained shower door twice to make sure he was okay. She brought him two frayed towels and a plaid flannel robe to wear.

As he carefully patted himself dry, he looked into the floor-length cracked mirror next to the rusted sink. He looked like he had lost weight. His thin face was covered in an unkempt beard and his hair had grown almost to his shoulders. Tilting his head, he decided he liked his new look. He also examined the rest of his body to see what damage had been done to him from the gunshot wounds and the fall over the cliff. He pulled his hair back and stared in the mirror at the jagged scar across his forehead. The two bullets that had scraped his shoulders had not caused any adverse affect and seemed to be healing. It was all the cuts and sores that were painful. Both of his knees were scabbed over and the calf of his left leg still showed a nasty wound that was beginning to ooze as he stood there. He wrapped a towel around his leg, put on the robe and called for help. Effy put a clean sheet on the bed and the room was already starting to smell better.

Lying back down on the bed, he still had no idea who these people were and what they intended to do with him. At the moment, all he wanted to do was sleep. The ordeal of taking the shower had worn him out. As he laid his head on an old floppy pillow, he could smell something cooking that made him realize how hungry he was. *He wanted food and he wanted it now!* If he were at the cabin he could whip up some chili and hot dogs.

Minutes later, his hunger pangs were answered as the younger of the two women, Maude, brought him a simmering bowl of beef stew and three pieces of bread covered in apple butter. She wanted to feed him, but he said he could do it himself. Lifting himself up on one elbow, he balanced the bowl on the edge of the bed and devoured every last bite of the stew and the bread in less than five minutes. Maude sat in silence and watched him until he was finished. She took the bowl and left the room. Now that his stomach was full and his body reasonably clean, he closed his eyes and slept until the next morning.

Sleeping and eating had become a daily routine for him without much in between. At times, he would lie in bed and listen to the conversations around him; loud voices that included a lot of cursing and yelling.

Fully awake now, he reached up and tapped the window pane; the blackbird flew off. Despite the fact that he didn't know the people who were caring for him, he was grateful that the two men had brought him here. If they would have left him in the woods he would have died. When Effy told him Dwayne and Arliss were his cousins, he was surprised. An even bigger surprise came when he was informed that Maude was his aunt. When he lived in the Iron Mountains as a young boy, Millard and Etta never spoke about their relatives and he had never met any of his mother's family. He wished that Conrad had told him about these people and also about Dana Beth. And then, of course there was Dana Beth's new baby. He had a family and he never knew it. Conrad must have been ashamed of him. Maybe things wouldn't have turned out so bad if he had known about his family.

Each day, Maude or Effy would tell him more about the family and as soon as he was on his feet, he would get to meet them all. He now knew that Maude was his mother's sister, and her first husband, Clovis, who was dead, had moved away from Tennessee for a long time and had no idea of what happened to Conrad and himself. When Maude married Otis, they moved back to Townsend and came to the Stroud place to live with Effy, who was Otis' mother. Maude told Russell that she was sorry Conrad had died. Russell was apprehensive about sharing too much information about his brother. Conrad had always told him to keep his business to himself and keep his distance from strangers.

Maude told him most of the family were none too happy that he was here, but, in time, she was sure when they all got to know him, their opinion would change. Maude was beginning to take a liking to him and for the first time in years, she felt like she had a purpose, even if it was only temporary. Since she and Otis had moved in with Effy, she felt like all she did was cook and work to take care of the family.

"Ya awake?" Maude asked, opening the door.

"Yes, Ma'am," answered Russell. "I'm just laying here."

Maude liked the idea of Russell addressing her as 'Ma'am.' It made her feel important. She was called the old lady or Maude by almost everyone on the property.

Puffing on a cigarette, Maude smiled, "I made me a mess of pancakes an' sausage. Ya hungry?"

Russell's face lit up. "Yes, Ma'am!"

"Let's see if we can git ya ta yer feet," said Maude, "so's ya can eat at the table in the kitchen."

Russell sat up painfully and felt the pain in every part of his body as he pulled the robe around him. He had been wearing it every day since he had taken the shower. He really wanted to take another shower but decided to wait until he could do it himself. He didn't like people going into the bathroom with him.

He sat on the edge of the bed and placed his bare feet on the cold floor. Light headed, he still had to try and get up. Grabbing hold of the wall to steady himself, he stood up slowly, a shot of pain racing up his left leg and into his hip. He closed his eyes and took a deep breath.

Maude flicked her cigarette out the open window. "Ya best be layin' back down. I'll bring yer vittles in here." Looking at his leg, she went on, "I'm worried a might about infection in yer leg." Placing her hand on his forehead, she confirmed, "Yup, jest what I thought. Ya done got yerself a fever. I'm gonna see if I can git one of the boys ta find some biotics fer ya ta take. That leg ain't gonna heal without 'em."

Maude yelled out the window to the children playing in the side yard, "One of you youngins go git Harmon. Tell him I need him. Go on...git!"

Two of the boys took off running around the side of the house and up the dirt road toward Harmon's trailer.

Minutes later, Harmon came busting in the front door and down the hall to the bedroom. He was eating a big turkey leg, the juice running down his bare arm. "What's so important ya need me right now? Loretty jest fried up a bunch of turkey legs an' I was havin' me a good meal."

Motioning toward the bed, Maude explained, "I need ya ta go inta town and git some medicine...some biotics fer Russell. He's got an infection in his leg."

"Hell fire! Why me? If I don't git back ta my place the kids are gonna eat all them legs."

Maude looked out over the top of her glasses as she answered sternly, "Harmon! When you ain't drunk ya got more sense than the whole lot around here. Yer the only one I can trust. I send one of them other boys and Lord knows what they'll come back with. I don't ask much of ya. This is important."

Harmon finished off the last bite of meat on the turkey leg and tossed the bone out the window and wiped his mouth with the tail of his shirt. The growling of dogs could be heard outside the window as they battled over the bone. "All right, dammit...I'll go, but I ain't happy about it! Where am I s'pose ta git these biotics. Ya jest can't walk into a drugstore and ask fer 'em. Ya need a script from a doctor and I ain't gonna go to no doctor."

Maude was getting frustrated, "Look, I don't care where ya go. Jest git 'em!"

Harmon turned and stomped out of the room, cursing, "Damn crazy woman. Why she's tendin' ta that man is beyond me. Hell, he ain't nothin' but a killer an' she's tryin' ta save 'em."

An hour later, Harmon returned with a white envelope which he handed to Maude. "I got these over at the vet's. Told him I had a good milkin' cow that got hung up on the fence and had a big oozin' cut on her side. He said ta give her one of these here pills twice a day."

Maude, opening the envelope, looked at the big white pills. "Hmm. I reckon Russell weighs about half a cow or thereabouts." That night she broke one of the pills in half and gave it to him.

Another week passed and Russell surprisingly was feeling better after taking all of the pills. The wound on his leg was healing and he no longer had a fever. He could now stand on his own, but walked with a limp. Maude gave him a pair of boxer shorts, an old white tee-shirt and a pair of bib overalls to wear. It felt good to Russell to be out of the ragged robe and into regular clothes, even though they were too big.

When he asked Maude for a toothbrush, she found a used one under the sink. Russell ran hot water over the seldom used dental tool and washed it with soap. Maude then gave him a box of baking soda to use as toothpaste. Conrad always told him to brush his teeth twice a day and if Conrad told him to do something then it was important and he would try his best to do it.

Conrad would have been upset at the sight of Effy's house. It was not only messy, but quite dirty. There were cobwebs everywhere and a layer of grime on the floor. Conrad had made a list for Russell when he had first moved into the cabin years ago. The list detailed everything Russell had to do in order to keep the cabin clean. Even though Russell had a habit of wearing the same clothes for days on end, he always made sure they were relatively clean. He wondered what Conrad would say if he could see this place.

Now that he was able to stand on his own, Russell was nervous about eating supper in the kitchen for the first time. He sat across from Otis who had already filled his plate. With his head just inches from the plate, Otis was shoveling food in his mouth, gravy and morsels of food falling onto the front of his shirt. Noticing no one was going to say grace, Russell silently blessed his food; another thing Conrad had taught him.

Effy sat at the head of the big wooden table, while several children wrestled for a spot on a long bench next to Russell. They all stared at him as they ate. Maude handed him a bowl of mashed potatoes and he ladled out several spoonfuls. The chicken and gravy came next along with a large wooden bowl of greens. The food was delicious and Russell tried to ignore the appearance of the kitchen where the meal had been prepared. There were pots stacked on the drain board and the sink was filled with dirty dishes soaking in grease covered water. A tattered curtain covered the broken window that was an access for the countless flies buzzing around the room. Effy had a fly swatter next to her plate and every so often would smack a marauding insect. Three dogs walked around the table, waiting for someone to accidentally drop something to the floor, occasionally stopping to scratch at the ticks and fleas in their matted hair.

On her way to her seat at the table, Maude slapped Otis on the back of his head as she scolded the man, "Ain't ya even gonna say hello ta Russell?"

Giving his wife a nasty look, he responded angrily, "What'd ya hit me fer woman? I see him. I'm eatin.' We can talk later."

Russell soon found out what Otis meant when he said they could talk later. When the meal was finished Otis took Russell into the living room, followed by Maude and Effy. The children were ordered outside and soon the room was filled with every adult on the property. Russell was seated on the end of a frayed brown sofa patched here and there with duct tape. There was an assortment of old chairs and sofas scattered around the room. Long unmatched floor to ceiling curtains created a gloomy effect, until an old floor lamp was turned on and three candles were lit. Sitting alone on the couch, Russell felt extremely uncomfortable. Back at his cabin, whenever he finished supper he'd always sit in his living room in front of the fireplace and he would enjoy the evening, smoking his pipe or doing some whittling. He was now the focus and center of attraction, something he always tried to avoid when he was around strangers. He looked around the room at the faces of the men and women who seemed to be waiting for him to speak.

Otis stuck a chaw of tobacco in his cheek and passed the pouch to Cletus who was seated in an old rocker. Cletus refused the pouch but pulled a beer from a six-pack and popped the top. Effy walked to the center of the room and spoke, "Before we git this meetin' under way it's proper ta make introductions." Looking at Russell she went around the room pointing to each person. "Ya already know me and Maude. This here be Otis, Maude's husband, that'd be Cletus, Maude's youngest. His wife, Ruby Jean, well, she done run off. Over there in the corner sits my oldest boy, Harmon and his wife, Loretty and his two oldest sons, Dwayne and Arliss." Pointing to an unshaven man sitting in the corner, she said, "That's my other grandson Ambrose and his wife Rosemary." Turning in a circle she finished up as she pointed her cane at Russell. "This here be Russell. If ya don't know by now, Russell here is kin ta us. All except fer me that is. His momma was Maude's sister, Etta Pender from over in the Iron Mountains. The rest of ya are uncles, aunts, cousins and the like. Now, when Arliss and Dwayne brought him here ta the farm, I never thought he'd see the next day, but here he sits, gittin' better by the day. What we need ta do is we got ta figure what ta do with him. Ya all heard all the stories goin' around the county sayin' he kilt nine or ten people. That bein' the gospel, we have ta decide if we want him ta stay around these parts. We've got enough trouble from time ta time with the law as it is. We don't need no more of that damned Chief Brody nosin' around up here. I figure the first thing ta do is ta let Russell speak." With that, Effy lowered herself down into a rocking chair and stared at Russell. "Go on boy, speak yer piece."

Russell, taken off guard didn't know what to say. He was nervous and didn't want to speak. He had never in all his life been required to speak in front of a group of people. With his head hanging down, he sat mute as the seconds ticked by until Effy slammed her cane down on an end table and gave Russell a look that scared him. "I said, speak yer piece boy!"

Maude, seeing that he was on edge walked over and placed her arm around him. "Now, I know ya ain't all that smart, Russell, but yer amongst family here."

Otis, who was leaning on the fireplace mantel, spoke up, using a mean tone, "Ya can at least tell us about all those men ya kilt!"

Russell didn't like Otis one bit. Why was he being so mean? Clenching his fists, Russell gave Otis a long cold stare then answered as if no one else were in the room, "I only killed those men because they were out to kill me! I never done them no harm." Starting to calm down, he explained, "I just wanted to be left alone, but they just kept coming after me. Them newspaper people and the police...they ain't telling the truth. They say I killed nine, but I only killed five and they was all mean men. They wouldn't leave me be." Hanging his head like a scolded child, he continued as he began to sob, "I'm...not a mean...person. I mind...my...own business."

Everyone sat in silence until Ambrose finally spoke, "Well. I fer one agree with Russell. A body needs ta be left alone if that's what they want. Ain't no call fer the law or anybody else ta come after ya, lessin' ya done somethin' real bad."

Rosemary, who was sitting at Ambrose's feet spoke up, "I say let him stay till he gits well enough ta leave on his own."

Effy placed her cane on her lap as she suggested, "All right then, I say we take a vote. Ambrose and Rosemary say yes. Anybody else agree, raise yer hand." Maude and Effy signaled yes as their hands went up, along with Cletus. "That's five," said Effy. "Harmon, Loretty...where ya at on this?"

"Don't make me no mind," said Harmon, "long as he don't bring us no trouble."

Loretty shrugged her shoulders. "I'll go with whatever Harmon thinks."

Otis, reluctantly agreed, "I'll say yes."

Dwayne stood up. "Look, me and Arliss is the ones who brought him here. I thought we was goin' ta turn him in for a reward. Me and Arliss say we do that."

Effy pointed her cane at Dwayne, "Shut up, boy. You and yer

dumb ass brother are outnumbered. Sit yer ass down!"

Turning to Russell, Effy smiled and stated as if she were some sort of judge, "Russell Pearl, ya git ta stay fer now, but ya got ta follow the rules. Ya can't be wanderin' off the property. If we tell ya to git out of sight, ya gotta do it. Understand?"

Russell shook his head yes, as he offered, "I can help around here. I can clean and do dishes."

Cletus let out a loud boisterous laugh. "Ain't that somethin'? He done kilt a whole mess of people and now he wants ta do women's work."

Maude walked over and slapped Cletus across his face. "Speakin' of women's work, how's things at yer place since Ruby Jean up and left?"

It was all Ambrose could do to keep from laughing but he didn't want to suffer the wrath of Maude. Otis spoke up, "I'll find somethin' fer ya ta do Russell. Ya don't have ta wear no apron around here."

Russell had no idea what was so funny but suddenly everyone started to laugh. Maude opened an old armoire and removed two jars of moonshine, passed one to Otis, unscrewed the lid of the other and took a long drink. She handed the jar to Russell. His refusal of the jar caused even more laughter. He watched as Dwayne and Arliss both took swigs, wondering what reward they were talking about and why they didn't seem to like him much.

Maude got Russell's attention as she hollered, "Russell...catch!"

Russell, taken by surprise ducked as he noticed a small item being tossed in his direction. The wallet bounced off of his right arm and fell to the floor.

"Ya can have yer wallet back. It's no use ta us."

Picking up the wallet Russell smiled, but then frowned when he opened it and looked inside. "I had money. It's gone."

"Ya did have some money in there," said Maude. "Twenty one dollars ta be exact. It cost a pretty penny ta nurse ya back ta health. Consider that money a down payment on what ya owe us. I put yer license back in there but I'm keepin' the picture of yer mother. If ya want a copy I'll have one of the boys run into town and have a copy made."

The next morning, Russell was allowed to leave the house for the first time. Stepping off the porch he surveyed the surrounding acreage. To him it looked like a tornado had blown through the property and no one had bothered to pick anything up afterwards. He tried to think of ways he could help around the farm, thinking that maybe he could pick up some of the junk laying around or maybe take care of the chickens. He wasn't strong or steady enough to tend to the cows and horses. He imagined that cleaning out the barn went far beyond shoveling out the stalls. He decided to look inside the barn later.

Limping out into the middle of the cluttered yard, he turned and looked at the house where he had spent the last month or so. It appeared to have been white at one time. Now, the two story structure was left with only a few scattered patches of faded white paint clinging to the marred and chipped boards. There were four large columns supporting the sagging front porch, where there were three rocking chairs and a whiskey barrel cut in half that was used as a table.

Feeling weak, he headed back to the porch and sat down in one of the rockers. He closed his eyes for a moment and had no idea that he was being watched by five children who were sitting on the side of the porch. When he opened his eyes, he was startled to find three boys and two girls, all dressed in tattered clothes and barefooted, standing in front of him. One of the girls boldly stepped forward. "My name's Valerie. Harmon and Loretty are my Ma and Pa. Granny Effy said we don't have ta be 'fraid of ya. Yer jest ugly...not mean. That true?"

Russell who had a fondness for young children, smiled and answered kindly, "Guess so."

Valerie plopped down in the rocker next to Russell while the other children sat on the porch steps. Fiddling with her long blond hair, she pointed at the other children. "Them three boys belong ta Ambrose and Rosemary and that there is Violet. Her Pa is Cletus. Her momma done run off. They say I talk too much, but I like ta know things. Why do ya talk so funny?"

Russell felt comfortable around the children. "I didn't know I talked funny," he said. "I talk the way Conrad taught me. He said I should always try to talk proper. Conrad was my brother, but he died."

"Well, what else can ya do," probed Valerie. "Do ya play the fiddle?"

"No, but I can whittle. If you want I can teach you how to make animals out of wood."

"Really," beamed Valerie. "Can ya make me a giraffe?"

"Sure, long as you give me a picture of what one looks like."

Valerie jumped down from the chair as she stood in front of Russell. "Well, we gotta go. My momma said I shouldn't bother ya." Running down the steps she stopped for a second and turned back. "I'll be tellin' the rest of the cousins that you ain't no monster man so they won't be 'fraid. See ya."

As the days passed, Russell learned all of the children's names, Violet was by far his favorite. She was like him; quiet most of the time. She kept to herself and didn't like to be around the other children all that much. She was content to sit in a tire swing under one of the large oak trees at the edge of the forest and hum songs to herself. On occasion, she would bring him magazines to look at. She helped him gather eggs from the chicken coop and he learned which hens were hard to get off their nests. He helped her shuck bushels of corn, which with his stiff fingers was not easy to do.

On a Sunday afternoon, sitting out in the woods in her secret place, which she shared with Russell, he asked her, "Why don't you play with the other children?"

Violet yawned and answered, "They play too rough and the boys are always hittin' on me, and they spit and curse when they git angry."

Russell became serious. "I've heard it said your Momma, Ruby Jean ran off."

Violet looked through the trees as if someone was watching and when she was sure no one was, she sat close to Russell. "I've got a secret. Well, our family's got one. I'm not s'pose ta tell *no one*. Since yer one of the family, I guess I can tell ya. But, jest in case. Don't tell no one I tol' ya."

Russell crossed his fingers. "Promise. I won't tell."

Violet looked at the garden twenty yards away and hesitated, but then finally spoke, "My momma didn't run off. She and my Pa had a fight. They was always fightin'. She hit her head and died. It was an accident. Effy and Maude says my Pa kilt her. We all have ta lie and tell everyone in town my momma run off. We can't tell no one the truth or the law will come and take me and Pa away. I miss my momma."

Russell noticed a tear run down the side of Violet's cheek. Reaching out, he gently touched her shoulder. "My momma was killed too. I wasn't much older than you when it happened. Her name was Etta and she was Maude's sister. She's buried up in the Iron Mountains. Where's your momma buried?"

Violet pointed in the direction of the garden as she answered, "Over there in the garden. I see her every day and I tell her I'm sorry she died."

Russell got a tear in his eye as he looked toward the garden and thought, *Maybe I'll kill Cletus for killing Violet's momma and making her so unhappy.*

The long summer finally at an end, fall had set in quickly. It was now October and Russell had been at the Stroud's place for over three months. Every morning following breakfast he would sit on the front porch with Effy and watch Mother Nature's magic as the leaves in the countless trees on the farm slowly changed from green to red, bronze, yellow and orange. He and Effy discussed many things and he found himself beginning to trust the old woman. One of the stories she told him was about the house. She said over a hundred and fifty years ago it had been a plantation with beautiful gardens and trees. The gardens were all gone now but some of the ancient trees still stood. When the Civil War came along the Yankees invaded the south, resulting in the master of the house, who happened to be an officer in the Confederate Army, getting killed in battle. His wife, unable to run the place herself, fled. The house was used as a military hospital by the Northern Army and eventually, when the war ended, the property was abandoned and sat empty for years. Then her parents, Charles and Edith bought the place. Effy explained to Russell that she had grown up in the house. When her parents died, she stayed on and married a man by the name of Lowell. They raised a big family, all of their children eventually married and moved away. Except for Otis, their youngest son, she had no idea where they had gone. Otis and Maude moved onto the place after Lowell died from the fever. She knew the place was deteriorating but she loved the old house. The second floor had been roped off because the upstairs floors were too rotted for anyone to walk across them, so now she,

Maude and Otis lived on the first floor. She hated the fact they had to live with her but she realized eventually she wouldn't be able to take care of herself.

Aside from sitting on the porch in the mornings and the few chores he was assigned, Russell spent most of his day roaming around in the woods that surrounded the farm. It was when he was alone in the forest with the sounds of the birds and woodland creatures that he felt comfortable. It was the only thing on the Stroud's place that remotely reminded him of back home. In spite of his limping gait, he walked the perimeter of the property several times each day.

As each day passed, the weather was beginning to get cooler and Russell was getting anxious. His wounds were healing and he was feeling like his old self. He was getting restless and he wanted to go home to his cabin. His had regained his strength and with the food he was given, his weight returned to normal. He had grown tired of listening to the constant bickering and all out fights between the men. They drank on a nightly basis and Russell would toss and turn in bed for hours waiting for them to quiet down.

Many a night, he lay in bed wondering if the men who had chased him up the mountain to the Cumberland Gorge were still looking for him. Surely, with all the time that had passed, they thought he was dead. As far as he was concerned, it was over. He wanted to go home and get back to a normal way of life. Whenever he mentioned it to Effy or Maude, he was told that it wasn't time yet. What were they waiting for? What did they want? Soon, it would be winter. He needed to get back to his cabin and cut wood and get it stacked so it could dry before the cold weather came. He wondered if his truck was still at the cabin. If it wasn't he would have to get another. He needed some new clothes. Looking off into the distant mountains, he decided, *It's time to go!*

The next morning, after spending time on the porch with Effy, he decided to tell both Maude and her he wanted to go home and that he needed someone to drive him to his cabin. Taking what he thought was one last walk out to the edge of the property and into the dense trees, he stopped at the barbed wire fence and discovered an old vine-covered shed he had never seen before. It looked abandoned and no one had ever talked about it. His curiosity was sparked.

Dwayne's old truck was parked next to the shed. Hiding behind a tall pine, Russell watched as Arliss and Dwayne came out of the shed and lifted something out of the bed of the truck. Russell could see that they were animal traps with long chains and metal teeth; the kind of traps that were used to catch animals and hold them until the poacher returned. Sometimes, in desperation, the snared animal would chew its leg off to escape and eventually bleed to death, while others would struggle for hours in the trap until they died a horrible death.

Russell clenched his fists and waited until they went back to the shed. Stealthily, he crept to the shed and peering through a missing board, had a clear view of the interior. The walls were covered with animal skins that had been stretched and nailed to the wood. All kinds of skins: deer, raccoons, fox, river otters, rabbits and others. A pile of traps filled one corner of the shed next to a wooden, blood-stained table where the animals had been skinned.

Russell's eyes began to fill with tears as he saw the skinned, dead carcasses of two river otters on the dirt floor. *No one eats river otters,* he thought. He couldn't recall ever eating any wild game meat since he had been at the Stroud's. They always served chicken, beef or pork. Then it came to him. *They were selling the skins of those poor creatures for profit.* He would never allow that to happen on his property up by his cabin.

His first instinct was to crash through the flimsy wall and kill both Arliss and Dwayne, but he knew they would probably overpower him. *No, he would wait. But not long!* He didn't want them to kill any more animals. He waited until they left and then he slowly walked back to the house on the opposite side of the property. He had to make a plan. Lying down in his bed, he removed a crayon drawing Violet had given him. He smiled as he ran his hand over the crude drawing. The smile on his face went away. His head was beginning to hurt; he was getting a headache. It was hard for him to concentrate.

CHAPTER SEVEN

FRANKLIN BARRETT STEPPED OUT OF HIS VINTAGE 1957 forest green Corvette. Standing back, he admired his latest purchase. Aside from the deep green, hand rubbed custom paint job and a few parts that he ordered, the fifty-five year old classic was original. Crossing the parking lot, he glanced up the road at the rustic GATLINBURG CITY LIMIT sign on the left hand corner of the last intersection before the two-lane paved road was swallowed from sight by the dense trees bordering Route 441.

The Park Grill Steakhouse was on the high end of the numerous restaurants lining the Parkway. The elaborate stone and timber eating establishment held a reputation for its rustic ambience and above average food; the expensive price tag that accompanied one's lunch or dinner tolerated by tourists as a dining experience. Climbing the stone steps, Franklin entered the log cabin interior, passed the massive bar and proceeded to the window table where he and Merle Pittman occasionally conducted business luncheons.

Merle was just returning from the salad bar, when he noticed Franklin approaching. Gesturing with his free hand, Merle pointed toward the buffet and spoke, "Grab a plate, Franklin. Lunch is on me."

Minutes later, after filling up a plate, Franklin seated himself at the table and spoke to his business associate, "Merle, what's the rush? You must be hungry. You couldn't even wait until I got here to eat?"

Merle pulled back his suit coat sleeve and looked at his Rolex. "For an individual who is quite anal about being punctual, whether you realize it or not, you happen to be thirty minutes late. I can't recall the number of times you've given me the third degree about being late for one of our meetings." Unfolding a white linen napkin he removed a stainless steel fork and stabbed a bite of salad. "I rest my case."

Grabbing his own napkin, Franklin acquiesced, "Alright, I guess I deserved that. I've had a chaotic week. I spent the better part of last week over near Mountain City, most of my time in the

Iron Mountains. Yesterday, I had a meeting with a newspaper columnist from Knoxville. I've really been busy." Cutting up a chicken strip, he explained, "Actually, this is the first good meal I've had in days so I'd appreciate it if I could partake of it without feeling like I'm in a court of law being cross examined."

Merle, realizing his long time friend was a bit stressed, suggested, "Should I order us something stronger than iced tea?"

"Sounds like a splendid idea," said Franklin. "I normally don't drink alcohol at lunch, but today...it's scotch on the rocks with a twist."

Merle looked for their waitress but she was at another table just beginning to wait on a large group who had arrived. "Listen, I'll be right back. Hell, we won't get to talk with our waitress for the next ten minutes the way it looks. I'll just go up to the bar and get our drinks."

Returning with two mixed drinks, Merle slid Franklin's drink across the table, took a sip of his and asked, "So why all of this running around the state. What's up? And please don't tell me you've been snooping around Mountain City hoping to cash in on some harebrained idea in regard to our old deceased friend, Hawk Caine?"

"Don't think the thought hasn't crossed my mind. Thing is, those mountain people aren't as stupid as folks make them out to be. If we had decided to cash in on the demise of Hawk Caine, they would have already beat us to the punch. I had lunch one day at the café where Caine and Pearl had their knock down; drag out fight. Can you believe it? They have the table where Russell Pearl had breakfast that day cordoned off with police emergency tape. For twenty dollars a couple you can dine at that table *and* they're running a special on what Pearl had for breakfast also. That's not the worst of it. Outside on the sidewalk they've got a red X painted on the concrete indicating the spot where Caine was shot to death. They have a pop-up tent set up just down from the X. Now get this, they stole our idea."

Merle took a drink and wiped his mouth, "What are you talking about?"

"Tee shirts! That's what I'm talking about. They're doing the same thing we did when your brother, Asa and Mildred Henks were killed. Their shirts read: HAWK CAINE X MARKS THE

SPOT. Then they have a large red X running right through the printing. Brilliant! There were people actually standing in line to get a shirt. Do you remember that stupid hat with the feather Caine used to strut around in? They're selling those type of hats as well."

Pointing his finger at Franklin, Merle smirked, "Listen, I don't want to hear about tee shirts. Remember, we still have two thousand Pittman-Henks Murder Tour shirts in storage."

Buttering a roll, Franklin went on to explain, "The main reason I went over to Mountain City stemmed from something I found in one my old file cabinets. Remember when I told you about that land deal I got into over in the Iron Mountains just after I graduated from college?"

"I do recall that," said Merle. "If I remember correctly you lost your ass on the deal."

"I did at that," admitted Franklin. "The land developer was a man by the name of Peabody. He turned out to be a shyster. The IRS stepped in and padlocked the property and Peabody wound up hanging himself up there on the property to avoid going to prison for income tax evasion and..."

Merle hesitated in taking another bite of salad as he interrupted Franklin in mid sentence, "Look, we've talked about that particular phase of your past life a number of times over the years. So, my question for you is, where is this going?"

"The thing that I found in my file cabinet was the original plans for the Iron Mountain Lodge: blueprints, plumbing and electrical schematics, construction costs, material lists, permits and so on. I guess seeing all that old stuff got me to thinking, so I took a run over there. I was thinking maybe about getting back on board with the original Iron Mountain Lodge project, but to be honest with myself I think that ship has already sailed."

Merle smiled as he agreed, "Starting that project up again would be insane. Almost as crazy as your idea was of the Pittman-Henks murder tours!"

Franklin put down his drink as he gave Merle a nasty glare. "How can you even insinuate that those tours were crazy?"

"Easy," replied Merle. "Don't forget we have two thousand tee-shirts that are now worthless sitting in storage not to mention that you're closing one of your riding stables you originally opened to handle the overflow of the tours."

"Opening an additional stable was simply a business decision that at the time made sense. The two stables I had couldn't handle all of the tour business that was coming our way. That stable made us quite a bit of money when you consider that tourists were shelling out over fifty bucks a head to take the tours. And while we're on the subject, you can't sit there and tell me those tee-shirts were not profitable. Do the math, Merle. We sold a little over forty-seven hundred shirts at ten bucks a crack. That's $47,000.00. We only have three dollars invested per shirt which means the shirts in storage equal a $6,000.00 loss. We made $41,000.00 just on the tee shirts alone."

Reaching into his coat pocket, Franklin extracted three cut out newspaper articles. "Remember, I also said that I just got back from Knoxville from talking to a newspaper columnist up there. His name is John Ladue and he writes a weekly column called, *What's Going on in the Smokies*? I always read his column. He's a bit of a radical. Back when we had all those murders Ladue wrote a scathing article every week about the inability of the local police as well as the Feds to catch the killer. But, back then every newspaper in the state had something to say about the killings. That's all over now. The murders have been solved, Russell Pearl was shot and things seem to be getting back to normal. Ladue won't let it go." Holding up one of the articles, Franklin went on, "Like this article written two weeks ago. It's titled *Where is Russell Pearl*? Then, last week his article is called *Is the Smoky Mountain Killer Still Out There*? The heading for his article this week is *Who Killed Luke Pardee?*"

On a roll now, Franklin took a drink of scotch as he continued, "So, I take a drive up to Knoxville and manage to get into see this Ladue. Now, after talking with him, I'd be the first one to agree that this guy is over the top. But, when you think about it, he's right. The authorities might have very well shot Russell Pearl, but still to this day *and* it's been over three months, they haven't found his body, so for all we know he could still be out there in the mountains somewhere. And another thing, who did kill Luke Pardee? Could it have been Russell Pearl? As long as Pearl's body is missing we can strike while the iron is hot and rake in the money."

"I'm still not sure where you're headed with this," remarked Merle skeptically, "but I'm listening."

"Tee shirts!" exclaimed Franklin. "It worked before and it can work again, only this time even better." Not giving Merle a chance to speak, he rambled on, "What we do is we get a couple of thousand shirts printed up for starters to see how it goes. We can have a couple of different shirts like, **Where is Russell Pearl** or **The Smoky Killer – He's Still Out There**? We can even have one that reads: **Who Killed Luke Pardee**? As long as the whereabouts of Pearl's body remains a mystery we can continue to make money. We could even start the tours back up again. You still own Asa's farm and I own the Henks' place. We could just simply change things up a little bit. We could have pictures of Russell Pearl made up and put them at the tour locations. Why, we could even have buggy rides that go past Pardee's place. This could be bigger than ever!"

Laying down his fork, Merle took a long drink as he stared at the ceiling in deep thought. Pointing his now empty glass at Franklin, he sat back in his chair. "You might just be on to something here, Franklin. You're right, we did make over $40,000.00 on the Pittman-Henks shirts, not to mention at least twice that amount on the tours. The way I see it, we could get started with less than a $10,000.00 investment. We could order, let's say twenty-five hundred shirts for $7,500.00, leaving us $2,500.00 for some point of sale literature with money left over to pay some kids to run the booths."

Franklin was getting excited once he saw Merle's interest. "That's right, we can hire some of the same kids that work for me over at my stables that we used before. We still have the three tents we purchased and plenty of wagons for the tours. I can have those shirts here in less than a week. We'll get that guy up in Knoxville we used before to print them up. We could be in business in less than two weeks. What do you say?"

Merle smiled as he removed his checkbook from his suit coat. "I'm going to write you a check for my end right now. That's five grand...right?"

"Correct," said Franklin. Suddenly, the smile on Franklin's face disappeared and was replaced with a look of great concern. "Hold on a minute, Merle. What about the authorities? I'm not the least bit concerned over Axel Brody, but about the Feds. They were able to shut down the tours before. Are we going to be faced with the same thing?"

Merle laid an ink pen next to his checkbook. "Two things: Brody wasn't a problem for us before and believe me, he won't be this time either. He doesn't know his ass from a hole in the ground, as they say. We can run circles around him. Now the Feds are a different story. Last time they shut us down because they were in the middle of a multiple murder investigation. There wasn't anything we could do. This time around, the murders have all been solved. They just haven't located Pearl's body. The only murder that's still outstanding or unsolved is Luke Pardee and that has nothing to do with the Feds. Don't worry, I'll have all of the proper licenses and documentation we'll need to open up. Now, let me write that check."

Two weeks to the day following their luncheon at the Park Grill, Merle and Franklin stood off to the side as they observed the activity on a grass lot next to the Parkway Grocery. A number of Barrett's employees were busy at work: two young men putting the finishing touches on the pop-up tent, another youth setting up eight-foot tables in a U-shape. An older man opened the back door of the truck and handed out box after box of tee-shirts to three girls. Franklin, dressed in jeans and fashionable cowboy boots proudly displayed the tee-shirt he was wearing: **WHO KILLED LUKE PARDEE?** Looking at Merle, he laughed and stated comically, "Merle, I can't recall the last time I saw you when you were not adorned in one of your custom made Italian suits. I have to admit the tee-shirt you're wearing befits you this morning."

Merle, standing next to his Mercedes frowned as he always took great pride in his appearance. Aside from his expensive cordovan loafers, perfectly pressed dress pants and thin leather belt, he looked down at his tee-shirt: **WHERE IS RUSSELL PEARL?** "Hey, as long as I'm making money, I'll be more than glad to advertise one of our shirts."

Looking at the crowd of people coming and going from the Parkway Grocery and all the tourists passing by, Franklin gestured toward the tent. "I think we might just sell out this weekend. I've got our tee-shirt guy on stand-by, not if, but *when* we need more shirts." Checking his watch, he walked toward the tent as he suggested, "Why don't you grab us a couple of coffees over at the Parkway. It's almost eight-thirty now. We should be open for business by ten."

Zeb Gilling turned right off Fox Hollow Road and entered the parking lot of the Tennessee Highlander Lumber Company in Townsend. For a Friday morning it was busier than usual. With all of the busloads of tourists flooding into town for the fall foliage, many of the locals, just like every year, were interested in sprucing up their properties; people were purchasing grass seed, winter fertilizer, fall plants and paint to touch up fences and lawn furniture. Parking in the only available spot at the far end of the lot, Zeb sat back in the seat and looked at the license plates on the line of customer cars. Every plate represented a car from Tennessee. He smiled as the lumber company was one of the few places a local could go without having to shove their way through the throng of visiting tourists.

Getting out of his truck, he noticed an old high school pal who he hadn't seen in ages loading a grass spreader and two bags of grass seed in the back of a car. Approaching the car, Zeb addressed his old friend, "Tab, Tab Hacker, you old fart! Haven't seen you in what, ten, twelve years?"

Tab closed the car door and turned as he smiled. "Well, if it isn't Zeb Gilling. Yeah, I guess it has been quite a while." Reaching for Zeb's hand he stated, "I see you're still here in Townsend."

Shaking Tab's hand, Zeb answered, "I was born here in Townsend and the way it looks I'll kick the bucket here as well. I thought you were still living out on the west coast?"

"I am. My sister still lives in Townsend. Her husband passed away a few weeks ago and I've been helping her with some home repairs. She's having a pretty rough time right now."

Zeb, concerned, thought for moment. "I remember reading about that in the paper." Watching a customer load six landscape timbers in the back of a truck, Zeb continued, "How long are you in town?"

"About two weeks. At least that's the plan. My sister is all by herself now. She's coming to live with me and the wife out on the coast. I'm here to help her get her house ready to sell. I just ordered some roofing shingles and some patio blocks. Next week her house goes on the market." Gesturing with his head at the entrance to the store, Tab mentioned, "Speaking of getting a house ready to sell, I ran into Buddie Knapp in there. He tells me he and his wife are moving down to Alabama. He was picking up a few things he needs to get his house ready to sell." Sticking his hands in his front pockets he frowned as he explained, "It's kind of strange to run into both you and Buddie. My sister over the past couple of years has kept me up to date with letters about what has been going on around here. Buddie told me he was glad he was moving out of Townsend. Growing up here in Townsend, I remember how peaceful it always was." Looking directly at Zeb, Tab asked, "I remember how you and Buddie hung out at the Parkway Grocery with Asa, Charley and Luke in the mornings having coffee and discussing all the local gossip. Do you and Buddie still go there now that there's only the two of you around?"

"Yeah, I still go a couple times a week. Buddie, well, ever since Luke was killed, he stopped going. It's kind of hard to sit by the front window by yourself, drinking one cup of coffee after another without anyone else to talk to."

Tab, seeing Zeb wasn't all that interested in talking about Buddie, politely excused himself, "Listen, I've got to get going. I've got a lot of work to get done at my sister's place. Maybe I'll drop by the Parkway next week and we can catch up."

"Sounds good," said Zeb.

He no sooner turned to head for the main entrance when he saw Buddie loading some lumber and paint in the back of his pickup. Zeb approached as Buddie flipped up the tailgate and started for the front of his truck. Zeb had to run the last few yards to catch him before he climbed in. "Buddie...hold on!"

Hearing his name mentioned, Buddie stopped and looked back, but frowned when he saw who had hailed him. Zeb noticed the look of negativity as he remarked, "Is that anyway to greet a friend?"

Buddie reached for the handle on the door and opened it as he responded coldly, "Gotta go...don't have time to talk."

Zeb, refusing to be put off, slammed the door shut and pointed a finger at Buddie. "Now look, this nonsense has gone far enough. I don't know what the hell's gotten into you but you've been avoiding me. I've been by your house to see you and I've called you a number of times. Your wife always tells me you're sleeping or not at home. Ever since Luke was killed you've been acting like a jerk. You'd think that with three out of the five of us being killed that we'd be closer than ever, but no! First, you refuse to see me and now you're leaving town and moving down to Alabama. What the hell's wrong with you?"

"I'll tell you what the hell's wrong!" barked Buddie. "You're not the same man, the same friend I've known all my life. Quite frankly, you scare the hell out of me! Luke's dead, and I think you had something to do with it. I keep thinking about that afternoon at the Parkway, the day before Luke was shot when he told us he was going to go to Brody and tell him what happened forty years ago. After he left the Parkway, we had no idea what we were going to do. Then, you said you were going to drop by and see if you could talk some sense into him. Luke's dead, Zeb! What kind of sense does that make?"

Zeb stepped closer to Buddie, "You almost sound like you're accusing me of killing Luke! Luke was just as much of a friend to me as you, but he was stupid!" Clenching his fists, Zeb stepped even closer. "I oughta bust you right in the mouth. Where do you get off accusing me of killing one of my best friends?"

Buddie, who wasn't the most aggressive individual, found himself pinned up against the side of his truck, Zeb only inches away from his face. Something snapped inside of him as he shoved Zeb roughly. Zeb, shocked at Buddie's reaction, smiled in a confident, cocky fashion as he placed his hands on his hips and gave Buddie the once over. Putting his finger into Buddie's chest, he raised his voice, "Buddie, you just better back off. In all the years we've known each other which borders on nearly seventy, even when we were kids, you couldn't lick me, so don't start thinking you can now!"

Before Zeb even realized it, Buddie drew back his right hand and punched Zeb on his right jaw, sending him plummeting awkwardly to the ground. Zeb, amazed that one of his best friends hit him, wiped blood from the side of his mouth as he started to get up, but was prevented from doing so as Buddie placed his foot on Zeb's nose and pushed him back down as he yelled, "Zeb, we ain't kids no more! You so much as move and I'm gonna push your damn nose through the back of your head... understand!"

Zeb remained silent as he stared back violently at Buddie. Buddie repeated himself as he applied more pressure on Zeb's nose, "Understand!"

Zeb nodded and Buddie raised his foot, opened the door to his truck, turned the ignition and sped out of the lot covering Zeb with loose dirt and gravel. Zeb slowly sat up as he stared at Buddie's truck speeding down Fox Hollow Road. Wiping the side of his mouth and waving dust away from his face, he said to himself, "Son of a bitch!"

Buddie stopped at the first stop sign he came to and realizing that he had been going seventy in a thirty-five mph zone, pulled over to the side of the road to compose himself. He couldn't believe he had hit Zeb, a man he had known since he was five years old. A friend of over seven decades. They had gone to elementary school, middle school and high school together. During his childhood years they had slept over at each other's house, had been in cub scouts and boy scouts, even played football together in high school. Zeb had been his best man at his wedding. They had gone on many a hunting trip together and for more years than he could remember, they had along with Asa, Charley and Luke shared a lot of good times in the morning at the Parkway Grocery. But, all of those good memories seemed to be now shadowed by what they had done forty years ago. He had thought that in time, it would have passed, but now it loomed bigger than ever. Luke was dead...murdered! The sooner he and his wife moved to Alabama the better. Wiping tears from his eyes, he pulled back onto the road.

Minutes later he found himself in the middle of a traffic gridlock on the Alexander Parkway, cars and buses backed up and at a standstill all the way to the Great Smoky Mountains Park entrance. Already frustrated, Buddie wasn't in the mood to sit in a long line of traffic. Turning on his left turn signal, he whipped across the highway and into the Parkway Grocery parking lot which was also crammed with cars. Parking near the back of the building, he decided that he needed a drink. He was going to take the rest of the day off from working on the house. He was too upset from his previous confrontation with Zeb. He'd just grab a six-pack, head on home, sit in the back yard, get drunk and then take a long nap.

Walking around the side of the building, he noticed a throng of people gathered around a tent in the adjacent lot. Just as he was about to enter the front door, he noticed a banner suspended above the tent, but was prevented from reading it as he bumped into a women coming out of the store. The woman politely excused herself, but Buddie just moved past her. He was too keyed up to be courteous.

Opening one of the glass fronted coolers near the back of the store, he overheard two couples with their backs to him who were getting coffee and donuts.

"These tee-shirts are great."

"I think we should consider taking one of those tours."

"How many donuts should we get?"

"Make sure you get some jelly-filled."

"I might go back over there and get another shirt to take back home for my brother."

Buddie didn't pay any attention to what was being said, but grabbed a six-pack and headed for the counter, stood in line for a few minutes, paid for his beer and exited the store. Outside he looked toward the tent and the group of people. The message on the banner caused him to stop, his mouth open in amazement, his eyes not believing what they saw: **WHO KILLED LUKE PARDEE?**

Two girls, standing next to their car were putting on tee-shirts which they modeled to their male companions: **WHERE IS RUSSELL PEARL?**

Standing just on the other side of the door, he didn't realize he was blocking the exit. The two couples he had overheard talking inside excused themselves as they squeezed by him. One of the men looked back at him displaying a look of dissatisfaction for his apparent rudeness in blocking the door. The front of the man's tee-shirt read: **THE SMOKY MOUNTAIN KILLER IS STILL OUT THERE!**

Buddie moved away from the door as another person barely nudged past. At the moment he could have cared less about where Russell Pearl was or that the Smoky Killer was still out there, but the fact that his best friend's name was plastered not only on tee-shirts but a bright yellow, ten foot banner reignited the anger he had experienced back at the lumber company. Walking across the lot, his eyes focused on the banner, he placed his beer on top of a trashcan and crossed the grass.

A teenage boy stood next to a car as he held up a tee-shirt he had just purchased as his friend asked, "Who the hell is Luke Pardee and why would anyone care who killed him?"

The boy with the shirt answered, "Some local hillbilly I guess."

Grabbing the shirt from the boy, Buddie pinned him against the side of the car as he grabbed the shirt and yelled into the boy's face, "He was my best friend...that's who he was!" Pitching the shirt to the ground, Buddie forced his way through the group of people surrounding the tent.

Two girls were making change for three customers, while Franklin Barrett cut open a new box of shirts. Merle Pittman stood at the back of the tent as he went about folding shirts into three neat piles.

Buddie didn't waste any time as he pushed his way to the front of the line and flipped over a table, shirts sliding to the ground. Moving beneath the tent, Buddie picked up a box of shirts and hurled it at Franklin who ducked to the left, the box bouncing off a customer's shoulder. The two girls who had been making change screamed and ran from the tent. Merle turned but was knocked over a table as Buddie body slammed him. Customers started to back away from the tent as Buddie picked up one of the corner posts and began to tilt the tent over.

Merle and two customers were trapped as the tent toppled over on top of them, the canvas top covering their bodies as they tried to escape. All of the customers ran for their cars except three who remained behind in order to try and free those beneath the canvas. Franklin, taken by surprise slowly got to his feet and pushed Buddie from behind, sending him toppling over some boxes. Buddie rolled and came up on his feet, but Merle who was now free of the tent clobbered him on his shoulder with his briefcase, causing him to fall sideways as he twisted his ankle. Everyone backed away as Buddie painfully stood. Looking around at all of the staring customers, Franklin's employees, Franklin and Merle, he realized that he had done all of the physical damage that he was capable of. Pointing at Franklin, he angrily stated, "What the hell's wrong with you people? Luke Pardee was my friend! You've no right to have his name splashed on tee-shirts and on that banner!"

Merle stepped forward, holding up his briefcase. "We have every right to sell tee-shirts, Knapp, and to display that banner. I have all the permits and licenses right here. We live in a free enterprise society and we also have freedom of speech in this country. We haven't broken any laws. You're the only one here who has broken the law: destroying public property, assault and battery, not to mention being a public nuisance!"

Sirens could be heard in the distance. Barrett smiled as he looked up the road. "That's no doubt the police, Knapp. When they get here we're pressing charges and your ass is going to jail. When you came in here and started acting like a lunatic, well, you messed with the wrong people."

Seconds later, both Brody and Grant simultaneously pulled into the lot from two different directions, the customers moving to the side so they could pull up next to the tent. Brody climbed out of his truck and stomped across the grass as Grant turned off the siren to his cruiser. Brody ordered some of the bystanders, "Move back, get out of my way!" By the time he reached the collapsed tent, Grant had caught up to him. Seeing both Franklin and Merle standing next to each other Brody smirked, "Well, well, what do you know, if it isn't the village idiots up to their old tricks again." Looking around, he gestured at the shirts scattered around on the ground. "See you're sellin' those damn shirts again."

Merle stepped forward. "Yes we are, Brody, and it just so happens there isn't anything you can do to prevent us from doing so. Remember the last time you tried to shut us down. We sent you packing and we went on with our business which is exactly what we're going to do today. Now, while you're arresting Mr. Buddie Knapp here for interfering with a legal business, we'll go about getting things back in order." Turning to the onlooking crowd, Merle announced, "It'll just be a few minutes before we have the tent righted and the tables set back up. We apologize for any inconvenience this unfortunate incident may have caused you."

Franklin stepped forward and held up one of the shirts. "And to show our appreciation for your patience during this disgusting display by one of our local citizens, for the next hour we're offering a twenty percent discount on tee-shirts."

"Not so fast," barked Brody. "You're not sellin' one more shirt today, because I'm shuttin' ya down until we git this thing sorted out."

"What is there to sort out?" asked Franklin politely, "Knapp comes busting in here, knocks over our tables, uproots our tent, physically pushes both Merle and myself, all the while disrupting our business."

Buddie walked over and picked up the rumpled banner and held it up for Brody to see. "They have no right to make money off of my best friend's death. It might be legal, but it's not right."

Suddenly, a customer walked up to Franklin and held out two shirts that he had purchased. "I think I'd like a refund on these shirts. I guess I really didn't realize what this was all about."

"Me too!" said a lady as she held out a shirt. "I want a refund as well."

"Another couple stepped up to one of the tables that had been set back up. Placing their shirts on the table, the man shook his head in disgust. "This just doesn't seem right. We want our money back."

Another woman threw her shirt on the table as she addressed Brody and pointed at Franklin and Merle, "These gentlemen did some pushing and shoving themselves." Nodding at Merle, she went on, "That one there hit this fellow with his briefcase."

"I think I've heard enough," ordered Brody. "Grant, slap the cuffs on Franklin and Merle here, put them in the back of your cruiser and take them back to the station and throw their asses in the clink."

Removing a set of cuffs from his belt, Grant started to move toward Franklin who objected as he walked toward Brody. "Axel, you better stop and think about what you're doing. I know you represent the local law in these parts but you can't arrest someone just because you feel like it."

Brody wasn't about to back down as he gave Grant a dirty look. "Officer Denlinger...I said cuff 'em...and I mean now!"

As Grant approached, Franklin backed away as he held his hands in the air, "On what charges?"

"How about resistin' arrest for starters?" stated Brody confidently.

Merle moved in front of Brody. "That'll never stick and you know it." Holding up his briefcase he stated, "I'm a lawyer and a damn good one. I'll have us out of your two-bit jail within an hour, then, on top of that I'll sue your ass! You'll be the laughing stock of not only Townsend but the entire county, not to mention the state."

"So, sue me," laughed Brody. "This is my last term anyways. All they can do is fire me. Maybe you will only spend an hour or so behind bars but I'll relish every second."

Brody reached for his set of cuffs as he moved toward Merle. "I think I'll cuff you myself."

Merle backed away as he threatened, "You're not putting those cuffs on me Brody!"

Axel, now inches from Merle's face looked Pittman up and down as he sneered. "Pittman, you better turn around and put your hands behind your back or I'll take you down to the ground and hogtie you like the pig you are!"

Franklin, seeing that their objections were getting them nowhere, strongly suggested, "Merle, just play along. Like you said. We'll be out in less than an hour. Right now, this is a battle we can't win. We can't reason with the likes of Sheriff Axel Brody. Just go with the flow. We'll have our day in court which will result in Axel's early retirement." Turning sideways, he smiled at Grant. "I'm sorry you work for that idiot. Go ahead and do your job. Cuff me. But, keep in mind you might just go down with the ship."

As Grant escorted Merle and Franklin to his cruiser, Axel addressed the still gathering crowd, "Ladies and gentlemen. I would like to apologize on the behalf of the City of Townsend for this unfortunate altercation, but I must ask that you clear this area. All of these shirts, the tent and the truck are being confiscated until further notification. No more shirts will be sold today, however. Anyone that would like a refund can get their money back...right now!" He then ordered the two young girls who had been operating the sales tables to set up the register for refunds only. Taking Buddie off to the side he explained that he would have to ride along with him back to the station, answer a few questions, but then he would be released.

As Grant was loading Merle and Franklin in the backseat of his cruiser Arliss and Dwayne Stroud who had been watching the entire tee-shirt fiasco, walked past. Arliss proudly displayed the shirt he had purchased earlier as he jokingly punched Dwayne on his shoulder. "Where is Russell Pearl? Hell, we know where he is...don't we!"

Dwayne shot Grant a strange look and gave his younger brother an elbow in the stomach as he whispered, "Watch yer mouth, dumb ass!"

Grant, thinking that it was an odd comment to make, stopped the two brothers. "Hold on there, boys! What exactly did you mean when you said, 'We know where Russell Pearl is?'"

Arliss stammered as he tried to answer, "Ah...well, we...ah..."

Dwayne recovered quickly and gave an explanation, "Don't mind Arliss none deputy. He don't know what he's talkin' about."

Grant, climbing in the front seat of his cruiser watched as the two Stroud brothers walked off as he thought to himself, *That sure was odd.*

CHAPTER EIGHT

DOUG ELAND KNELT DOWN AND TIED HIS RUNNING shoes. Looking west, he smiled as he viewed the low hanging, smoky blue mist that covered the crest of the mountain range. Taking a deep knee bend, he watched his wife carry her fourth load of handmade walking sticks into their newly acquired gift shop. Glancing down at his Casio sports watch, he noted the time at 8:07 in the morning. Standing up, he stretched his shoulders, legs and arms. Max, now back outside for her last load looked at her own watch and reminded her husband, "Doug, make sure you get back here no later than ten. Our grand opening is at twelve noon. I think we're really going to be busy, especially with all the tourists in town. I've had a lot of the locals dropping by and calling. After I get these walking sticks in place the only thing I have to do is mop the floors and clean the windows." Snapping her fingers, she asked, "Did you remember to get two hundred dollars worth of small bills and change from the bank?"

Giving his wife the thumbs up, Doug responded, "Did that yesterday. Money is in the bottom of the register beneath the change drawer." Saluting Max, he started to jog out of the small parking lot, and shouted, "See ya in about an hour."

Max waved, "Be careful and I love you."

Running down the sidewalk that ran parallel to the Parkway, he took a right down a paved alley, traversed a large grass-covered field, cut through Burns Cemetery, crossed a small wooden bridge and turned left onto the Little River hiking trail. With the small river on his left, he followed the paved path occasionally passing another runner or walker out for some morning exercise.

Running up a slight rise, he gazed down at the river below and the surrounding trees. The leaves were especially colorful this year with the brilliant yellow and gold of the Sugar Maples along with the Pin Oak's russet and orange shades and his favorite; the striking crimson of the Red Maples. There was a slight nip in the morning, the warm breath escaping his mouth quickly vaporizing into thin air.

Running down the opposite side of the rise he was just two feet from the river's edge, the pleasant babbling of the water moving over and around large rocks music to his ears. A rabbit darted quickly across the path in front of him and disappeared into a small thicket of brush.

Taking a right, he left the trail behind and started up Cedar Creek Road which was a two mile loop that would lead him back to the Parkway. Passing an old abandoned barn that was one mile into his run, he picked up the pace now that he was warmed up.

Eight minutes later he was at the halfway point on the loop when he passed the Caylors Chapel Cemetery on the right, a small herd of cattle grazing peacefully on the left. The last half of the loop was his favorite part of his morning runs, the road flanked on both sides with tall trees, their limbs creating a roof of colorful leaves that resembled a tunnel. The wind suddenly picked up, blowing thousands of red and gold leaves in every direction. Running along, he tried to catch some of the flying foliage but the colorful leaves seemed to avoid his grasp.

Coming to the end of Cedar Creek Road, he turned left, running next to the Parkway which would lead him back to town. He thought about how lucky he was. Thanks to Mr. Callibrizzi and his wife, he and Max were able to purchase not only the gift shop but a log home nestled in a group of tall pine trees just off Route 73 directly across the road from the Great Smoky Mountains Park. He couldn't imagine living anyplace else. He felt blessed.

Looking at his watch, he noticed the time at 8:41 a.m. In approximately nineteen minutes he'd be back at the shop and his morning run would be complete. He'd check with Max to see if she needed any help, then drive home for a quick shower, jump into jeans and one of his flannel shirts, then it was back to the shop and last minute preparations for their grand opening.

Stepping from the sidewalk, he entered the parking lot of the IGA, Townsend's largest grocery store. The store sat back at the far end of the lot, only a few cars parked near the main entrance as it was too early in the morning for most people to be grocery shopping. At the farthest edge of the lot away from all of the other cars sat an older, faded blue Chevy, its light blue paint streaked with spots of rust, some areas of the metal completely eaten away.

The rear bumper was pitted with rust and secured with four bungee cords, the left rear tail light broken out. The two tires he could see were missing hubcaps, the front tire low on air. The car was in such poor condition that Doug couldn't imagine anyone driving it. Maybe the car had been abandoned. He ran the same route everyday for the past week. The car had never been parked there before. He stopped running as he stared at the dilapidated vehicle, his curiosity getting the best of him.

Walking around to the other side of the car he noticed the rusted plate on the front of the car depicting a rebel flag. The passenger side door handle was missing and the tires were in just as bad condition as the first two he had seen. At the rear of the car he noticed Tennessee tags from Blount County. Bending down, he noticed the small tag positioned in the corner of the plate. The tags were current. Moving away from the car he placed both hands on his hips as he looked around the lot. If the owner of the car was shopping at the IGA why would they park all the way out at the edge of the lot? Maybe the owner wasn't even around. Maybe the car *was* abandoned.

Stepping close to the car he peered in the rear window. What he saw not only took him completely by surprise but caused him to back away from the window in amazement. Moving back to the window, he looked inside again hoping that what he had previously seen was nothing more than his imagination. It wasn't his imagination, it was real! *A baby wrapped in an old blanket laying on the backseat.* Checking the front and backseats there was no one else in the car. Next, he checked the parking lot to see if anyone was close by—no one!

Looking back in the window it appeared the baby was sleeping. Then, he had a horrible thought. *What if the baby is dead!* He had heard the news on numerous occasions where people had left a child in a car while they were shopping and the child had died from lack of air or heat exhaustion. Thank God it wasn't that hot out. He tried the door but it was locked. The front passenger door was missing its handle so he couldn't open that door either. He tried both doors on the opposite side. Same thing—locked! Looking around the parking lot once again he wasn't quite sure what he should do. This was one of those things you heard about, but never experienced. But, *this was real!* It was actually happening right before his eyes. He had to do something—but what?

Running around to the side the baby was on, he tried to calm himself as he thought, *Calm down...use your head...do the right thing...call the police. No! That might be too late. Check and see if the baby is alive first, then call the police.* He shoved the car, but the baby remained perfectly still. Shoving the car more violently he spoke to himself, "Please let the baby be alive."

Suddenly, the baby girl opened her eyes and began to cry, the jarring of the car bringing her out of a nap. Doug let out a sigh of relief, realizing she was alive. He felt bad for waking the sleeping child, but at least now he knew she was alright. Now, all he had to do was to get hold of the police. He ran to the curb of the street and tried to flag down three cars in a row. Realizing that no one was going to stop for a man wearing a perspiration soaked sweat shirt and pants on the side of the road, he looked across the lot toward the IGA. A young high school age boy was busy gathering grocery carts left on the lot the previous evening. Running across the lot, he yelled at the boy, but was still too far across the lot to get his attention.

Another twenty yards passed and he yelled again, "Hey you...hold on there!"

The boy turned and looked in Doug's direction as he noticed a man running toward him waving his arms and yelling, "I need your help!"

Finally, Doug stopped directly in front of the boy. "Look, I need you to go into the store and tell the store manager that there is an abandoned baby in a car at the far end of the lot."

The boy, confused, looked around the lot and gave Doug a funny look. Doug could see the boy didn't quite get the message. Grabbing the boy by his shoulders, Doug repeated himself, "Listen, I don't have time to explain this to you. Go into the store and tell the manager that there is an abandoned baby in a locked car in the parking lot. Tell the manager to call the police...now!"

The intensity in Doug's voice caused the boy to back away as he started for the store more concerned over Doug's aggressive behavior than what he had been told. The boy wasn't moving fast enough for Doug, who yelled at the boy, "Move...get the manager! I'm going back to the car and check on the baby."

As Doug watched the boy run toward the store, he wondered if he had scared the boy to the point where he would simply inform the manager that there was some nut out in the parking lot rather than telling them about the baby. Turning, Doug ran back toward the car, praying the boy would follow the instructions he had been given.

Back at the car, Doug peered in the window. The baby's eyes were closed again. He shoved the car and the baby's eyes opened. This time she just stared out the window at Doug. There were no tears. *She's still okay,* thought Doug. He looked back toward the store. Nothing was happening. It had only been twenty seconds since he had left the boy. As the seconds seemed to slowly tick by, Doug began to get nervous as he asked himself a series of questions. *What if the boy didn't believe me? What if he doesn't tell the manager what I told him? What if the police don't come? What if the baby dies right before my very eyes? Is there something else I should do? Maybe I should break in and rescue the child. But, how can I break in?*

Looking around, he noticed a small pile of two by fours, some bags of concrete and some metal rebar that were stacked next to the road where some construction had been taking place on repairing the sidewalk. Looking toward the store, no one was approaching. He couldn't wait any longer. He had to do something. Running to the curb, he grabbed a short section of rebar and a two by four and returned to the car. Laying the section of lumber on the ground he decided to break out the driver's side window furthest from where the baby was laying. Just as he raised the bar, he was interrupted by a female voice, "You the man who reported the baby in the car?"

Looking across the roof of the car he saw a woman running toward him, a grave look of concern on her face. With a sigh of relief, Doug moved around to the front of the car and pointed at the rear window. "Yeah, she's in the backseat. All the doors are locked. No one seems to be around. I was just about to break in and get her out. Are you the store manager? Did you call the police?"

Holding up her cell phone, the woman answered, "Yes, I'm Phyllis Woods. I just called. They said they'd have a cruiser here in a few minutes."

Doug looked up the street. "I don't know if we can wait a few minutes. It's been over five minutes since I discovered her. Who knows how long before that she's been in there. From the looks of this car, there's no telling how long she's been here. I was just about to break in the front window."

The manager looked in the rear window, stepped back and strongly suggested, "Break out the glass, but be careful. We don't want any glass to get near the baby."

Moving back around to the passenger window, Doug raised the rebar as he spoke, "Well, here goes! Keep an eye on the baby." Starting at the low front corner of the window, he rammed the bar into the glass, the first attempt accomplishing nothing, but the second glance pushed the glass inward, small cracks forming and running up the window. On the third attempt, the glass caved in, leaving a small two inch opening, the broken glass falling onto the floorboard. Looking across the roof, Doug asked, "How's the baby doing?"

"Fine, just fine," said Phyllis. "Keep going. The sooner we get her out of there the better."

Once Doug realized the baby was alright he became more aggressive on breaking out the glass. Moving the bar up a few inches he repeated the process, more glass falling inside the car. The manager didn't notice the man and the two small children when they approached as she was concentrating on the baby. Doug was grabbed by the back of his sweatshirt and jerked backwards, his feet leaving the ground. Phyllis let out a scream as she watched the large man throw Doug to the ground and kick him in the side. The man yelled at Doug, "Who the hell do ya think ya are? Break my window, will ya!" The two children dropped the bags they were holding and ran to the side of the car.

Doug, realizing that he had to defend himself started to raise the rebar, but the man stepped on his arm preventing him from doing so. Phyllis started around the rear of the car, not sure what she was going to do, but she had to try and do something. The man ordered her roughly, "Stop right there or I'll break his damn neck!" He kicked Doug again in the side and then placed his large boot on Doug's neck and pointed at Phyllis. "Back away from the car or I'll give ya more of the same!"

Trying to reason with the rough looking man, she spoke calmly, "Look, we're just trying to get the baby out of this car. Someone abandoned her."

The man sneered at her as he pointed at the car. "This is my car *and* that's my baby girl layin' in the backseat. Yer breakin' the law by tryin' ta kidnap her."

Phyllis looked at the two little girls who were huddled together, "Kidnapped! Are you kidding? You abandoned this child. We had no idea how long she had been left alone in the car, which in case you didn't know, is against the law."

Doug tried to get up, but the man applied more pressure to his neck as he ordered, "Move and I'll snap yer neck like a twig!"

Phyllis breathed a sigh of relief when she saw a Townsend police cruiser pull into the far end of the lot. "You're in trouble now. The police are here."

"I ain't gonna be in no trouble," snapped the man. "Yer gonna be arrested fer breakin' inta my car and tryin ta kidnap my daughter!"

Grant pulled up next to the old car and got out, his hand on the butt of his gun, not sure what he was going to be confronted with. At first glance, he could only see the store manager and Ambrose Stroud standing on opposite sides of the car. Looking quickly at the two small girls, he approached Phyllis, "You the woman who called about an abandoned baby?"

"Yes," she answered as she pointed at Ambrose. "And that's the father who abandoned the baby."

Grant's first concern was the baby. "Is the baby all right?"

"Yes, she's laying in the backseat."

Grant was stopped from looking in the rear window as the manager suggested strongly, "The baby's okay for now. You need to get that big lummox's foot off of the man who found the baby!"

Walking around to the front of the car, Grant's confusion was quickly cleared up when he saw Doug Eland laying on the ground with Ambrose's size twelve boot across his neck. Instantly, he ordered, "Stroud! Let him up...now!"

Ambrose gave Grant a snide look and then laughed, "Ya ain't gonna do nothin' Denlinger. The last time we met up I thought ya was nothin' but a weasel. Remember, when that damn tourist ran inta my truck. Ya left 'em go. Scott free! Not this time. This asshole busted in my window and was gonna kidnap my little girl. I want him arrested. Ya put the cuffs on him and I'll let up my boot."

"Doesn't work that way, Ambrose. You abandoned your little girl in a locked vehicle and went into the store leaving her unattended. That's against the law and furthermore, it's just plain stupid!"

"You callin' me stupid?" He pressed down with the boot, Doug struggling to breath.

Phyllis started around the back of the car as she directed her stern comments at Ambrose, "Since you're on the store's property, I'm going to press charges and furthermore, you'll never be allowed to shop here again!"

Grant unsnapped the strap on his gun. "Ambrose! This has gone too far. Back off and let the man up."

Ambrose pointed at Grant "Ya ain't got no right to pull a gun on me, Denlinger! I'll let him up when you cuff him and not a second before." He nodded at Phyllis and added, "And while yer at it ya might want to tell that fat assed store manager to shut up before I walk over there and slap her silly!"

Phyllis, boldly walked over and picked up the two by four and stated confidently, "I've had enough of this crap!"

Before Grant could react she brought the section of lumber down over Ambrose's shoulder. The blow was glancing but did manage to knock him back away from Doug, who instantly got to his feet and ran to the rear of the car as he held his neck, trying to regain a normal pattern of breathing. For a big man, Ambrose was quick. He reached out and backhanded Phyllis, sending her to the ground like a rag doll. Grant pulled his gun, but before he could level it, Ambrose picked up the two by four and slammed it across Grant's wrist knocking the gun from his hand. The next thing Grant realized, he was picked up like a sack of potatoes and tossed over the roof of the car. As Ambrose started around the front of the car to inflict more damage on Grant, he didn't notice Brody's truck pulling to the curb. Ambrose, wielding the broken section of lumber like a club raised it to bring it down on Grant's legs but the two hundred and forty-five pound Brody slammed into Ambrose driving him to the pavement. Both men rolled and Brody managed to get Ambrose in a neck lock, his huge arm locked around Ambrose's throat. Ambrose was livid, thrashing his arms and legs, all the while cursing up a storm, "Son of a bitch...Got damn, I'll kill ya!"

Grant, slow to get to his feet, could see Brody wasn't going to be able to contain Ambrose for long. Placing his foot on Ambrose's chest, Grant aimed his gun at Ambrose as he ordered, "You make one move and you're a dead man!"

Brody released his grip and stood as he removed his cuffs from his belt, all the while Ambrose yelling, "Get your foot off me! I can't breathe! I'll kill all of ya! Mess with my family!"

Axel struggled to roll Ambrose onto his side, then snapped the cuffs around his thick wrists.

Grant holstered his gun and backed away as Ambrose tried to get to his feet but his uncontrolled anger made it difficult for him to stand. He got to his knees but then fell over onto his side. Brody ordered Grant, "Come on, let's get this animal loaded in the cruiser before he causes us any more trouble."

Phyllis, who was now holding the baby approached Brody as she spoke, "Chief Brody, I'd like to press charges."

Brody gave her an odd look. "That's fine, but what charges can you bring? The only thing we have on him is child abandonment and aggravated assault on an officer of the law."

"A lot happened before you were on the scene," interjected Grant. "Ambrose backhanded Phyllis and tried to strangle Mr. Eland to death so we can actually charge Stroud with three different instances of assault."

Doug was now standing next to Phyllis. "I'd like to press charges as well."

Lee Griner pulled his cruiser into the lot, hopped out and joined the group. "What we got, sir?"

Brody was short and to the point. "Ambrose Stroud here left his baby in this locked car. When Grant tried to arrest him he attacked Grant with a two by four, hit Phyllis here and tried to squeeze the life out of Mr. Eland. Here's what I want done. Grant, I want you to call Maryville and inform Sheriff Grimes to send over a car to haul Ambrose to the county jail. You also need to tell them to send someone from Child Protective Services. They'll know what to do with the baby and the two girls. Lee, I want you to take statements from Phyllis and Mr. Eland."

Ambrose, still laying on the ground suddenly stood and charged toward Doug and yelled at him, "Yer responsible fer all this. Ya can't take my kids away from me!"

Lee, who was on the muscular side, intercepted Ambrose before he even got close to Doug and body slammed him to the ground.

Brody and Grant rushed to help restrain Ambrose as he rolled on the ground and looked directly at Doug. "You haven't heard the last from me Eland!"

As Lee and Brody were stuffing Ambrose in the backseat of Lee's cruiser, Ambrose yelled at his twin daughters, "Go on git...run on home. Tell Effy what happened!" Before Grant could react, the two little girls ran across the lot, disappearing in the trees behind the store.

Brody, with a look of disgust on his face ordered Grant, "Leave them go. We know where they're headed. I'll pay the Stroud's a visit later this mornin' to make sure they got home okay."

Axel walked to Grant's side and looked down at his bleeding wrist. "You need to get over to the Immediate Care Center and get that wound tended to." Turning to Doug, he asked, "You gonna be all right?"

"I think I'll be fine," said Doug. "Who is that crazy bastard?"

Brody answered, "That's Ambrose Stroud. And, you're right. He is a crazy bastard. His family lives east of here on a farm. They're all a bunch of loonies. I'll go have a talk with them. But still, you need to be careful."

Twenty minutes later, Brody pulled off the road down from where Maude and Otis were setting up their goods beneath the tent. Otis popped his first beer of the day as he inspected his handy work. Everything they wanted to attempt to sell sat on the four picnic tables. The golf cart and attached trailer was parked at the back of the tent, a case of iced down beer sat next to his lawn chair. He was looking forward to relaxing in the chair and watching the tour buses and countless cars pass by on Wears Valley Road as he drank one beer after another.

Maude pointed her cane across the road as Brody stepped out of his truck and adjusted his hat. "Wonder what that idiot wants? Dammit all ta hell! The last person I wanted ta see this mornin' out here by the road turns out ta be the first one I git ta see. Damn ol' Axel Brody!"

"Take it easy, Maude," suggested Otis as he swilled down his beer. "Mebbe he jest wants a few tomatoes."

Maude lit up her fourth cigarette of the day. "Tomatoes...my ass! Brody never drops by our place unless he's got a bone ta pick with us. I gotta feelin' this is gonna be a bad day."

Otis plopped down in his chair, pitched his now empty can in a trash container and reached for a second beer as Brody approached. "Mornin', Sheriff. How's about a cold one?"

Brody nodded at Otis, but his main focus was centered on Maude who he knew ruled the roost. Tipping his hat, he spoke, "Mornin', Maude." Turning, he looked at the goods beneath the tent. "Looks like you're set for a busy day."

Maude spit on the ground, took a drag of her smoke and answered sarcastically, "Cut the crap, Brody! You and I both know ya didn't drive out here ta pay us no social visit. What's on yer mind?"

Axel walked past Otis, flipping him a quarter, then selected a Macintosh apple from a basket on one of the tables. Polishing the apple on his shirt, Axel placed his foot on an empty crate, took a large bite and spoke as he chewed, "We, or I guess I should say you, have a problem."

Maude puffed on her cigarette. "That so."

Brody didn't like Maude or her attitude as he answered smartly, "It seems your idiot son, Ambrose, went and left his baby girl in the backseat of his car while he went into the IGA. The car was locked, all the windows were rolled up. The child could have died, but thanks to one of our local citizens and the manager at the IGA, she was rescued. Ambrose didn't take too kindly to their efforts. He nearly choked the citizen to death, backhanded the store manager and assaulted one of my officers. Right now, your son is on his way to jail in Maryville. Aside from the assault and battery charges, he's facin' resistin' arrest and child abandonment. The baby has been taken into custody by the Blount County Child Protective Services until they decide the best course of action needed for the safety of the child."

Maude pointed her cane at Axel and spoke calmly, "Brody, I'll be the first ta admit my three boys ain't the sharpest tools in the shed and if what yer tellin' me is the gospel, well, then I reckon my dumb ass son should sit in jail. But, this is my granddaughter yer talkin' about. Ya done us wrong by not bringin' that little girl to me. I'm her grandma. Child Services ain't got no right ta take her off somewheres. Now, you've done yer job by comin' out here ta tell us what happened and now me, Otis and Effy are gonna drive over ta Maryville, bail out Ambrose and git my granddaughter back."

Taking another bite out of the apple, Axel explained, "Maude, it doesn't work like that. This is serious. It's not like a speedin' ticket you pay and everythin' is forgiven. Bail hasn't even been set for Ambrose yet. He has to appear before the Blount County Judge, which may, or may not happen today. Maybe tomorrow. It wouldn't make a difference if you went over there with a million dollars. Your son has to go before the judge, then bail is set. And, as far as gettin' your granddaughter back, well, the judge will have to talk that over with Child Protective Services. They're not gonna hand that child over to you. They'll conduct an investigation, more than likely pay you folks a visit. They'll want to talk with Rosemary, the child's mother...not you. If after that, they feel the child's safety is not in any jeopardy, then they'll release the child to Rosemary, but that's gonna take some time."

Otis, surprisingly agreed with Brody. "Axel's right, Maude. Don't make no sense in goin' over ta Maryville and makin' things worse than they is."

Knocking the beer out of his hand with her cane, Maude snapped, "Shut the hell up, Otis! If I want yer opinion, I'll ask!"

Brody was surprised at Maude's agreement with him that her son should sit in jail but he also knew the next bit of information he had to share with her would not go down as well. "Maude, there's another reason why I came by this mornin'. Ambrose had his twin daughters with him. When we mentioned gettin' Child Services to come by and pick up the children, Ambrose ordered them to run back home and tell Effy what happened. They took off runnin' before we could stop them. And besides that, we had our hands full tryin' ta calm Ambrose down. So, I just wanted to make sure they got home okay."

Maude stepped closer to Axel and stuck her cane in his chest. "Ya mean ta tell me two of my granddaughters, Jasmine and Opal are between here and town somewheres on their own?"

Brody, not one to be pushed too far, grabbed the cane and pointed it at her. "Yeah, that's what I'm tellin' you. Ain't my fault. Their father, Ambrose, your stupid ass son, ordered them to run home. Weren't none of my doin'. Hell, they were off in the woods before we knew what was happenin'."

Otis stood and approached Brody. "Ya ain't got no right ta talk ta my wife that way!"

Axel, using the cane, pushed Otis back down in his chair, then threw the unfinished apple at him and spoke directly into Maude's face, "You people just don't seem to grasp what has happened here! I have to report those two little girls runnin' off. I guarantee you, Child Protective Services will be over here lookin' for them as well. Ambrose will take the fall for that also. The authorities aren't goin' to take too well to a father tellin' his two seven-year-old daughters to run off into the woods and make their way home on their own. Ambrose put their lives in danger. You better just pray those two little girls make it home alright."

Maude turned to Otis and ordered, "Git up ta the house and round up Cletus, Harmon, Arliss and Dwayne. Tell 'em ta spread out and start searchin' the woods between here and town. Otis, you take one of the trucks and search up and down the road."

Axel handed the cane back to Maude and interjected, "I'll put everyone I have available on the lookout for your granddaughters."

As Brody was walking away, Maude shouted after him, "Ya better pray they show up or you'll have ta deal with not only me but all us Stroud's!"

Grant sat on the end of an uncomfortable couch in the Immediate Care Center. The cut on his right wrist had stopped bleeding and the nurse at the reception desk after looking at the small wound said it would only be a few minutes before the doctor on duty would take a look at him. More than likely, the way it looked, he'd have to get stitches.

Flipping through an outdated Field and Stream magazine, Grant looked up just as Buddie Knapp was coming through the swinging doors from the back where patients were seen by the doctor. His right arm was in a sling and he didn't look like he was in the best of moods. "Hey, Buddie!" shouted Grant. "What happened to your arm?"

Buddie really didn't look like he wanted to talk as he reluctantly walked over to where Grant was sitting and held up his slinged arm. "Fell off the damn ladder while I was trying to put up new fascia boards on the house. Broke my damn arm." Motioning at Grant's injured wrist, Buddie asked, "Looks like a nasty cut. What'd ya do? Trip over something at the office?"

"No, actually I had a run in with Ambrose Stroud."

The mention of Ambrose suddenly changed Buddie's attitude. "It's funny you should mention one of the Stroud's. My six-year-old granddaughter was just talking about the Stroud's the other day. She goes to school with some of the Stroud kids, one being Violet Stroud, Cletus' daughter. Everyone in town by now knows that her mother, Ruby Jean ran off and left her and Cletus. Well, anyways, my granddaughter tells me that she told Violet she was sorry her mother had run off. Violet answered by saying her mother didn't run off and that she gets to see her every day. I don't know what to make of that. Ruby Jean's been gone for weeks now, nobody in town has seen her and yet her daughter claims she sees her daily. Seems kinda strange."

"There's a lot of strange things going on around here lately," stated Grant.

"What could be stranger than a woman who's reported as running off and her daughter still seeing her every day?"

"I'll admit, this business with Ruby Jean does seem odd, but we have bigger fish to fry...like *who* killed Luke Pardee."

Grant's answer took Buddie completely by surprise as he stammered, "Look...I gotta...go! I've got...to get...my house...finished, so me and the wife...can get the hell...out of ...Townsend."

Grant wanted to continue the conversation about Luke's murder but was interrupted by the nurse, "Officer Denlinger, the doctor will see you now."

CHAPTER NINE

MAUDE OPENED A PEANUT AND THREW THE SHELL ON the floor. Popping the nut in the side of her mouth, she handed the wooden bowl to Effy. Taking the bowl, Effy looked at Russell, "Ya want any more?"

Russell shook his head. "No, had enough."

Motioning with her head toward the road, Maude smiled. "Rosemary was sure happy when her two girls showed up. I guess we can be expectin' them Child Protective people any time now."

"I can tell ya she ain't all that happy over it," said Effy. "Her husband is locked up and there's no tellin' when they're gonna release him."

Lowering her head, Maude spoke sadly, "Out of my three boys, Harmon's the only one with any sense. Cletus beat Ruby Jean all the time and now Ambrose leaves his daughter in a locked car."

Pointing to the yard where Dwayne and Arliss were laying under their truck, Effy remarked sarcastically, "What the hell are them two doin'?"

"Seems like their truck got two flat tires," cackled Maude. "I reckon they's waitin' fer a gust of wind ta blow some air into 'em. They think somebody slit 'em on purpose, but them tires were balder than Otis' head."

Russell, who had been watching Dwayne and Arliss, spoke up, "I have a truck! I bought it earlier this year. It's red."

"Well, that's mighty nice," said Maude as she pitched a peanut shell off the porch. "Where's it at, Russell?"

"It's parked over by my house. I'm sure it's still there. I got a lot of good things at my house. My brother bought me a television, but I never watch it much. I got a real neat refrigerator, cook stove and a bed."

Maude smiled at Effy. "That a fact? I'll bet it's right nice at yer place."

"It is and when I get to go home, you, Effy and Otis can come visit me. I can make you something to eat and..."

Russell was interrupted as Dwayne crawled out from beneath the truck and holding the side of his head, yelled, "Dammit. I jest busted my skull! Damn ol' truck!" Still holding his head he kicked at the flat tire.

Arliss, who was now out from under the truck, spit out a chaw of tobacco as he spoke, "Here, lemme see." Pulling Dwayne's hand away from his head, he inspected the small gash, "Aw, it ain't nothin,' jest a scratch." He turned and looked at the porch, lowering his voice so Effy and Maude could not hear what he was saying. "Look at them three, sittin' there stuffin' their faces with them peanuts. When was the last time, the ol' lady made a batch of boiled peanuts fer us? Look at that damn Russell starin' at us. He gives me the willies. Every time I turn around, he's givin' me the evil eye. There's somethin' strange about him."

Showing no concern over what Arliss said, Dwayne shrugged, "I ain't worried about Russell right now. What we got ta do is git some tires or we're gonna be doin' a lot of walkin'. Ya got any money?"

"About four dollars," replied Arliss.

"Dammit, that won't even buy a lug nut. Tell ya what. You git down ta the shed and start pilin' up some skins and I'll go ask Cletus if we can borrow his truck till tomorrow. If we leave in the next hour we can be down at Sutter's place before midnight. He'll buy everythin' we got."

"Ambrose said we ain't s'pose ta sell any of those skins. He said we need that money ta git us through the winter."

Dwayne was getting aggravated, "I ain't worried none about Ambrose. We was the ones who trapped them critters and skinned most of 'em. He ain't our boss. 'Sides that he's sittin' in jail. I'll bring Cletus' truck down and we'll pack the skins up. Now, go on...git!"

Minutes later, Arliss walked around the back of the house and opened the gate leading to the back field. Walking through the tall weeds, mumbling to himself about the fact that Dwayne always had the last say, he was startled by a shadow that crossed his path. Turning quickly, he almost ran into Russell who was standing behind him. "Russell! What the hell's wrong with ya. Ya scared the crap out of me! Almost pissed my pants."

"I was just taking a walk," said Russell. "Where're you going?"

"Ain't none of yer business," snapped Arliss as he continued on through the weeds. Realizing that Russell was right behind him, he stopped. "Ain't no need fer ya ta follow me either. I got ta go down ta the shed and see if I can find me some tires. Ya go on back ta the house."

Russell looked in the direction of the shed. "Is that's what's in there...tires?"

"Yeah, amongst other things. Mostly junk. Old bed springs and bottles. Stuff like that."

Arliss stomped off through the weeds, Russell following. "I'll go with you and help to find some tires."

Realizing Russell was not going to go back to the house, Arliss stopped. "On second thought, I think I'll wait till tomorrow. It'll be dark soon. I don't like ta go down there in the dark. Ya know...snakes and rats. Let's go back ta the house."

Dwayne was heading away from Cletus' trailer when he saw Arliss and Russell walking toward him. Arliss stopped, but Russell just kept on walking as he nodded at Dwayne. When Russell was out of earshot, Arliss pulled his brother to the side. "That damn idiot followed me down ta the field. I don't trust 'em. He's always snoopin' around."

Dwayne watched as Russell walked up onto the porch of the house and sat in one of the rocking chairs. "Change of plans. We can wait and git the skins early in the mornin'. 'Sides that, it's startin' ta rain. We better git some sleep so we can git up early."

Walking toward their trailer, Dwayne continued, "Cletus said we can borrow his truck, but we have ta have it back by noon tomorrow. We're gonna have ta pull out of here no later than five in the mornin'."

It was two in the morning when Maude was awakened by the cold rain beating on the window pane. Deciding to walk down the hall for her nightly visit to the bathroom, she looked out the hallway window and let out a piercing yell, "Otis...git up! There's flames shootin' up out in the back field. Somethin's on fire!"

After she shook Otis out of a deep sleep, they ran out the back door to get a better look at the fire. Within seconds, Rosemary and Loretty were at their side. Rosemary pointed at the flames. "Looks like the skinnin' shed's on fire. How'd that happen?"

Harmon came running out of his trailer, still pulling his pants over the top of his long johns. Hopping on one foot, he yelled for Arliss and Dwayne, "Son of a bitch! We got us a rip roarin' fire right in the middle of the rain!"

Otis looked up into the falling rain and commented, "That fire won't last long. Rain'll put it out soon's those ol' boards burn off."

Maude stared at the reddish-orange flames. "Well, there goes all our pelts."

Harmon, Dwayne and Arliss were now at Otis and Maude's side. Dwayne looked around and asked, "Where's Russell?"

A voice from behind startled him, "Right here." Russell stood a few feet away concealed in the shadow of a large tree, once again causing Arliss to jump and move away from him.

Effy, who was now outside thumped Arliss on the side of his head. "Ya seem nervous boy. Why ya worried about, Russell?"

Arliss gave Russell a nasty look. "Somethin' or someone started that fire. It jest didn't start on its own."

Harmon stepped forward and asked, "Any of the damn kids been sneakin' off ta the shed ta smoke?"

Effy waved her hand. "Naw, they's all in bed this time of night. Could have been a rat chewed through a wire or mebbe one of ya left somethin' electric on." Giving Arliss a hard stare, she explained, "Russell ain't got no call ta burn down the shed if that's what yer thinkin'."

Arliss could see that his accusation toward Russell was falling apart quickly. "Naw, I was jest askin' ta make sure ya was safe...that's all." Changing the subject, he looked across the field. "Ya think anybody else saw the fire? We sure don't want no fire engines comin' out here."

"Don't rightly think so," said Otis. "Fire's already dyin' out." Looking around, he asked, "Where's Cletus?"

Harmon pointed his thumb back over his shoulder. "He's passed out drunk in his trailer. Been hittin' the bottle all day. Since Ruby Jean ain't around no more he's been a mess."

Maude walked over and slammed her oldest son up against the side of a tree. "We don't mention Ruby Jean around here no more. Ya know better than that." Turning, she placed her arm around Effy. "We might as well all git back ta bed. We're gittin' soaked out here. Ain't nothin' we can do till mornin'. If the fire company shows up jest stay in bed and pretend like ya don't know nothin' about no fire."

As everyone started to walk away, Arliss pulled Dwayne around the side of the house and pointed out, "I know damn well Russell started that fire, jest like he slit our tires. He doesn't like us one damn bit. I don't know what he's up to, but we gotta git him before he gits us. When I was up at the house earlier today, Effy starts tellin' me Russell's got a bunch of good stuff at his cabin...plus a truck. That piece of crap truck we have is on its last leg. We could use another truck. Since we ain't got no pelts, I think you and me oughta take Russell back ta his place. I figure if we don't git the stuff in his cabin, someone else will. That cabin ain't gonna sit that long before somebody breaks in and takes everythin'. Russell is dumber than a box of rocks. He thinks he can go on back home like nothin' happened. I bet the police are still keepin' an eye on his place. We need ta find out where his cabin is, git in, grab everythin' and then git out real quick like."

Dwayne gave his brother an odd look. "What in blazes are ya gittin' at Arliss? I'm wet and tired. Right now all I wanna do is ta crawl in a warm bed. All this talk about Russell. Ya think he's gonna stand by and watch you take all his stuff?"

"Hear me out, Dwayne. We can still borrow Cletus' truck and when we git ta the cabin we can make quick work of Russell. Hell, everybody thinks he's already dead anyways. We can strip the cabin and put everythin' in the two trucks. We can make a killin'. Maude told me he's got a television, furniture, dishes, bed clothes and all kinds of stuff. We can run it over ta the flea market out on Route 40 and sell it. Whadda ya think?"

Dwayne shrugged. "Well, I am tired of Russell hangin' around here. If we could make some good money and git his truck then we'd be set fer awhile. But, here's the thing. It'll take us more than one day ta git the stuff and then sell it. Remember, we have ta git Cletus' truck back here by noon or he'll be raisin' hell. And another thing; how are we gonna git Russell out of here without Effy and Maude knowin'?"

"Effy can't hear a damn thing and both Maude and Otis snore so loud ya could slam a door and they wouldn't wake up. Besides, when I tell Russell we're gonna take him home, he won't give a lick about them ol' ladies."

Dwayne rubbed his calloused hand across his stubbled face.

"Gimme a minute ta think." Whenever he took time to think something over, it always pissed Arliss off to no end. "Hmm...let's see. If we do git the stuff and sell it, we'll split the money fifty-fifty, but who gits the truck?"

"Dammit Dwayne, I don't care! You can have it. I'll fix up our ol' truck and drive it. Stop hemin' and hawin' around. Sometimes, you really piss me off!"

"Alright," said Dwayne, "let's do it! After I git out of these wet clothes, I'll go down ta Cletus' and git his truck, some ropes and blankets. You go git Russell. Make sure, and I mean damn sure, no one sees you two leavin' the house. We'll meet up, in let's say about fifteen minutes down by the front gate."

Arliss watched as his brother ran up the lane. *Finally,* he thought. *We'll be rid of Russell and have some money in our pockets from sellin' all his stuff.*

Creeping around the other side of the house, Arliss checked to see if anyone was watching, then tapped on Russell's bedroom window. Russell, a light sleeper, sat up quickly and looked around, his ears always attentive to sounds. This sound was unfamiliar to him. Arliss tapped on the glass again and Russell got up and went to the window. He just stood there staring at Arliss who signaled by raising his hands for him to open the window. Skeptically, Russell slowly opened the window but remained silent. He stepped back, not trusting Arliss.

Leaning in the window, Arliss began to talk in a low voice, "I got some good news fer ya, Russell. Me and Dwayne talked it over and we think it's time fer ya ta go home. I know ya miss yer place and we're willin' ta take ya there...right now! How's that sound?"

Russell gave Arliss a strange look and asked, "Why do you want to take me home? I know you and Dwayne don't like me much. Why would you do that for me? Why now? It's dark and it's raining."

"You got me and Dwayne all wrong. We had a long talk and we think you should be allowed ta go back ta yer place. It ain't fair that ya have ta stay here. We know ya ain't happy here and now with the fire and all, we don't want no one blamin' you. Now, if ya can git yer clothes and git out this window, we'll be leavin' right now."

Russell looked toward his bedroom door as he pulled on his pants. "I gotta tell Maude and Effy good bye. I need to at least do that."

"No!" objected Arliss. "They don't need ta know yer leavin.' I'll tell them when we git back from takin' ya home. I think they want ta keep ya here forever...like a prisoner. You'll never be able ta go anywhere. I hear tell Otis is goin' ta stop ya from goin' back in the woods. He don't like ya wanderin' around."

Arliss was getting nervous. It was taking too long to convince Russell to leave. If he got caught by Maude or Effy he'd get the beating of his life. Just as he was about to forget the idea for the night, Russell spoke up, "Move!" as he climbed out the open window with his large boots in his hand.

"That all ya takin'?" asked Arliss

"This is all I got. Ain't got nothin' else worth takin'. I got everything I need back at my cabin...back home." Looking back in the window, Russell whispered, "Let's go!"

Dwayne was waiting by the main gate as he leaned against the truck, smoking a cigarette. Signaling for them to hurry, he whispered, "I put the truck in neutral and pushed it down the road with the lights off." Reaching in the back window, he put his shotgun on a rifle rack just behind the seats, along with a burlap gunny sack.

As the three climbed in the truck, a small light came on near the back of Cletus' trailer. Pulling back the curtain, Violet watched as the truck pulled though the gate.

Russell was uncomfortable sitting between Dwayne and Arliss. He felt trapped. Their bodies were touching his and he disliked being anchored between them. He wrinkled his nose at the acrid odor of sweat and tobacco that lingered in the truck. He wondered how long it had been since either one of them had a bath.

Turning onto the highway, Arliss asked, "What'd Cletus say about us takin' his truck?"

"He don't know about it," answered Dwayne. "I jest took the keys without tellin' him. He was drunk as a skunk, passed out on the couch." Dwayne started to laugh which turned into a nasty cough, spewing brown liquid on the windshield. He opened the window and spat out a small chaw of tobacco.

"Are you crazy?" said Arliss. "He'll kick our asses when we git back! Hell, he might even report his truck stolen. We could wind up in deep crap!"

"He ain't gonna do that. His license and plates are expired. He ain't gonna want ta pay no fines. 'Sides, when we git back if we give him fifty dollars and a tank full of gas he'll git over bein' mad right quick."

"What do ya think about that, Russell?" asked Arliss. "Ya know, gittin' this truck and takin' ya home jest cause we like ya?"

"I guess it's okay," said Russell. "My truck has good plates and I have a license."

Dwayne leaned forward and looked past Russell as he winked at Arliss, "Well, that's real good, Russell. Now, when we git ta Jellico, yer gonna have ta tell me how ta git ta yer place. Ya know the way...right?"

Russell was annoyed by the question. "I ain't stupid. I know where I live! I gotta question to ask."

"You betcha." said Dwayne. "Ask away!"

Russell hesitated, but then blurted out, "Why did you kill those animals and then skin them? Why did you do that? I looked in the shed. I saw them skins. That's bad!"

Dwayne's mood suddenly changed. He didn't like the direction the conversation was going. Arliss spoke up, "So, ya was snoopin' around. Well the truth is we kilt 'em ta eat 'em and then we sell the skins so we can buy food in the winter. That's what most mountain folks do. All those fox and raccoons were raidin' our chicken house every night. They was killin' our chickens and eatin' all them eggs. We need them eggs fer the youngins ta eat. Now, that ain't bad...right, Russell?"

Russell objected, "You killed more animals than you needed for food and people don't eat river otters or skunks. You use them steel traps. That's still bad!"

Arliss, trying to sound sincere put his arm around Russell's shoulder. "I reckon yer right, Russell. I'll tell ya what. From now on me and Dwayne won't kill no more critters except when we need food and we'll git rid of them traps. How's that sound?" Before Russell could answer Dwayne reached over and turned the radio on. He didn't want to talk with Russell any more. He just wanted to get to the cabin, kill Russell and take everything they could haul from his place. As they turned onto Route 40 West, a country song filled the cab of the truck.

Just as the sun broke over a distant ridge, Dwayne spotted the sign that read: JELLICO 3 MILES. Yawning, he asked, "Okay, Russell, which way do I go from here?"

Pointing up the road, Russell gave simple instructions, "Go past the town about seven miles. There'll be a road on the left called Buck Point. Go on up that road."

Entering the tree lined dirt road, Dwayne maneuvered the truck up the winding one lane path, the truck making a constant grinding noise as the gears struggled with the steep incline. A half mile into the deep woods, Russell tapped Dwayne on his shoulder. "I gotta pee. You can pull over at a clearing that's just around the next bend. There's plenty of room to park."

"Pee! Can't ya wait?" growled Dwayne. "Yer house can't be that much farther."

"It's a couple more miles. I don't think I can wait that long. I have to go real bad!"

Dwayne slowed the truck as they went around a hairpin turn and then pulled into the small clearing. Sitting back in frustration he held the steering wheel with both hands. "Go on, take yer piss, but don't be all day about it!"

Arliss got out of the truck and let Russell slide out. Limping on his bad leg, Russell walked to the rear of the truck, but was stopped by Arliss who removed his jacket and spoke, "Hey, Russell, whadda ya think of this shirt?"

Russell hesitated at the edge of the road as he looked back at the tee-shirt which read: ***WHERE IS RUSSELL PEARL?*** Arliss could tell from the expression on his face that he was surprised. Jokingly, Arliss poked at Russell, "Yer famous! Everyone wants ta know where ya are. Right now, me and Dwayne are the only ones in the whole world who know where you are."

Arliss laughed as Russell started down a steep embankment, holding onto the trees to prevent him from sliding in the soft, pine needle covered earth. Ten yards down, he stopped at a large boulder and waited.

Three minutes passed when Dwayne stuck his head out of the truck and yelled, "What the hell's takin' him so long? Go down there and see what he's doin'."

"Why me," argued Arliss. "You go!"

"I can't dumb ass! I'm afraid ta take my foot off the brake or me and the truck might end up down there." Pointing down the ravine, he ordered his younger brother, "Git down there!"

Walking a few feet down the road, Arliss peered down through the trees where he saw Russell standing next to the rock. "Ya done? Come on back up."

"I need some help," lied Russell. "I slid in the pine needles. I need some help getting back up the hill."

Arliss turned sideways and placed his left foot on the side of the embankment and grabbed a low hanging tree branch for support. He slid the rest of the way down to the rock, finding it difficult to keep his footing. Brushing dirt and pine needles from his pants, he scolded Russell, "Why'd ya come down here fer? How in the hell are we s'pose ta git back up ta the road?"

"Turn around and grab that tree branch, Arliss," said Russell. "I'll hold on to your waist. All I need to do is steady myself so I can get my footing."

Arliss wasn't happy as he turned and grabbed the branch. "I swear ta God, Russell, if ya pull me down and we fall into the ravine I'm gonna break yer good leg!"

It was swift and unexpected. Russell's left arm wrapped tightly around Arliss' neck and his right hand went over his mouth. Arliss' feet dangled in the air, his hands trying to pry Russell's arm from his neck. It only took one swift jerk from Russell when the snapping of Arliss' neck signaled his sudden death. Arliss went limp and Russell watched as the body crumbled to the ground. Placing his boot on Arliss' neck, he pushed down making sure Arliss was dead. Going to the other side of the body, Russell kicked it and watched it bounce and roll down into the ravine below.

Making his way back up the steep embankment using tree limbs to pull him upward, he hid behind a tree next to the road. Peering around the thick trunk, he saw Dwayne still sitting in the truck. His left arm hung out the window as his fingers drummed impatiently on the side of the door. Russell stepped from behind the tree and started to walk to the truck. Dwayne, seeing him in the rearview mirror, looked back as he stated with an irritated tone, "Well, it's about damn time!" Noticing that Arliss was not with him, he asked, "Where the hell's my dumb ass brother?"

Russell pointed over the side. "He got his foot stuck in between two rocks. He needs your help. I tried to get him loose, but I couldn't get a good foothold with my bad leg."

"Son of a bitch," snarled Dwayne as he wrestled his heavy body out of the truck and started down the road toward Russell.

"He's down over the side, right down there," pointed Russell.

As Dwayne peered through the trees, Russell walked to the truck, reached in the window, grabbed the shotgun and followed Dwayne.

Dwayne was concentrating on the steep ravine as Russell silently approached. "Where? I can't see him."

Dwayne heard the click of the gun as he turned, but it was too late. The first shot hit him directly in the chest. His face froze in a state of shock and disbelief. Falling back against a tree, his vision was starting to blur as he watched Russell step closer and aim the gun once again. The second shot was point blank, hitting him full in the face nearly tearing his head off. Pulling his slumping body from the tree, Russell pushed it over the side of the embankment and watched it roll and careen down the ravine, stopping a few feet from where Arliss lay. Russell smiled, put the gun over his shoulder and walked to the truck. He'd be back home is less than thirty minutes.

The first thing he noticed when he pulled into the clearing was that the grass was long and needed cutting. He could take care of that tomorrow. Pulling around to the back of the cabin, he could not see his truck. It wasn't under the carport where he had left it or anywhere in the clearing. *Who took my truck?* thought Russell. *I need my truck. It isn't right for anyone to take my truck. What is all that yellow tape around my yard? Who put it there?*

Some of the police tape was still hanging on the stakes that had been driven in the ground, while other streamers of yellow tape hung from the bushes and low branches of the trees. Russell began pulling the tape from the stakes and bushes and wadding it up as he went. Reaching up, he grabbed a large piece hanging on the side of the deck. He was furious.

Walking up the deck stairs, he kicked away piles of fallen leaves that had accumulated from the surrounding trees. The backdoor had a metal bar across it, secured with a heavy duty padlock. Tugging on the bar he realized that the only way he could remove it was with a crowbar. He lumbered back down the stairs and went into the shed next to the cabin. All of his tools that once had been hanging neatly on pegboard fastened to the wall were scattered across the dirt floor. The drawers of his toolbox had been pulled out and the contents dumped in a sloppy heap in the corner. He slowly bent down and picked up one of his screwdrivers and laid it on a workbench. After a few minutes of picking up tools, he located a crowbar and returned to the deck.

Wedging the tool under the bar, he began to slowly pull back on the crowbar. The pain in his shoulder was a reminder that he was not completely healed. After three attempts, the bar broke loose from the door frame pulling shards of wood along with it. Throwing the crowbar on a nearby plastic chair, he opened the door of his home.

Standing in the doorway, he surveyed what at one time had been a clean and orderly house. The room was now in complete disarray: all of the kitchen cabinets had been opened and everything thrown on the floor, the refrigerator door stood open and the smell of rotten food made him cover his nose with his hand. As he moved from room to room, there was not one thing that hadn't been moved, tipped over or scattered about. He could feel the anger building inside himself.

Sitting on the edge of the bed, he thought, *If I find out who did this...I'll kill them! First, I'll make them clean my house and make it the way it was, then I'll kill them!* Getting up from the bed, he kicked a small trashcan across the room and went to find his broom which was always in the front closet.

Broom in hand, he opened all the windows and began to methodically put his house back in order. It was a daunting task to say the least. He tackled the kitchen first, then moved to his bedroom. Once those two rooms were straightened up, he systematically moved through the rest of the house putting everything back in order and in its proper place. The entire time he worked, his only thought was if and when he found out who had destroyed his house, he was going to kill them.

Following six hours of nonstop work the house finally met his expectations and he was satisfied with the way it now looked. Suddenly, he felt hungry. He found an unopened jar of peanut butter and a box of stale crackers. Opening the jar and the crackers by means of his fingers, he lathered the crackers with the peanut butter and ate the entire jar and all the crackers, followed by a long cold drink from the kitchen spigot. Now that he was no longer hungry and was satisfied with the way his house looked, he decided to survey his land and see if all his animal friends were all right.

When he opened the door, he saw a small flock of turkey buzzards circling above. As he climbed the embankment that led up the side of the mountain, the buzzards reminded him of the Stroud brothers laying twenty some miles away at the bottom of that ravine. He smiled to himself as he looked up at the circling birds of prey once again and thought: *The coyotes, vultures and all the other flesh eating critters will have enough food to last them for a few days as they feast on the bodies of Dwayne and Arliss.*

CHAPTER TEN

MAXINE ELAND SET A PLATE OF BACON AND EGGS IN front of her husband as she sipped at her glass of grapefruit juice. Walking back to the kitchen counter, she spoke back over her shoulder, "I think our grand opening yesterday was a big success. Last night when we got home I was so tired I just put the cash box on the nightstand, then crashed and burned. I was really bushed. I noticed that you conked out rather quickly too."

Doug stabbed a strip of bacon and answered, "Yeah. It was a long day and..."

Before he could finish his sentence, Max interrupted him, "I got up early and counted our proceeds. Turns out we made a little over nine hundred dollars and that's just what we took in. I know of at least two couples who said they were coming back today for some of your wildlife pictures and then there was that one lady from Wisconsin who wants three walking sticks for Christmas gifts. I think I'll pack us a lunch. If today is anything like yesterday we won't have a chance for either one of us to slip out and grab something." Snapping her fingers, she remembered, "One of us has to run to the bank just after we open. We're low on twenties and ones and we probably need quarters."

Turning to face Doug, she noticed a look of concern on his normally jovial face. "Did I say something wrong? You look like you're off somewhere else."

"Well, I was just about to tell you how long the day really was," said Doug, "but you didn't let me finish."

Sitting at the kitchen table, Max apologized, "I'm sorry, I guess I'm just so excited about how well we did, I didn't notice I had cut you off."

Doug sat back in his chair and took a drink of juice and a long deep breath. "Yesterday was longer than you can possibly imagine. Something happened to me when I was out on my run. I didn't want to say anything about it yesterday because it would have put a damper on the opening and I know how much you were looking forward to having a great day. I just didn't want to ruin things for you...that's all."

Now it was Max who wore a look of concern. "Something happened to you on your run...what?"

Shaking his head, as if he still couldn't believe what happened, he blurted out, "I got attacked!"

Leaning across the table, Max placed one of her hands over his right hand as she inquired, "Attacked? How, when, where?"

"Look, it's not that big of a deal. I just happened to be in the wrong place at the wrong time. No, let me rephrase that. I was in the right place at the right time."

Cocking her head, Max smiled in a confusing manner. "You're not making any sense."

Setting down his juice, Doug patted her hand. "Okay, here it is. I was running across the IGA parking lot when I noticed an old, what looked like abandoned car near the end of the lot. For some reason, I looked in the backseat and there low and behold was a baby. The car was locked, all the windows were up and no one was around. At first, I didn't know what to do. This is one of those things you hear about from time to time. It never happens to you, it's always somebody else. The long and short of it is I told a grocery store employee to tell the store manager to call the police. While I was waiting for the police I got nervous and was afraid something might happen to the baby before they arrived, so I broke out the window with every intention of rescuing the baby."

Max raised her hand for Doug to stop talking. "I'm confused. How could you possibly be attacked trying to rescue a baby from a car?"

"Easy!" exclaimed Doug. "The owner of the car who just happened to be the baby's father showed up as I was in the process of breaking out the window. He grabbed me and threw me to the ground, then kicked me a number of times and finally pinned me to the ground with his foot on my neck. I thought for a moment I was going to choke to death."

Max couldn't believe what she was hearing. "Then what happened?"

The store manager tried to help me but the father hit her and she went down. Finally the police show up, and of all people Grant

Denlinger, the man we met with his wife at Lily's a couple of weeks back is the officer on duty. The father went berserk and attacks Grant, throwing him over the top of the car. Two other officers showed up and in the end it took all three of them to subdue this guy."

"So, what happened to the baby?"

"Child Protective Services was called and they came over from Maryville and took the child after the father was hauled off to jail."

"Who was this man? Do you know him? Have you ever seen him before?"

"No, I've never laid eyes on him. Turns out his name is Ambrose Stroud. He lives around here somewhere. Chief Brody said he was a crazy bastard and after dealing with him I'd say he's right."

"This whole thing sounds scary!"

"Well, it was until the police finally got there. There is one thing that kind of bothers me though. When they were trying to put Stroud in the cruiser he lunged at me and told me that I hadn't heard the last of him."

"What does that mean?"

"Well, I'm not really sure. Brody said not to worry. He'd have a talk with the Stroud's."

Getting up and walking around the table, Max gave Doug a hug and then inspected his bruised neck. "Oh, my God! You're injured!"

"It's all right. It's not nearly as bad as it looks. I pressed charges and so did the store manager."

Standing back and looking at Doug, Max asked, "Do you think that was the right thing to do?"

"Of course, it was the right thing to do. I mean the guy left his baby all alone in a locked car. He not only assaulted me, but the manager and an officer of the law."

"Aren't you the least bit concerned about his threat about not hearing the last of him?"

"Well yeah, at the time it was rather scary, but Brody assured me he would handle it. What else am I supposed to do? Walk around for the next few days or months constantly looking over my shoulder? What kind of a way is that to live your life? Chief Brody said he'd take care of things and I'm sure he will."

"Maybe we made a mistake by moving here, Doug. You told me that it was so peaceful here in the mountains, then once we get here I hear about all these murders they've had over the past two years and now this: you're attacked by some crazy bastard who threatens you by saying you haven't heard the last of him. What are we going to do now?"

Doug walked to the sink and rinsed off his plate as he finished his juice. "I think we should just put this to rest. I'll finish dressing, then we can head on over to the shop and another great day."

The early morning sun was just a sliver as it started to rise above the eastern foothills. Maude, sitting in an old foldout chair pulled the collar of her overcoat up around her neck as she stared at the still burning embers of what was left of the shed. The all night rain had slowed to a few sparse drops here and there. Lighting up a cigarette she thought about her son, Ambrose, who according to Chief Brody was sitting in the Blount County Jail in Maryville. All three of her sons had at one time or another been in jail for disorderly conduct or public drunkenness, but this was much more serious. Ambrose had made the grave mistake of leaving his baby girl in the backseat of his car as he went into the IGA. *What A fool thing to do,* she thought. Looking off toward the pinkish-red sky in the distance she realized that there was little they could do for Ambrose at the moment. Brody had told her that before he could be bailed out he had to go before the Blount County Judge, at which point bail would be set. Not all that familiar with the law, she wasn't even sure if they were going to have enough money to get her son released. There was no sense in worrying about something that she couldn't do anything about at the moment, but she couldn't get the baby off her mind. She was confident that the child would be alright in the hands of those who worked for Child Protective Services, but the fact still remained that someone else, a group of strangers was caring for her six-month old granddaughter and that kept grinding away at her.

A voice from behind her pierced the semi-darkness, "Maude! What the hell are ya doin' out here so early?"

Maude, looking over her shoulder noticed the ruby red glow of a cigarette as Otis' skinny frame slowly emerged from the shadows. Talking another puff on her smoke, she stated hopelessly, "Couldn't sleep. Hell, I even tried some warm milk with a shot of Jack. Didn't help. I just laid there in bed worried about Ambrose and the baby, not ta mention the damn shed. Then, there's Rosemary. I thought we'd never get her calmed down when we told her that her baby girl is with Child Services." Pointing her cane at Otis, she went on, "We're gonna have ta keep a close eye on her when Ambrose gits out of jail. She's hot, ta say the least. When she found out that Ambrose left April May in the car all by herself, she said she was goin' ta kill Ambrose. We can't afford ta have another family spat that turns inta someone gittin' kilt. Hell, the way we're goin' we're gonna have more dead bodies out there in the garden than we have tomatoes."

Picking up a nearby branch, Otis approached the edge of what was left of the shed. Running the branch through the red-hot embers, they ignited, a few small flames flaring up, but then quickly going out. "Looks like this could be simmerin' fer days. I think it'd be best if at first light we git everyone down here with some shovels and some water hoses and make sure this is completely burned out."

"I reckon yer right on that," said Maude as she slowly stood and stretched. "I'm gonna head on back up ta the house and git us a good breakfast goin'. Why don't ya round everyone up and we'll make us a plan fer the day over some mornin' vittles."

Pitching a handful of diced onions into a frying pan of what would soon be scrambled eggs, Maude stirred the mixture then flipped the sizzling sausage patties on the stove as Effy entered the kitchen. "What's all this racket out here? Somebody pounding on Russell's door, pots and pans rattlin'. It's too early fer breakfast. Can't a body git some sleep around this house?"

Salting the eggs, Maude looked out the kitchen window as she noticed lights coming on in Cletus' trailer. "I was up all night worryin' about Ambrose and April May. Couldn't sleep, so I went out and kept an eye on the shed. It's just about burned out what with the rain. Me and Otis decided that we need ta git the family together and come up with a plan fer everythin' that's goin' on."

Effy wiped her nose with the back of her hand and opened one of the kitchen cabinets. "Sounds good. I'll git the table set."

Just then, Harmon, Loretty and their three children walked in the front door and made their way down the hall to the kitchen.

Harmon yawned as he flopped down in a chair. "What the hell, Maude! Otis comes down beatin' on our door tellin' us ta git down here fer breakfast. Ya know, I'm always up fer a good meal, but the sun ain't even hardly up yet."

Loretty told the kids to go into the living room and sit, then went to Maude's side asking, "Anythin' I can do?"

"Matter of fact, there is," said Maude. "Ya can git a bunch of taters out of the bin."

Cletus and his daughter, Violet joined the group in the kitchen. Cletus stretched and asked, "Any coffee yet?"

"Be a few minutes," said Maude as she nodded at the old time percolator on the end of the cracked counter.

Violet, always one to keep to herself looked around the room and asked, "Where's Russell?"

"Probably still in his room," answered Effy. "I'm sure Otis got him up. He'll be along soon. That boy never misses a meal...especially breakfast."

Cletus pulled out a chair and took a seat while Violet sat on the floor in the corner. Rubbing his hands across his face, he corrected Effy, "Russell ain't in his room. At least that's what Otis told me when he got me and Vi up. The last time I saw Otis he was walkin' up the road with a flashlight. Said he was goin' ta find Russell. Russell is on the weird side anyways. Probably out walkin' around in the dark."

Violet got up, walked over and hugged Effy's leg and looked up at her great grandmother. Effy always knew when something wasn't right with Vi. "Now what's this all about?" said Effy as she looked into the child's eyes.

Violet looked at Cletus then back to Effy as she spoke softly, "Russell ain't out walkin' around. He went with Arliss and Dwayne in daddy's truck."

Just then Otis walked in the kitchen as he wiped the rain from his face. "Startin' ta rain again. Couldn't find Russell nowhere's and it seems that Arliss and Dwayne ain't around either."

Violet tugged on Effy's dress. "Arliss and Dwayne took Russell and they left in Pa's truck. I seen 'em through the window. They left in the middle of the night."

Effy bent down and asked, "Ya sure about this child?"

"Yes, Ma'am."

"Well, that's it then. I've never known this child ta lie...especially ta me. But why would Arliss and Dwayne take off with Russell?"

"Come ta think of it," said Cletus, "Dwayne come down and talked with me last night after we discovered the shed burnin' and asked if he and Arliss could borrow my truck. I tol' 'em as long as they had it back by noon...then okay. When Otis got me and Vi up I didn't even notice the truck was gone. They musta came and got the keys durin' the night when I was sleepin'."

Otis grabbed a coffee cup out of the cupboard. "That answers why Arliss and Dwayne ain't around. They's off somewheres doin' somethin'."

Harmon shook his head. "I don't know what I'm gonna do with those two boys. There ain't no reason ta be out in the middle of the night. They's up ta no good."

Rosemary, who had remained silent, added, "Remember the last meetin' we had when Arliss and Dwayne said we should turn Russell in fer a reward? Well, mebbe that's what they's doin'."

Effy sat in a chair and held Violet by her thin shoulders. "Listen ta me child. I need ya ta tell me what ya saw. Was Arliss and Dwayne fightin' with Russell when they was gittin' in the truck? Did Russell look happy?"

Violet ran her foot back and forth across the floor as she answered, "It was kind of dark. I couldn't hear what they was sayin' either. It didn't look like they was mad or anythin' like that."

Maude looked at Harmon as she pointed her cane, "Harmon, if those two stupid ass sons of yers hauled Russell off ta collect a reward, they's gonna have ta answer fer what they done. Ya know that...don't ya?"

"That couldn't be the reason. Russell wouldn't agree ta go along. He's slow, but he ain't stupid! Ya all know that he's been wantin' ta git back ta his cabin up near Jellico. Mebbe that's where they went."

Effy patted Violet on her head and gently ordered her, "Go on in the livin' room with the other children. We'll be eatin' soon." Standing, Effy adjusted her eyeglasses then addressed the family, "Here's the way I see it. Arliss and Dwayne couldn't of taken Russell in fer a reward in the middle of the night. I agree with Harmon.

They mighta went up ta Jellico. Hell, those two boys might come back here any moment tellin' us they took Russell back home. Ain't no sense in worryin' ourselves about this right now, cause there ain't nothin' we can do about it. Now, I say we eat us a good breakfast and then git down ta the shed and git that mess cleaned up. We'll deal with Arliss and Dwayne when they git back."

Police Chief Drake Houseman looked up from the papers he was reviewing when he heard the rapping on the glass of his office door. Officer Jerry Flynn entered as he excused himself. "Sorry to bother you Chief, but we just received a call from a couple of hikers up near Buck Point Road. They claim that they stumbled across two bodies up there."

Chief Houseman gave Flynn a look of disgust as he shook his head, got up and grabbed his hat and coat. "Well, I reckon we better head on up there and see what's up." On the way out of the office, he pointed at Katy, the office secretary and ordered, "Katy, I want you to contact Sheriff Turnbull and tell him to meet me with the County Coroner up on Buck Point Road. Tell him that we're on our way up there to investigate two bodies that were found. We'll call him with an exact location when we get there."

Leaving the Jellico town limits, Houseman removed a cigar from the console, bit off the end and spit it out the window. "Seems every year someone gets shot in these mountains, especially this time of year...hunting season. Some fool hunter takes a potshot at something he sees moving in the trees. Ninety-nine percent of the time, if they're lucky, they bag a deer. But that other one percent always amazes me. Hunters normally wear bright orange. How in the world some idiot can take a shot at another hunter is beyond me. If it was up to me, I'd ban hunting. It's not like we're living back in the pioneer days when a man had to go out and hunt to provide meat for his family. It's nothing more than a sport: man against animal, the poor animal usually coming out on the losing end."

"I don't hunt myself," said Flynn. "My brother does. Gets his limit every year, has the deer butchered, hangs the antlers on the wall of his den and gives me some venison. I don't like the taste of it. My kids and wife love the stuff."

Looking out at the passing forest, Houseman puffed on his

stogie and commented, "We've been right lucky the past three years. Not one hunting accident. Guess we were due."

Flynn looked across the seat at his chief. "Don't forget about ol' Lamont Devers last July and how Russell Pearl snuffed out his life."

"That's different," said Houseman. "Pearl was a serial killer."

"Speaking of that," offered Flynn, "I was reading an article about that very subject earlier in the week. Some crazy newspaper columnist from Knoxville stills thinks that since Pearl's body was never found that he's alive and well and running around up here in Campbell County in the mountains."

Houseman, pointed his cigar at Flynn. "Well, I've got news for ya. Just because we couldn't come up with a body doesn't mean that Russell Pearl is still up here somewhere. The damn newspaper keeps everyone on edge. I think they should ban the news media just like they should hunting, but as long as people continue to commit crime and create what I call, bad news, I guess they'll keep selling papers from one end of this county to the next."

Making a right hand turn onto Buck Point Road, Houseman looked out into the dense trees that surrounded the dirt road. As the cruiser bounced out of a deep rut, he commented sarcastically, "This is one of those roads there is no reason for. It leads to no cabins or hunting lodges. It just continues on for eight miles until it dead ends into an abandoned radio station tower." Turning to Flynn, he asked, "Did the hikers who reported the bodies say anything else?"

"No," said Flynn. "The man who called sounded quite nervous and when I tried to get more information from him, he just kept saying we needed to get up there right away. He said he'd stay by the road to flag us down when we arrived then we were disconnected."

Placing his cigar in the ashtray, Houseman dodged another rut in the road as he spoke, "That doesn't give us much to go on. We'll just have to wait and see what we find."

The going was slow for the next ten minutes, the curvy, rutted one lane road preventing the cruiser from going more than ten miles per hour, at times the car barely moving forward as Houseman negotiated one turn after another. Coming out of a hairpin turn, Flynn pointed up the road to a man standing just on the side of the road who was signaling them to stop as he waved his arms anxiously. Pulling to the side of the road, Houseman commented, "That must be one of the hikers."

Before they were even out of the car, the slender man who turned out to be what looked like a twenty-year-old boy walked up to the cruiser. Chief Houseman no sooner had the door open when the boy started to speak in an excited tone. "Boy, are we glad to see you guys." Brushing long blond hair away from his face, he continued, "We weren't all that excited about staying up here alone too long."

Houseman stepped out and asked his first question, "Who's we?"

"Oh, I'm sorry," apologized the boy. "Conner, my friend is down with the bodies. We flipped a coin to see who got to come up to the road and I won." Motioning with his head down over the side of the embankment, he explained, "It's a ghastly site. I've never seen a dead person, let alone two before. Actually, we'd like to get back to town as soon as possible. The killer might still be in the area."

"Two questions," said Houseman. "What's your name and how did you determine that these people you refer to were killed?"

"I don't know if they were killed. It just sort of looks like they were. Well, for one thing the one man has a nasty wound in the middle of his chest and almost a third of his head looks like it was blown off."

"Enough said. Guess we better go have a look. Listen, you need to stay up here on the road for now. Officer Flynn will get your name and some other information." Grabbing a tree at the edge of the embankment to support him on the way down, Houseman ordered Flynn, "Call Turnbull and give him our location. He's probably already on his way here."

Turning his attention back to the steep hillside he was about to traverse, Houseman planted his foot next to a small boulder and started down. Twenty yards down the side he saw the other hiker seated on a boulder next to the two bodies who were laying side by side up against a fallen tree trunk. The boy stood as Houseman approached when he slipped in the leaves and slid the last few feet. Stopping next to the bodies, he got up and brushed off his pants and picked up his hat which had fallen from his head. Looking back up the hill, Houseman took a deep breath, then introduced himself, "Chief Houseman, you must be Conner."

Conner reached out to shake the Chief's hand but Houseman was already bended on one knee as he inspected the closest body. "Your friend back up on the road told me you fellas think these people were murdered." Dwayne who was wedged up against Arliss was laying on his back, the gaping wound in his stomach surrounded with dried blood, muscle tissue and assorted insects who were crawling in and out of the wound. Snapping on a pair of plastic gloves, Houseman gently turned the head and made a horrible face as he inspected the head wound. The left side of the face was practically missing. Sitting on the tree trunk, Houseman motioned toward the boulder. "Have a seat, Son. I need to ask you a few questions."

Seated, Conner looked back up toward the road and asked, "Didn't Terry fill you in on what we found."

"Sort of," said Houseman, "but I want to get your version also. So, first of all what are you two doing out here hiking this time of year?" A shot rang out in the distance and echoed through the valley below. Raising his eyebrows Houseman nodded in the direction of the gunshot and stated. "Are you and your friend not aware that it's hunting season?"

Looking down into the valley, Conner lowered his head and removed a ball hat he was wearing. "To be honest with you we really didn't even think about it until we were two miles down the trail. We thought if we stayed close to the road we'd be alright."

"Where are you hiking from and where were you headed?"

"Our girlfriends dropped us off over near Newcomb and we were planning on hiking into Jellico where they are going to pick us up."

"Did you see any hunters or for that matter, anyone in the area?"

"We didn't see anyone on the trail, but we did hear occasional gunshots in the distance. We were walking pretty fast. We just wanted to get to Jellico after we figured that we messed up going on this hike in the first place. When we came across these bodies we just wanted to get the hell away from here, but Terry insisted that we call the local authorities first."

"After you discovered the bodies did either of you touch them in any way?"

"Hell no! We were scared out of our wits! We figured that whoever did this might still be around here somewhere. Terry said it might be that Russell Pearl, that serial killer that disappeared up near here."

Houseman shot Conner a strange look. "What on earth could possibly lead to that conclusion?"

Conner pointed at the lifeless body of Arliss. "Take a look at the tee-shirt that one is wearing."

Scooting over next to Arliss he read the part of the shirt that was exposed: *PEARL*?

The conversation was interrupted from a deep voice from above them at the edge of the road. "Drake! Do we need body bags down there?"

Looking up, Houseman saw not only Sheriff Turnbull but the County Coroner, Bernard Dougherty, peering down through the trees.

Cupping his hands around his mouth, Houseman yelled back up, "Bring two bags. We've got two bodies down here. One's a mess, the other, I'm not sure yet."

Houseman turned to Conner and suggested, "Why don't you go back up to the road and tell Officer Flynn what you told me. You can call your girlfriends and tell them that we'll be dropping you off at the police station in an hour or so."

On the way up the embankment, Conner nodded at the two men who were descending the steep incline. Turnbull and Dougherty arrived much in the same manner as Houseman had, as they slid in the numerous leaves. Turnbull looked back up the hill and asked, "Who the hell was the kid we passed on the way down?"

Houseman shook hands with Dougherty and answered, "One of the hikers who called the incident in." Looking down at the bodies, he went on, "The one, as you can plainly see was shot in the stomach and then in the head. Looks like close range. I haven't had much of a chance to check the other one out."

Placing the two black body bags on the ground, Dougherty knelt next to Arliss and gently examined his neck. After a few seconds of turning and twisting the head gingerly, Bernard gave his prognosis, "Neck's broken, but it wasn't caused from the fall.

There's no bruising in the neck area from where it collided with any objects, at least enough to cause the damage that was inflicted on the victim. Patting Arliss on his lifeless shoulder, he explained, "This one here had his neck snapped, possibly by the same person who shot the other one. I can tell you one thing. This was no hunting accident. The shooter was no more than a couple of feet from this one when he pulled off two shots. It couldn't have been an accident at that range even if some hunter misfired. Maybe one shot, but not two. Did you check for any ID yet?"

"No," said Houseman, "We wanted to wait for your arrival before we started to move the bodies around too much."

Dougherty nodded his head in a silent answer indicating that Houseman had done the right thing as he slowly rolled Dwayne to his side and reached for his back jeans pocket. Extracting a wallet, he removed a driver's license and handed it to Turnbull who read the name on the plastic coated card, "Dwayne Stroud. 1329 Wears Valley Road. Townsend, Tennessee. Blount County."

As Dougherty was searching Arliss for any ID, Chief Houseman spoke up, "That's odd."

Turnbull gave Houseman a confused look, "How's that?"

"Think about it. Wasn't Blount County where Russell Pearl killed most of those folks?"

"Come to think of it, it was," responded Turnbull, "but I don't see how that seems odd."

Dougherty, now in possession of Arliss' wallet pulled out his driver's license and read the information to himself then commented, "I can see what direction the chief is going here. Pitching the wallet to Turnbull, he went on, "Read the license in there."

Catching the wallet, Turnbull flipped it open and extracted the card as he read: "Arliss Stroud, 1329 Wears Valley Road. Townsend Tennessee. Blount County. Hmm. Sounds to me like we have two brothers here who live at the same address. This does border on odd. It hasn't even been four months since we supposedly killed Russell Pearl, who killed some folks down in Blount County, and now, two more people from Blount County show up here...dead!"

Standing, Dougherty spoke in a professional manner, "You can't be suggesting that Russell Pearl is still alive and responsible for these killings...that's insane! Pearl was shot three times and fell over a two hundred foot drop. Now, I'll be the first to admit that it's strange that we never located the body, but my professional opinion still stands that the man is dead. There has to be some other logical explanation in regard to the death of these brothers. Saying that there might be a connection here is stretching things a bit...don't you think?"

Turnbull gave the coroner a look of disdain and commented, "Look, Bernie, you need to concentrate on what you do, which is determining how someone is murdered. Let Drake and I handle the who and why. Now, how long do you estimate the bodies have been here?"

Bernie, blowing off Turnbull's sarcastic remark, inspected Dwayne's chest wound and then examined the bruise on Arliss' neck. He stated, "I'd put the time of death about twenty four hours or so ago. We can't be exactly sure. Victims that are found outside, especially where the elements and the local wildlife can get to them, have a tendency to make time of death estimates difficult. That being said, I think a day or so is rather close."

"There isn't much more we can do here at the moment," said Turnbull. "We need to get these bodies bagged up and over to Jacksboro where Bernie can get a better handle on how they died. I'll give Sheriff Grimes down in Maryville a call and let him know that we have two Blount County residents up here on ice."

Chief Houseman looked off into the distant trees as he heard another gunshot from somewhere across the valley. "Damn hunters!" Turning to Turnbull, he asked, "Look, do you think on your way through Jellico you could drop off those two boys at the station. Their ride is waiting there for them. I think Jerry and I are going to have a look around the area to see if we can find anything that might tip us to what happened up here."

Chief Brody was just exiting the bathroom, when Marge stopped him from walking down the hall to his office. "Chief, you have a call from Sheriff Grimes."

Rolling his eyes, Brody who wasn't in a good mood, ordered her, "Put the call on my office phone. I'll answer it back there."

Seconds later, Axel flopped down in his swivel chair and picked up the receiver, "Burt, what's up?"

"Just got some bad news," answered Grimes. "I got a call from the County Sheriff from up in Campbell County. Says they located two bodies up there that appeared to have been murdered. The victims names are none other than Dwayne and Arliss Stroud. They've transported the bodies over to Jacksboro where they'll keep them until the Stroud's can get up there and ID the boys. After that, they'll take care of the embalming procedures, then they'll transport the bodies back down here to Blount County."

Axel turned in his chair and looked out the office window as he spoke sarcastically, "The Stroud's! Couldn't have happened to a nicer family. You said that the boys appear to have been murdered?"

"Yep. One took two shots. One to the chest and the other to the head. The other one had his neck snapped. They're ruling out a hunting accident. Listen, since they live in your jurisdiction, Axel, you're going to have to go tell the family. Probably won't be an easy task what with everything that's going on with them recently. If you want to hold off, I'll drive up and go along with you."

Axel swung back around in the chair. "I appreciate it, but I reckon I can handle the Stroud's. I'll take Officer Griner with me."

There was silence on the other end of the phone, then Grimes spoke, "That's just part one of the bad news. The second part, the part that could make your visit over to their place, let's say, uncomfortable is that Ambrose was just released from jail. Merle Pittman just bailed him out. Paid cash on the barrelhead. Ambrose never even had to go before the judge. Pittman contacted the judge and armed with his usual legal documentation got both Ambrose and the baby released due to some technicalities. The judge told me that Ambrose will still have to appear and will probably still get some jail time but for now he's free. He and his wife, Rosemary left here with the baby not fifteen minutes ago. My point is, Ambrose more than likely will be there when you show up. I don't think he'll cause any problems, but with the Stroud's...you never know, so my offer stills stands. I can be at your office in half an hour and we can head on over to their place."

"Thanks again," said Brody, "but I can handle, not only Ambrose, but their entire nutcase family. I'll call you when I get back and let you know how things went down."

Hanging up the phone, Brody grabbed his hat and walked down the hall, hesitating at Marge's desk. "Get Lee on the horn and tell him to meet me at Frank's Market. We've got to go over to the Stroud's place and tell them that Dwayne and Arliss have been found murdered up near Jellico." Axel was out the door before Marge could respond.

Frank's Market wasn't even a five minute drive. Axel figured he had time to slip inside and grab a cup of coffee before Lee arrived. Parking his truck near the front of the lot, he got out and entered the market. Dumping two packets of sugar into a cup, he was interrupted by a familiar voice, "Chief Axel Brody!"

Pouring coffee into the cup, Axel looked to his left where he saw Franklin Barrett leaning up against a bread rack. "Barrett. The last time I saw you, you were in one of my holding cells down at the station. How's the tee-shirt business?"

Barrett smiled as he inspected his manicured fingernails. "Axel, your attempt at trying to insult me today falls short of the mark. I've decided that I have to live here in Townsend and as long as you're the Chief of Police, my days of trying to get over on you have come to an end. You'll no doubt find what I'm about to say hard to believe, but I'm heading in a new direction. I've cut any ties at all with Merle Pittman. Over the years we've made some rather good money together, but that's all over now. I don't need Merle's legal abilities anymore. I had money before I met him and I've got enough to get along without him. As a matter of fact, I'm getting out of the tee-shirt business so you needn't worry about that anymore."

Sipping at the coffee, Brody asked, "Why the change of heart?"

"Simple! Merle is about to wage a war he can't win. When we were sitting in your jail cell, which I might add only lasted for an hour before Merle had us bailed out, it seemed like he was running right on the edge of the cliff. He vowed that he would do everything in his ability to bring you down. That's when I decided to go down another road. So, you won't be having any more problems from me."

Brody laughed and said, "Well, it all makes perfect sense now."

Barrett, confused, asked, "What makes perfect sense?"

"We just got word that Dwayne and Arliss Stroud were found murdered up near Jellico. Sheriff Grimes informed me that I had to go on over to their place and give the family the bad news. I'm just about to head there as soon as Lee Griner gets here. Grimes told me that Ambrose had been bailed out and set free, by none other than Merle Pittman. Ever since I got that call I've been trying to figure out why a high roller like Pittman would want to associate with the likes of the Stroud's. It's clear to me based or what you've told me that he bailed Ambrose out because I'm the one who nailed him on that child abandonment charge. He's dealing with the Stroud's in order to attempt to make me look bad."

"I can't believe it," remarked Barrett. "If Merle starts running with the Stroud's, well, I just can't believe that. I guess I cut the ties with him just in time."

Lee Griner walked up, interrupting the conversation, "Chief, what's up?"

Brody shook Barrett's hand as he motioned toward the door. "I'll see ya around, Franklin. I think you're doin' the right thing." Placing his hand on Lee's shoulder he continued, "Come on, we'll take your cruiser. We're goin' up to the Stroud's. I'll fill you in on the way."

Leaning on the side of the cruiser Brody pitched the remainder of his coffee to the ground. "Dwayne and Arliss Stroud were found murdered up in Campbell County. We get blessed with having to go down the road to their place and tell Harmon and Loretty that their two oldest sons are dead. On top of that, if Maude happens to be there, which I'm sure she will, we have to tell her that two of her grandsons have been murdered. Ambrose was just released from jail and I have no doubt that he's not gonna be all that enthused about you and I bringin' the news."

Lee, who was standing by the driver's side door remarked, "Yeah, we did give him a good thumpin' over at the IGA...didn't we."

Brody climbed in the passenger seat. "That's right, and he deserved it, but I don't think he's gonna look at it like that. We're not gonna be exactly welcomed guests."

"You don't think he'll try anything, do you, Chief?"

"I doubt it, but you can never tell when you're dealin' with the Stroud's. When we get there I'll do all the talkin'. You just need to keep your eyes open and be ready to react if any of the Stroud's try somethin'." Motioning toward Wears Valley Road, Brody ordered, "Let's go!"

When they arrived at the Stroud's, traffic was backed up with three cars pulled to the side of the road, three sets of tourists rummaging through the assortment of goods beneath the old tent. Cletus and Ambrose were busy carrying items from the shed to the tent while Maude and Otis were in their usual positions in their lawn chairs, Otis drinking a beer and Maude nursing a cigarette. Maude noticed the cruiser as it slowly passed and then turned in the dirt driveway. Parking the cruiser just off the side of the road, Brody climbed out and ordered Lee, "Get out, but stay over here with the cruiser. Keep an eye on Ambrose and Cletus. If anythin's gonna happen, it'll be one of those two. I can handle Maude and Otis just fine. Just keep a watch on those boys. If any tourists stop and approach the tent, just tell them they are temporarily closed."

Brody walked across the grass, stopped at the tent and spoke to the customers, "I'm sorry folks, but you'll have to leave. They're gonna be closed down for a few minutes. Ya might wanna come back later."

Otis, hearing what Brody said was on his feet as he threw his can of beer to the ground, "What the hell! Ya can't close us down like that! We ain't done nothin' wrong!" Looking past Brody at the customers, he spoke with confidence, "Ya don't need ta leave. Ya jest stay right where yer at and keep shoppin'."

Brody tapped the badge pinned on his shirt and stated very firmly, "Like I said...they're closed!"

The customers, sensing that trouble was brewing quickly walked to their cars and pulled out.

Maude was now standing as she pointed her cane at Brody. "Well that cuts it, Brody! You jest can't come waltzin' in here and shut us down!"

Brody smiled. "Relax Maude, it's just for a few minutes. When you find out why I'm here you won't want any customers around. Got some news for Harmon and Loretty. They around?"

Ambrose and Cletus stopped beneath the tent and Ambrose approached Brody and stopped just inches away from him. He didn't say a word but the anger on his face said it all. Brody, brazenly stepped even closer as he looked up into Ambrose's face. "Don't do anythin' stupid, Ambrose. You've only been out of jail for what, maybe an hour. Don't get smart with me or I'll have you right back in there!" Looking at Cletus, Brody emphasized, "That goes as well for you."

Maude rapped her cane on the top of a crate as she ordered her two sons, "Back off! I'll handle this!"

Cletus took a seat at one of the tables while Ambrose retreated back to the edge of the tent and remained standing as he glared at Brody.

Brody turned his attention back to Maude and spoke calmly, "Like I said, I have need to talk to Harmon and Loretty."

Maude objected, "Harmon is my oldest son. Anythin' you got ta say ta him ya can say ta me."

"Doesn't work that way. I'll just go on up to their trailer."

Brody turned to go back to his cruiser, when Maude stopped him, "Jest a minute! I'll call 'em and tell 'em ta come on down here. You jest stay put!"

Axel, not one to be told what to do, objected, "Alright, but I think I'll wait over by the road."

Minutes later, Harmon and Loretty appeared at the edge of the woods as they walked down the road. Brody walked back toward the tent to meet them. Both Harmon and his wife looked like they had just climbed out of bed: hair every which way, rumpled clothes. Seeing Brody standing by the tent, Harmon groaned, "What the hell kinda trouble am I in now?"

Axel removed his hat out of respect for the news he had for the couple, even though they were the Stroud's. "Your two boys, Arliss and Dwayne were found murdered up in the Jellico Mountains. Dwayne was shot in the chest and the head and Arliss had his neck snapped."

Loretty collapsed in Harmon's arms. Maude lowered her cane and sank back down onto her chair as if the air had been let out of her. Otis took offense as he exclaimed loudly, "I knew it. That damn nephew of yer's kilt them two boys!"

Maude reached over and rapped Otis across his knuckles with her cane as she ordered him, "Shut yer trap, Otis. Ya don't know what yer talkin' about!"

Otis, suddenly realizing that he almost divulged that Russell Pearl had been staying at their place just sat quietly with a dumb look plastered across his face. Brody noticed that Ambrose and Cletus shot each other a look of concern. Facing Maude once again, Axel squinted his eyes and asked, "Maude, I just saw somethin' not only in your eyes, but in the faces of Ambrose and Cletus that doesn't sit right. If you know anythin' about the murders you better tell me now."

Maude, now once again composed, shot back at Brody, "We don't know nothin' about no murders."

"Who's this nephew that Otis claimed killed those two boys?"

"That don't mean nothin'! He don't know what he's talkin' about. We had some man come by lookin' fer work. We let him stay overnight out in the barn, then the next mornin' he moved on. He was jest a drifter. Nobody we ever seen before."

Brody gave Otis a long hard stare. Otis, after a few seconds turned away as he opened another can of beer.

"If I find out you're hidin' somethin' about these murders," said Axel, "I'll come back up here and throw the whole lot of ya in jail."

Maude lit up a cigarette as she answered smartly, "Well if ya ain't got nothin' else ta say I reckon ya can be on yer way then, Brody!"

"Yeah," snapped Cletus. "We need ya ta git so's we can git back ta business."

Axel turned to leave, but was stopped as Ambrose stood and asked, "How's come that Denlinger boy didn't come along with ya. Guess he's afraid of me what with me tossin' him over that car and all. Make sure ya tell 'em that if I run into him and he's off duty, he better watch hisself."

Axel looked at Maude and spoke, "Yer son ain't all that smart is he Maude? That sounded like a threat ta me." Turning to Ambrose, Axel took off his hat and laid it on one of the tables. "If you have a problem with me or any one of my officers we can settle it right now, Boy! If I was you, I'd be thinkin' more about losin' your two nephews than what's goin' on with one of my officers. You need to start thinkin' about some burial arrangements."

Maude was on her feet again. "Now there ain't no need fer any of that, Chief Brody. My son is jest upset over what happened, what with him bein' tossed in jail and all and his little girl bein' taken by Child Services." Using her cane as a directional pointer she ordered Ambrose and Cletus, "Git on back ta the shed and do what ya was doin' before. After Brody leaves we'll have customers comin' in here."

As the two turned and walked off, Maude asked, "Brody, we're all upset about the news of Arliss and Dwayne. We'll pray for them boys tonight and make sure they git a proper burial. Look at Harmon and Loretty. They're torn ta pieces! So when can we go git my two grandsons?"

Brody, now more relaxed that the two short tempered brothers were not in the conversation, answered, "What you need ta do is call the County Sheriff's office in Jacksboro and see when you can go up there and ID the bodies. Shortly after that, they'll release the bodies and they'll be transported down here to Townsend and then you can make arrangements for their burial."

Back in the cruiser headed down Wears Valley Road, Lee asked, "I couldn't hear everything that was said but it looked pretty intense from where I was standing. How'd they take the news?"

"I think they know more than they're lettin' on," said Brady. "Otis was about ta say somethin', but Maude stopped him. I have a feeling they know who killed those two boys. Now, provin' it...that's somethin' else."

CHAPTER ELEVEN

GRANT WALKED INTO THE KITCHEN WITH A BROAD smile on his face. Dana Beth, sat at the table reading a recipe book while Ruth stood at the sink peeling potatoes. Coming up behind his wife, he kissed her on the head. "Guess what? Since ol' Brody gave me some time off because of my injured hand, that means I've got two more days off before I have to report back for work." Walking to the sink, he placed his hands on Ruth's shoulders. "And if this sweet lady would be kind enough to watch our little angel for us, maybe my wife and I can get out of town for two whole days."

Putting down her paring knife, Ruth placed her hands on her hips and beamed, "Of course, I'll watch her! I think it'd be great for both of you to get away."

Dana Beth closed the book and stood. "I don't know, Grant. Mom has been taking care of Crystal Ann an awful lot lately. Maybe she's the one who needs a break."

Wiping her hands on her apron, Ruth objected in a friendly manner. "Nonsense! I don't need a break! I love taking care of Crystal and I want you to go off somewhere and have a good time. Now, there'll be no argument. You kids go on and get out of here for awhile."

Dana Beth smiled limply. "Well, if you're sure."

Before Ruth or Dana Beth could utter another word, Grant interjected, "I thought we could pick somewhere close so we don't have to spend all of our time driving. How about Nashville? Maybe we could even do some dancing or if you don't like that idea, we could rent a cabin."

Dana Beth hesitated for a moment. "I know this might sound crazy but I've been thinking about this a lot lately. I would like to go and see the cabin where Russell lived. We already have the keys and Mr. Case said we could go there if we wanted to. It's only a couple of hours up to Jellico."

"Why would you want to go there?" asked Grant. "I would think that place would be full of bad memories for you, what with

Russell being your uncle and all."

"Not really, Grant," said Dana Beth. "It's just the place where he lived. I think if I saw the cabin I might be able to get rid of some of the bad feelings I have. If I could see where Russell lived, where he slept and how he spent his days maybe then I could get rid of all of the bad images I have of him. I mean, he was my uncle. I'd like to think of him as a human being rather than a serial killer."

"Don't make the man out to be something he wasn't," said Grant. "He was a killer and had little regard for human life. I stood face to face with him up on that ridge. I thought the same thing. I thought I could talk him into giving himself up. If it wouldn't have been for Chief Blue pulling the trigger, I might not be here today. I looked square in Russell Pearl's eyes, Dana Beth. Believe me, he'd have killed me and wouldn't have batted an eye."

Dana Beth could see that Grant was on the verge of getting angry and besides that she had spoiled his surprise. Smiling, she suggested, "Well maybe we could just ride by the cabin and then go on to Nashville. How does that sound?"

Grant, frustrated, waved his hand as he headed for the stairs. "Whatever you want to do is fine with me. I'm going to change clothes."

Dana Beth lowered her head. "I upset him, didn't I, Mom?"

Ruth tried to console her daughter as she walked over and placed her arm around her. "I don't think he quite understands why you wouldn't want to put all the murders behind you rather than reliving them."

Slamming the recipe book down on the table, Dana Beth began to cry. "Nobody really understands the way I feel."

"You can't keep all of this bottled up inside," pointed out Ruth. "Perhaps you should talk with Grant instead of closing him out by always telling him you're tired or you've got a headache or you don't want to talk about it."

Dana Beth turned and gave her mother a hug. "I'm sorry I've been such a pain."

Ruth wiped Dana Beth's tears from her face with a dish towel. "Well then! Go talk with your husband...right now!"

When she entered the bedroom, Dana Beth could see the opaque image of Grant in the shower. She sat on the bed and waited for him to come out. Opening the shower door, he was surprised to see her sitting there. Grabbing a nearby bath towel, he started to dry his hair and asked sarcastically, "What's wrong now?"

"Look, Grant," said Dana Beth, "I didn't mean to upset you downstairs. We need to talk. I know the kind of work you do and maybe you can let things go easier than I can. Everything that has happened has stayed with me and I can't seem to shake loose of it. It was bad enough losing dad, but then all those murders started up again. How would you feel if you discovered you had an uncle who was a serial killer and you weren't one hundred percent sure that he's dead? It scares me to death and I have to face my demons in order to try and get these crazy thoughts out of my head. Every time I leave the house I get anxious. I'm afraid I'm going to turn around and see Russell standing there. Last week I almost had an accident with Crystal Ann in the car. I thought a man crossing the street in front of me was Russell. I just can't keep doing this."

Grant wrapped the towel around his waist, walked to the bed and knelt down in front of her. "I'm sorry. I had no idea all this stuff was bothering you so much. Russell Pearl is dead. There is no way he could have survived that fall. You have to put all this behind you. I know it's easier said than done, so if going up to that cabin will help, then we'll do it. We'll leave tomorrow morning, drive up to Campbell County, visit the cabin then drive on over to Nashville." Dana Beth rested her head on his shoulder as Grant reached up and touched her face. "You know I love you and I'll do everything I can to protect you and our family." Standing, Grant motioned toward the bedroom door. "Why don't you head back downstairs and help Ruth with dinner. I've got a call to make, then I'll be down."

After Dana Beth left, Grant, using the phone on the nightstand called information. Hanging up, he dialed the number for the Campbell County Sheriff's Office. Following three rings someone on the other end picked up. "Campbell County Sheriff's Office, Helen speaking."

"Hello, Helen. This is Officer Grant Denlinger from down here in Blount County. Is Sheriff Turnbull around?"

"No, at the moment he's out of the office. Can I take a

message?"

"Yes you can. Listen, Helen. I have a favor to ask Frank. My wife and I are going up to Russell Pearl's cabin tomorrow. I know Frank was with the FBI when they searched the place. Do you know what kind of condition the cabin is currently in?"

"They did a pretty good job of taking the place apart according to Sheriff Turnbull. He said they searched every nook and cranny in the house and the shed. I recall Frank saying the place was a mess when they finally left. They impounded Pearl's truck and then someone from our office had to drop by the cabin every week to check things out. I just received a call from them this past weekend, telling us we could run over there and take down the tape. The electricity is still on, but the gas tank in the back is empty. Do you have any idea of what's going to happen to the property? I've already had a few people ask me if I knew if and when it was going to be sold."

"As a matter of fact, I do know. Believe it or not my wife and I will be the owners. It was deeded to my wife by a lawyer who took care of her father's estate. I'm not really sure what we're going to do with the place, but my wife wants to go up there and have a look at it. I know this is a lot to ask, but do you think you could ask Frank to arrange to have someone take a run over there and spruce the place up some? I think it would really freak her out if she walked in and the place is turned upside down."

"No problem, Mr. Denlinger. We'll get someone to put it back in order. There is a padlock on the door. We have the key. I'll make sure that whoever goes up there takes the lock off and leaves the key."

Early the next morning, Dana Beth and Grant kissed Crystal Ann good bye, and thanked Ruth once again. Ruth handed them a tote packed with food she had prepared for them. Thirty minutes later, they pulled over at a drive-thru and ordered breakfast burritos and hot chocolate and headed for Jellico. The last of the fall leaves were clinging to the trees giving an occasional burst of color to the passing landscape lining the highway. Looking out the passenger side window, Dana Beth commented, "These mountains seem much more rugged than the area we live in."

"There aren't nearly as many hiking trails up here and not too many people live in the wooded areas," replied Grant. "There are some scattered cabins, but you need a four-wheeler to get up most of the outlying roads. A lot of people like to hike up here for some reason, but you have to be careful in these parts. I'd hate to get lost in these mountains."

Dana Beth downed the last of her drink and remarked, "I've always heard that it's best to stay put if you get lost in the mountains."

"I've heard that philosophy also, but I think it's better to try and walk out. If you move off you need to try and leave clues behind, like bent twigs or marks in tree trunks. You know. Like the old Hansel and Gretel trick where they used bread crumbs."

Thumping Grant lightly on his shoulder, Dana Beth joked, "Yes sir...Scout Master Denlinger. I'll try and remember that the next time I decide to take off in the deep woods."

Grant let out a laugh. "This is nice. I can't remember the last time the two of us had an opportunity to get away from everything and just laugh and joke around. I think the last time we laughed in the car was a couple of weeks back when we went to the grocery store. We're getting to be like two old married people. We need some fun in our lives."

"I agree," said Dana Beth. "This past year or so hasn't exactly been a walk in the park for either of us. It seems like ever since the first murders we had and then the death of my father our lives have been turned upside down. I feel it's time for us to get some closure and that's why I decided I'm going back to the psychiatrist for a while. Now, hear me out before you give me an opinion. It seems like he keeps wanting me to talk about the past. He keeps going over my childhood and my interaction with my father. I had a good childhood and a great relationship with dad. I'm really going to make an effort to work through my own problems. If I can't figure it out, you'll be the first to know."

"Alright, if that's want you want, then I'll go along with it. Just don't shut me out if something is bothering you."

"I promise!" responded Dana Beth. Turning on the radio, she laid her head back on the seat and looked out at the passing trees that engulfed both sides of the road.

Nearly an hour passed when Grant made the final turn onto

the dirt road that led to Russell's cabin. The anticipation of seeing Russell's cabin made Dana Beth focus on every curve and slope as she waited for the cabin to come into view.

Minutes passed and Grant slowed the Jeep as he pointed through the trees. "There it is." He maneuvered the Jeep up the road leading to the cabin.

Dana Beth stared out the front windshield and commented, "Oh, it looks nice! Much nicer that I thought it would be. Can we take a look inside?"

"Don't know why not. It seems a shame to drive all the way up here and not go in."

Getting out of the Jeep, Grant was not as eager to go in as Dana Beth. The last time he was here he was part of a manhunt for a serial killer. Looking up the gradual slope at the right of the cabin he recalled how he and the others had charged up the hill after hearing gunshots only to find Officer Devers shot. He thought about that day, months past, when Devers eventually died and he and the others weren't too sure if Russell would appear and kill them all. It was all coming back to him: how he got nicked in the ear and how Agent Gephart had been wounded. He recalled that face to face moment with Russell at the edge of the Cumberland River Gorge and how he had tried to talk him down.

His concentration on the past was interrupted by Dana Beth, "Grant! Did you hear me? Grab the tote bag."

"Oh, sorry, Hon! I was just thinking about something."

The dry leaves crunched beneath their feet as they walked across the yard and up onto the front porch where they were confronted by a large padlock on the door.

Grant, starting around the side of the wrap-around porch, suggested, "Let's try the back."

At the rear of the cabin, Dana Beth rubbed her hand over the broken door frame. "I wonder how this happened. Looks like someone tried to bust in."

"I doubt it," said Grant. "The FBI could have done this when they searched the cabin." Grant tried the door but it was locked. *Strange,* he thought as he looked around for a key. *Helen said that she'd have whoever cleaned the place up leave the key.* Taking the key that Marshall had given them, he inserted it and swung the door open. Dana Beth boldly walked past him and entered the cabin. Her eyes traveled around the interior taking in as many details as she could.

Turning in a complete circle, she held out her hands, "It's nice, Grant. This really looks cozy. I was expecting it to be a shabby mess. This is so organized. Russell must have been a clean freak."

Grant placed the tote on the kitchen counter as Dana Beth walked into the living room. "Grant, look at this. Come in here. I want to show you something."

Touching the edge of a quilt on the back of an old couch, she went on, "My father bought this quilt at a flea market over in Sevierville years ago. I remember he told mom and me that he was buying it for a co-worker. And that rocking chair over there by the fireplace. That was my mother's. It was always on the sun porch. Dad told her one summer years ago it was broken and he was going to throw it out." Looking around in amazement she held her hands out in wonder. "What else did my dad give Russell?"

After touring the remainder of the cabin, she returned to the kitchen and sat at the table. "Well, this really wasn't as hard as I thought it would be. Somehow, it's just a house. I'm not feeling sad and I'm not afraid of anything. It's so plain and aside from the quilt and the rocking chair there's nothing here to feel like I'm actually in Russell's house." Sitting back in her chair, she stretched. "I'm feeling a little hungry and besides that I'd like to hang around for awhile. Like I said...it's nice! I have an idea. Rather than driving to Nashville why don't we spend the night. We have the food my mother packed for us. All we need is some snacks and something to drink. Maybe after we eat we'll take a walk in the woods. Later tonight, we can have a fire or play some cards..."

Grant, totally surprised at her reaction to the cabin couldn't seem to get a word in as Dana Beth was rambling. "Maybe you could even pick us up some beer and a couple of bags of popcorn."

Finally, Grant, able to speak, asked, "Are you sure?"

"I'm sure."

"Okay then. Why don't we take a ride over to Jacksboro and pick up a few things: coffee and donuts for the morning, maybe a bottle of wine and some snacks. You know me. I'm always hungry."

Making herself comfortable on the couch, Dana Beth wrapped herself in the quilt. "Why don't you go, Grant. I can stay here. I'd really like to take a short nap. We did get up pretty early. I want to stay up with you tonight instead of going to bed at nine like always."

Grant objected, "I think you should go with me. I don't want to leave you here alone."

"Don't be silly! I'll be fine. You'll be back in less than an hour. Besides that, I have my cell phone." Crisscrossing her heart, she smiled. "I promise I won't leave the cabin."

Grant realized that once his wife made up her mind about something it was nearly impossible to change it. Something was telling him that she wanted to spend some time alone in the cabin. Maybe she wanted to have a good cry without him being around. He didn't like the idea but finally relented. "Okay, I'm not real keen on this. I'll go as fast as I can so I can get back here so we can get our eventual evening started. Are you sure you don't want to go with me?"

"No, just go on. I'm going to lie down." Getting up, she pushed him toward the door and remarked. "I'll lock the door after you if it'll make you feel better. And, don't call me!" She kissed him on the cheek and he left, all the while feeling an uneasiness that wouldn't go away.

Climbing into the Jeep, Grant took one last look at the cabin and thought, *Everything seems okay. Surely Helen would have told me if anything was going on up here.* He pulled away, planning on making it a quick trip.

Alone, Dana Beth began to look around once more to see if she could find signs of Russell in the house. She wanted to know more about him. Walking into the bathroom, she opened the medicine cabinet. There was a razor, a can of shaving cream and a box of Band Aids, nothing else. Russell's bedroom was devoid of any personal effects. There were no pictures, old cards, letters, nothing. Just a dresser filled with folded shirts and underwear. The second bedroom was much the same. Just the bare bones, nothing else.

Stepping back into the front room, she opened the drawer of a small table sitting next to a rocker. There were two pipes, a pouch of Peach Brandy smoking tobacco and a deck of playing cards. Taking a deep whiff, she smiled. The Peach Brandy scent reminded her of her father. Under the cards there was a pad of paper with separated initials at the top: R and C. They must have played cards when her father had visited Russell. It appeared that the last time they played, father had been winning according to the running score.

Going to the kitchen cupboards, she opened the first cabinet and discovered a set of Greenleaf designed dishes her mother had placed in a box to be given to Goodwill. Attached to the inside of the door was a sheet of old paper written in her father's unmistakable precise handwriting detailing a list of chores Russell was to perform each day, week and month. A post-it note was stuck to the bottom of the paper as a reminder to Russell that his gas tank would be filled on Friday. The date on the note indicated that the note was written two days prior to last Thanksgiving. Her father had been here with Russell just two days before his death. Dana Beth recalled that her father had told she and her mother that he had a lot of work to catch up on at the university on Tuesday and Wednesday and that he was staying over in Knoxville since he would be working late each evening. All that time, he was here with Russell."

Frustrated and confused, Dana Beth sat at one of the kitchen table chairs as she tried to sort things out in her mind: *My father had a second life I never even knew of. How many other lies had he told Mom and I in order to conceal the identity of Russell? Why? Why didn't he tell us about how his parents had died and then why did he hide Russell away all those years? Maybe things could have been different or maybe dad knew that Russell was a dangerous person and wanted to protect us. It makes no sense either way.*

Just as she closed the cabinet door and started to open another, she heard the back door open. Thinking that Grant had already returned, she spoke without turning around. "You're back already. I thought…."

She was interrupted by a low, angry sounding voice, "What are you *doing here? What are you doing in my house?*"

Dana Beth froze and then turned ever so slowly. What she saw sent a shiver through her body. The figure standing in the doorway filled the entire space, a black shadow against the late morning sun. She could feel her heart pounding in her chest as she tried to regain some sense of what was happening. Suddenly, she realized: *It must be Russell!* He looked entirely different from the first time she had seen him. Her body was trembling and her mouth was so dry she could hardly speak. He was wearing the same black hat. A shotgun was slung over his massive shoulder.

Be calm. Don't panic! she silently told herself. She stumbled over her words, "Russell, it's me...Dana Beth. You remember me! I'm your niece. You came to my house in Townsend to see me and now I've come to visit your house. I...I thought...everyone thought you were dead." Russell just stared at her with a blank look as he turned his head slightly as if he were sorting things out. His silence was unnerving. Dana Beth wrung her hands together as she thought, *Oh God...try and stay calm!*

Russell spoke very loudly, which caused Dana Beth to jump. "Where is your car? How did you get here? Who's here with you?"

Dana Beth thought quickly and answered, "A friend of mine dropped me off here. She went into Jacksboro to pick up a few things. She should be back any minute."

Russell, still angry, spoke loudly again, "Why do you want to see my house?"

Praying her answer would be satisfactory, she nervously answered, "I...I just wanted...to see where you lived and where my father, Conrad, spent time with you when he wasn't home with me in Townsend."

The mentioning of Conrad seemed to have a calming effect on him. He removed his coat and hat and hung them on a hook next to the door. Next, he leaned the gun against the doorframe and Dana Beth breathed a sigh of relief. As he turned toward her, she noticed how horrible he looked. There was a jagged scar running across his forehead. His face was covered in a shaggy beard and his hair appeared greasy and unkempt. She watched him carefully as he walked toward the sink. She took note of the way he limped and the strange way he held his left hand. She imagined that whatever happened to him after he had fallen over that cliff had obviously taken its toll. Trying not to stare too long, she watched him as he turned on the spigot and began to wash his hands and then splashed water on his face. It was almost as if she weren't there. Looking around she thought to herself, *My cell phone! Where did I leave my phone?* Scanning the room, she saw the small black devise sitting at the edge of the counter on the opposite side of where Russell stood. *Somehow, I've got to get to my phone. It's right there on the counter!*

She jumped again as Russell turned, his loud voice scaring her. "Where's your baby?"

Dana Beth was trembling again as she did her best to answer his demanding question. "She's at home with my mother, Ruth. Ruth was Conrad's wife. She's taking care of my baby."

Speaking again, Russell seemed to be calming down. "I don't know your mother. I would like to see her and your baby." Holding up his index finger as if she should not move, he limped into the living room where he opened a drawer of an old hutch. Dana Beth realized this was her opportunity to get to her phone. Russell's back was to her. It would only take her a few seconds to silently cross the kitchen and scoop up the phone. She looked into the living room again. Russell was occupied searching for something. Looking at the closed door she thought, *Maybe I should get the gun. Then I can keep him at bay until Grant returns. No, that will never work. I've never even held a gun before. I don't know if I'll know how to operate the thing. If it comes down to it, could I shoot Russell? Right now he seems calm. The one thing I don't want to do is piss him off. Grant said the man had no concern for human life. He could take the gun from me and kill me! Maybe I should just run out the door. With the way he limps maybe I could run down the road and he might not be able to catch me.*

Keeping her eye on Russell, she moved to the door. Just as she reached for the doorknob, Russell spoke without turning around, "Found it!" His voice startled her and she lost her nerve as she returned to the kitchen counter. Russell walked back into the kitchen with a look of satisfaction on his face. Holding up what looked like a newspaper clipping, he smiled and repeated himself, "Found it! I cut this out of the paper when you had your baby." He handed the article to Dana Beth with great pride.

Dana Beth took the clipping. She was speechless. She didn't know what to say. Leaning against the counter, Russell spoke again, but this time softly, "I like babies. People with babies won't let me look at their babies. They act like they are afraid of me." Reaching for the article, he continued, "Next time you come you bring the baby...okay?"

Dana Beth breathed deeply as she tried to relax. Russell had mentioned the next time she came which meant he had no intention of harming her. She knew Russell was slow and that if she used her head she could control the situation. She handed him the article then reached for the tote bag, asking, "That would be nice. I'll bring her with me the next time I come to visit. Are you hungry, Russell? I brought some food. I have some sweet tea also."

Russell's answer was childlike. "Yes, I am hungry. I would like to eat."

As Russell limped to the table, Dana Beth turned her back and opened the tote bag at the same time slipping her cell into her pocket, turning it on vibrate. Next, she took the bag and a thermos and set them on the table. For the moment, she felt as if the wheel had turned and now she was gaining control. Opening the tote, she started to remove items, describing each one. "Let's see, we have fried chicken, some tuna fish sandwiches and some cookies." Opening the container of chicken she sat it in front of him then lowered herself down into a chair on the opposite side of the table.

Russell pulled out a chair and sat down and stared at the chicken. She could tell from the look on his face that he was hungry. Pushing the container closer, she offered, "Go on, take all you want. I'm not really all that hungry. I had breakfast." Russell began to eat as if he hadn't eaten in days. Wolfing down one of the sandwiches, he then devoured three pieces of chicken in what seemed like record time and downed half of the tea directly from the thermos. All the while, he kept his head down, not uttering a single word.

Dana Beth removed another sandwich from the tote and asked, "Care for another sandwich?"

Sitting back in his chair, Russell shook his head no. Unwrapping the cookies from two folded napkins, Dana Beth dumped them on the table. "How about a cookie? They're peanut butter. Conrad's wife made them."

Russell smiled and picked up three cookies. "My brother, Conrad used to bring me cookies all the time. My favorite is chocolate chip, but these are good." Dana Beth watched as he stuffed an entire cookie in his mouth, chewed it, then followed in the same manner with the other two treats. Finished, he sat in silence staring out the kitchen window. The silence was killing Dana Beth. She had to remain in control until Grant got back. *What time is it?* she wondered. *How long has Grant been gone? I have to get out of the house and warn him somehow. Should I keep him talking? I don't know what to do!*

"Can I ask you a question, Russell?"

Russell's attention was now back on the cookies. "Can I have more cookies?"

"Yes," said Dana Beth, "You can eat them all."

"No," said Russell. Picking up a cookie he handed it across the table to her. "I want you to eat one with me."

Dana Beth took the cookie and bit into it and repeated her previous question, "Can I ask you a question?"

Russell, with a mouthful of cookie nodded yes as he reached for another.

Dana Beth knew she had to be careful what she said as she started, "How did you survive the fall from that cliff and how long have you been here?"

"I don't remember the fall." said Russell, "but I do remember being tangled up in some vines. I crawled up the side. Some men found me and took me to their house. I stayed there a long time. They brought me back here a couple of days ago."

"Did they just leave you here? Where are they now?"

"I killed them both over on the mountain. They were mean, nasty men. They made fun of me and they killed animals."

Dana Beth was stunned at how calmly he had made the admission. It was as if he were discussing the weather. She chanced another question. "Russell, did you kill all those people because they killed animals?"

"Yes...some. Some others I killed because they were trying to kill me. They wouldn't leave me be. I killed the man who took those turtles and the man who put that bear in a cage. They deserved to die. They were hurting animals. I had to kill Arliss and Dwayne. They told me they were not going to kill any more animals, but they lied. They thought I was stupid. They were going to kill me. They were the stupid ones." Russell took another bite of cookie and added, "Conrad killed some of them, too."

Dana Beth couldn't believe what she was hearing. Any composure that she had gained was lost as she slammed her hand down on the table and shouted, "No! My father never killed anyone! He couldn't have done any of those terrible things!" Tears began to run down her face.

Russell stood up as he seemed to be annoyed that she didn't believe him. Pointing his finger at her, he shouted back, "Conrad told me to never lie. I don't lie! Conrad killed all those people before I came to his funeral. Those people made him mad. He got sick and died. I miss him! I wish he was still here!"

Dana Beth's head was spinning. *This is insane,* she thought. *I'm sitting here talking to this man about my father being a killer.* Was Russell making all of this up? Was he smarter than everyone thought? *Oh God, Help me! I need to get away from Russell and warn Grant.* If she could convince Russell to go outside then maybe she could run down the road and escape. She stood and wiped her eyes. She had to take control of the situation before it developed into something more serious. "Russell! I think we should take a nice walk and calm down. Maybe you could show me around your land. I hear you have ten acres. Maybe we could see a bear or some other animals that live near here."

Russell instantly smiled, the suggestion he show her his land and some of his animal friends was the medicine that ended his sadness. "Yes, let's go see if we can see some of my friends. I would like you to meet them."

Perfect, she thought. *Once we get outside I'll wait for an opportunity to run off. I need to distract him so that he doesn't take his gun along.*

Russell was walking toward the door before she could say anything. Scooping up the last two cookies she wrapped them in the napkins and stuffed them in her pocket and spoke, "I'm taking these cookies with us. Maybe we can eat them as we walk." Russell looked back and smiled in agreement.

Approaching the door he put on his coat and hat and much to the dissatisfaction of Dana Beth grabbed his gun. Opening the door, he suggested, "Put on your coat. It's getting cold."

Russell held the door open as she walked past him, uncomfortably close. As he closed the door she stood on the back porch steps and looked off into the dense trees and thought that if she did manage to get away from Russell she would not be able to stay put. She'd have to walk out just like she and Grant had talked about when they had been joking about Hansel and Gretel. It was then that she realized that if she and Russell got too far from the road, then it would be impossible for Grant to know where she had gone. Then she remembered the cookies in her pocket. She could leave cookie crumbs behind, but would Grant be able to see them? Fingering the two napkins in her pocket, she thought, *No wait! I'll use small sections of the napkins. They'll be more noticeable.* Tearing off a small one inch section of one of the napkins she dropped it nonchalantly on the porch.

Russell closed the door and waved his hand in a westerly direction and started around the side of house. "Come on, I want to show you something. It's only about a ten minute walk from here."

Walking down the steps, Dana Beth objected in a friendly manner, "I'd really rather stay on the road, Russell. The shoes I'm wearing are not designed for walking in the woods and besides that, I'm not very good at climbing."

Her objection was quickly overruled as Russell held out his hand to assist her. "Don't worry, I'll help you. I know every inch of these woods."

Dana Beth knew she was pushing it by not agreeing with Russell, but she had to try and manipulate him to remain on the road. "Wouldn't it be better if we stayed on the road?"

Russell's tone suddenly changed as he grabbed her arm roughly and ordered loudly, "No! I want to show you something!"

Dropping another small section of the napkin on the ground, she reluctantly followed Russell up the ridge, dropping another piece halfway up and then on the top. Overlooking the cabin below, she dropped another section, praying that Russell would not discover what she was doing.

Walking along the top of the ridge, she left another small piece fall to the ground as she tried to distract Russell. Zipping up her jacket, she asked pleasantly, "You really like it up here, don't you?"

Russell nodded yes, but remained silent and focused on where they were headed as they began to climb upward again into the tall pines.

Dana Beth tore off another small piece of napkin and dropped it as she asked, "Can you tell me why Conrad never brought you to see us in Townsend?"

Russell still had hold of her arm as he pulled her forward, but with less aggressiveness. The mentioning of Conrad seemed to calm him once again. He smiled and answered, "Conrad always took care of me. He was afraid people would find out I killed the bus driver and that we hurt Mr. Pearl. He decided that it would be best for me if I just stayed here at the cabin. He would come and visit me and we would play card games and talk."

She had no idea what he was talking about as she thought, *Bus driver? What bus driver?*

Depositing another portion of napkin on the ground she tugged on Russell's sleeve with her free hand. "You're my uncle, Russell. You're family. You can trust me. You can tell me the truth. My father didn't kill anyone. Did he?"

Russell didn't answer, but just kept plodding up the side of the incline going deeper and deeper into the forest. Trying to calm him, she offered, "How about one of the cookies, Russell?"

He refused, "No, not now! Maybe when we get there."

Climbing higher, she realized Russell was in a mood where he wasn't going to speak unless she asked him a question.

Another section of napkin fell to the ground as she asked, "Do you remember my husband? His name is Grant. He was mentioned in that newspaper article you showed me. Remember?"

Russell stopped, turned and looked directly into her eyes as he answered defiantly, "I remember him! I met him on the ridge above the river. He was going to kill me! But then...he didn't! That Indian policeman shot me."

Dana Beth took a chance and asked her next question. "Would you have killed Grant, my husband, a man who is part of your family?"

Russell pulled on her arm as he started climbing once again as he spoke roughly, "I have to protect myself from mean people. That's why I killed that man in the alley and that bounty hunter. They were mean and wouldn't leave me alone. Grant and those men who chased me up this mountain wouldn't leave me alone either. They were going to hurt me! Your husband was raising his gun. He had no right to try and hurt me. I don't like him. We need to kill him, Dana Beth so that we can be safe! Then we can go to Townsend and get your baby. She can live with us here at the cabin. I'll take care of you both."

Any sense of control that she had over Russell seemed to have slipped away. Grant was right about not making him out to be something he wasn't. She was helplessly being pulled up the mountain, further and further from the cabin. She still had her cell phone but was there reception this high up? Falling down on purpose seemed to be the only way to stop him. Falling in the leaves, she cried out, "Russell! I can't keep going. I'm getting cold. Let's go back to the cabin."

Russell pulled on her arm and started climbing once again. He spoke loudly, "No, you come with me!"

Tears started to stream down her face as she looked back down the side of the mountain. The cabin was out of sight. She knew she had to remain calm as she dropped another piece of the napkin.

CHAPTER TWELVE

GRANT BEGAN TO RELAX AS HE MADE THE LAST TURN on the mountain road that led to the highway. Reaching into his jacket pocket, he removed his cell phone, and then remembered what Dana Beth had said, *'Don't call me.'* He smiled and thought, *If I call her she'll probably get upset. Anyway, what is there to worry about? Everything looked fine at the cabin. I'll just run into town, grab a few things and be back in no time.* Laying his cell on the seat next to him, he continued to think, *There's probably a Wal-Mart or another store in Jacksboro where I can get everything I need.* Mentally, he began to make a list of what he needed, watching the road so he wouldn't miss the turnoff. When he got on 25W it would be a straight shot into town.

Twenty minutes later, on the outskirts of Jacksboro, just like he had anticipated, a Wal-Mart sat on the right. Locating a spot near the front where a customer had pulled out, he parked the Jeep and headed for the main entrance. Once inside, he grabbed a shopping cart and started down the main aisle. The store was busy with Friday shoppers as he zigzagged up and down various aisles picking up items and tossing them in the cart. Placing a second box of crackers back on a shelf, he decided he had enough food to last them the night when he spotted a fresh flower counter. Dana Beth loved flowers. *Perfect,* he thought. *A secluded cabin, a roaring fire, flowers. This is going to be a nice evening. Maybe I should pick up a bottle of wine.*

Satisfied he had everything, Grant took his place in line behind an elderly couple. The woman smiled when she noticed the red asters and yellow mums as he carefully laid them on the counter. He was surprised to hear someone calling his name. Turning, he saw Frank Turnbull standing in the checkout line two customers back. Backing up, Grant spoke to the lady behind him, "I'm stepping out of line. Here, you go next." Placing the flowers back in the cart, Grant walked back to where Frank stood. "Sheriff Turnbull, good to see you. I'd shake your hand but I see your arms are full."

Motioning at his arms, Turnbull answered, "Yeah, picking up coffee and supplies for the office. It's good to see you, too. What brings you up to our neck of the woods?"

"Just picking up a few things. Me and the wife are spending the night at Russell Pearl's cabin. By the way, thanks for having the place straightened up. It really looks nice."

With a look of confusion, Turnbull asked, "What are you talking about?"

"Yesterday morning," said Grant. "I called you, but you weren't in. I left a message with your receptionist. She said she'd leave you a voicemail. When we got to the cabin, I assumed..."

Frank interrupted him, "I'm sorry, Grant. I haven't listened to my voicemails since Thursday night. I don't know who cleaned that cabin up, but it wasn't anyone I sent up there. Glad it was in good shape. Why on earth would you and your wife want to spend time in Russell Pearl's cabin?"

"It's a long story. The short version is that the cabin was left to my wife after Russell's death. So, we decided to take a run up here and have a look see. It was so nice my wife decided she wanted to stay the night."

"Well, I'm glad that worked out for you," Frank said. "To tell you the truth, I've been so busy I haven't had time to take a leak! Some hikers found two bodies on Thursday up near Buck Point Road. That's about twenty some miles from here over on the other side of Jellico. Turns out they were murdered. They were from down your way. Maybe you know them, Arliss and Dwayne Stroud. One had his head half blown off and the other one had his neck snapped. In fact, I called Sheriff Grimes about it. He's supposed to be taking care of notifying their next of kin. I'm surprised you don't know about the murders."

Holding up his bandaged hand, Grant confirmed, "I've been out of the office for a few days. Had me an accident, so I've been out of the loop."

"One of the victims was wearing a tee-shirt that read: Where is Russell Pearl? I thought that was rather odd, especially seeing as how we haven't located Pearl's body yet. Maybe it's just a coincidence. I don't know..."

Grant wasn't listening anymore. All he could think of was, *Who cleaned the cabin? Arliss and Dwayne Stroud...murdered.*

One was wearing a Russell Pearl tee shirt! Grabbing Turnbull's arm, Grant asked, "How far away were those murders from the cabin?"

Frank, with a look of concern at Grant's reaction answered, "About twenty miles, I guess."

"I have to go, Frank!" said Grant. "I shouldn't have left Dana Beth up there all by herself." He pushed the cart to the side and with a look of great concern on his face, stated, "I think she might be in danger!" Pushing his way past the customers in front of him, he started a slow trot and then broke into a run, rushing past customers, excusing himself the best he could.

The older lady standing in front of Turnbull asked, "Is there something wrong? That young man didn't even take his flowers."

Frank, taken completely by surprise at Grant's reaction to their previous conversation placed his purchases on the counter and answered somewhat dumbfounded, "I don't know."

Back in the Jeep, Grant backed out of the parking spot and headed for the highway, trying his best to control both his speed and thoughts. *Who could have cleaned up the cabin? Nobody had keys to the place except Sheriff Turnbull and I. Could it have been Russell? It couldn't be...he was dead. Or was he? God, please let me get back to the cabin before anything happens to my wife.* He beat on the steering wheel with his free hand. *Dammit! Why did I let her talk me into leaving here alone? If anything happens to her I'll never forgive myself.*

Speeding down the highway, his thoughts switched back to what Turnbull had said, *Arliss and Dwayne Stroud were found murdered a little over twenty miles from the cabin. They were probably up there poaching. What other reason could they have had for being in Jellico?* Suddenly, he remembered something else Turnbull said—*one of the victims was wearing a tee-shirt that read: Where is Russell Pearl?* Then, he remembered something else that at the time seemed insignificant, but now loomed as important. Right after the tent fiasco with Merle Pittman and Franklin Barrett when Buddie Knapp had tried to destroy their tee-shirt sales tent, Arliss had on a shirt that read: Where is Russell Pearl? He had made a strange comment about how no one knew where Russell was...but they did. Dwayne had given him a jab in his chest indicating that he shouldn't have said anything.

When he asked them what they were talking about, they just blew him off and walked away awkwardly. Something strange was happening, but he couldn't quite put his finger on what it was. *Who killed Arliss and Dwayne Stroud? Was Russell still alive? Did he kill the Stroud's? And if he did...why?* He reached for his cell phone and punched in Dana Beth's number. A message flashed across the tiny screen: No Service! Tossing the phone back on the seat, he rounded a curve then pressed the gas pedal to the floor. He had to get back to the cabin and put his mind at ease.

Looking at the red needle on the speedometer he realized he was traveling at eighty miles per hour. Taking his foot off the gas, he let the Jeep slow to fifty-five. He thought to himself, *I've got to keep calm. I'm letting my crazy thoughts rattle me. I don't have a minute to lose. If Russell, is somewhere around here, Dana Beth could be in big trouble.*

He passed two hunters who were securing a deer they had shot to the top of their vehicle on the side of the road. Then he remembered, *It's hunting season. How had that slipped my mind? I should have known better than to bring my wife to the woods during this time of the year. When I get back to the cabin I'm going to suggest that we move on to Nashville.*

Still climbing up the side of the mountain, Dana Beth was losing hope that Grant would find her. Tears filled her eyes as she thought about Crystal Ann back in Townsend. She had to find a way to get away from Russell even if it meant that he might take a shot at her. *Look at him,* she thought. *Plodding along, his head down, focused on getting to his destination. He keeps mumbling to himself. He really is crazy! The man belongs in an institution. I'm so mad at my father! Why didn't he put Russell in a hospital or somewhere where he couldn't hurt people? But then again, if Russell was telling the truth about Conrad, then her father as well, should have been in a mental hospital. She didn't know what to believe. Right now, she couldn't worry about what Russell had said about her father. She had to find a way to escape from the situation she found herself in.*

Russell stopped suddenly and pointed at an overhang of vines and branches to the right of where they stood. "Here we are," he

announced proudly. "This is what I want to show you." Guiding
Dana Beth toward the vines, he pulled back some of the hanging
foliage. "This is my cave. Come on, I want to show you the
inside."

Dana Beth stared into the black hole as she hesitated, not
wanting to enter. Russell, sensing her fear of the darkness smiled.
"I'll light a lantern and it won't be so dark and then you can see
how nice my cave is." Seconds passed, when a soft yellow glow
filled the entrance of the cave as Russell took her by the arm and
gently pulled her inside. He seemed pleased to show her the
cavern. "It's a big cave. I don't know how far it goes back. I never
go past the first turn. I always stay up here near the front. There's
a stream along the wall and then it gets narrow. It's nice in here.
It's always the same temperature and it's very quiet. I like quiet. I
have two sleeping bags and three lanterns. I keep firewood and
kerosene in here most of the time. I usually have food here but I
ran out. I was really getting hungry. I watch my animal friends
from here and make sure they're all right. Sometimes they come
right up to the entrance. They know they can trust me." A smile
crossed his face. "Isn't it nice here?"

Being careful what she said, Dana Beth stood just inside the
entrance, her arms wrapped around her. "It is nice, Russell, but I
think we should go back to the cabin. You can eat another
sandwich and we can talk. My friend should be coming back soon
and she'll wonder where I am. You wouldn't want my friend to
worry about me...would you?"

Russell objected, "No, I want to stay here!   We can eat the
cookies."

Seeing that he was getting agitated again, she began to slowly
edge her way back out of the cave. "Where are you going?" he
demanded in a loud tone.

Dana Beth thought quickly and answered, "The fumes from the
lantern are burning my eyes. I need to get some fresh air."

As she stepped out of the cave, she didn't realize that Russell
was right behind her. She felt the vibration of her cell phone in her
pocket. Quickly pulling it out, she hit the On switch. She could
faintly hear the crackling sound of Grant's voice:

Dana Beth...are you okay? I'm on my way!

As Russell's hand shot out to grab her phone, he knocked her to the ground. Russell's face grew dark with anger and he threw the phone down and began to stomp it with his heavy boot. "You lied to me! Your husband is up here with you...not a friend! You're not my friend. You lied!" With one hand he picked her up off the ground and threw her back inside the cave.

Scrambling to her feet, Dana Beth began to cry as she pleaded, "Russell stop! I didn't lie to you! I didn't know Grant was going to call me. Remember, we're family. You're my uncle!"

Russell shook his head as if he were confused. "It doesn't matter anymore! Those men are after me again and when they find me they'll put me in a cage for the rest of my life! I would rather be dead. I'm tired and hungry and I have no place to go, but here. I can't go to the bank and get money. I can't go into town and get food. If I stay at the cabin, they'll come for me."

Grant, trying his cell again, got service, but the call was short-lived and he was instantly disconnected after leaving his quick message. He drove up the mountain road as fast as he could but the hairpin turns and curves constantly slowed him down. *Take it easy,* he thought. *You're getting all worked up over nothing. Soon you'll be back at the cabin and find that Dana Beth is just fine.*

When he reached the cabin road, his heart was pounding despite the fact he had tried to calm his thoughts. He pulled the Jeep to the side of the road before the cabin was in view just to be on the safe side. Checking to see if his revolver was fully loaded, he stuck it in the back of his pants and started jogging up the road, looking to his right and left for anything that seemed unusual. When the cabin loomed into sight, he slowed down to a walk. Hesitating for a moment, Grant took in the surroundings. Everything seemed peaceful just like when he had left an hour ago. Birds were chirping in the tall pines, a squirrel ran across the front porch, a few stray leaves blew in the air. Then he heard a distant shot ring out. He cringed, but then remembered it was hunting season.

Staying low, he went around to the left side of the house and crossed the front porch. Looking into the bedroom window, nothing seemed out of place. He listened but there was no sound coming from inside. Working his way around the side of the house to the back steps, he carefully raised his head and peered in the kitchen window. The open tote was sitting on the table. That seemed odd as they hadn't opened the tote when they arrived at the cabin. Maybe Dana Beth opened it after he had left. Turning the knob on the door he slowly pushed the door open and stepped just inside. He withdrew his revolver and called out, "Dana Beth, I'm back! Where are you?" No answer.

Looking at the kitchen table, he noticed that all of the chicken and one of the sandwiches had been eaten plus there were cookie crumbs scattered across the table and on the floor. The thermos was half empty. Dana Beth couldn't have eaten all that food. Something was wrong. Carefully, with his revolver at the ready, he ventured into the living room as he called out her name again, "Dana Beth." Again, no answer.

Searching the two bedrooms and the bathroom, he walked quickly back out to the kitchen where he noticed that her jacket was not hanging on the hook. For some reason, she had left the house. She couldn't have possibly taken a walk. She had promised him that she would not leave and she would lock the door after he left. The door had been unlocked when he returned. Trying to control himself, he took a deep breath. He had to find out where his wife was.

Walking out the back door, he started down the steps. He noticed a small one inch section of white napkin on the last step. Recalling something he had seen just outside the door he went back up the steps where he saw another small section about the same size. Picking up the ripped napkin he put it to his nose. It smelled like peanut butter cookies. It was part of the napkin that Ruth had wrapped the cookies in they had brought along. Looking down over the side of the steps, he saw yet another section of napkin. Bounding down the steps, he walked up the side of the house where he spotted another torn napkin section. It couldn't have been more obvious. Dana Beth was leaving him a trail. As he bent down to retrieve the piece of napkin, he saw something out of the corner of his eye. Beneath the steps, shielded on two sides by redwood latticework, there was a concealed carport. He could see the front end of a pickup truck. He wondered if the truck had been there before they first arrived or had it been parked there after he left for town? Peering through the latticework, he thought, *God, why didn't I take a better look around when we first got here. If the truck was already here, I never would have let Dana Beth go into the cabin. I have to find her.*

The next piece of napkin was at the bottom of the ridge leading up the side of the mountain. She had to be with someone. Why else would she leave clues as to where she had gone? As he ventured up the side of the slope he had to be careful. The last time he had climbed this ridge, Russell Pearl was up there waiting for them. Once again, he contemplated the idea of Russell being alive. It seemed impossible, but at this point he couldn't rule out the possibility.

Staying low, using occasional trees and the thick weeds as cover, he found the next napkin section hanging on a low tree branch. He knew he was on the right trail, but where was it leading him? He had to be careful. He was an easy target. He noticed fresh mud on the side of a protruding rock indicating that someone had recently passed by. It might have been an animal. He couldn't be sure. A few yards further on, he discovered where the weeds had been matted down by two different set of footprints, one much larger than the other. Kneeling down, he ran his fingers across the matted weeds and thought, *They must have passed by this way recently.* A few feet further on, he saw another piece of torn napkin. He was still on the right trail.

Coming to a small clearing flanked on the right by a steep cliff, he pushed a low hanging branch to the side. Kneeling down he picked up another section of the white napkin. When he stepped on a branch, a loud snapping noise penetrating the quiet forest.

Russell jerked his head toward the cave opening when he heard the sound. He could tell from the sound that it was not created by an animal. He raised the rifle toward the opening and stated, "I heard a noise. Someone is coming!"

Thinking it might be Grant, Dana Beth followed Russell and screamed, "No!" as she pushed him forward, his gun misfiring, sending a loud echo through the thick forest.

Grant stopped in his tracks. For a moment he was frozen in thought: *My God! Dana Beth's been shot! My wife has been killed!"* Turning in the direction of the gunshot, Grant ran as fast as he could as he looked to the left and right. Arriving at the cave entrance, he saw Russell standing over Dana Beth who was laying on the ground. Just four feet from Russell, Grant pointed his revolver directly at him and ordered, "Drop the gun, Russell! Step away from my wife...now!"

Russell was caught off-guard as he responded, "I didn't hurt her! She tried to grab my gun and it went off accidentally. I pushed her and she went down."

"Drop the rifle," repeated Grant sternly." Stepping carefully to the side in order to get a better view of Dana Beth, Grant kept his eyes on Russell. He tried to keep focused on his wife, all the while his revolver trained on Russell. Kneeling down he placed his free hand on her forehead. She let out a low moan and Grant breathed a sigh of relief. She wasn't dead. Standing, he pointed the revolver at Russell's head. "All right, Russell. It's over! Put the gun down and place your hands above your head. Do it now!"

The frown on Russell's face slowly turned to a sad smile. His right hand tightened around the rifle as he spoke softly, "You won't shoot me. You didn't shoot me the last time we were on this mountain. You made that Indian policeman shoot me. I'm family. You wouldn't shoot me! You go away and leave me alone." His fingers wrapped around the trigger as he started to raise the rifle. His right hand grabbed the barrel as the gun came even higher.

"This is your last chance, Russell. I told you before. There are people who can help you. It doesn't have to end with your death. Put down the gun and come back with me. I'll make sure you get the help you need."

The gun was raised higher as Russell sneered, "No, they'll just put me in a cage for the rest of my life. Conrad always told me people would be mean to me. Go away and leave me be!" He aimed the gun directly at Grant, but before he could squeeze the trigger, Grant pulled off two shots, both penetrating Russell's chest. Russell staggered and then fell to one knee then over onto his face, a pool of blood seeping into the dirt surrounding his body. Keeping his revolver pointed at Russell, Grant knelt down and placed his hand on Russell's neck. There was a weak pulse, but then it stopped. Russell Pearl was officially dead."

Walking over to where Dana Beth was laying, he put his hand on her forehead. Placing his ear next to her mouth, he discovered that she was breathing evenly. Blood was coming from the side of her head. Picking her up, he spoke softly, "I'm here, Dana Beth. Just hold on!" Putting his revolver back into his pants, he cradled her in his arms and walked out of the cave and began the long difficult journey back down the mountainside to the cabin. Dana Beth drifted in and out of consciousness as he spoke to her, telling her how much he loved her and that she was going to be alright. Thirty minutes passed when he was standing on the ridge overlooking the cabin below. He heard sirens in the distance and by the time he got to the bottom of the ridge two Jacksboro patrol cars pulled into the small clearing. Grant let out a sigh of relief when he saw Sheriff Turnbull step out of one of the cars. Grant yelled, "Frank, over here. I need help!"

Frank sprinted across the yard as Grant stepped down from a small ledge of rocks and laid Dana Beth gently on the ground. Looking up at Turnbull, he explained, "She fell Frank. She's got a nasty cut on her head and it knocked her out. I need to get her to a hospital right away! My Jeep is parked down the road."

Frank reached into his pocket and took out his keys. "Here, take my car. One of my officers will take you into Jellico. What happened up here?"

Picking his wife back up, Grant looked back up the side of the mountain. "I killed Russell Pearl. His body is about ten to fifteen minutes up the side of the mountain. There's a cave where I left him. He's dead for sure this time."

Turnbull shook his head. "So he really was alive all this time we thought he was down there somewhere in that gorge. I'll be damned! Listen, you go on and get your wife to the Community Hospital in Jellico. My officer knows the way. Leave me your Jeep keys. I'll make sure it gets delivered to the hospital. I'll take care of Pearl's body."

As Grant placed Dana Beth in the backseat, he addressed Turnbull once again, "There's a pickup truck in a carport down beneath the back porch. I really didn't get a chance to check it out. It probably belongs to Russell. I gotta go."

The time spent in the emergency room seemed endless. Grant paced back and forth as he waited for the door to Dana Beth's room to open. A doctor and nurses were going in and out, technicians bringing in x-ray and CT machines, but no one would let him see her or go into the room. Any thoughts about Russell Pearl had completely left his mind for now. He was overwhelmed with emotion about what had happened to his wife.

When the doctor finally came out of the room and approached, Grant stood to meet him and asked, "Is my wife alright? When can I see her?"

"Calm down, Mr. Denlinger. My name is Doctor Morton and your wife is going to be fine. She has a bad cut on the side of her head which required six stitches. Probably hit her head on a rock or something. She also has a slight concussion, but with bed rest that will heal in about a week. I have given her a sedative and she'll be asleep for some time. You can go in and sit with her, but I would suggest that you keep any conversation to a minimum. I would like to keep her here at least overnight for further observation to make sure she doesn't develop any other symptoms. You understand, it's just a precautionary measure. Now, go see your wife." He patted Grant on the shoulder and moved off down the hall.

Grant pushed open the door and slipped behind the long white curtain that shielded Dana Beth from view. She looked so small laying there in the hospital bed. A large white bandage was wrapped around her head. Tears filled his eyes as he sat down in a chair next to the bed. He took her hand and placed it by his face. Even though he knew she was asleep, he spoke to her in a soft voice. "If I lose you, I lose everything. I'm so sorry for putting your life in danger. I'll spend the rest of my life making it up to you. I know how scared you must have been up there on that mountain with Russell. You were so brave. I love you." He laid his head down on the side of the bed and sobbed.

Dana Beth woke up momentarily, reached over and touched his head. He looked up at her as she spoke weakly, "I'm going to be okay. We've got a lot to talk about. I love you..." Her voice trailed off and she closed her eyes, sleep once again taking over.

A nurse pulled back the curtains and motioned to Grant. Once outside she spoke, "Chief Turnbull and two FBI agents are waiting for you in one of our offices down the hall. They want to talk with you. Please follow me."

Entering the office, Grant did not recognize the two agents. They introduced themselves as Ron Riley and David Radison from the Knoxville office. They were much younger than Agents Gephart and Green and had more businesslike mannerisms. Sheriff Turnbull sat off to the side while a gentleman by the name of Phil went about setting up recording equipment.

"How is your wife, Mr. Denlinger?" asked, Riley.

Grant smiled and answered, "Aside from a concussion and a cut on her head, it looks like she'll be fine. The doctor assured me she'd make a full recovery."

"That's good news. The media is starting to show up out front of the hospital. By now, the news is starting to spread about the shooting up by Pearl's cabin. We're going to have to give them some kind of report on what happened up there. Sheriff Turnbull filled us in on what he knows, but there are still some holes that need to be filled in. We were hoping we could get things cleared up by talking with you."

For the next thirty-five minutes Grant explained in detail everything that transpired from the moment they arrived at the cabin up until he delivered his wife to the hospital. He answered every question the Feds asked him and reiterated a number of times when asked about what happened at the cabin during his absence, that he didn't know as he hadn't had an opportunity to speak with his wife yet.

Satisfied with the interview, Riley stood and motioned toward Phil. "You can shut down. I think we have enough information to satisfy the press for now. They can run the story about Officer Denlinger shooting Russell Pearl but they'll probably want a lot more answers, which at this point we are unprepared to supply them with. I have a few more questions myself but for now I'm going to go out front and make a brief statement based on what we have so far. The death of Russell Pearl is news that's been a long time coming."

Grant stood and walked to the door but was stopped by Riley. "Officer Denlinger. We're going to have to speak with your wife as soon as possible. She's the only one who knows what happened at the cabin after you left."

"I realize that," said Grant. "But for right now, I'd just like to go spend some time with her."

Riley nodded in agreement. "I'll have agent Radison check back with you later and see if your wife is in condition to give us some insight on this matter."

CHAPTER THIRTEEN

IN THE DREAM, SOMEONE WAS SHAKING HIM. THEN HE heard a voice, "Grant! Grant, wake up!" Slowly opening his eyes, he saw the large round face of Sheriff Turnbull staring down at him.

Grant rubbed his hand across his face and looked up into the dim white ceiling of the hospital room, asking, "What time is it?"

Turnbull walked over and pulled back the drapes, the morning light seeping into the semi-dark room. "It's just after eight thirty."

Grant made an odd face as he licked his dry lips, a pasty taste hung inside his mouth. Reaching for a pitcher of water next to the bed, he poured a glassful and gulped it down, then sat up in the uncomfortable chair he had spent the night in. Running his hands through his hair, he looked at Dana Beth who at the moment was sleeping peacefully. Rotating his neck, he remarked. "I fell asleep around one o'clock last night." Getting up from the chair he continued, "This chair isn't the most pleasant way to get a good night's rest."

Turnbull nodded toward Dana Beth. "How's the wife? What did the doctor say?"

Grant walked to the window and looked out. "Same as before. According to the doctor, she'll be fine. He was in last night around eight. Said what she needed most is some bed rest. They're going to run a few tests."

Turnbull removed his hat and tossed it on the chair. "Did you get a chance to speak with her about what happened after you left her at the cabin?"

"No, not really. That still remains a mystery. Yesterday afternoon she was awake for a few minutes. She had some pudding and a glass of juice, then dozed off again. But she did say we needed to talk. So, I guess maybe later today or tomorrow we'll find out exactly what happened."

"Let's step outside," said Frank. "Is there a lounge on this floor? I sure could use a cup of coffee."

Outside in the hallway, Grant remarked, "I'm really worried

about my wife. Maybe it's just my imagination, but she doesn't seem to want to talk about what happened at the cabin right now. When I ask her about it she just stares off into space or closes her eyes. I'm her husband. I just can't understand why she won't tell me what happened."

The lounge was down the hall and around the corner. Except for a nurse who was drinking a cup of tea, the small room was empty. She nodded and smiled at them as she left. After preparing a cup of black coffee, Frank settled into one of the comfortable lounge chairs as he continued with the conversation they had out in the hall, "Whatever happened to Dana Beth had to have been a frightening experience. I can only imagine being alone with a serial killer and not knowing if you were going to live or die. She was probably worried about you also. I'm no doctor, but maybe it's too hard for her to talk about right now. Then again, maybe the concussion is causing her to forget some of what happened. Either way, the next few days are going to be a pain in the ass for both of you. The press will be camped on your doorstep searching for any scrap of leftover meat that the vultures missed. Be careful what you tell those people. They could take a simple recipe for apple pie and turn it into the worst piece of crap you'd ever want to taste. As you can tell, I'm not all that fond of the media."

"That reminds me," said Grant. "I've got to give my mother-in-law an update on Dana Beth's condition. I'd hate for her to find out what happened second hand. Would you please excuse me for a moment?"

Grant stepped into the hallway and punched in his home number. Ruth answered the phone in her normally pleasant manner. "Denlinger residence."

"Ruth, it's Grant. Dana Beth is still in the hospital. She has a slight concussion, but the doctor said she's going to be fine..."

Before Grant could finish talking, Ruth broke in, "Should I drive up?"

"No, that won't be necessary. We should be home later today or maybe tomorrow. Listen, there's something else I need you to know about. If they haven't shown up already, the press and the media might show up at the house. I shot Russell Pearl up here near the cabin. He's dead and the media are going to be after the story like hounds. If they show up, don't tell them anything. Now, don't worry. We'll be home soon. Give Crystal Ann a hug from both of us. I've got to go now. There's a lot going on up here. See you soon."

Back in the office, Turnbull asked, "Is your mother-in-law alright?"

Grant sat at the table and answered, "Yeah, I think she'll be fine. I just hope I get home before the media starts surrounding our home."

Sipping at his coffee, Frank spoke up, "Speaking of the press, after the Feds get Dana Beth's statement, there will be another press conference. I spent most of yesterday at the cabin and at the cave with six people from my department. They went over the area with a fine tooth comb. We checked out the truck you told me about. The registration and plates were expired. It's registered to a Cletus Stroud. We dusted the interior and the door handles and found a number of different fingerprints: Arliss and Dwayne Stroud along with two other apparent members of their family, Cletus and Ambrose Stroud. We also found a set of prints that we didn't have on record. We fingerprinted Russell Pearl and got a perfect match, which indicates that Russell was recently inside the truck. We can't rule out the possibility that he could have killed those two brothers. They were killed approximately twenty some miles from the cabin and yet a truck registered to one of their family members is found at the cabin. It's safe to say we've found a connection between Russell Pearl and the Stroud's."

Grant, amazed that the truck belonged to Cletus Stroud and not Russell, raised his hands in confusion. "I thought when I shot Russell this whole mess was finally over, but apparently there's some dots we haven't connected yet."

Shaking his head in agreement, Turnbull asked, "What can you tell me about the Stroud's?"

Grant sniffed and wiped his nose with the back of his hand. "You mean Arliss and Dwayne?"

"Well yeah, I'd like to know what you can tell me about them, but also their family. Six of them dropped by my office last evening to ID their kin. Now, we've got our share of rough mountain people up here, but those Stroud's. Talk about a freak show! There were two older women with them: I believe the older one was referred to as Effy and the other one Maude. They seemed to run the show. Then there was an older man and three other younger men, maybe in their forties. Effy calls all the shots for the most part," said Grant. "She's Maude's mother-in-law and the older man was probably Otis, Maude's husband. The three other men were no doubt Maude's sons: Ambrose, Cletus and Harmon, who's the oldest. Arliss and Dwayne were his sons. The Stroud's have been giving us fits recently. Cletus' wife Ruby Jean has disappeared. They claim she ran off but there's something fishy about her disappearance. Then, just recently, Ambrose leaves his six-month old daughter alone in a car while he goes into a grocery store. He was arrested and believe me, he put up quite a fight." Holding up his bandaged hand, he explained, "That's how I got this. They threw his ass in jail but he got out on a technicality. He threatened one of our local citizens and hit the manager of the store. I think he'll still wind up serving some time but for right now, he's out."

Turnbull looked at Grant in amazement. "When they first came into our headquarters they approached our receptionist. Effy did all the talking at first, explaining that they were the Stroud's and they were up from Townsend to get their two boys and take them home. I just happened to be in the office and I saw them walk in. When the receptionist buzzed me that we had visitors, I went out to the front desk and introduced myself. The one called Effy repeated herself in a demanding fashion, the other five staring at me like they wanted to kill me, especially after I informed them they could follow me over to the Coroner's office where they could identify the bodies, but we weren't prepared to release the bodies just yet as we were still in the process of sorting things out. When I told them we were pretty sure those boys were murdered based on some of the prints we lifted from Cletus' truck, the one called Maude slammed her cane down on the desk and demanded, 'Who killed my grandsons!'"

"What did they say about Cletus' truck winding up at Russell's cabin?"

"When I told them where we found the truck, they all seemed to clam up except for Cletus who mentioned that Arliss and Dwayne had borrowed his truck and were supposed to return it by noon the next day."

"The finger of the law seems to be pointing at Russell Pearl as their killer but there are still some unanswered questions as far as I'm concerned. Arliss Stroud was wearing a tee-shirt that read:

Where is Russell Pearl? That's just plain weird!"

"It's not as weird as you may think," said Grant. "Two of our local citizens from the Townsend area came up with the idea of selling those tee-shirts. It was just another method in a long string of ideas for them to cash in on what has been a tragic situation. Some people will try and make money at any costs."

"The other thing that strikes me as extremely strange happened when I mentioned to the Stroud's that Pearl might have killed those boys. The older fella, I think the one you said was Otis, spoke up angrily and blurted out, 'I knew Russell kilt them boys!'

"Maude, I guess his wife, clobbered him with that cane of hers and told him to shut his trap! It was an awkward moment for a couple of seconds. Finally, Effy speaks up and says not to mind anything Otis says because he's not all there. I think she was trying to say he was slow witted. Well, I didn't buy it! I knew Otis had said something they didn't want mentioned but at the time it didn't seem appropriate for me to question them. They had come to identify and collect their kin. That family is hiding something. I think they know more about why Arliss and Dwayne were killed and from the way they all reacted I think they already knew Russell was responsible."

Grant looked across the room at Frank. "You may be right. I think there's a possibility that Russell might have killed them."

Snapping his fingers as if he had forgotten something, Frank reached into his pocket and removed his wallet and took out an 8½ by 11 folded, wrinkled piece of construction paper. Unfolding the paper, he spoke to Grant. "We found this in Russell's wallet. Does it mean anything to you?"

Grant took the paper and placed it on the table, smoothing out the edges. It was a crude childlike drawing done in crayon: three stick figures; one very large, one very small and the third laying down in what appeared to be flowers, a large tree with what appeared to be a hanging tire swing. The crayoned printed wording on the paper read: russell, me and momma. A name was printed at the bottom: violet.

"This is very interesting," commented Grant "If this is the Violet I think it is, she's Cletus Stroud's daughter. It appears to me that the big stick figure on the drawing is probably Russell, the smaller one represents Violet and the one that is laying down might be her momma. This drawing might mean that Russell knew the Stroud's. He may have even had contact with them recently, which throws a whole new light on things."

Frank got up and refilled his cup. "I'm going to see if Riley and Radison are here yet. You might want to check with the doctor and see if Dana Beth is well enough to speak with them."

Walking down the hall toward Dana Beth's room, Grant heard familiar footsteps behind him: the unmistakable, heavy gait of Chief Axel Brody. The steel brads on the heels of his boots made a double clicking sound that had always been an irritation to Grant.

Catching up with Turnbull and Grant, Brody yelled, "Hey...hold on! I want to talk to you two! How's come nobody called me about what's goin' on up here today? Why should I be the last one to know? You're one of *my officers* Denlinger, and I should have been the first one you called!"

Grant wasn't in the mood to screw around with Brody. "Wouldn't have done me any good, Axel. I needed help and I needed it right away. Besides, this is Frank's jurisdiction."

"That's a lot of bull!" snapped Brody "You guys just didn't want me in on the picture! Well, I'm here now and I've got a lot to say. First off, Wonder Boy! You're on leave until further notice...until we get this shootin' sorted out. Seems kinda strange how you knew where Russell Pearl was and then came up here and tracked him down without sayin' a word to me!"

Grant turned and got in Brody's face. "Look, Axel! I had no idea Pearl was near his cabin. I thought he was dead just like you and everyone else thought."

"Sounds shady to me," barked Brody. "Turn in your badge and gun tomorrow mornin' at the office in Townsend. We'll discuss this later."

Frank rescued Grant from Brody's wrath as he interjected, "I just found out. The Feds are waiting to question Dana Beth." Giving Brody a cocky smile, he stated, "You can give us the rest of your lecture later on."

I'm sorry, Mrs. Denlinger, but as long as you're a patient here at the hospital you are required to use a wheelchair." The nurse smiled and pleasantly ordered, "Please sit."

Dana Beth lowered herself into the chair and placed a white blanket across her lap. With Grant walking by her side, she was wheeled down the hall to the office where Grant had previously been interviewed.

Both agents, Riley and Radison, along with Frank Turnbull stood when she entered the room. Brody who was allowed to attend the questioning, remained seated in the far corner.

"Thank you for your time, Mrs. Denlinger," stated Riley professionally. "I'm sorry for what happened to you and I hope you're feeling better."

Following some brief introductions, Riley continued, "We just have a few questions to ask you. We'll be as brief as possible as I know you're anxious to go home. Our conversation is going to be recorded so we don't miss any of the details." Looking at Phil who was making an adjustment to the recorder, Riley asked, "Are we on line, Phil?"

Phil gave a thumbs up, flipped a switch and announced, "We're live!"

Radison shuffled some papers lying in front of him and then cleared his throat. "For the record, would you please state your name, address and state you reside in."

After Dana Beth complied with his request, he spoke again, "Now, I will reiterate the facts your husband told us. If at any time you disagree, please feel free to interrupt me. When I finish reading his statement, I would like you to tell us what happened from the time you encountered Russell Pearl up until the moment he was shot and killed."

Axel crossed his arms across his broad stomach and listened with great interest as Grant's statement was read aloud. At times, he wanted to interrupt, but was prevented from doing so as Agent Radison held up his hand for silence.

Radison was no sooner finished, when Brody spoke up, "It appears that Mrs. Denlinger, nor does anyone present have any questions about officer Denlinger's statement. Well, I do! Let me set the record straight. I'm the first one to stand in line and say, 'Good Riddance' to the likes of Russell Pearl. The man deserved to die after all the people he killed. I don't have a problem with his death, but I do have some serious questions for Officer Denlinger about how he went about accomplishin' this feat. In the next few days he'll be regarded as a hero, but based upon what I've been told, that may not be the case."

Turnbull was clearly disturbed at Brody's statement. "What the hell are you getting at Brody?"

Axel pointed at Turnbull as spoke sharply, "This might be your jurisdiction, but Officer Denlinger happens to work out of *my jurisdiction* so maybe you oughta sit there and listen to what I have to say."

Riley jumped in, "Sheriff Brody, what does any of this have to do with Grant's statement?"

"It could have plenty to do with it. I have it from a very reliable source that Officer Denlinger may have had an ulterior motive for killing Russell Pearl."

"That's insane!" objected Grant.

Brody, now the center of attention, stood and walked to the front of the room as he pointed at Grant. "My wife has a sister who works for an attorney right here in Knoxville. They keep in touch by calling one another from time to time. Recently, my wife finds out the Denlinger's stand to inherit not only Russell Pearl's cabin, but approximately five million dollars! But there's a problem. As long as Russell Pearl's body is not found the money and the cabin cannot be touched for seven years or until the body is found. Don't you gentlemen find it strange that Grant drives up to the cabin, tracks down Russell Pearl and kills him, which immediately entitles he and his wife to the five million?"

Grant stood and placed his hands on his hips as he directed his words at Brody, "Look, Axel! You heard my statement. I mentioned that the cabin was left to my wife along with some money according to her father's will."

"Yeah, but you forgot to mention *how much money!* Five million dollars is a lot of cash. Money can do strange things to people. Now, that Russell Pearl is *most definitely dead,* you and the wife don't have to wait seven years to cash in! Wait until the press gets hold of this tidbit. They'll have a field day questionin' the integrity of the Townsend Police Department. You should have come to me and discussed all of this *with me!*"

Riley stood and stepped between both men. "Gentlemen, if you would please stop talking, we can get back on track. Let's get back to the reason we are here today; to get a statement from

Dana Beth. We need to get it right this time before we go to the press. Last time they made a mockery out of all of us because we couldn't come up with Pearl's body. Anything else at this point, as far as I'm concerned needs to be put on the back burner. Now, if everyone would please return to their seat then we can continue."

There was complete silence in the room for a few seconds then Riley turned to Dana Beth. "Mrs. Denlinger, you can begin your statement."

As soon as she began talking, Dana Beth had no problem remembering every detail from the time Russell entered the cabin up until he was killed. She spoke slowly and precisely, and at times was asked to speak louder. Occasionally, she would glance over at Grant and he would give her a knowing smile as if to say, 'You're doing fine!'

There were a number of times when Riley or Radison would interrupt her and ask a question. They wanted to know Russell's physical condition and as a layperson, did she feel that he was stable? Riley asked her whose idea it was to leave the cabin. Radison asked if she ever felt that Russell was going to kill her. They wanted to know how Russell discovered that Grant had brought her to the cabin.

Fifteen minutes into the interview, Riley spoke very seriously, "This next question is very important, Mrs. Denlinger. Did Russell Pearl indicate to you that he was going to kill your husband and did you see at any time where Pearl aimed his rifle in the direction your husband was standing?"

Dana Beth knew the Feds were searching for any mistake that Grant might have made while at the cave. Confidently, she smiled and answered, "Russell told me he was going to kill Grant. He pointed his rifle at my husband who up until that point tried to get Pearl to surrender. I lunged at him, he knocked me to the side and then Grant shot him. I must have gotten knocked out, because I don't remember anything after that until I woke up in the hospital."

Riley asked the next question. "Did Russell Pearl give you any explanation of where he had been for the past four months?"

"Yes and no," was her answer as she explained, "He told me two men had found him in the woods and he stayed with them until he got well. He never indicated where the men lived." Tears welled up in her eyes as she went on, "He said he killed them when they were bringing him to the cabin. He said they were mean men."

"And where were these two men killed?"

"He didn't say."

Grant was getting nervous, thinking to himself, *What else are they going to ask her? God, I hope Conrad's name doesn't come up.*

Riley turned to Chief Brody and remarked, "This next question *does* have to do with your jurisdiction. Mrs. Denlinger, did Russell Pearl ever mention Luke Pardee?"

Her answer was short and to the point, "No."

Radison thanked her for her time and signaled for Phil to turn off the recorder. "If we have any more questions we'll get in touch with you. Please get some rest and I wish you a speedy recovery."

Grant stood. "I'm going to take my wife back to her room. The nurses told me that after our meeting she would be released."

Riley, Radison and Phil packed quickly and walked out the door followed by Brody, when Grant stopped him. "Axel, if you're not in a hurry I was wondering if you and Sheriff Turnbull could hang around for a couple of minutes. I have something I want to discuss with both of you." Pushing his wife toward the door, he politely stated, "Stay here. I'll be right back."

Moving down the hall Dana Beth looked up at Grant. "I really want to go home now. I want to see Crystal Ann."

Grant reassured her, "I promise I won't be more than ten minutes. The nurses will help you pack and get dressed then we'll be on our way home."

Frank and Axel stood in the corner discussing something when Grant entered. When Brody saw him, he sarcastically asked, "Okay, Wonder Boy! What's on your mind now? Make it quick. I have to get back to Townsend."

Grant closed the door and then spoke, "Looks like Russell Pearl had us all fooled, didn't he? There is still a part to this story that we are not aware of." Looking at Turnbull, he elaborated, "Frank and I had quite a discussion yesterday about not only Arliss and Dwayne Stroud, but their entire family. I think that somehow they may be involved in this. I'm not sure just yet, but things are starting to add up. As hard as it is to believe, Russell Pearl survived that fall from the gorge. He told Dana Beth that some men found him and that he stayed with them. We know now it was the Stroud's who found Russell and nursed him back to health. He had been staying at their place. Russell killed Arliss and Dwayne and took their truck. Since that's the case, then the ball is right back in our court, Axel. The Feds are on the verge of wrapping this thing up. The Stroud's are our problem! Since I'm required to hand over my gun and badge, I guess you'll just have to deal with the Stroud's with one less deputy! So, what I said before about the Stroud's being our problem seems to be incorrect. It's *your* problem, Axel!" Grant turned to Turnbull and shook his hand. "Thanks for all your help, Frank. I'm going to take my wife home now."

Frank followed Grant out the door leaving Brody alone. Axel kicked at a nearby chair and sent it skidding across the tile floor. "Son of a bitch! Just about the time I think we've got this thing under control, the Stroud's pop up their ugly heads! The day when I'm no longer the Chief of Police in Townsend can't get here quick enough!"

CHAPTER FOURTEEN

FRANK TURNBULL WAS RIGHT ABOUT THE NEWS MEDIA being camped on their doorstep. When Grant pulled on to the street where they lived, there was hardly room for the Jeep to make it through the line of vans and cars parked haphazardly on both sides. Electrical wires crisscrossed the street; a tent at the end of the block had been set up where a local caterer was serving hot coffee and sandwiches. People were huddled together in the mixture of snow and rain. Grant had to stop while a technician ran a wire across the street. Dana Beth, who had slept the entire trip from Knoxville was startled as she awoke only to find a woman reporter staring in the window who asked loudly, "Mrs. Denlinger...how do you feel about your husband killing Russell Pearl?"

Another reporter approached the driver's side and signaled for Grant to roll down his window. Grant honked the horn and waved the technician out of the road as he slowly moved forward, ignoring both reporters walking alongside the Jeep. Dana Beth, not quite awake stared out the window at the female reporter as she exclaimed, "Grant! What's going on? Who are all these people and what are they doing here?"

Honking the horn again, Grant rolled down his window and sternly warned the reported on his side, "Back away from the vehicle. Get out of the street and back onto the sidewalk!" Turning his attention to Dana Beth, he answered her question, "It's the damn news media. Sheriff Turnbull warned me they might be here when we got back, but I didn't think it'd be this bad!"

The reporter on Dana Beth's side spoke loudly again, "Mrs. Denlinger, what can you tell us about what happened at the cabin?"

Grant honked the horn a third time as he said, "Just ignore her. We'll be in the house soon."

Finally, at their driveway, Grant was confronted by two television vans parked on the front lawn and a radio van partially blocking the driveway. A crowd of onlookers was gathered together on the sidewalk across the street. Grant noticed some of them as his neighbors. Dana Beth was starting to panic as a group of reporters began to surround the Jeep. "Oh...my God, Grant. Are we going to be able to get into the house without talking with these people?"

"Yep, it's gonna happen right now!"

Rolling down the window, Grant pushed away the microphone that was shoved at him as he yelled at the driver of the van blocking the drive. "Move that van or I'm gonna push it out of the way." The driver gave him an odd look but did not respond to his demand. Grant laid on the horn and slowly nudged forward until his bumper was touching the side of the van. Putting the Jeep in neutral, he gunned the engine and yelled at the driver again, "Move it...now, or I will!"

The driver backed onto the grass as he gave Grant a nasty glare. Grant slowly inched forward, constantly honking the horn as reporters and cameramen reluctantly moved to the side allowing them to pass. Grant pushed the garage door opener and the double doors slowly raised, a signal for the crowd to gather next to the garage. Pulling in, Grant got out of the Jeep and ordered three reporters who followed them inside, "Get the hell out of my garage! This is private property!" As they backed away, Grant hit the door closer and walked around to the other side to help Dana Beth out. She already had the passenger door open as she asked, "How are we going to get inside the house?"

Grant placed his hands on her shoulders and apologized, "I'm sorry about all this. You're just going to have to trust me for the next few minutes. When we go outside to the driveway, just keep your head on my shoulder and your eyes closed. You're probably going to hear a lot of people shouting questions at us plus you might hear a few choice words from me, but believe me, we'll be in the house before you know it. Okay?"

Dana Beth smiled. "Alright...let's go."

Standing at the garage door entrance, Grant hugged his wife and asked, "Ready!"

Laying her head on his shoulder she wrapped her arms around him. "I'm ready."

He opened the door, only to be met by a wall of people and the flashing of numerous cameras and shouts:

"Officer Denlinger! How did you know where Russell Pearl was?

"When do you get the five million?"

"Did Pearl say anything before you shot him?"

Grant forced his way past the initial group as he shoved a cameraman and a number of microphones to the side. The reporters moved in unison and continued to fire questions at them:

"Mrs. Denlinger! What can you tell us about your fall?"

"How does it feel to be a millionaire?"

Arriving at the rear of the house, Ruth rescued them from the crowd. She opened the kitchen door and let them in as one last question was asked, "Did Pearl kill Luke Pardee?"

Grant instantly guided Dana Beth to the table where she took a seat. Ruth, with her back to the door took a deep breath. "Thank goodness you're home! This place has been a zoo all morning. I'm afraid to even go out and get the mail. I was so stunned when you called and told me what happened." Going to the table, she wrapped her arms around her daughter. "I was so worried about you two!"

Dana Beth looked around the kitchen and asked, "Where's Crystal Ann?"

"She's sleeping. I put her down about an hour ago. Are you hungry? I can make you something."

Dana Beth got up and headed for the stairs as she answered curtly, "No, I just want to see my baby!"

Turning to Grant, Ruth asked in a quiet voice, "Did I do something wrong? Is she alright?"

"I'll think she'll be alright," assured Grant. "She's been through quite a lot. We'll talk about all that later. She slept all the way home. I guess all the media people were a bit much for her." Walking to the picture window, he drew back the curtains. "Why don't you put on a pot of coffee. I'm going to wait a few minutes and then I'm going out front and get those people out of our front yard."

Once upstairs, Dana Beth opened the door to the nursery. She gently ran her hand through Crystal's soft hair and bent down next to the crib as she whispered, "You're so beautiful and I love you so much. I will never leave you alone again." Crystal let a out a gentle sigh and turned her head.

Dana Beth stood as Grant entered the half open door, asking, "Is she alright?"

"Yes, she's okay."

Closing the door, Grant spoke in a low voice, "Your mother has no idea what happened at the cabin. She's really on edge. I think maybe you should come back downstairs and have a cup of coffee with her. She's your mother...she's worried about you."

"Look, Grant. My mother has always been there for me and my family, but right now, I'm tired. I would just love to take a hot shower, put my pajamas on and sleep in my own bed. I'll come down later, when I feel better."

"I understand," said Grant. "I'll tell her. Listen, did the doctor give you anything to help you sleep or to calm your nerves?"

She nodded yes and answered, "He prescribed some medication for me, but I don't think there's a pill made that will help me at the moment. I'm going to take that shower now." Moving past him, she left him standing in the darkened room.

At the bottom of the stairway he was met by Ruth who held out a cup of steaming coffee to him. Turning to walk in the kitchen she explained, "I'm having a shot of Wild Turkey in mine...how about you?"

"Good call," said Grant. "Dana Beth is really tired. She said she'd come down later and talk." Looking out the window, he asked, "When these people out front started to show up did you happen to give Brody a call?"

"No, I figured they had a right as the media to be here and besides that, I was so shocked when they started ringing the doorbell and looking in the windows. I just locked the doors and closed the drapes."

Setting down his coffee, Grant went into the kitchen, opened the Wild Turkey, took a long swallow and stated, "They do have rights, but they cannot trespass on our property. I'm going to put a stop to this...right now!"

Grant no sooner opened the front door when the group standing on the front lawn moved quickly toward the porch like a school of piranhas chasing an injured swimmer. One particularly brazen reporter climbed the steps as her cameraman set up a tripod mounted camera at the edge of the porch steps. "Officer

Denlinger. Alexis Canett of the—"

Grant cut her off before she could finish. "I don't care what your name is or who you represent. Get the hell off my porch!" Looking past the reporter he shouted at the group of reporters standing in the yard. "All of you need to leave and move back out to the street. This is private property and you're trespassing. Those of you who refuse to get off my property will be arrested by the local authorities. You have five minutes to vacate my lawn."

The cameraman, ignoring Grant's request, asked brazenly, "Could you please move back just a tad. You're a little too close to the camera. If you'll move just a little, I can get a much better shot."

Rather than backing up, Grant moved forward as he pointed at the reporter and spoke strongly, "If I were you I'd get off this porch...now! And take that camera with you!"

The reporter objected, "We just want to ask you a few questions about the Russell Pearl killing and..."

Grant wasn't interested in what she had to say. Moving toward the reporter he removed his wallet and flipped it open displaying his badge. "I really don't have to wait for the police to get here to start arresting folks, because I'm a police officer. I know you think I'm just another local citizen who has information that you seek but that can all change in an instant. I can simply walk back inside my house and return with my gun and a set of handcuffs. As an officer of the law I would be perfectly within my rights."

The woman reporter nor the cameraman budged. Grant shrugged and walked to the front door when the reporter spoke, "That won't be necessary, Mr. Denlinger. We'll move back to the street and I'll see what I can do about getting the others to move as well."

Grant smiled and said, "Thank you."

Back inside, he went to the picture window and looked out. The female reporter was talking to some other reporters as she motioned toward the house. After a few seconds the group started to walk toward the street. Grant turned and spoke to Ruth. "I don't think they'll be giving us any more trouble. At least for now."

"But what happens if we try and leave the house to go

somewhere?" asked Ruth.

"Like you said, they do have rights as the press," answered Grant. "As soon as we step off of this property they'll be on us like a bear on a bee hive, but let's not worry about that now."

Stretching, he yawned, "If it's alright I think I'll head up and take a nap with Dana Beth. I didn't get much sleep at the hospital."

"Go right ahead," said Ruth. "I might take a short nap myself. I'm going to plop down on the couch for an hour or so."

The bedroom was dark. Dana Beth had pulled all the blinds shut. Removing his shoes, he slipped beneath the covers and put his arm around her shoulders. Instantly, she shrugged and pushed his arm away. Grant, surprised, sat up and turned on a table lamp next to the bed. "What's wrong? Are you mad?"

Dana Beth pulled her legs up toward her stomach in the fetal position and jerked the covers up around her neck.

Grant insisted, "I know you're wide awake. You said at the hospital, we had a lot to talk over. I think right now might be a good time."

Without turning over, she asked, "How long have you known the truth about my father?"

Here it is! Thought Grant. *The moment I've been dreading! There's no use to pretend I don't know. Russell must have told her about Conrad.* "I've known since the day before your father died. He told me everything on Thanksgiving day last year out on the porch."

Dana Beth sat up and kicked off the covers as she stared directly at Grant. "So, it's true then. My father was a serial killer! He killed those four people! God! I was hoping Russell was lying, that he made the whole thing up. I can't believe this!"

Grant wanted to hold her—to tell her how sorry he was for keeping the secret, but most of all because it was true. He searched for the right words but the only thing he could think to do was to be honest. "I was hoping you and Ruth would never find out. I wanted to keep the terrible part of your father's life a secret and let you and Ruth, along with everyone else believe that Russell was responsible for all the murders. I was only trying to protect you and your Mom from knowing the truth."

Dana Beth looked up at the ceiling as if she couldn't believe what she was hearing. "What were you trying to protect me from, Grant? My father was already dead! Did you think I couldn't handle the truth?"

"You had just recently found out you were pregnant and I knew how much you loved your father. I remember how you grieved for months after he died. I was worried that the stress would be too much for you and I had no idea how Ruth would react when eventually the whole town would find out that Conrad was a murderer."

Dana Beth shook her head. "Who else knows?"

Chief Blue and Dalton. I had to tell Chief Blue so he could help me cover up what really happened and so that we could catch Russell. I went to Dalton for advice. I told him on Labor Day."

"That's what you were talking about when I surprised the two of you out in the barn. I knew something was up. Why do I feel so betrayed?" She began to cry as she rocked back and forth, tears rolling down her cheeks. "My father just didn't go out and shoot those people. He had to torture them and make them suffer! What kind of a sick person was he? The father I knew was kind and gentle and I know he loved me! He loved my mother and animals and he loved his work. Who was this man I called dad? He hid away his brother and his past. This man did horrible things to people! This man you speak of couldn't have been my father!" She buried her face in her hands.

"Dana Beth. Your father was sick. He was a psychopath. He was leading a double life, just like the second financial life that Marshall Case told us about...only much worse. Your father never connected what he did in his secret life with you or your mother. I know all this is hard to believe but it's the truth." He tried to put his arms around her once again, but she pushed him away. Trying to rectify the situation he found himself in, he explained, "I love you, Dana Beth. I know it's going to be hard for you to accept what has happened and it may even be harder for you to know that I kept all this a secret. I wish I could just take away all the pain you must be feeling, but I can't! I did what I thought was best at the time. It's too late for me to take it back. I can only say I'm sorry and I'm here to help you in any way I can to make sense of this."

Giving Grant an icy stare, Dana Beth spoke slowly and firmly, "You can't help me, Grant. I need to figure this out by myself. All those years my father led a secret life and ever since he confessed to you, you've had your own secrets! It's just too much for me to handle right now. Please don't tell my mother any of this. I'll tell her when the time is right."

Grant sat on the edge of the bed. "I know you think this is all about you, but you're wrong. How do you think I felt carrying around this burden all this time? You don't have any idea how many times I just wanted to come to you and tell you the truth, but I couldn't bring myself to do it. Something else: the last couple of days hasn't exactly been a cakewalk for me. Between worrying about you when you were in the hospital, not to mention the fact that I had just recently killed a man, I've been a nervous wreck!"

Grant stood and turned out the light. "You need to try and get some rest. Sitting here in bed arguing is getting us nowhere." Leaning over the bed he kissed her on the forehead. "Let's not forget what's really important in our lives. We'll get through this...I promise."

Dana Beth slept through the night and awoke to the smell of bacon. She had no idea what time it was. Grant's side of the bed looked as if he hadn't slept there. She threw on her robe and walked into Crystal Ann's room. The crib was empty. Going downstairs to the kitchen she saw Ruth standing at the stove, "Good morning, Mother."

Ruth returned a good morning of her own and then smiled as she said, "You slept all through yesterday and through the night. I hope you're feeling better."

"I do feel better, thank you." Crystal Ann was sitting in her highchair eating Cheerios. Dana Beth picked her up and planted a number of kisses on her cheeks. "Good morning, my sweet pie!" The baby giggled and reached down for another Cheerio. Dana Beth placed her back in the highchair and sat next to her.

"I have scrambled eggs, bacon and toast," announced Ruth. "Can I make you a plate?"

Dana Beth nodded, "I'm starving, that sounds great. Where's

Grant. Did he go to work this morning?"

"No, he's running some errands for me. I'm afraid to go out the door with all those reporters hanging around out front. I needed a few things from the store and I wanted him to stop by a newsstand. I want to read what people are saying about us."

"Why do you care, Mom? They'll print whatever they want, even if it isn't the truth as long as it sells their magazines. We know what really happened and that's all that matters!"

Ruth set Dana Beth's breakfast down in front of her then sat on the opposite side of the table. "That's the problem! I don't know what happened and from the way you reacted when you got home yesterday, I don't think you want to answer any questions."

Pushing the plate of food to the side, Dana Beth leaned on the table. "Okay, tell me what you want to know and I'll try to answer your questions."

Ruth stammered for a moment, but then began, "I want to know what happened when Russell came to the cabin and I want to know about him. After all, he was your father's brother. I just can't believe how different they were."

Not as different as you may think, Dana Beth thought. "When Russell first came in the cabin, I was scared to death. Here I was face to face with a man who I thought was dead. Besides that, he looked terrible. I had no idea what he was going to do. He was so loud and angry at first, but then he calmed down when I told him who I was. He was hungry so I let him eat the food you packed for us." Giving Ruth a smile, she explained, "He loved your cookies. We talked for a few minutes and I actually felt sorry for him. He was like a child in a man's body. He seemed confused and not really sure what he was going to do. He talked with me about dad. He really missed him and I think he felt totally lost without someone to look after him."

"Did he say anything about me?" Ruth asked.

Dana Beth nodded, "He only said he wished he had got to know you. He seemed to be more interested in me and Crystal Ann. When we went outside his mood changed and I began to worry about what he was going to do. I don't think he planned on doing me any harm, but he made it clear that he was going to kill Grant."

Ruth sat back and placed her hand across her heart, "Oh my!"

Dana Beth continued, "I had to stop him, so when Grant got to the cave, I pushed Russell, and well, you know the rest. I fell down and Grant shot him."

Ruth placed her hand over her mouth. "This is all so horrible! I know Grant must be having a hard time himself. He had to realize even though Russell was your uncle and my brother-in-law that he was a total stranger to us. Russell was Conrad's secret."

"Mom, it's really hard for me to believe that in all your years of marriage dad never mentioned him."

"Oh, there were times when he acted like he wanted to tell me something, but then he would always back off and say 'never mind.' I never mentioned this to you before, but Conrad had his dark side. There were times I remember when he'd lock himself away in his study for hours on end, sometimes a day or two. He'd only come out to eat or go to the bathroom. Other times he would go off and not even let me know where he was going or when he was coming back." She stopped talking for a moment as if she didn't want to say the words that were on her mind. Finally, she spoke again, "For awhile, I thought he was having an affair. When I confronted him with it, he became very angry and for the first time in my life I was a little afraid of him."

"And you just let it go? You're a better person than I am! I think I would have been even more determined to find out what he was hiding."

"Looking back I suppose I should have. But, most of the time your father was a wonderful, loving husband. I know he loved me and we shared a lot of good times together. For sure, he loved you more than anyone. So, I just let it go in order to keep peace in the house. I guess it was wrong, but there is nothing I can do about that now."

Dana Beth remained silent as she thought, *I want to scream at my mother! I want to tell her that her husband was a murderer! Conrad was much worse than Russell who may or may not have realized the severity of his crimes. But my father knew! He planned the murders and carried them out like judge and executioner! I can't say the words. I can't tell her!*

The front door slammed, causing both Ruth and Dana Beth to jump. Grant marched into the kitchen and set two bags of groceries on the counter. "Dammit! I'm just about at the end of my rope! If one more of those reporters gets in my face, I'm going to punch their lights out! When I left, they followed me all the way into town. Inside the IGA they dogged me everywhere I went asking me questions. When I finally got back outside, I had one hell of a time getting out of the parking lot." Walking to the front window, he looked out. "Those bloodsucking bastards are still out there parked on the street!"

"Grant please, watch your language," remarked Ruth as she pretended to cover Crystal Ann's ears. "You don't want your daughter's first words to be bastard!"

"I'm sorry," apologized Grant. "I just want this to be over. Axel called me and said he wanted me to come back to work today. Hell, those newshounds will be trailing me all day." Looking at Ruth and Dana Beth he apologized again, "Look, you guys, I'm really sorry!" He kissed his wife on top of her head and walked back to the kitchen where he started to put up the groceries. Pulling two magazines and the morning paper from one of the bags he tried to hide then behind the toaster.

"Give me those," Dana Beth said. Taking the baby, she grabbed them from Grant and headed up the stairs.

After laying Crystal Ann on the bed she flipped open one of the magazines to an article entitled: SERIAL KILLER KILLED FOR THE SECOND TIME? Another article read: HUSBAND KILLS HIS WIFE'S UNCLE IN STANDOFF! Just as she threw the magazine against the wall, the doorbell rang. She heard Grant cursing again as he went to the front door.

A few seconds passed when Ruth came into the room and spoke softly, "Grant needs you downstairs right now. I'll watch the baby. There are some men here to see you. Grant says it's important."

At the bottom of the stairs Dana Beth saw two well dressed men sitting in the living room. They politely stood when she entered the room. Pulling her robe close to her body, she shot Grant a look as if to say, *You could have at least told me to get dressed first!*

Grant made the introductions, "Dana Beth, these two gentlemen are from Marshall Case's office. Mr. Case is going to be out of town for a month and he wants you to sign some documents that would transfer Russell's estate over to you. According to these gentlemen, it's going to take a while to get all the paperwork done, but this will give Mr. Case the authority to get things rolling. This is Mr..."

Dana Beth interrupted Grant, "I don't need to know their names. I really think this is all very premature. I don't want to sign anything right now! I'm sorry you had to make the trip down here for nothing, but all of this can be handled at a later date!" With that, she turned and left the room.

It wasn't even a minute later when Grant bounded up the stairs two at a time and then entered the bedroom. Confronting his wife, he asked, "Could you please tell me what that was all about? All they wanted was a couple of simple signatures, but you sent them on their way!"

Dana Beth, sitting on the edge of the bed, picked up the baby. "I don't give one iota about the money. As far as I'm concerned, they can just give it all away to charity."

Ruth, who was folding some towels, seemed confused as she asked, "What money?"

Dana Beth waved her hand in the air, "Oh, just five million dollars! Money and investments that dad put in Russell's name and now that he is dead, it belongs to me. Isn't that wonderful!" she said sarcastically. "I get all the money that dad could have been sharing with you instead of keeping it in a bank and supporting his half-wit brother!"

Grant was stunned. Ruth was speechless. "I guess we'll talk about this later," said Grant as he left the room. He had never experienced the level of anger that now encompassed his wife.

Ruth was about to speak, but was prevented from doing so as Dana Beth raised her hand. "Mom, I know I've got a lot of explaining to do, but now is not the time. Please be patient with me. I want to ask you a question. Does Aunt Grace still have her condo in Fort Meyers?"

Ruth nodded. "Yes, she does."

"Would you please call her and see if it would be alright if we spent some time down there. I really need to get away from here...soon! I want you and the baby with me. Will you do that for me?"

"I guess, I mean if that's what you want...sure. Let me give

Grace a call."

Later that morning, sitting in the living room, it wasn't easy telling Grant she was leaving. She could see the hurt and the sadness in his eyes. "Why?" he asked.

"I just need to get away for awhile, Grant. This pain that I'm feeling is hard to explain. I can't touch it or taste it or smell it, but I can feel it! It's constantly on my mind. I feel like I have a huge weight pressing down on my shoulders and if I don't find some way to deal with it, it'll eventually crush me! Right now, I can't be the person I was a week ago. I can't talk to people I know or our friends and tell them I'm doing fine. I don't want to answer the questions I know people are dying to ask me: How are you feeling? How does it feel to know that your uncle was a serial killer and your husband had to kill him? And let's not forget: How does it feel to be a millionaire? I don't know how it feels to be any of those things. Let's face it. I'm the daughter of a serial killer! I can't answer the questions people want to know." Dana Beth stood and walked to the large front window. "They're still out there, Grant. I need this time away so I can become human again and stop being a robot going through the motions of trying to act normal after everything that's happened. Forgive me, but I've got to do this. Ruth, Crystal Ann and I are going down to Ft. Meyers to Aunt Grace's condo. I promise you, I'll be back. I'll call you when I get there."

Grant leaned forward trying to understand. "I just don't see how running away is going to make things any easier for you."

"I really wish you could, Grant. Like I said, I'll call you. Don't worry, I'll be with Mom and Crystal. We'll be okay. Considering all of the media that doesn't seem to be leaving any time soon, it might be for the best if you just close up the house and go stay at Dalton's. Once we're gone for a few days, then maybe they'll pack up and leave."

Grant stood. "How long do you think you'll be gone?"

Walking over to her husband, she kissed him on the cheek and started up the stairs to the bedroom. "I don't know, Grant. I just don't know. Please be patient with me and try to understand."

CHAPTER FIFTEEN

THE HOUSE LOOKED THE SAME: TWO STORY, WHITE siding, black window shutters, fieldstone chimney. The white wicker furniture was still there on the front porch where he had spent many an evening enjoying a cup of coffee or glass of iced tea. The house held quite a few good memories for Grant. How many times during high school had he driven up the driveway, bounded up the front porch steps only to be greeted by Dana Beth at the front door? How many times had he kissed her good night on that porch after bringing her home following a date? More recently, over the past two years, how many meals had he shared with his wife, daughter and mother-in law inside the house? How many evenings had he tucked Crystal Ann in for the night?

Staring at the house, Grant noticed seven rolled up newspapers scattered across the front porch, the two trashcans laying on their side in the driveway; signs that clearly stated life had stopped in the house. Getting out of his Jeep, he realized that along with all the good memories he had experienced in the house there were also things that were not so good. Secrets, that at least for the moment seemed to be destroying his life. Stepping up onto the porch, he gathered up the newspapers as he stared at the chair Conrad had sat in that evening over a year past and had confided in him about not only the fact that he had cancer and would soon die, but that he had killed four people. Walking around the side of the house, Grant remembered something Chief Blue had told him shortly after they had first met. It was an old Cherokee Indian saying: *If you don't tell the truth, someone else will tell it for you.* In this case, despite the fact Grant had managed to keep the truth from his wife and mother-in-law, Russell Pearl was that *someone* who revealed the truth about Conrad. He glanced at the garage and thought about yet another secret hidden in the overhead storage area: all of the incriminating clues about Conrad.

Righting the trash cans, he placed the newspapers inside, walked to the side door and unlocked the house. Stepping into the kitchen, he missed the smell of Ruth's cooking. He missed Crystal

Ann's toys scattered all over the house. He missed his wife's great smile. He missed lying in bed next to her at night.

He sat in his favorite chair in the living room and looked around the interior of the house. Everything was the same. The grandfather clock still stood in the corner. Dana Beth's homemade flower arrangement sat on the coffee table. Her collection of wooden angels still graced the mantel over the stone fireplace. The house was full of material objects and memories, yet still seemed cold and empty. His wife, child and mother-in-law had left him. He had no one to blame but himself. If he would have been honest from the beginning maybe then this wouldn't have happened. Picking up the framed photograph of he, Dana Beth and Crystal Ann, he laid the picture on his chest and wept. Despite the fact Dana Beth had called him from Ft. Meyers and assured him they had arrived and were okay, still, he couldn't recall a time in his past life when he had felt more alone.

Backing out of the driveway, he wondered how long he was going to be able to keep the fact that his wife and family were no longer in town. The newspaper boy had no doubt already noticed that the papers had not been taken inside for a week. The neighbors would soon notice there was no normal activity around the property. Since Grant was staying at Dalton's farm for the past week, his Jeep would not be parked in the driveway. Dana Beth's car would not be present either. It was just a matter of time until someone started asking questions.

He had to stop as the traffic was backed up on the Parkway. Looking to his left, he saw Zeb sitting alone at his table in the front window of the Parkway Grocery nursing his morning coffee. From all appearances he and Buddie were still on the outs. Grant slouched back in the seat and gazed at the distant Smoky Mountains. All along he had been of the opinion that when Russell was finally declared officially dead things would begin to return to normal. *Not so!* There were still too many unanswered questions that continued to haunt Townsend. Who killed Luke Pardee? Were Zeb and Buddie somehow involved in his death? Were they part of the hunting party that had killed the Pender's forty some years ago? If it was true that Russell killed Arliss and Dwayne, were the

Stroud's involved with Russell in some fashion? What happened to Ruby Jean Stroud? What did the crayon drawing that Turnbull had given him mean? Would peace ever return to his life? Sooner or later he was going to have to tell Brody and Marge that Dana Beth had left town. Of course, he didn't have to tell them, or anyone as far as he was concerned, the truth. He could simply say she and the baby went with Ruth down to the shore for a couple of weeks. But then again, if they were gone for more than a month, people were going to get suspicious and ask questions. He knew Dalton and Greta wouldn't say a word. He could trust them.

Finally arriving at the Townsend Police Department, Grant sat in the Jeep for a minute and tried to regain some level of normalcy. He knew he could continue to fool Brody, but Marge would notice as soon as he walked in that something was wrong. For the past week at work he had been able to pull off the charade that everything in his life was normal, but as the days wore on he wondered how long he could shield what was really going on with his immediate family. The one good thing that had happened was that Brody had rescinded his order for Grant to hand over his gun and badge. Lee Griner was off sick with the flu and Kenny was out of town at his uncle's funeral. Axel was too short handed to put Grant on leave until things got, according to Brody, *sorted out.* Taking a deep breath he thought, *Time to go to work!*

Marge, as usual was positioned at her desk. When Grant walked in the office she was on the phone. She mouthed a silent, "Good morning!" Entering Brody's office, he was surprised to find Doug Eland seated across from Axel's desk.

"Ah...just in time," said Axel. "Have a seat, Grant. Doug was just about to tell me about a potential problem he's havin'."

Grant pulled a folding chair up to the desk as he reached for Doug's hand. "Morning, Doug. How's that new business going?"

"Not that well," answered Doug with a troubled look on his face. "Remember last week when I gave you a call and told you some strange things were happening to me?"

"Yeah, I do recall that. That was the night I brought Dana Beth home. You'll have to forgive me. I had a lot on my mind that evening. Things around the ol' house were not exactly what one would call normal. But I do remember what you told me. Let's see, you said that over the past few days your mailbox had been destroyed, your riding lawn mower had been stolen and some windows had been busted out at your shop."

"That's right, and I think Ambrose Stroud is living up to the threat he leveled at me that day you guys hauled him off for child abandonment. He said that I hadn't heard the last of him. You said, at the time of my call, you had a lot on your plate and that I needed to give Chief Brody a call. Well, when I got to thinking about it, I figured it was just some small town vandalism so I let it slide. This week hasn't been any better, if anything it's gotten worse. Our dog was poisoned on Monday, but luckily we got him to the vet in time and he managed to survive. Last night our shop was broken into and then this morning, the worst yet. My wife, Max, is over at the IGA shopping when none other than Ambrose Stroud runs into her with a shopping cart and knocks her on her ass. We took her over to the hospital. She suffered a broken wrist, twisted her ankle and lost two teeth in the process."

Axel held up his hand, asking, "And you think Ambrose Stroud is responsible for all these things?"

"Yes, yes I do! I think he's trying to get even with me for breaking into his car and trying to save his daughter. You heard what he said...you were standing right there when he threatened me. You also said you were going to go out to the Stroud's and have a talk with them. I don't know what you said to them, but it looks to me that it made no difference. It costs me two hundred dollars to get my tires replaced, another fifty bucks to get my mailbox repaired and the mower that was stolen was brand new. I had just purchased it. Cost me eight hundred. Replacing the busted windows in my shop wasn't any big deal, but when it was broken into, well hell, I haven't even calculated the damage as of yet. It's gonna run me thousands with all the damage that was done to the merchandise and the building. The vet bill ran me nearly one hundred fifty and who knows what the hospital bill will run me. Ambrose is costing me a small fortune, but that's not the point. After this morning at the IGA I feel our lives are in danger."

Grant spoke up as he apologized, "Doug, I'm so sorry that I didn't take your phone call more serious. I should have come to Chief Brody myself and discussed the situation with him personally."

Brody interrupted, "Now just hold on a sec! First of all, there is no one in this county who hates the Stroud's more than me. If it was up to me I'd run the whole lot out of here on a rail. But, I have to uphold the law...for everyone! Let me ask you this, Mr. Eland. Do you have any actual proof other than Ambrose's verbal threat?"

"Proof! You heard what the man said. He's doing exactly what he said he'd do. Our pet almost died! My wife got injured! What's next? I can replace tires and windows and mailboxes. I can't replace a life. I feel my family is in danger!"

"Mr. Eland...Doug. Calm down," said Axel. "I get the feeling that you'd just as soon have me drive out to the Stroud's, throw the cuffs on Ambrose and haul his ass off to jail. Believe me. I'd like nothin' better. But you have to understand, I just can't arrest someone for just sayin' somethin'. I have to have solid proof."

"What more proof do you need other than what happened at the IGA parking lot?" said Doug loudly. "Ambrose Stroud nearly choked me to death!" Pulling his shirt collar to the side he pointed to his wounds. "You can still see the abrasions on my neck. He hit the store manager and tossed Grant over top of his car. He was like a wild man. You yourself, Brody, said he was a crazy bastard!"

"Ambrose might be a crazy bastard," said Grant, "but he's not as stupid as we might make him out to be. If he or the members of his family have done all these things you claim, they haven't left a clue behind. Now, you say Ambrose knocked your wife for a loop over at the IGA. What did he do, what did he say after it happened?"

Doug scooted forward on his chair as if he had a revelation. "You're right, Grant! Ambrose may be smarter than we're giving him credit for. My wife said that after he knocked her over, he actually helped her to her feet and apologized and told one of the employees to call an ambulance. She said he couldn't have been nicer. Of course, at the time she had no idea who he was. She knew about the incident involving Ambrose abandoning his child and how he threatened me, but she had never met him. It wasn't until they were on their way to the hospital when she mentioned how nice the man was who knocked her down, that one of the paramedics told her it was Ambrose Stroud." Doug held up his index finger to make his point. "He's a lot smarter than we think. He abused my wife and yet has everyone at the store thinking it was an accident. Well, I'm here to tell you it wasn't an accident. He ran into her on purpose! Something has to be done...and now! Ambrose Stroud cannot be allowed to continue to hassle my family. It's not right. It's against the law and you, Chief Brody, have to do something about it before somebody gets killed!"

Axel made a face. "You can't really expect me to believe Ambrose Stroud would kill you or your wife because of what happened over there that day in the IGA parking lot?"

"That's exactly what I mean *and* when I said someone could get killed I was not just referring to my family. I have a registered handgun and a license to go along with it. I carry it with me when I go on remote photo shoots. I mean hell, when you're out in the woods there's no telling what you might run into. Like last year over in Virginia. I was taking some photos when three black bear cubs come running out of nowhere. Before I knew there was their mother, a three-hundred pound female. When she saw me in the same close vicinity to her cubs she started for me. Three shots in the air chased both her and the cubs off. That's the only time I ever had to fire that gun, but I swear to God if Ambrose Stroud ever so much as puts his hands on me or my wife again, I'll take him out!"

Grant interjected, "Doug, ease up some! If you shoot Ambrose Stroud and there's the slightest chance you were mistaken, you'll go to prison for murder. Let the law take care of this."

"That's what I'm trying to do!" Looking directly at Axel, Doug slammed his fist down on the desk. "What are you going to do about this Brody?"

Axel pointed his finger at Doug and suggested strongly, "Grant's right, you need to ease up. Now, I suggest that you go home and let us take care of the situation. Grant and I will pay the Stroud's a visit this afternoon. But, I've got to tell you until we catch Ambrose in the act there's nothin' else we can do. The law is the law and believe it or not, I hate to say this, but Ambrose Stroud has rights just like anyone else. We can't go marchin' up to his place and start accusin' him of somethin' we have no actual proof of. Now, considerin' what's happened to you I can see where you might find that hard to believe. This isn't the ol' west where a person could just go out and shoot a man and be justified in doin' so. I guess we've become more civilized. Like I said, I have a deep dislike for the Stroud's and if I had the power to make them disappear, I'd be the first one to wave the magic wand. But the thing is, I represent the law and there are boundaries I cannot cross...and neither can you! Now, go on and get out of here and don't worry so much. We'll take care of this."

Doug stood, reached out and shook Brody's hand as he apologized, "I'm sorry, Chief Brody. I didn't mean to go off on you like that. I'm just concerned...that's all. My wife has really been on my case. I guess I can't blame her. I told her how peaceful it was here. Then, she hears about all the murders we've had here the past two years, plus Ambrose Stroud nearly chokes the life out of me and now all these strange things that have happened to us, especially her getting injured by Ambrose himself. Things haven't turned out quite the way I told her they would here in Townsend. Listen, at least give me a call will you? Let me know how you made out up there at the Stroud's."

Doug no sooner left the office when Grant took the chair he had been sitting in as Brody asked, "So you already knew about this?"

"Just the first few things he mentioned about the mailbox and the mower. I guess maybe I should have called you. When he called I had my own problems to deal with. My wife was still recovering from her concussion plus I was still dealing with shooting Pearl up there in the mountains. I figured he'd come speak with you like I told him."

Axel stood and walked to the window and looked out. "The Stroud's! Looks like they might turn out to be our next round of turmoil here in Townsend. With everythin' we think we may have discovered about them recently, this recent turn of events concernin' Eland might just be the straw that breaks the camel's back." Walking to the water dispenser in the corner, Axel poured a cupful and gulped it down in seconds. "The Feds have backed off for now, especially since Russell Pearl is dead. Like you told me when we were in Knoxville. The Stroud's are our problem." Taking down the crayoned drawing from a small corkboard, Axel stated, "I've been goin' over everythin' we have on the Stroud's this past week and it still doesn't add up. Like this drawin'. It would seem that Russell Pearl was in contact with Violet, Ruby Jean's daughter. The word is that Ruby Jean ran off, but then you told me what Buddie said about Violet claimin' that she sees her mother every day. I keep thinkin' that the stick figure in this drawin' that's layin' down in these drawn flowers represents Ruby Jean. Maybe she didn't run off. Maybe she's actually buried up there on their property. On top of that, we find Russell's fingerprints in Cletus' truck which is found parked under the cabin, approximately twenty miles from where Arliss and Dwayne are found murdered. Russell Pearl is dead and yet we're still missin' somethin' here. Nothin' adds up. The one thing I'm sure of is Ambrose hasslin' Doug Eland has nothin' to do with any of this. It's a separate incident."

"I agree," said Grant. "It is a separate matter, just like Luke Pardee's murder. I don't think Luke was murdered by Russell Pearl. Now that Pearl is dead I plan on following up on some suspicions I have, but for now we need to handle the situation currently at hand: Ambrose Stroud."

Brody grabbed his hat. "We'll take my truck up there. Oh, and one other thing I need to mention. When I said that I'd talk with the Stroud's about Ambrose's initial threat. I didn't. When I got to their place and gave them the news about Ambrose being hauled off to jail and his daughter being taken into custody by Child Services, plus the fact that Ambrose's two seven-year-olds ran off into the woods, it slipped my mind."

"So what you're telling me is this will be the first warning the Stroud's have gotten from us in regard to Ambrose's threat."

"That's right, and this visit will be just as unpleasant as any other time we've had to go over there. It could wind up being a waste of time. Ambrose might not even be at home."

"If he is at home," stated Grant, "but not out front selling with Maude and Otis we're going to play hell getting to talk with him. We don't have a search warrant to go onto their property. If that's the case, then we'll have to talk with Maude about something else one of her stupid sons may have possibly done."

Brody pulled out of the parking lot. "Maude might not even know about this. If what Doug says is true this might be a personal vendetta that's being waged by Ambrose himself."

Grant, fastening his seatbelt, looked to his right and saw Doug and Max's gift shop sitting back from the road. "Ya know it's a shame. Doug is one of the nicest people I've ever met and his wife seems like a peach. They were so excited about moving here to Townsend, buying a house, opening up their own business and what happens? The bottom falls out. You have to admit, Axel, that in just two weeks they've had more than their share of unfortunate instances."

Turning on the truck heater, Axel coughed and answered, "We'll get to the bottom of all this."

Grant did a double-take as he tapped Axel on his shoulder. "That might be sooner than you think, Chief. You must be living right. I swear I just saw Ambrose Stroud changing a tire on that old car of his."

Surprised, Brody exclaimed, "Where?"

"Back there on the side of the road. Ironically, just down from Eland's shop. Turn around. This might be our lucky day. We might get to talk with Ambrose without having to deal with Maude."

Brody turned into a restaurant parking lot and started back down the parkway. Just as Grant said, there was Ambrose on the side of road kneeling down next to the driver's side tire. "Well, I'll be dipped," said Axel. "This *is* our lucky day. We get to talk with ol' Ambrose Stroud without his nutcase family bein' present."

Pulling to the side of the road in a lot of a business that had been closed for some time, Axel and Grant got out and crossed the street. Ambrose picked up a tire iron from the ground and began to unloosen a lug nut. Stopping at the rear of the car, Axel spoke, "Well, well, of all the folks to meet on the parkway with car troubles, if it ain't my ol' friend Ambrose."

Ambrose turned and looked up, seeing both Grant and Axel standing by the road. With a look of disgust on his face, he spit on the ground and commented, "Yeah, well there's all kind of vermin on the side of the road: dead skunks, groundhogs, an occasional cat, but I'm lookin' at Townsend's finest. The fat assed Chief of Police and one of his stupid sidekicks." Continuing to loosen the lug nut, Ambrose kept right on talking, "Officer Denlinger, the last time I saw ya, ya was flyin' over the top of this here car over at the IGA. How'd that work out for ya?"

Ignoring Ambrose's cutting remarks, Axel ordered, "Get up, we need to talk."

Pitching the nut to the side, Ambrose placed the tire iron on another and began to loosen it. "I do somethin' wrong, Brody? Is it against the law ta have a flat out here by the Parkway? Mebbe ya wanna have a look in the backseat for abandoned children!"

Axel took a step forward and ordered again, "I told you to get up and I ain't gonna say it again!"

Ambrose threw down the iron, stood slowly and walked toward Brody, stopping just inches from his face. "I reckon yer right. I should git up. If I don't I might jest git another beatin' from ya and yer dumb ass deputy." Looking down into Brody's face, he sneered, "What's yer problem?"

Brody, not about to back down, put his hand on his holstered revolver and ordered sternly, "Back up some Stroud or you and I are gonna dance right here in the street!"

Glancing quickly toward Grant who unsnapped his revolver, Ambrose stepped back and leaned against the side of his car as he laughed. "Without those guns both of ya couldn't whup me!"

Now that it appeared that Ambrose had calmed down at least for the moment, Axel removed his hand from his gun. "We got a complaint late this morning that might involve you. You remember Doug Eland?"

"Yeah, I know who he is," said Ambrose sharply. "That bastard who broke out my window and tried ta kidnap my daughter. He's the one ya shoulda thrown in jail. I was jest protectin' what's mine! I got rights jest like anybody else around these parts."

"That's right, Ambrose, you do have rights and so does Doug Eland. He came into my office this morning reportin' that he's had quite a few strange things happen to not only him, but his family as well."

"A lot of things happen ta a lot of people. What's that got ta do with me?"

"The day we took you over to Maryville, you verbally threatened Mr. Eland by sayin' he hadn't heard the last of you."

Ambrose spit again. "So, that don't mean nothin'!"

"That's where you're wrong Ambrose. "If you act upon what you say, that's against the law."

Looking Brody square in the eyes, Ambrose smirked, "Don't have no idea what yer talkin' about."

"Eland claims he had his mailbox smashed, his lawn mower stolen and some windows at his shop broken out," explained Axel. "That was last week. This week he claims his dog was poisoned, his shop was broken into and ransacked and his wife was run down at the grocery store by none other than you. She suffered a broken wrist, twisted ankle and some missing teeth. Can you explain any of those things?"

Ambrose smiled as he answered, "Don't know nothin' about any of those things except the grocery. I run into her, but that was an accident. I didn't even know it was Eland's wife until ya jest mentioned it. I helped her up, even apologized. That some kinda crime?"

Brody moved closer to Ambrose and pointed his finger up into his face. "Eland thinks you're the one responsible for all the problems he's been havin'. Claims you're tryin' to get even with him. He feels he and his wife are in danger. I can't let somethin' like that just slide on by. Here's the deal, Ambrose. If I find out you had anythin' to do with hasslin' Doug Eland or his wife I'll be on you like green on grass!" Poking his finger into Ambrose's chest, Brody emphasized, "Understand!"

Ambrose looked down at Axel with a distinct look of hatred on his bearded face. Jabbing Ambrose in the chest again with his finger, Axel smiled confidently, "You don't like that do ya, Ambrose? You'd like to take a swing at me...wouldn't you? Well, go right ahead. There's nothin' more I'd like to do than toss your hillbilly ass back in jail. I know for a fact that Merle Pittman bailed your ass out last time but he can't keep your type out of jail forever." With that, Axel got right beneath Ambrose's face and stated, "Ya just can't fix stupid!"

Backing off, Axel bent down and picked up the tire iron and handed it to Ambrose. "Now if I was you I'd get that tire changed right quick. Then you can move your sorry ass and that piece of crap car of yours. We've got enough trash on the side of the road. We'll be drivin' by in the next fifteen minutes. You better be gone or I might change my mind and really get pissed!" Turning to Grant, he ordered, "Come on, I don't like the stench around here!" Halfway across the street, Axel yelled back at Ambrose, "Remember Stroud...fifteen minutes! Move it!"

Back in the truck, as they pulled out, Grant asked, "You've got more guts than I do, Axel. There's no way I would have handed that man that tire iron. He'd of beat you to a pulp before I could of pulled my gun."

"We got lucky," said Axel. "I could tell from the look on his face that we had the upper hand. He was intimidated." Tapping the badge on his chest he commented, "A badge and a loud voice can at times be very convincin'. If he is responsible for what Eland claims, at least we gave him somethin' to think about."

Looking back at Ambrose, who was now on his knees once again, Grant probed, "So, do you think that'll be the end of it?"

"I'm not sure," said Axel. "With everythin' that seems to be pointin' at the Stroud's right now with their possible involvement with Russell Pearl, we might be headed for a war with that family. Today was just a battle, but a battle we won!"

CHAPTER SIXTEEN

THE BUZZING OF HIS CELL PHONE AWOKE GRANT AS he stared up into the dark ceiling of his room. The glowing red numerals on the alarm clock on the nightstand indicated the time at two-thirty in the morning. His first thought was that it might be Dana Beth calling. Who else would have a reason to call him in the middle of the night? He hoped it wasn't Brody. Something might have happened that required him to go into work. Rolling to the side of the bed he scooped up the phone, flipped up the cover and answered in a sleep filled voice, "Hello."

Doug Eland's voice sounded stressed as he spoke, "Grant! This is Doug. I need your help! My wife and I were attacked! We just got back from the hospital. I need to talk with you as soon as possible!"

Turning on a small table lamp, Grant wiped the sleep from his eyes and tried to comprehend the words he was hearing. "Grant! Did you hear me? We were attacked!"

"Attacked? What are you talking about?" asked Grant as he sat on the edge of the bed.

"I don't want to discuss this over the phone," said Doug. "The Stroud's attacked us earlier tonight. Max and I are at our wit's end. Please! I need to talk with you. Can you drive over to our house?"

"Of course I can. Give me the address. I'll be there as soon as I can get dressed and on the road."

Supplying Grant with the address, Doug added, "And don't tell Brody I called. He doesn't know about any of this. I'll explain what happened when you get here. See ya in a few."

Grant got up and walked down the hall to the upstairs bath where he splashed cold water on his face. On the way back to his room he ran into Dalton, who was coming down the hall. "Dalton, I've got to run over to Doug Eland's place. He and his wife were attacked. I'll be back as soon as I can."

Dalton, not quite awake, asked in a confused voice, "Attacked? By who?"

"I'm not really sure yet. I'll fill you in when I get back. I've gotta run."

It wasn't even ten minutes later, dressed in jeans, sweatshirt and sneakers, when Grant jumped in the Jeep, backed down the driveway and headed down the Parkway. Rolling down the driver's side window, the cold night air hit him in the face bringing him to a state of total alertness.

Locating Doug's address, he spotted the lit sign in the front yard that read: ELAND'S WILDLIFE PHOTOGRAPHY. Turning onto the gravel drive it was only thirty yards when he pulled up in front of the two story log home, every light in the house burning brightly. Doug was sitting on a porch swing as he awaited Grant's arrival. Grant was no sooner out of the Jeep when Doug stood and signaled him, "Come on, inside…quick!"

Grant stepped into a small foyer, while Doug looked back across the front yard, closed the door and locked it. Leading the way, he motioned toward a large living room. "Let's go in here where we can sit and talk."

Max was sitting on a couch in the vaulted room, her right wrist in a sling, a baseball bat centered between her legs. Before Grant could say anything, Doug ushered him to a large cushioned chair across from the comfortable looking fire in the stone hearth. "Have a seat. We've got a lot to talk over."

Doug took a seat next to Max on the couch as he laid his gun on the armrest and took a deep breath. A moment of silence followed, which was finally broken when Grant asked, "What the hell's going on? You two look like a demented Norman Rockwell painting; both of you sitting there with your right arms in slings. You, Doug, with a black eye and what looks like a broken nose and on top of that, a gun at your side. Max, you fared no better. Looks like you've got a severe cut on your mouth and you're holding that bat like a weapon."

Max started to tear up and Doug placed his good arm around her shoulder. "Like I told you on the phone we were attacked. I know it was the Stroud's."

"When did this happen?"

"Just after midnight," said Doug. "We've been working day and night trying to get the shop back up and running. Last night we finally got things back in order. We locked the backdoor of the shop and were taking out two bags of trash. There's no light back there so it was on the dark side. The next thing I know I get pushed from behind and down I go. I was kicked repeatedly and punched in the face once. I couldn't see who they were, but there were two of them, plus the one who was holding Max. She didn't get a look at the one holding her, but did see the two that were working me over. She was fighting to get away from him when he swung her around and she hit her face on the side of the dumpster."

Looking at Max, Grant asked, "You said it was the Stroud's. Did you see their faces?"

"No, they were wearing some crude burlap sacks over their heads and besides that, it was dark. All I can tell you is that they were both big men."

"Can you describe their clothes?"

"Vaguely," said Max. "It was over in less than a minute. I think one was wearing denim coveralls and the other looked like he had jeans and a dark shirt."

"How about the man who was holding you?"

"I never saw him. He grabbed me from behind right after Doug was knocked down. He had one hand over my mouth and with the other held me back. Just before they left, the man wearing coveralls walked over and slapped me across the face." Dabbing at her lip, she remarked, "Those bastards!"

"Then what happened?"

Seeing that his wife was beginning to calm down, Doug walked over to the fireplace and placed another log on the fire. "They just left...never said a word. I know it was the Stroud's."

Grant waved his comment off as he remarked, "We'll get to that later. Right now I want to make sure you're okay."

Seated once again on the couch, Doug answered the question. "After they left and I discovered my arm was broken we went to the hospital. We finally got home about two fifteen and then I called you."

"Now, wait a minute. You said you went to the hospital. Based on your injuries didn't they fill out a police report?"

"No," said Max. "We lied about what happened. We told them Doug fell two stories from a ladder onto his face and right side, hence his broken arm, nose, two fractured ribs and black eye. They bought it, bandaged him up and sent us home. They never even called the police. There was no reason to. It was documented as a simple in-home accident."

Pointing at Max, Grant asked his next question, "They didn't question you about that cut on your mouth?"

"They asked, but we had that covered as well. I told them I got hit in the mouth with the ladder. They gave me two stitches and that was that. The only other injury I sustained were some bruises on my arm where I was held. The other injuries I have," as she displayed her broken wrist, "were from the run-in with Ambrose Stroud at the IGA."

Grant stood, walked to a nearby window, pulled back the drapes and peered out. "How can you be so sure it was the Stroud's?"

"Come on, Grant," said Doug. "You're starting to sound like Brody with all that crap about how the Stroud's have rights and that nothing can really be done until they are caught in the act. Look at us. We look like a train wreck. What more proof do you need?"

Grant returned to his chair and sat. "I'll be the first to admit that Brody isn't the most compassionate man I've ever known, but he does know...and follow the law to the tee. All you can tell me about what happened as far as the assailants are concerned is that two of the three men were on the large size and some vague comments about what they were wearing. If we try and pick the Stroud's up based on simply that, they'll be out of jail in no time *and* you might be facing a law suit."

Max slammed the bat down on the end of the couch. "I'm getting tired of hearing about the Stroud's rights! You've got to be kidding me. Sue us! We haven't done anything wrong! You're telling me that Ambrose Stroud and his family can run around this town doing whatever they please to Doug and me and there's nothing that can be done!" Looking at Doug, she remarked, "I have a feeling that we should have never moved here in the first place; a place where criminals have more rights than law abiding citizens."

"Townsend is no different than any other town. The law is the law. No lawman in their right mind would go after someone without proof. I know it's a hard pill to swallow, but the truth is in today's world, people who don't follow the law have to be stopped by those in law enforcement who *are required* to follow the law to the letter. Believe me, at times, it's not easy to do."

Doug spoke up, "We're not getting anywhere sitting here going back and forth. We need to figure out what we need to do now. I've got an idea. Max, why don't you whip up some breakfast? Maybe after we have something to eat and calm down then we can come up with a solution."

Max smiled. "Breakfast does sound good. I'll get started. It'll probably be about forty-five minutes. I'll put on a pot of coffee."

After Max left the room, Grant asked, "So, at this point I take it you have no intention of telling Chief Brody about the attack?"

"I don't want Brody involved and I hope you'll keep this between you, me and Max," answered Doug. Lowering his voice, he continued, "Let me ask you something I never thought I would say in my life." Holding up the gun, he went on, "What do you really think my chances are of killing Ambrose Stroud and getting away with it?"

Grant buried his face in his hands and mumbled, "My God! This is like a bad movie." He looked at Doug and stated, "I can't condone that. I'm an officer of the law in this town. When you say things like that it makes you just as bad as Ambrose. You can't threaten someone's life like that. I'm your friend, Doug, and there is no way I'm going to let you kill Ambrose Stroud. What if you get caught? He's not worth spending the rest of your life in prison."

"So what you're saying is that I can't threaten Ambrose Stroud's life but he can threaten mine! God, is it any wonder why people want to take the law into their own hands. What other option do I have, Grant? Brody talked with Ambrose just recently and look what it resulted in. My wife and I *were attacked!*"

"Brody is doing everything he can based upon what he has to go on. I was with him when he talked with Ambrose. Believe me, he went up one side of him and down the other. I thought Axel was going to go at it with him right there on the street. Brody wants this to stop just like you, but his hands are tied without something more solid to go on."

Doug and Grant continued to discuss the attack for the next half hour, Grant trying to establish the smallest thing that might indicate the identity of the Stroud's, Doug constantly saying that he had no doubt it was them. Their conversation was finally interrupted when Max announced, "Soup's on!"

Sitting in a small breakfast nook, Grant surveyed their early morning meal: scrambled eggs, sausage, sliced tomatoes, toast, orange juice and a pot of coffee. Max, displaying the table suggested, "Dig in!"

Pouring himself a cup of coffee, Doug spoke to Max, "Grant and I have been discussing what can be done. He has agreed not to go to Chief Brody just yet and I have agreed not to go after Ambrose with my intent to kill him...just yet!"

Scooping some eggs onto her plate, Max shook her head in wonder as she commented, "I can't believe we're having this conversation. If you would have told me months ago when we first met, that we would get married this year, purchase a house and then be up at four in the morning discussing your killing someone from right here in the town where we live, I would have said you were loco! Just listen to yourself, Doug. You take wildlife pictures and I make walking sticks out of branches. We're way out of our league here. There's got to be a rational, more civilized way to deal with this."

Grant, biting into a sausage, remarked as he pointed his fork at Max, "I agree, but then again on the other hand I don't think the Stroud's are the type of people who can be dealt with rationally. They're hard people; people who live in a different world than we do. They hold themselves to a different set of values, one obviously being that if they feel someone has done them wrong, they're bound and determined to get even and feel justified in doing so. If we do decide to report this to Chief Brody all he can do is go and talk with them again. He can threaten them with going to jail, fines and a host of other things, but that's just talk, which at this point I think the Stroud's will let roll off their backs like water."

"What else can we do?" asked Doug. "Do you think it would do any good if I went out there and talked with them, maybe apologized to Ambrose?"

"I don't know," said Grant. "I had a couple of run-ins with Ambrose and I've gone up there to talk with Maude and Otis. They're not the easiest people to deal with. First of all, an apology from you might be misconstrued as an accusation from their point of view. Then again, they might back off and consider things even. But, you realize if that happens then they've won."

"I don't like the idea of them coming out on the winning end of this," said Doug. "If we allow them to get away with what they've done to us and go unpunished, who will be next? They physically hit both my wife and me. I say they need to be stopped!"

Max sat back hopelessly and asked, "How can we, two normal citizens, stop a group of people like the Stroud's?"

"I've got an idea," said Grant. "We need some advice from someone who's been around the block a few times."

Doug sipped at his coffee and asked, "And who might that be?"

"Someone we both know and are friends with...William Blue!"

Max looked at Doug. "Who is William Blue?"

Answering her question, Doug smiled. "William Blue is the Chief of Police over in Cherokee. I introduced Grant to him right after the murders started last year. He is one of the most intelligent men I've ever met. If anyone would know what to do, he would."

"I agree," said Grant. "He's got more insight that the three of us combined. Let's finish up our breakfast and relax for a couple of hours. We can jot down some things we want to discuss with him. I'll give him a call around seven and then if he's in, Doug and I will drive over."

"What about Max?" asked Doug. "Do you think it'll be safe to leave her here by herself?"

Getting up from the table, Max walked to the kitchen counter and picked up the gun and the bat. Holding one in each hand, she had an evil smile. "Just let one of those Stroud's try and break in here. It'll be the last thing they ever do!"

Grant finished his coffee. "It's settled then. I'll give Blue a call at seven."

Max put the gun down and asked, "But don't you have to report for work today?"

"No, it's my day off."

Max interjected, "What about Dana Beth? Won't she mind you running off to Cherokee with Doug?"

"It'll be fine," lied Grant. "She's got her hands full at home with Crystal Ann. Besides that, she doesn't need to know about any of this." Lying again, Grant explained, "I'll just give her a quick call on my cell before we leave."

The clock on the fireplace mantel chimed the time at seven o'clock. Grant located Blue's number on his cell and made the call. It was answered on the second ring. "Good morning. Cherokee Police Department."

Grant got right to the reason for his call. "This is Officer Denlinger from over in Townsend. I was wondering if Chief Blue is in his office yet."

"Yes, he is. He just walked in the door a few minutes ago. I'll put your call back to his office."

Seconds passed when a familiar voice answered, "Chief Blue."

"William, this is Grant. Don't have a lot of time for chitchat. Something's come up over here in Townsend. It involves Doug Eland. We need some advice. Do you think if we drove over this morning that you could give us some time?"

Blue joked, "Are you kidding me? I'd be honored. The man who killed the Smoky Mountain Killer and the best wildlife photographer in the country coming to see me. When can I expect you?"

Grant smiled at Doug and Max who were standing next to the fireplace. "We're leaving in two minutes. We'll see you within the hour."

"See you then," said Blue. "I'll have fresh coffee."

Shortly after eight o'clock they pulled into the Cherokee Police Station. They no sooner entered the one story brick building when the receptionist recognized them. "Chief's waiting for you back in his office down the hall."

Chief Blue was busy at the coffeemaker cleaning up a mess he had made. Tossing a wad of coffee-stained napkins into a trash container, he smiled when he saw Grant and Doug walk through the door. "I should have let one of the girls out front make coffee. The wife is always telling me about how undomesticated I am." Gesturing at two chairs in front of his desk, he continued to sop up coffee, "Have a seat boys. It'll just be a minute for me to get this cleaned up."

Grant took a seat but Doug remained standing as he looked at the various Indian photographs and artwork on the walls and commented in a joking manner, "You're really into this Cherokee stuff, aren't you, Blue?"

William placed his hand on a sheaved knife attached to his handmade belt and gave Doug a sideways glance. "You betcha, paleface. I've never scalped a white man but that can change rather quickly."

Doug laughed and took a seat as Blue asked, "The word is you got married to some good looking woman who should have her head examined."

"Yeah, it's hard to believe," admitted Doug. "You know what they say, there's someone out there for everyone!"

William, frustrated with his inability to make coffee, picked up the phone and called the front desk. "Justine, will you have someone run up the street and bring back three coffees. I made my usual mess back here."

Sitting at his desk, Blue leaned back and placed his hands behind his head. "So, what's all this about? The last time you two came to my office was October a little over a year past. Right after that I got involved with the murder investigations. When you take the time to think about it that was a pretty wild ride…wasn't it?"

Grant smiled and responded, "Yeah, I guess you could say that. The reason we've come to pay you a visit today is because we are faced with another dilemma. We need some advice. I think the best thing to do at this point would be to let Doug explain."

Blue remained silent and nodded at Doug to commence.

Doug hesitated, but then began with his detailed story, "It all started a couple of weeks ago when I went out for my morning run…"

Nearly an hour later, Doug finished, "I called Grant after the attack, he came over to my place, we discussed what happened, decided to give you a call and here we are!"

Blue crushed his empty cup and threw it into the trash container as he commented in a state of disbelief, "That's quite a story; a frightening story, especially the part about you wanting to kill Ambrose Stroud. I assume you came to see me for advice because you'd rather go down another road; a more logical way of handling your problem. I can tell you this, any advice would be better than killing Stroud."

Removing his gun from his coat pocket, Doug laid it on the corner of the desk. "If I thought there was any other way, William, believe me, I'd gladly take that direction. Hell, I've only fired this gun three times in my life and that was to scare off a bear. Frankly, I don't know if I'd even be able to pull the trigger on Stroud, but I'm scared. That family has imbedded a very real sense of fear in my wife and me. Fear can drive people to do strange things."

Blue stood up and closed his office door. "Put that gun away! There are other ways to deal with Ambrose Stroud and his family and it doesn't involve gunplay." Seated once again, Blue placed both his hands on top of the desk. "Based on what you've told me, leaves little doubt that it is indeed the Stroud's that have perpetrated a string of malicious deeds aimed at your family. If the same thing were to happen here in Cherokee, my efforts to put a stop to it would be hampered just like Axel's. I'd be faced with the same problem that Brody has had dumped in his lap. We, as members of the law enforcement community cannot go after someone who is accused of something without the evidence to support our suspicions. So, don't be so hard on Brody, Doug. I'm sure he wants this situation to end as much as you do. The problem is, the longer you sit around and wait for the law to take action, the more danger your family may be in. I know that must sound ridiculous, but that's the way it works sometimes."

Doug slumped in his chair as if he had been scolded. "Are you saying that it's impossible to stop the Stroud's? I can't believe that!"

"I didn't say that," said Blue. "What I meant to say is that if you sit around and wait for the law to collect enough proof to go on, the more danger your family may be in. What I am about to tell you, you didn't hear from me. There are two different roads you can take if you choose. Both are on the illegal side, but depending on how things turn out, the law might turn its head if the situation is solved."

Grant spoke up, "Now you've really got me confused. Are you suggesting that we do something illegal?"

"I'm not suggesting anything. You came to me for advice so I'm giving you two options for you to consider."

Doug held up his hand and interrupted Grant who was about to speak again. "Wait...I want to hear these options. I don't care if they are illegal. What Ambrose Stroud and his family have done to my wife and me is illegal. Maybe it's the only way."

Grant sat back in his chair and crossed his legs. "If anyone else rather than Blue was having this conversation with us, I'd probably walk away, but his wisdom and advice in the past have always proved effective, so I'm willing to listen."

William nodded his head then held up an index finger. "Option one. There are people, men, who live amongst us in our society who appear to lead what most folks would refer to as a normal life. Most of these men live in nice peaceful neighborhoods. They have children and pets and even mow their yards. If you were to meet them on the street you probably wouldn't give them a second look. But, underneath their veil of normalcy lies a special talent; a talent for making problems like the Stroud's *go away!*"

Grant interrupted Blue. "You're not suggesting we bring in another Hawke Caine type of person? The last time that happened, we all know what the result was. Caine got killed. He didn't fit into our small town way of life in Townsend. He was like a fly in the ointment."

Blue smiled and answered, "Hawke Caine, even though he got results for the most part was a buffoon. The kind of man I'm talking about is very discrete and professional."

Doug spoke up, "Do you know of such a man?"

"Yes, I do," said Blue. "He lives in Nashville. His name is Albert Shellheimer. He's quite intimidating, nearly seven foot tall, close to three hundred pounds; a huge man. Doesn't have a hair on his head. No eyebrows, no facial hear. In general, one scary dude. He's helped me out on several occasions. I guarantee you, if you have a problem, for the right price, he can make it go away! He knows his business well and will be up front with you. If what you want done, can't be accomplished, he'll tell you straight away. As far as I know, he's never killed anyone, but that's a question I'd never ask him. Men like Albert Shellheimer take the law to another level that we as lawmen are not taught. They make problems, that at least for the moment, we can't seem to make go away...disappear!"

Grant and Doug stared at one another for a moment, not believing what they had just been told. Finally, Doug asked Blue, "What kind of money are we talking?"

"Well, I guess that depends on the job. If I were to guess I'd say you can probably figure on a few thousand."

"A few thousand!" exclaimed Grant. "That's pretty steep."

Doug spoke up. "Now just wait! Hell, I've already spent a couple of thousand just repairing the damage the Stroud's have done to property I own. It's not the money that causes me to hesitate in dealing with this Shellheimer. It almost feels like I'd be dealing with organized crime."

"I don't know if the man is connected to those type of people or not. But let me ask you this? How much is it worth to have a level of peace back in your life?"

"It's not just the money," said Doug. "I'm just not so sure that's the right thing to do. You said there were two options. What's the second?"

"The second option involves getting your hands dirty."

Doug frowned, "I don't understand."

"It's simple," explained Blue. "If you go with a man like Shellheimer, he'll do all the dirty work. That's what you're paying him for. If you go with option two, then you have to stick your hands into the garden, so to speak. You have to get your hands dirty!"

Grant, finishing his coffee, shook his head. "I still don't understand where you're heading with this."

Blue grinned. "What you have to do is reverse the situation. Go after the Stroud's with a vengeance! Make them feel uncomfortable. If you will, give them a taste of their own medicine. Make their lives miserable."

"And we do this...how?" asked Doug.

"You don't have to physically injure them, just hit them where it hurts. I'm guessing that would be in their wallet. Maybe their tires get slashed, or something from their property is stolen or destroyed."

"So what you're saying is that I do the same thing to them they are doing to me?" asked Doug.

"Yes, that is what I'm saying, but it could be dangerous. You have to make sure the Stroud's are not aware that you are the culprit, at least until they figure it out"

"What prevents the Stroud's from going to Brody and reporting me?"

"Their own guilt will prevent them from going to anyone in authority. It's like this. If a thief steals money and then that money is stolen from him, who in their right mind is going to have any sympathy for his problem. In a case like that the law will most likely look the other way. If anything, this could work to your advantage. The Stroud's might get frustrated and stop hassling you because they might feel that things are settled or they might get overly upset, make a mistake and show their hand, in which case Brody can then nail them. You have to make them go on the defensive rather than the offensive. Give them something to think about."

"The concept sounds logical, but I need some time to think this over."

"Whatever you decide to do, don't take too long. From what you told me the Stroud's seem to be getting more violent as the days go by. You don't want to put this off until it's too late." Blue crossed his arms and continued, "There's one last thing I'm going to tell you two young bucks and that's just this: In any situation in life, good or bad, there are always four different kinds of people. There are people who make things happen as well as those who don't know what's happening. There are also those who wait for things to happen and folks who allow things to happen. Now, it seems to me that you two do not fall into the category of not knowing what's happening. That's evident from what you've told me here today. You two fall into the group that most folks tend to lean towards and that's just this. By not taking action, you are allowing the Stroud's to continue to get over on you and the other thing you're doing is you're waiting for Brody or the law to take action. You *must* become men who make things happen and despite whether you go with the likes of Shellheimer or do this thing yourselves, you have to step up to the plate. And that, gentlemen, is my advice."

Grant stuck out his hand and Blue gave it a hardy shake. "You never cease to amaze me, William. I would have never guessed you would give us the information you have."

Blue grinned. "Hey, remember when I was a kid I played cowboys and Indians just like you fellas did, but in my case the Indians always won!"

As Grant guided the Jeep over the mountain back to Townsend, he asked Doug, "Do you think we're coming back with our answer?"

"Yeah, I think Blue was honest with us. I'm just not sure which direction I want to go. I need to talk this over with Max and see how she feels."

Grant looked out at the passing forest. "This conversation with Blue reminds me of something Brody said to me after we talked with Ambrose. He said that this could be the beginning of a war with the Stroud's, but that we had won a battle. If you decide to start your own personal war with the Stroud's, I just want you to know, I'm with you.

CHAPTER SEVENTEEN

THE SLEET WAS JUST STARTING TO FALL WHEN Grant pulled into Dalton's driveway. Getting out of the Jeep, he noticed the barn door wide open. Thinking that his grandfather forgot to shut it, he walked to the barn only to find Dalton inside busy at his workbench. "Dalton, what's up?"

Dalton turned as he held up a short section of lumber. "I decided to get those shelves put up in the pantry for Greta." Pointing at the pot-bellied stove in the center of the barn, he asked, "Mind throwing some of that scrap wood on the fire. It's a bit nippy out here today."

Walking to a bin full of smaller pieces of cut boards Grant pulled out a number of sections, opened the metal door on the small black stove and placed them over the leaping flames. Backing slightly away, he held his hands in front of the stove and commented, "That really does take the edge off the cold."

Dalton, sanding the shelf asked, "How'd things go with the Eland's?"

"They were attacked out behind their shop. They said there were three of them."

"Did they get injured?"

"Yeah, they suffered some injuries, but I think they'll be okay."

"Do they have any idea who attacked them?"

Grant hesitated for a moment. It seemed as if he was always confiding in Dalton. Yet he knew there wasn't a better person he could talk to. He knew that anything he told Dalton would always be kept between the two of them. "They're really not sure," he answered. "They were attacked in a dark alley." Before he could tell him more of the story, Dalton asked "What's ol' Brody think about it?"

"Doug hasn't said anything to Axel yet. I'm not sure what he's going to do, so if you wouldn't mind, just keep this to yourself."

Shrugging, Dalton changed the subject. "Have you talked with Dana Beth lately?"

"No, not since she called me after she got down to Florida..."
The buzzing of Grant's cell phone interrupted the conversation.

Grant dug the phone out of his jacket pocket and answered,
"Hello."

"Grant. It's Doug! It didn't take long for Max and me to decide
what direction we're going to take. She's still pissed as hell! When
I got home, she met me at the front door with that damn bat she's
been carrying around. She didn't like the concept of Albert
Shellheimer, but she did agree with us turning the tables on the
Stroud's. As a matter of fact, she came up with a great idea or how
and when we can get started. Can you meet us at the shop?"

"When?" asked Grant.

"As soon as you can get there. If we're going to act on Max's
idea we have to strike tomorrow morning. I don't have time to
explain it over the phone, but if we can pull it off, it'll cost the
Stroud's a lot of money. When you get here, pull around the rear.
You can come in the back door."

"I'm on my way," said Grant. Waving his phone at Dalton, he
started to back out of the barn. "I've got to go, Dalton. Tell Greta I
should be back tonight for supper."

Pulling around the back of the gift shop, Grant parked the
Jeep. Before he could even get out, Max was standing at the back
door as she gave him a wave. Inside, Grant was amazed as he
looked around the interior: toward the rear of the shop, there was
a display of handmade log furniture, which included chairs, end
tables, lamps and rockers. The front of the shop walls were graced
with a number of Doug's wildlife photographs, each one numbered
and signed. A glass counter next to the cash register housed Max's
homemade jewelry and a rack full of walking sticks sat next to the
front door. Putting his hands on his hips, Grant gave his approval.
"This is really nice. I thought you said the Stroud's damaged a lot
of stuff."

"They did!" said Max. "But for the last couple of days we've
busted our asses to get the place back in order."

"The shop might be back in order, but we're not," remarked
Doug. "We're going to wait a week before we reopen. You were
right when you told us earlier at the house this morning that we
looked like a demented painting, what with all our bandages, cuts

and bruises. We need some time to heal up a little bit so we don't scare the hell out of our customers."

"So, what's this plan that Max has?" asked Grant.

Offering Grant a seat in one of the log chairs, Max and Doug sat down as Doug explained, "While we were over in Cherokee talking with Blue, Max decided that she wasn't going to live her life hiding from the Stroud's, so she took a drive over to Home Depot near Sevierville."

Grant looked at Doug as he commented, "I've only been here for a couple of minutes and I'm already confused."

Max took over the conversation. "When we purchased the house from the Calibrizzi's we bought it *as is*. What I'm trying to say is that a lot of things in the house are really dated, one being the light fixtures. So, like Doug told you I took a drive over to Home Depot to see about getting some newer lights. When I got there they were taking all of the light fixture displays down and the stock from the shelves. I asked a clerk who was working there what was going on. He explained to me that they were discontinuing their current light inventory with a newer selection. I asked him if they were going to discount their inventory and he told me all the lights were already spoken for. One customer had purchased the whole lot for $2,500.00 cash."

Moving forward on her chair, Max went on, "Now, here's the interesting part. The clerk was a rather talkative sort of individual and he went on to tell me that the Stroud's were the ones who brought all the lights. Said he didn't care much for the Stroud's, especially the two brothers that always dropped by the store at least once a month like vultures to see what kind of a deal they could get. He went on to say the store manager loved them because they always paid cash for clearance inventory that he didn't have to keep around the store for months on end. The clerk told me the Stroud's would be by tomorrow morning at six o'clock, which is when they always showed up to pick up whatever they had purchased. He was going to have to be there to help get them loaded. He said they were getting around $19,000.00 worth of merchandise for their $2,500.00 and could probably sell the stuff and make around a $10,000.00 profit. He added that he always hated to deal with Ambrose and Cletus. They were rude and course and not very friendly. He also told me that they always have breakfast at a place called Daily's Diner which is just down the road from the store after they make a pickup. That got me to thinking, so I took a short drive down to this Daily's. It's a small place just off the road. Sits about thirty customers. Now, here's the best part. They have a paved parking lot."

Grant shook his head. "Now I'm really confused. I know there must be some logical explanation for all this but at this point I'm not picking up on it."

"It's really quite simple," said Max. "If the Stroud's pick up their load at six there's a good chance that they'll be out of there by six-thirty or so. Let's say they get to Daily's at seven or maybe even seven-fifteen. It'll still be dark out for another thirty to forty-five minutes." Rubbing her hands together she got a devious grin on her face. "Alright, here's the plan."

Ten minutes later, Max sat back after explaining and asked Grant, "Well, what do you think?"

Grant stood and walked to the front window of the shop and looked out. "As elaborate as your plan is, I think we could pull it off, but there are still a lot of what ifs involved. For instance; what if the Stroud's pick up their load later than six? What happens if they don't go for breakfast? What happens if you're noticed in the parking lot? And another thing, Doug, you know I said I'd back you on whichever way you went. But, I've got to be careful in how I participate. As an officer of the law I can't just go around breaking the law, which is what you're actually going to be doing. I can only participate from a legal standpoint; things like pulling them over for a trumped up traffic violation or hassling them about not having their County Vendors License. What you're planning on doing, and that's if it works will no doubt piss the Stroud's off to no end. I'm willing to turn my head, but I just want you to know that I can't be involved in any direct illegal activities."

"We understand your position, Grant," said Max. "If the Stroud's don't go to the diner then we just cancel the whole idea, but if everything falls in line with the way I think it will, we can strike a hard blow to the family. And while I'm talking, I have an idea how you can help us out at the diner and no one will know the difference!"

At precisely 5:00 a.m. the following morning Grant pulled into an abandoned fruit market fifty yards down the road from the diner. Doug and Max were already parked in the empty lot next to an old boarded up shanty. Grant was no sooner parked when Doug got out of their car and Max drove off as she waved good bye.

Climbing in the Jeep, Doug held a gym bag and two cups of steaming coffee. Handing Grant one of the cups he removed the lid from a cup of his own and threw the bag in the backseat. "With any luck Max should be calling us from Home Depot in the next hour or so with an update. Now, all we can do is wait." Looking at Grant's uniform he asked, "What time do you have to report for work?"

Removing the lid from the coffee, Grant answered. "Nine o'clock. If everything goes according to plan I should have plenty of time to get to work and you and Max should be back home well before nine."

Doug looked at the glowing face of his watch as he announced, "It's five-fifty. Don't you think the Stroud's should have gotten there by now?"

"Take it easy," said Grant. "The clerk said they usually show up at six to pick up their load. They've still got ten minutes before the store opens. If they don't show by six then we can give Max a call." Looking across the seat at Doug, Grant stated, "If you're getting nervous, we can always back out and forget all this."

"I'm not nervous, it's just that so many things have to fall in place for us to pull this off."

"Relax," said Grant, "We can pull out at any point if things don't pan out."

Doug's phone signaled an incoming call. "Doug, it's Max. It's six o'clock on the dot and no Stroud's. Maybe they cancelled. What do you want me to do?"

"Let's wait a few minutes," answered Doug. "Maybe they're just running a little..."

Max interrupted him as she spoke excitedly, "Wait! An old flatbed just pulled up to the front door." Peering through a set of binoculars while holding the phone she continued to speak, "I can't quite make out who's inside the truck. There's too many shadows. Okay, they're getting out. Two men...big men. The one on the driver's side is completely bald and the other one is definitely Ambrose. Gotta go. I'll call you back after they get loaded up. Let's just hope they go to the diner."

Doug closed his cell and spoke to Grant. "They just arrived. Max said she'd call us when they get ready to leave with the load. I'm gonna get dressed."

Confused, Grant asked, "Dressed?"

"Yeah, dressed," repeated Doug. Reaching back for the gym bag he unzipped it and removed a black sweater and dark blue ski mask. Pulling the sweater over his head awkwardly due to his slinged arm, he remarked, "I thought this was the way people dressed when they did this sort of thing."

Despite the seriousness of what they were about to attempt, Grant managed to laugh. "I think you've seen too many espionage movies. But if you feel safer dressed like a ninja, then so be it."

Laying the gym bag on the seat, Doug sorted through the tools inside. I think we have everything here we need."

It wasn't even ten minutes when the two brothers came back out of the store, climbed in the flatbed and drove around the side of the building. Max drove around the opposite side of the lengthy structure and parked at the far end of the rear back lot. Peering through the binoculars she watched as the two men got out and watched as a driver on a forklift began the process of loading the first of eight skids of lighting merchandise. She was just about to give Doug a call when a rapping sound caused her to look at the side window where a uniformed officer with a flashlight stood as he motioned for her to wind down the window. Allowing the binoculars to fall to her chest, she hit the automatic window button and the glass slowly lowered. The officer smiled pleasantly as he inquired, "Excuse me, Ma'am. Could you please show me some identification."

Laying the binoculars on the seat, Max reached up and removed her driver's license from the visor and handed it out the window as she asked, "Have I broken some sort of law, officer?"

Reading her license, he handed it back to her and answered, "That depends, Mrs. Eland." Shining the flashlight on the binoculars, he politely asked, "What were you looking at?"

"Oh those. I can explain the binoculars." Thinking quickly, she opened the glove compartment and grabbed one of Doug's business cards and handed it to the officer as she explained, "My husband is a professional wildlife photographer. He's done quite a bit of work for National Geographic Magazine. I'm sure you've heard of the publication."

The officer remaining patient, responded, "Yes, I have heard of it, but what does that have to do with sitting behind Home Depot at six-thirty in the morning watching some customers being loaded up?"

"My reason for being here has nothing to do with any of their customers. I was bird watching."

"Look, Ma'am, I just didn't fall off the back of a turnip truck. It's too dark out here to see any birds this time of the morning."

"I was just getting an early start. You see, it's been reported that there are some bald eagles roosting back over there behind the store. I wanted to check it out before my husband made a run over here. I guess I just got here a little early."

Handing the card back to her, the officer smiled and spoke. "Home Depot has reported a lot of theft out here behind the store in their lumber area. I'm simply going to suggest that you return to the front of the store or leave and return when the sun comes up."

Max, relieved, smiled and answered, "I can do that and I apologize if I've caused a problem."

"As long as you move your vehicle, they'll be no problem. Good day to you, Ma'am."

As the officer turned and walked back to his cruiser, Max let out a breath of relief, realizing how close she came to screwing up their plans. The officer waited until she backed up and drove around the building. He followed her to the parking lot, then made a right hand turn on the road as she drove across the street to a gas station and parked. Picking up her cell phone, she dialed Doug.

Doug picked up his cell when it bussed. "Max, what's up. It's been awhile since you called."

"I almost got caught by the police!"

Doug, surprised, asked, "Almost got caught. What do you mean?"

Looking out the front windshield, Max noticed the flatbed as it pulled around the side of the store. "I gotta go," said Max. "The Stroud's are pulling out with their load. They just made a right hand turn heading your way. They should be at the diner in less than five minutes. I'm going to follow at a safe distance. If they drive by the diner I'll follow them. If they drive straight home, then we'll have to scrap the plan. Hopefully, I'll see you soon."

Doug, with a look of amazement tried to explain to Grant what Max had told him. "The Stroud's are headed this way. Max said she almost got caught!"

"How?" asked Grant.

"She didn't have time to tell me. She's following them right now. We better get ready. Doug got out and Grant opened the back of the Jeep. Tossing the gym bag inside he climbed in the back.

Looking in the rearview mirror, Grant spoke, "Max should be calling us soon, that is if they stop at the diner."

Keeping the red taillights of the flatbed in view, Max followed and finally smiled to herself when she saw the left hand turn signal blinking. *Perfect,* she thought, *they're going to the diner!*

Pulling over to the side of the road, she watched as the truck was parked near the back of the lot. After the two men entered the diner, she pulled in, parked near the front of the lot and made her final call. "Doug! They just parked and went in."

"Alright," said Doug, "We'll be there in less than a minute." Looking over the rear seat, he ordered. "Grant, let's hit it. They're inside the diner."

Following the short drive up the road, Grant pulled in next to Max. Checking to make sure no one was outside in the lot, she got out of her car and walked to the rear of the Jeep where she met Doug and Grant. Doug held up the gym bag as he remarked, "Let's go...I'm ready!"

As Doug ducked into the nearby tree line, Max reminded Grant, "Alright, you're on. When you get in there make sure the Stroud's don't come out for at least twenty minutes. I don't think we'll need that much time, but still, you need to keep them occupied."

Grant started across the lot for the diner as he saluted, "Shouldn't be a problem. You guys be careful."

As Grant entered the diner, Doug and Max made their way through the trees to the rear of the lot, stopping when they got to the back of the flatbed.

The diner was nothing to write home about: cedar planked walls, dim lighting, five sets of unmatched tables and chairs and a sit down counter with six barstools.

Two of the tables were occupied with what appeared to be locals, Ambrose and Cletus sat at the two barstools near the end of the counter.

Kneeling down, Doug opened the gym bag and removed a heavy-duty hunting knife as he motioned to Max. "I need you to stay back in the trees but where you can keep an eye on the diner and the parking lot. If anyone pulls in or comes out of the diner let me know." Max hid behind a large tree as she watched the diner. Doug walked to the front driver's side of the flatbed and jammed the knife into the tire, a low hissing noise indicating the slow release of air. Seconds passed and he moved to the rear tire, repeating the process. Max glanced at the glowing face of her watch: 7:10. They had plenty of time before it started to get light out.

Grant went directly to the old Wulitzer juke box. He put a dollar in the slot and selected four songs. The diner was filled with the twang of a country ballad. Taking a seat on a barstool, he left one space between himself and Cletus. A blond waitress pushed open a set of café doors and set two plates of food in front of Cletus and Ambrose. Looking at Grant, she asked, "What can we get for you this morning, officer?"

Cletus was the first to notice Grant and before he could even bump his brother on his arm, Grant spoke up, "Mornin', Boys. Coffee any good here?" Ambrose stared past his brother at Grant in disbelief. Nodding at the waitress, Grant ordered politely, "I'll just have a cup of coffee, thank you."

Ambrose cut into a slice of ham, took a large bite then looked at Grant again as he remarked sarcastically, "Officer Denlinger, what brings ya over here ta Sevier County? Run outta folks ta hassle over in Blount County?"

Grant smiled and answered, "Just running a few errands for Chief Brody."

Nodding at Grant's bandaged hand, Ambrose asked snidely, "How's that hand comin'?"

Holding up his hand, Grant smiled. "Coming along just fine."

Ambrose, dipped a section of toast into his sunnyside eggs, some of the yoke running down his chin. "Ya know, Denlinger, I tol' yer boss that if I ever run inta ya and ya was off duty that I'd finish up what I started over at the IGA."

Displaying his uniform, Grant answered, "Well, I guess you'll just have to wait on that. I'm definitely on duty this morning."

All four tires punctured, Doug tossed the gym bag up on the back of the flatbed and then jumped up. Using the knife, he began to cut the first of four heavy straps that secured two old faded blue tarps. Despite the lack of use of his right arm, it only took thirty seconds to cut though the canvas strap, then he moved on to the second, when Max signaled him, "Doug, customer just pulled in!" Laying flat on the tarp, Doug stopped cutting. Seconds passed when Max gave him the go ahead, "All clear!" On his knees again he began cutting the second strap.

Grant's coffee was placed in front of him. He dumped a packet of sweetener in and stirred it as he addressed Cletus, "How long has it been since Ruby Jean ran off. Seems to me it's been, what, about two months or so. Do you think she'll ever come back?"

Cletus gave Grant a dirty look, then responded, "She ain't never comin' back. I guarantee ya that!"

Grant pushed as he asked, "How can you be so sure? Folks around town have said all along that it seemed so strange that she left and didn't take Violet along with her. How can you explain that?"

Ambrose interrupted Cletus as he was about to answer. "Ain't none of yer business or nobody else fer as that goes. She done run off and that's the end of it! My brother is better off without the likes of her around!"

Grant smiled as he sipped at his coffee. "All I'm saying is that it just seems odd, but it doesn't make a difference to me either way."

Cutting the fourth and final strap, Doug spoke to Max, "Come over here and pull down the tarps and put them back in the trees after I throw these loose straps over the sides." After the tarps were hidden in the trees, Max returned to her watchdog duties as

Doug smiled and said, "Here goes. It's gonna get a little noisy so keep a close watch." With that he lifted up the end of one of the skids and tipped it over the side, the sound of busting globes, light bulbs and glass piercing the silence of the darkness. The noise caused Max to crouch down as she concentrated on the door of the diner and the parking lot. In the next few seconds two more skids crashed down onto the pavement, glass scattering in every direction.

Changing the subject again, Grant spoke to both brothers, "Sorry to hear about Harmon's two boys getting killed up near Jellico. Some people feel that it was Russell Pearl who killed Arliss and Dwayne. What do you fellas think?"

Cletus answered instantly, "Russell Pearl was a slow-witted dumb ass if I ever seen one!"

Grant knew he had pushed a button as he went on, "How would you know that? Sounds like you met the man."

Ambrose broke in on the conversation, fearing that his younger brother had said too much. "We never met the man, we just heard about him, that's all!"

The fifth and the sixth skids crashed to the pavement as Max shuddered as each skid hit the ground. She stopped Doug from tipping another skid as she noticed a group of four men leaving the diner. "Doug...stop!" Doug instantly laid down flat as he watched the men walk over to two parked cars. Rather than getting in the cars and leaving, they congregated at the front of one car and were discussing something. Doug swore beneath his breath, realizing the longer the men remained in the lot that he could not continue. He silently prayed that no one would look toward the rear of the lot. It was still dark out, but he couldn't be sure what they could see from where they were standing. Finally, after two long minutes the men broke up, climbed in the cars and drove out of the lot. Max gave Doug a thumbs up and said, "Finish up and let's get the hell outta here!" Doug stood and tipped the last two skids down over the side of the truck, the noise reverberating back through the trees.

"Speaking of Arliss and Dwayne, did Maude and Otis get up to Jacksboro and bring those boys back home yet?" asked Grant.

Cletus answered, "Brought them back home yesterday. The

funeral is gonna be at ten tomorrow mornin'.'"

Ambrose looked past his brother at Grant. "What do you care? Yer the big hero around these parts! The man who killed the Smoky Mountain Killer!"

Grant's cell phone buzzed. Taking it out of his jacket pocket, he answered, "Denlinger here."

The voice of Max on the other end was music to his ears. "We're finished. Mission accomplished! We're in our car. We'll see you at the abandoned fruit market."

"That's affirmative," said Grant. Laying two dollars on the counter, he turned to leave but then stopped as he wanted to mention one more thing. "You boys need to talk with Otis and Maude about filling out that County Vendor's License. If you don't ol' Brody's gonna come up to your place and shut that tent of yours down." Smiling he headed for the door as he commented, "Just sayin'."

Outside, he glanced at the rear of the lot. It was still too dark for him to see what damage the Eland's had done. Pulling out of the lot, he drove the fifty yards up the road and made a right hand turn into the abandoned lot and pulled up next to the Eland's car. Doug rolled down his window and reaching out gave Grant a high five. Max leaned across the seat and looked out the window. "Thanks for all your help, Grant. I don't think we could have pulled this off without you."

Doug added, "We flattened all four tires and dumped eight skids of merchandise. Man, are they going to be pissed!"

Max spoke up again, "Listen, I've got another idea for the next thing we can do to the Stroud's."

Grant held up his hand. "I think I've had enough excitement for one morning. You guys need to go home or back to your shop and forget this ever happened. In the next couple of days you're going to hear about this. Just ignore it and act like it's news to you. We need to cool it for a couple of days and see what happens. Be careful. I've got to get to work."

Grant pulled out behind the Eland's and headed for Townsend. Turning on the radio, he smiled when he thought about the well deserved revenge the Eland's had secretly inflicted on the Stroud's. At the moment he was glad he wasn't Ambrose or Cletus as they were going to have to face the wrath of both Effy and Maude. Twenty-five hundred dollars down the drain, not to mention all the money they would not get to make on the resale of the clearance lighting. He wondered if the Stroud's would put two and two together and somehow figure out that he had been at the diner, not from mere coincidence, but that he had been part of the attack on their truck. They weren't that smart and besides that, they couldn't prove he was involved.

Ambrose got up from the barstool and threw a twenty on the counter and nodded at the waitress, "Keep the change!"

Outside, the sun was just starting to filter through the dense trees at the end of the lot, the pavement still appearing as a black void. Making their way across the lot, Cletus asked, "Back there in the diner you sounded like yer not finished with Denlinger. If I was you, I'd be careful, Brother. Ya know, ya still got ta serve some time cause of what happened over at the IGA. Did ya talk with that lawyer, Pittman lately?"

"I haven't talked with him, but Maude said he called a couple of days back and said it looked like I was goin' ta have ta serve thirty days and it could be soon. I've got lots of time ta git even with Denlinger. Hell, I might wait fer a year or so. I'll run inta him sometime in the future when he's off duty, and when I do, he'll have ta worry about a lot more than just his hand, I can tell ya that!"

Almost to the truck, Cletus felt a crunching beneath his shoes. Ambrose experienced the same thing. Looking down at the pavement as their eyes began to focus in the early morning sunlight, Ambrose cursed, "What the hell. Somebody broke a bunch of beer bottles out here or somethin'."

Thumping his brother on the arm, Cletus shook his head as he pointed to the empty truck. "It ain't beer bottles, Ambrose...it's our lights!"

Ambrose was silent as he walked over the scattered glass and approached the four empty skids surrounded by broken lights. Cletus at his side, asked, "Who coulda done this ta us?"

It was then that Ambrose noticed the two flattened tires. Picking up one of the cut straps, he looked around the lot and then into the tree line. "This weren't no accident. Somebody done this on purpose!"

Walking to the other side of the truck, Cletus yelled, "They flattened the tires and dumped the skids on this side too. Whoever done this drug the tarps back inta the trees. Ya think there was more than one person that done all this? Do ya think it was just a bunch of kids or vandals?"

Joining Cletus, Ambrose picked up a globe that had not been broken and threw it against a tree, the glass shattering. "This ain't the worst of it."

Cletus, not understanding, asked, "What could be worse that this?"

"I'll tell ya what's worse than this! We gotta call Maude and try ta explain what happened. She gave us $2,500.00 in cash and she expects us ta bring back eight skids of lights that we coulda sold fer mebbe ten times that much. Ya know how she gits when we mess up somethin'."

"Mebbe we could go ta Home Depot and explain what happened. Mebbe they'll give us our money back."

"That ain't gonna happen. Once we left their parking lot everythin' on the truck is our responsibility."

"Come on, Ambrose, Maude surely will understand that it weren't nothin' we done wrong. We was the victims here."

"Use yer head, Cletus. She'll say we shouldn't have left the truck unguarded and went in the diner. This whole thing is gonna come down on us. Hell, I might be better off sittin' in jail than ta go through the hell of dealin' with Maude over this." Walking toward the diner, Ambrose ordered Cletus. "Stay here with the truck. I'm gonna give Maude a call. We're gonna get our asses kicked good!"

Grant walked in the door at the Townsend Police Station fifteen minutes early. Marge, as usual was making coffee. "Good morning, Marge," said Grant as he hung his hat on a hook by the door. "Anything going on yet this morning?"

Marge, placing a filter into the coffee machine answered as she smiled, "As a matter of fact, there is! The Chief is in a great mood, which we both know for this early in the day is a miracle! He just got off the phone with Maryville. According to Sheriff Grimes, he and two of his deputies are heading up to the Stroud's later in the day to pick up Ambrose and haul him off to jail. He's been sentenced by the county judge to serve thirty days. Axel was so excited after he got off the phone, that he said he was going to buy my lunch today. To tell you the truth, I think the reason for his happiness is due to the fact that his arch nemesis, Merle Pittman, couldn't keep Ambrose out of jail with all of this legal savvy and connections."

"Well, I guess at times there is justice in this world, Marge," said Grant as he walked down the hall to Brody's office.

"Morning, Chief. Marge told me the good news you got from Maryville. What time are they going up to the Stroud's?"

Brody, busy taking some stick pins out of his small bulletin board answered, "He didn't give me a specific time. Grimes told me we didn't even have to be involved. He said he and his deputies would handle it. I'm kinda glad we don't have to tag along. Maude, even though she knows Ambrose has to serve time will, as usual, be hard to deal with."

Grant smiled. "If there's nothing else then I think I'll head out on patrol." Hesitating at the doorway, Grant turned as he remembered something. "Speaking about the Stroud's, the word is that they're having Arliss and Dwayne's funeral tomorrow. You planning on going, Chief?"

"Not on your life! When someone runs over a rattlesnake in the middle of the road...no one mourns!"

Back out in the main office, Grant grabbed his hat and waved at Marge. "Enjoy your lunch with the Chief."

The day passed quickly for Grant. Townsend was packed with tour busses, RVs, cars and motorcycles. The restaurants were busy, there was an unending line of cars at the gas stations, all of the local businesses were thriving. There wasn't much for Grant to do except drive around town. In two weeks it would be Thanksgiving and people would begin to start putting up Christmas lights and decorations. The leaves for the most part had not only changed colors but had fallen to the ground, most of the trees appearing as black skeletons. Bored, Grant drove down the street where Buddie's house was located. Buddie was nowhere in sight on the property and Grant figured he had completed the repairs to his house. The FOR SALE sign had an additional sign above it that read: SOLD. With everything that was going on,

Grant had put Luke's murder temporarily on the back burner. He still hadn't forgot about the hunch he had about Zeb and Buddie.

While eating a Parkway hotdog and bag of chips, he decided to take a drive past the Stroud's place. He wasn't the least bit surprised to find them closed for the day. Ambrose and Cletus had no doubt called Maude and gave her the bad news about the truckload of lights that had been destroyed. More than likely they were over in Sevier County trying to get to the bottom of the vandalism that happened at Daily's. Later that afternoon, he drove past Doug and Max's gift shop. No one was there. They had probably gone home to lay low like he had suggested. Just prior to four o'clock he was called to a local restaurant as someone had skipped without paying their bill.

Sitting in the parking lot of the restaurant filling out a complaint form, he received a call on his cell, "Grant, it's Doug!"

"What's going on?" answered Grant.

"We might have trouble, that's what!"

"What are you talking about?"

"We just got a call at the house from your boss, Chief Brody. He wants Max and me to drop by his office at five o'clock. What do you think he wants?"

"I don't have a clue. Why do you think it's trouble?"

"It's just too ironic that Brody wants to see us the afternoon after our little escapade...don't you think?"

"Well yeah, maybe."

Just then, Grant got a radio call. "Hold on a sec, Doug. I've got a call coming in."

Laying his cell phone on the console, he answered the radio, "Grant here. What's up?"

Marge's voice was pleasant as she explained, "Axel wants you back here at quarter to five. He wants to talk with you about something. He also said that we're going to have two visitors here at five. He wants you in on a meeting he's going to have with them."

"I'll be there," said Grant as he turned off the radio and picked up the cell. "Looks like you might be right," said Grant. "I just got a call from Brody. Apparently, I'm going to be at this meeting also."

There was panic in Doug's voice, "What do we do now?"

"Just show up on time and tell Max to get herself together. If

Brody gets the slightest inclination that either one of you are nervous, then he'll start digging. Right now, we don't have any idea what Brody wants, but I think we have to assume it might be about what happened this morning. Like I said, you guys need to stay cool and act like it's news to you. Hell, we could get there and it might have to do with something completely different. Let's not jump to any conclusions. And another thing: all of us, have to act surprised when we see each other at the office. Brody might act like he is just a good old boy running a small town police force, but believe me, sometimes he can be sharp as a tack. If we so much as miss a beat, he'll pick up on it. I'll see you guys about five."

Grant no sooner closed his cell when he got another call. "Hello."

"It's me. I just wanted to check in with you and let you know we're doing fine. Crystal Ann loves the beach. You should see her. Right now she's covered with sand, and oh yeah, she loves to feed the seagulls."

Grant wanted so much to talk with Dana Beth but her timing couldn't have been worse. "How about you? How are you doing?" he asked.

"I've been doing a lot of thinking. I'm feeling better about the entire situation, but I'm still not quite out of the woods. I'm not ready to come back just yet. Mom and I have quite a bit of talking to do. I've been putting it off, but I'm going to have to tell her the truth about Conrad. That's not something I'm looking forward to. Give me about a week and then...I think we'll come back home. Crystal Ann really misses you. I do too! Oh, I've got to go! Crystal Ann is headed for the water. I love you!"

The conversation had been fortunately short, which was a blessing as Grant had to get himself together for the mystery meeting. Pulling out of the lot, Grant headed for the office and possibly a touch and go confrontation with Chief Brody.

As soon as Grant entered the police station, he went to the front desk. Speaking in a low voice so that Axel could not overhear their conversation, he asked, "Marge. Any idea why Axel wants to see me?"

Marge, who was getting ready to leave for the day was wiping down the desk as she answered, "I'm not sure, but it might have something to do with the Stroud's. Maude Stroud and her husband, Otis, were in here about two o'clock. They were here for about forty minutes. There was quite a bit of yelling on Maude's part: something about a truck getting damaged over in Sevier County and then there were nasty words swapped about Ambrose being picked up and hauled off to jail in Maryville. I didn't hear everything that was said, just bits and pieces. After they left, Axel didn't say much. It's strange. Despite all the rough language they were throwing around back there in his office, he really didn't look all that pissed. I think confused would be a better way to describe his attitude. He told me to give you a call and you know the rest from there."

Looking at the clock on the wall, Grant shrugged his shoulders and started down the hall. "I guess I better go back and see what he wants."

Entering Axel's office, he found the Chief sitting at his desk looking over the crayon drawing they had found in Russell's wallet. Axel noticed Grant standing in the doorway and gestured for him to come in. "Have a seat. I was just looking over this drawing we found on Pearl. The more I look at this the more I think it really does have something to do with the mysterious disappearance of Ruby Jean Stroud. I'm not quite sure what it means, but I'm leaning toward your interpretation. Ruby Jean might just be buried up there on that farm. Of course, just based on this crude drawing, we can't be sure that this even represents an area on their property." Folding the drawing, he stuck it back in his desk drawer, yawned and gave Grant a puzzling look.

Grant, guessing that the meeting had to have something to do with the attack on the Stroud's truck asked, "How did Grimes make out with picking up Ambrose?"

"According to Burt it went rather smoothly. Ambrose went peacefully and Maude didn't have all that much to say. If you ask me, Ambrose got off easy with just thirty days, thanks to Pittman. Later on in the afternoon I got a visit from her and Otis."

The conversation was interrupted as Marge stuck her head in the door and announced, "Chief, your visitors are here."

"Send them back...thank you."

Within seconds Doug and Max walked into the office. Grant sprang into immediate action as he jumped up and shook Doug's hand. "The last time I saw you was right here in this office. We have to stop meeting this way!" Moving to a chair in the corner, Grant offered the two chairs in front of the desk to Doug and his wife.

Doug and Max joined in on the charade as Doug introduced his wife to Axel and Max commented that the last time she had seen Grant was over at Lily's and that she still had to call Dana Beth about getting together. Grant could tell that Brody was trying to read their faces for anything out of the ordinary.

Brody folded his hands on top of the desk as he asked Doug. "What's with the bandaged arm and broken nose?"

Holding up his arm, Doug explained, "Just fell off of a ladder at the house."

Max jumped in before Brody could speak as she pointed at her mouth. "I got hit with the ladder on the way down."

Brody smiled slyly, "You wouldn't be hidin' anythin' from me now would ya?"

Doug gave Brody an odd look as he stated, "What are you talking about?"

Axel grinned. "I thought that just maybe you had another one of your run-ins with Ambrose Stroud!"

With a confused look, Doug answered, "No, not since we last talked."

Looking down at the desk, Brody half smiled and shook his head as if he didn't believe them.

Max brazenly spoke up, "Chief Brody! If you don't believe us go ahead and call the hospital. They should have a record of the report that was written when we were there."

Brody waved off her comment and sat back in his chair. "That won't be necessary. The real reason for this meeting today is in regard to a visit I had earlier from Maude and Otis Stroud. Maude told me that her two sons, Ambrose and Cletus were at Home Depot early this mornin' pickin' up a load of discontinued lights. While they were eating at a diner down the road, their truck was vandalized. Someone dumped over the skids and broke all the lights, and then slashed all four tires. Seein' as how there's no love lost between me and the Stroud's, I sent her and her husband on their way. I told them it was none of my business because it happened over in Sevier County, not Blount."

Max, who obviously didn't care much for Axel, spoke up again, "I don't see what any of this has to do with us."

Brody smiled as if he had some sort of inside information. "I didn't say that it did have anythin' to do with you *or your husband!* However, I did receive a call from the sheriff over in Sevierville who said that one of his officers found a Mrs. Eland parked out behind Home Depot at six-thirty in the morning watching some customers who were getting loaded up in the back through a set of binoculars. He went on to say that she said she was bird watchin'. The officer thought it was rather strange so they gave me a call to see what I could tell them about you two. The other strange coincidence that occurred was Maude told me her two boys while inside the diner ran into none other than Officer Denlinger here. Don't you think it's strange that both Mrs. Eland and you, Grant, were in the same close vicinity to where they parked their truck." Leaning forward, he became very serious. "What I'm sayin' here is that if I find that any one of you or the three of you turn out to be involved in any way with the damage that was done to that truck, I'll be forced to come down on you."

Max stood and pointed her finger at Axel. "If you're accusing us of anything why don't you just come out and say it. Yeah, I'll admit that it is coincidental that I was at Home Depot while the Stroud's were being loaded up, but I really didn't even know they were there! Like I told that officer...I was bird watching. I got there a little early...that's all!"

Grant jumped in on the conversation and directed his statement at Axel, "I guess you might think it strange for me to be at a diner where the Stroud's just happen to show up that early in the morning over in the next county, but I had a reason for being there. Dana Beth and I are remodeling my daughter's nursery. We planned on getting the work done when my shift was over so I ran over to Home Depot early in the morning and picked up a few things we needed before I had to report for work. I stopped by that diner for coffee. I had no idea the Stroud's would be there having breakfast. I'll admit that it does seem strange that Mrs. Eland and myself were at the store about the same time as the Stroud's, but it's nothing more than a coincidence...nothing more!"

Doug stood up next to Max and stated firmly, "If that's all you have to say, Brody, if my wife and I are not under arrest, then I think we'll just part ways for today!" Stepping closer to the desk, Doug emphasized strongly, "I'm going to give you some of your own advice, Brody. When I came to you about how Ambrose Stroud was hassling my wife and me, you said there wasn't much you could do without solid proof. You can think whatever you want about my wife and me, but until you have proof of our involvement, I would suggest that you just let us be. We've got enough problems with Ambrose Stroud and we certainly don't need the law in this town tipping the scales in his favor, Brody!" Doug took his wife by the arm and they walked out of the office.

Grant stood and asked, "Is there anything else, Chief?"

Axel glared at Grant and then spoke, "Somethin's goin' on here and I don't like it one bit! If I was you, Wonder Boy, I'd watch my Ps and Qs. Now, get the hell out of my office!"

CHAPTER EIGHTEEN

IT WAS JUST AFTER MIDNIGHT WHEN GRANT FINALLY dozed off. In the last twenty four hours he only had three hours sleep. The last thing he remembered as he closed his eyes was thinking about Dana Beth and Crystal Ann. He was glad she had called. Pulling the covers up around his neck he turned his head sideways on the soft pillow when his cell phone rang. Opening his eyes, he fumbled for the phone and answered in a tired voice, "Hello."

"Grant! This is Lee. I'm sorry to call you this time of night. Brody told me to give you a jingle. I'm on my way over to the Stroud's'. We got a call about a fire up at their place. Brody's on his way over there as we speak. I guess you need to meet us out there."

"I'll be there as soon as I can," mumbled Grant. Getting slowly out of bed, he threw on a pair of jeans and a flannel shirt, slipped into a pair of shoes and grabbed a coat, his gun and the phone.

Walking across the yard to where his Jeep was parked, he noticed the thermometer hanging on the side of the barn, the bright light above the double barn doors illuminating the temperature gauge. The red mercury line was just about the thirty four degree mark. Pulling the collar of his coat up around his neck, he thought about the warm bed he had left behind up in his room.

It was only a fifteen minute drive to Wears Valley Road then another two minutes to the Stroud's place. As Grant pulled to the side of the road it was just starting to spit snow. Crossing the highway, he took in the scene. A fire truck was parked on the grass, a floodlight on the side of the vehicle shined brightly on what was left of the Stroud's tent and picnic tables. A powerful stream of water was directed on the smoldering remains by a fireman as two other local volunteers stood off to the side. The Stroud's, dressed in their nightclothes were all gathered together by the tree line, the children huddled next to their parents. Lee Griner was busy talking with Maude and Effy, while Brody stood next to Buck Hiller, the Townsend Fire Chief.

Walking across the grass, Grant stepped over a fire hose and approached Brody and asked, "What do we have, Chief?"

Brody looked in the direction of the Stroud's as he answered, "Somebody set fire to the Stroud's tent and their tables."

The first thought that came to Grant was, *Doug and Max!* He wondered if they had struck again. He recalled what Max had said to him when they left after the diner incident in regard to having another idea about what they could do to the Stroud's.

Buck spoke up as he brought Grant up to speed, "It looks like arson. Someone threw gasoline on the table and the tent and lit it. It went up quick." Addressing Brody, he explained, "We'll probably only be here another ten minutes or so. It looks like it's pretty well contained. I'll drop off the fire report at your office later in the day."

As Buck walked back to the fire truck, Brody pointed at the large metal shed where the Stroud's kept a lot of the merchandise they sold. "Somebody not only set the fire but defaced that shed with spray paint."

Grant looked at the shed. The previous gray metal of the shed was now streaked with yellow, pink and brown paint. "Looks like a case of vandalism, Chief."

Brody put his arm around Grant and walked him back to the edge of the highway. "Look, Grant. This situation could get real ugly. First, we have the Stroud's truck gettin' sabotaged and now this! Remember what I said about gettin' into a war with the Stroud's? If you know anythin', you need to let me in on it before this gets out of hand."

Grant looked back in the direction of the burned out tent and answered, "I don't have a clue who's doing this or why it's even happening. Have you talked with Maude yet?"

"Yeah, when I first got here. She didn't have a lot to say, but she did make it clear to mc that if we didn't get to the bottom of who's responsible for the fire and their truck bein' damaged, then she and her family would." Looking back at the destroyed tent, Axel ordered, "Looks like everythin' is under control here. I'm gonna head back home. I want you and Lee to hang around about fifteen minutes after the fire company leaves just to make sure everythin' is alright. I won't be in the office when you get there in the morning. I've got to go over to Maryville and talk with Grimes.

He wants to talk with me about this business of the Stroud's possible involvement with Russell Pearl. Personally, I don't think it's gonna go anywhere, although I'll say this: It'd be nice if we could tie them in with Pearl somehow. If we could, then my long awaited dream of bein' rid of the Stroud's for good would become reality. At this point I don't think that'll ever happen, but it's a pleasant thought. Good night."

Grant walked over to where the tent had been located, bent down and picked up part of one of the burned picnic tables. Taking the small section of charred wood to his nose, he agreed with what Buck had said. It was arson. He could detect the faint scent of gasoline.

Looking up, he noticed Maude making her way across the grass in his direction. Stopping just short of where the tent had been she leaned on her cane. "My boys told me ya was at the diner while my truck was bein' messed with. They said ya asked them a lot of personal questions about Ruby Jean, Russell Pearl, Arliss and Dwayne. I'm here ta tell ya them things ain't none of yer damned business!"

Grant stood and stated, "First off, I just dropped by for coffee. I had no idea your boys were there. Secondly, why would you be concerned about anything I asked your sons in regard to Russell Pearl unless you knew the man? Your son, Cletus acted like he'd met Pearl before."

"None of us ever met that man. Like I told Brody. Ya better git on the stick and find out who's been pesterin' my family. I'm a patient woman, but I gotta tell ya, if somebody messes with me or my family, I ain't gonna just stand by and let it be." Without waiting for a response, she turned and walked away as she lit up a cigarette.

Real smart, thought Grant. *Lighting a cigarette in the area where they just had a fire ignited by gasoline. The sooner I get away from here the better.*

Arriving back at Dalton's farm at 1:45 in the morning, Grant collapsed in his bed. He was too exhausted to think about the Stroud's, Doug and Max, Brody or anyone or anything else other than sleep.

It seemed like he was no sooner asleep when the alarm on the nightstand went off at six o'clock, its annoying buzz bringing him out of a deep sleep. Following a long, relaxing shower he dressed, walked outside into the cold morning air, climbed in his Jeep and headed for the Parkway Grocery and a cup of morning coffee.

Preparing his coffee, he saw Zeb sitting by the front window by himself which as of late had been a common sight. Paying for his coffee at the counter, Grant thought not only about Zeb, but Buddie. The hunch he had about Luke Pardee's murder seemed to have taken a backseat with everything else that was going on. Looking at his watch, Grant realized he had fifteen minutes before he had to report for work. Walking over to Zeb's table, Grant pulled out a chair and flopped down. "Morning, Zeb. What's the latest around town?"

Zeb, eager to talk with someone about the local goings on, smiled and answered, "Actually, quite a bit! I'm sure you already know about Ambrose being hauled off to jail."

"Yep, already know about that," said Grant.

"Well, I guess you already know about the fire over at the Stroud's last night?"

"Yeah, know about that, too. I was out there for about an hour."

Zeb gave Grant a strange look as he commented, "Seems like the Stroud's have had a run of bad luck lately. First, their truck gets vandalized over in Sevier County and now last night's fire...and that's just the beginning! Later today, they'll be burying Arliss and Dwayne. Their Pa, Harmon was in here about twenty minutes ago. Sat right there in that chair you're sitting in and had a cup of coffee with me. I've known Harmon for years. I've had quite a few business dealings with him. As far as I'm concerned he's the only one of the Stroud's with a lick of sense."

Looking out the front window at the early morning traffic, Zeb went on to explain, "He told me that Effy fell off the porch last night after the fire and hit her head. They couldn't bring her around so they called an ambulance out to their place. Turns out she had a brain aneurism which unfortunately burst on their way to the hospital. When they got there she was DOA. Harmon told me that after the funeral for his two boys later on this afternoon he and Loretty are packing up their kids and moving down to North

Carolina. He also told me that, Rosemary, Ambrose's wife and their kids are tagging along. That just about wipes out the Stroud clan when you figure that leaves Maude, Otis and Cletus to run the place. To tell you the truth I really don't see them hanging around either. Maude's tough, but she can't keep that place up by herself. Otis is too old and Cletus is just too lazy. I bet they wind up selling the place."

Grant stood as he finished his coffee. "If that happens ol' Axel will sure be happy. According to him, he's been looking for a reason for years to run them out of the county. Looks to me like they all might just leave of their own accord. Look, I gotta run. If you happen to see Buddie tell him I said hey!"

Grant only spent a few minutes at the station as he swapped some pleasantries with Marge. He grabbed the crayon drawing from Brody's top desk drawer then headed out for a day of patrolling the streets of Townsend. Aside from a routine day ahead, Grant had two specific things he wanted to accomplish. One would have to wait until later in the afternoon, but the other could be handled within the next hour. Sitting in the parking lot of the station he punched in Doug's home number. After a number of rings and no answer he figured they were either still in bed or not at home. Looking up Doug's cell number on his phone's contact list he made the call.

"Hello, this is Doug."

"Doug, it's Grant! Where are you right now?"

"Max and I are over here at the shop. We decided to go ahead and open up rather than waiting a week. What's on your mind?"

"Don't go anywhere," said Grant. "I'm gonna drop by. Got something I want to discuss with you and Max."

Five minutes later, Grant pulled around to the back of the shop, got out of the cruiser and entered the building. Max was busy cleaning the front windows while Doug was going about dusting off his framed wildlife pictures. Giving Grant the high sign by waving his feather duster in the air, Doug gave him a greeting, "Mornin', Grant. Looks like it might get up into the high forties today."

"Forget the weather," said Grant. "I need to know if you set that fire at the Stroud's last night?"

Max climbed down off of the stool she was standing on. "I thought you were going to be supportive with us on this. I already told you I had an idea for the next thing we were going to drop on the Stroud's. You didn't seem all that interested so we just went ahead on our own. Besides that, there was nothing you could have done last night to help us out. It came off smooth as snot on a skillet."

Grant sat in one of the log chairs. "I got called out to the fire last night."

Interested, Max asked, "How did it turn out? After Doug lit the tent we took off through the woods."

Sitting back in the chair, Grant crossed his legs. "If your intent was to close them down, if for nothing else, temporarily, you succeeded! By the time I got there is was all but over. The tent was completely gone and the tables were destroyed beyond repair." Looking at Doug, he asked, "I suppose the artwork on the side of their shed was your handy work as well?"

Max proudly spoke up, "No, that was all my doing! Doug set the fire, I did all the creative painting."

"Look, you guys, I think you need to back off. Mathematically, you've caused the Stroud's more financial damage than you have experienced. They lost the $2500.00 they spent on that lighting, not to mention the money they'll lose on the resale of the merchandise. They have to replace four tires on their truck and now you've shut them down, which will no doubt cost them money to get started back up again."

"It's more than just the money involved," said Doug. "They beat both Max and myself. How do you put a price on physical damage?"

"I understand what you're saying," agreed Grant, "but I think your troubles with the Stroud's might be over. Think about it? Has anything more happened to you since the attack here at the shop?"

"No," answered Doug. "But why should we stop now when the roles have been reversed?"

"Because I feel it's over. Ambrose is now in the process of serving thirty days and if he is the one who has been orchestrating everything that has happened, nothing is going to happen to either of you as long as he is incarcerated. The truth is, the Stroud's are running out of time and resources, and by resources, I mean members of their family. Now, we don't know if any of the other members aside from the night you were attacked by three men, were involved or not. Their numbers are decreasing rapidly. Arliss and Dwayne are being buried this afternoon and last night Effy died from a brain aneurism. I just got some information this morning that you might be interested in. Harmon, his wife and children are leaving for North Carolina after the funeral. Rosemary, Ambrose's wife and children are going with them. That leaves Maude, Otis and Cletus to mind the store. They're going to be too busy just trying to keep their place up, let alone seeking revenge for what's happened to them lately."

"So what are you suggesting?" asked Max.

"I think you need to back off and wait and see what happens. Brody is over in Maryville this morning talking with the County Sheriff about some suspicions regarding Russell Pearl. I'm not exactly sure right now how things are going to pan out, but I think the Stroud's are going to have a lot of questions to answer. If things turn out the way I hope they will, the whole lot could wind up behind bars."

"What exactly are you talking about?" asked Doug.

Grant stood and walked to the door. "I'm afraid that's something I really can't discuss with you. Trust me! Just back off on this revenge kick you're on and let's see what happens in the next week or so."

Doug placed his arm around Max and stated. "Okay, it's business as usual for us here at the shop. We'll wait until we hear from you."

The morning seemed to drag on forever as Grant drove up and down the streets of Townsend. It was an odd time of the year in the Smokies. In two weeks it would be Thanksgiving and for the most part the locals caught a break from the hoards of tourists. After Thanksgiving business always picked up again as countless tourists flocked into Gatlinburg, Pigeon Forge, Townsend and the surrounding area as Christmas season was in full swing, tourists cramming into the shops for unique Smoky Mountain gifts.

Pulling into Arby's to grab a roast beef sandwich and a drink he thought about the fact that he hadn't even given any thought to what he was going to get his wife, daughter and mother-in-law for

Christmas. It was hard for him to imagine his family sitting around a Christmas tree, the house decorated with lights and holiday ornaments. They were three states and hundreds of miles from where he was. Even though Dana Beth had promised him that soon she would come back home, a sense of loneliness settled in over him. Sitting in the cruiser in Arby's lot, he slowly ate his lunch thinking about how strange his life at the time seemed to be. His immediate family had left him, he had just recently shot and killed a man, he was indirectly involved in Doug and Max's illegal revenge activities and despite all these things, depending on how Dana Beth felt when she returned, he could wind up being a multi-millionaire!

It was times like this that he had half a mind to drive back to the station, confront Brody and tell him he was quitting. Then he would drive down to Ft. Meyers, locate his wife and child and bring them home. He wanted some normalcy in his life. But then again, he was an officer of the law, an occupation that at times revealed the ugliness of what people were capable of. But the thing was, he couldn't throw in the towel just now. He had to see this thing through. Quitting now, would be like dropping out of a race before you reached the finish line or not finishing the reading of a book and not knowing the eventual outcome. No, he had to hang in until he reached the finish line, until he read the final page.

Swallowing the last bite of the sandwich he finished his drink and looked at his watch, 12:50. It was time to accomplish the second thing he wanted to get done before the end of his shift. Once on the Parkway he drove about a mile out of town and made a right on Webb Road. Cutting across two different back roads he came to Dunn Road where he made a right, traveled for a quarter mile and then pulled off into a small dirt clearing next to a large field bordered on three sides with trees. Looking through the binoculars he had borrowed from Dalton he peered across the field at the distant tree line that marked the north end of the Stroud's property. There were three breaks in the trees. Hopefully, in one of these breaks he would find what he was searching for. Just like he had figured, he was going to have to get out and walk across the field for a closer look. Changing into some civilian clothes he brought along, he tucked his gun into his jeans, grabbed his camera and notebook, the binoculars hanging from his neck.

Hugging the tree line on his right would allow him to travel across the field without being easily noticed. Five minutes into his short hike, he heard the snapping of a twig from somewhere in the trees. He stopped and peered into the tree line. There wasn't a sound. Was someone watching him? It couldn't be one of the Stroud's because they were all on their way or at Arliss and Dwayne's funeral. A small flock of wrens flew from the top of a tree. Shrugging off his thoughts, he continued down the tree line, the intersecting barbed wire that marked the Stroud's property line just thirty yards away.

Making a left at the rusted fencing he continued until he came to the first of the three clearings. It was nothing more than a power line that was cut through the dense trees, two power line towers and an old rutted dirt road.

Continuing on forty yards further he stopped at the second clearing where there was a large pile of cut logs, an old rusted, dilapidated car and what looked like a makeshift shooting range. There were a number of empty shells on the ground and twenty yards away there were four bullet shredded targets hanging on the side of two trees. There was only one clearing left. If he didn't find what he was looking for there, then he might have to venture onto the property; something he really didn't want to do.

Fifty yards on he stopped at the final clearing. A dirt road ended at the corner of an old storage shed. A backhoe was parked next to the shed, along with an assortment of garden tools: shovels, rakes and hoes. A thirty by ten foot weed infested garden ran along the edge of the barbed wire fencing. The cold weather and the time of year dictated that the garden had been abandoned until the coming spring. A few tomato cages stood at the far end of the garden; a number of rotted tomatoes laid on the ground. Looking past the shed in the distance Grant saw a small herd of grazing cattle and an old dog as it crossed a small field. Then, he noticed what he had come to discover: an old tire swing hanging from a large oak tree. Pulling the crayon drawing from his pocket he smiled as he was sure this was the spot that had been drawn. He took a quick picture of the shed and the garden, then the tree swing when he was interrupted by a soft voice, "Hello."

Grant, startled, looked to his left and there stood a young ponytailed girl in a pink dress. Her feet were encased in filthy white galoshes. The girl appeared to be about six or seven years old. Grant, surprised that anyone was on the property, looked around for any adults, but the child seemed to be alone. Grant smiled and responded, "Well, hello there yourself. What's your name?"

The girl pulled a piece of red licorice from a pocket in her dress, took a bite then answered, "My name's Violet. I live here." Holding the licorice out toward him, she offered, "Want some?" Grant, still looking around for someone else was surprised that he had run into the very person who had drawn the picture he was holding. Reaching out, he took a bite of the candy and handed it back as he spoke, "I know your daddy. His name in Cletus. I've talked with your grandmother, Maude. Are they at home right now?"

Taking another bite. she answered, "My Pa is but Maude and Otis went to a funeral for Arliss and Dwayne."

Grant, not wanting to confront any of the Stroud adults asked, "Where is your Pa right now?"

"He's asleep in our trailer."

Holding up the drawing so that Violet could see it, Grant smiled. "I think you were the one who drew this picture."

At first Violet seemed confused but then she grinned and asked, "Where did you get it?"

"I got it from a man named Russell. Do you know him?"

The grin on her face grew even larger as she exclaimed, "Yes, I know Russell. He stayed with us for a long time but then he left without even sayin' good bye ta me! I miss Russell. He was my friend."

Pointing at the drawing, Grant spoke again, "Maybe you could help me." He pointed at the large stick figure and asked, "Is this Russell?"

"Yes, and that's me," as she pointed at the small stick figure.

Grant pointed at the figure that was laying down in the drawing as she probed, "And is this your Momma?"

Violet smiled proudly, "Yes!"

"Why is she laying down? Is she resting or asleep?"

Walking across the garden, she stopped a few feet down the fence line and pointed at the ground. "She's down there. I come to visit her everyday!"

"Does she talk to you?"

"No, she can't talk because she's in Heaven. Looking around she placed her index finger over her lips. "I have a secret, but since you know Russell, I guess I can tell ya. My Pa and my Ma had a bad fight. I saw the whole thing. My Ma got kilt by my Pa and Maude and Effy said we had to bury her here in the garden." Kneeling down, she patted the ground. "She's right here!"

Grant, had not only gained the information he had come for but much more. Violet walked to the tire swing and jumped on as she asked, "Maybe ya could push me like Russell did?"

"I'd love to, but I have to go," said Grant. "I won't tell anyone that you shared the secret of your momma with me if you promise that you won't tell anyone that I was here. If you can do that, the next time I see you I'll bring along some red licorice."

Violet smiled. "Okay!"

Grant turned and jogged back across the field. Back at his cruiser he looked through the binoculars at the clearing where he met Violet. She was nowhere in sight. He quickly changed back into his uniform and called the station. "Marge...is Brody back from Maryville?"

"Yeah, but he's not in the best of moods. Apparently, things didn't go all that well. He came in mumbling something about how Sheriff Grimes felt they didn't have enough to go on just yet."

Grant pulled out of the clearing. "Tell Brody to stay put. I've got some news that will make his day."

CHAPTER NINETEEN

THE CLOCK SOFTLY CHIMED THE TIME AT FIVE O'CLOCK.
Grant was just finishing his morning coffee when Dalton entered
the kitchen. Wiping sleep from his eyes, Dalton yawned and
opened the cabinet where the cups were kept. "Going in earlier
than usual today?"

"Yeah, indeed I am," answered Grant. "Looks like we're finally
going to put this Russell Pearl business to bed. I had a very
interesting meeting with Brody yesterday afternoon. For the first
time, I think he and I are on the same page."

"I thought that fiasco was over when you shot him up there in
the mountains."

"Not quite. We have a few loose ends that need to be tied up.
I don't have time to tell you what's going on right now. I'll fill
you in when I get home tonight. By the end of the day it's going
to be big news around these parts." Tipping his cup at Dalton,
Grant walked to the door and grabbed his coat off of a hook.
"I've got a meeting at the station in twenty minutes. I better get
going."

Grant was the last one to arrive at the station as Marge
gestured down the hall. "Everyone's back there. This should be an
interesting day."

Entering Brody's office, he found Axel sitting at his desk, Lee
Griner and Kenny Jacks standing near the far wall and County
Sheriff Burt Grimes seated across from Brody. Grimes reached out
and shook Grant's hand, "Morning Officer Denlinger. I understand
you have an interesting photograph!"

Grant removed an envelope from his coat pocket and laid it on
the desk. "Right here it is. Got it developed last night at Wal-Mart
on my way home."

Axel opened his desk drawer and laid the crayon drawing next
to the envelope. "I haven't seen the photo yet, but according to
Grant this drawing is the location on the Stroud property where
Ruby Jean Stroud might be buried."

Grimes opened the envelope and matched it up with the drawing, then turned to Grant. "And you say you had a conversation with Cletus Stroud's daughter who drew and signed this drawing?"

"That I did," said Grant. "Her name is Violet just like her name indicates on the drawing."

For the next half hour, Brody, Grimes, Lee and Kenny listened intently as Grant put all the puzzle pieces in place: From the information he had gathered, he was sure Russell Pearl had stayed at the Stroud's at some point after he was thought to be dead. Violet had admitted that her father, Cletus, killed her mother, Ruby Jean. The family tried to hide this fact by burying her in their garden. Along with the fact that Russell Pearl's fingerprints had been found in Arliss and Dwayne's truck, Russell most likely killed them.

Grimes removed an envelope from his coat pocket and laid it on the desk. "I just happen to have an envelope myself; an envelope that contains a search warrant for not only the Stroud's main house but all of the buildings on their property and the acreage itself." Tapping the envelope, he went on to explain, "Yesterday Axel and I had quite a discussion about the Stroud's, but when it was all said and done I didn't think we had enough to go over there and arrest anyone. After talking with Grant last evening, Brody gave me a call and told me what Grant had discovered, so I went to the County Judge and had him issue a search warrant." Picking up the envelope, he addressed Axel directly. "Chief Brody, even though I'm the County Sheriff, all of this is happening in your backyard so I'm going to leave this up to you. If you want to get a team together and head on up to the Stroud's, then…so be it!"

Axel smiled. "We have our team right here in this room. I assume you want to tag along?"

"I'd like nothing better. The Stroud's have been a constant problem not only here in Townsend, but throughout the county. What's the plan?"

Brody looked around the room and addressed each officer, "Kenny, you'll be staying here in town on patrol, but be ready in case we need you later. The rest of us will head over to the Stroud's at first light. Burt and I will drive up in his cruiser and Grant and

Lee will drive separately. It's now six forty-five. We leave at seven sharp. Any questions?"

Lee spoke up, "Exactly what are we going to be looking for?"

Axel answered the question as he stood and picked up the crayon drawing. "Ruby Jean's body, which reminds me. I've got two shovels, a pick axe and some heavy duty cuttin' shears in the back of my truck that we need to take along. Check your weapons and make sure you've got a full chamber. I don't expect anythin' to go wrong, but this is the Stroud's were talkin' about. If everythin' works out the way I think it will, they'll get backed into a corner like the rats they are. So, dependin' on how things go down, they might come out swingin'. We don't want to get caught with our pants down."

As everyone exited the building, Brody stopped and ordered Marge, "We're goin' up to pay the Stroud's a visit. Be ready for us to call. We might need the County Coroner or possibly Child Services."

Brody was out the door as Marge wished him, "Good Luck!"

In the parking lot, everyone congregated around Brody's truck as he unloaded the shovels and other tools, continuing to give orders, "When we get up there we might have to cut a chain or a padlock on the main gate. When we get back to where they live, Grant and I will roust Cletus out of his trailer. Sheriff Grimes and Lee need to head on up to the main house and collect Maude and Otis. Accordin' to information Grant received, they'll be the only family members on the place. That bein' said, we still need to check the other two trailers just in case. After that, we'll head on back to the suspected burial spot." Walking toward Grime's car, Axel hoisted the tools over his shoulder. "Let's hit it!"

Grant, who was bringing up the rear of the three car convoy, turned on the windshield wipers as large snowflakes began to fall. By the time they arrived at the intersection of the Parkway and Wears Valley Road it was practically a white out. Grant's radio crackled followed by Brody's voice, "We might have to pull over when we get there and wait this weather out. I don't want to take any chances on blowin' this opportunity."

Making a right onto Wears Valley, Grant crept along at no more than ten miles an hour, the wind whipping the white swirling snow in every direction. Then, suddenly as if by magic the blinding whiteness disappeared and was reduced to large falling flakes. Three minutes later, Grant followed the other two vehicles onto the dirt road that led to the Stroud's.

The sun was just starting to come up, but the snow clouds were preventing the natural sunlight to penetrate the semi-darkness. Grant watched as Brody and Grimes got out. The headlights from the lead car illuminated the cattle gate that blocked the road. Axel made quick work of the chained lock on the gate and Grimes pushed it open. Walking back to the car Axel, gave a thumbs up to the others that they were going in.

Driving up the dirt road flanked on both sides by tall pines, Grant peered through the falling snow as a murky shadow of an abandoned car or old appliance loomed into view. A deer ran quickly from one side of the road to the other in between Lee and Grant's vehicles. Grant felt on edge as if he were invading the Stroud's privacy. He wondered what kind of trouble, if any, laid ahead. There was no reason for him to be nervous. Their team consisted of four armed officers. Legally, they had every right to be on the Stroud's property, but how would the Stroud's view the legal invasion of their farm? If Grant had learned anything during his short stint as an officer it was that the best laid plans could change rapidly. Things could take longer than planned, people didn't always cooperate and there was always the unknown; that silent unseen fact that anything could happen at any time. He could only control his actions. He had to be ready to react to the Stroud's who would no doubt look at the invasion of their property from a different viewpoint; a viewpoint of anger.

Finally the three cars broke into a clearing, a security light mounted on a telephone pole next to Cletus' trailer piercing the early morning dim sunlight. Grimes stopped the lead car and Brody got out and signaled Burt and Lee forward toward the main house. Grant climbed out of his car and joined Axel in the front yard of Cletus' place. Axel unsnapped his holster and withdrew his revolver as he ordered Grant, "I want you to go the back and see if there is another entrance to the trailer. Wait there until I call you. We don't want Cletus to run out the back or crawl out a window. Ready?"

Grant drew his revolver and answered, "Yes, sir!"

Brody walked across the yard and stepped up on the

cinderblocks that led to the front entrance. He yelled as he banged loudly on the door. "Cletus Stroud...open up, this is the Townsend Police Department!"

At the rear of the trailer, Grant shined his flashlight on the back of the home. There were three windows but no back door. He heard Brody yell again, "Cletus Stroud, this is the Townsend Police...open the door... now!" Stepping to the side of the door to prevent being shot, Brody yelled to Grant. "What's it look like back there!"

Grant yelled back, "Three windows, no door."

"Beat on the side of the trailer and identify yourself. We have to get him outside. We don't want to get involved in a standoff."

"Grant, using the butt end of the flashlight banged loudly on the side of the mobile home as he yelled, "Cletus Stroud...Townsend Police Department. Open up!"

Brody banged on the front door again. "Cletus, come out now, or we're comin' in. We don't want anyone injured!"

A deep voice from inside the trailer answered, "What do ya want? Ya scared the hell out of my daughter! Go away and leave us be!"

Banging on the door again, Brody yelled back, "Can't do that Cletus. You either come out or we're bustin' in. I have a search warrant with me that says I can come in. Now, don't make this harder than it has to be. Come on out!"

The door slowly opened and Cletus peered out. "What do ya want, Brody? Do ya have any idea how pissed Maude's gonna be when she finds out ya scared my little girl?"

Brody stepped forward, displaying his revolver. "Yeah, well you can talk with her about all that in a few minutes. Sheriff Grimes is gettin' her and Otis up as we speak. Now, move back and I'm comin' in while you and your daughter get dressed." Yelling around the side of the trailer, Axel ordered, "Grant! Come around front. We're goin' in!"

Cletus backed up as Axel shoved the door completely open. "Move back, Cletus. As soon as my deputy gets in here you need to get dressed and get your daughter out here. Don't try anythin' funny. Don't give me a reason to use this gun!"

Cletus reminded Brody of a sumo wrestler. Dressed in nothing more than a pair of white boxer shorts, he backed up slowly as Axel entered the trailer with Grant right behind him. Suddenly,

Violet appeared in the hallway and wiped her eyes as she began to cry. Grant moved past Brody and walked down the hall as he spoke softly. "Remember me? We talked yesterday out by the back fence. You shared your licorice with me. I told you the next time we met that I'd bring some red licorice." Reaching into his jacket pocket, he produced three strands of the twisted red candy. "I've got some right here. If you come out here in the living room with me your daddy can get dressed."

Violet sniffled and wiped her eyes, then slowly walked down the hall to the adjoining room where Grant gave her the candy. Brody nodded in approval and then ordered Cletus. "Alright, let's walk back to your bedroom where you can get some clothin' on."

Cletus backed up further into the room appearing like he was not going to cooperate. Brody motioned at a blanket lying on the couch. "Officer Denlinger. Why don't you wrap Violet in that blanket and take her out to the cruiser where she can keep warm. Cletus and I are goin' to have a little discussion about what's goin' to happen in the next couple minutes."

Grant, sensing that Brody had enough of Cletus, grabbed the blanket and wrapped it around Violet as he ushered her outside, Brody closed the door behind him. Axel looked Cletus up and down and remarked, "You really are one stupid ass son of a bitch! I told you months ago that if I ever had to come back over here because of you beatin' on your wife, I'd haul your ass off to jail."

Cletus gave a cocky smile. "So, that's what this is all about. Well, Ruby Jean ain't here. Everybody knows she run off. If that's why ya came out here, well then ya can just turn around an' git! I can't beat on a woman who ain't even here, now can I?"

"We'll talk about that later. Right now, you need to get dressed so we can join the others."

Cletus looked at the revolver in Brody's hand and sneered. "If ya didn't have that gun ya wouldn't be so tough, Brody!"

Axel cocked his head and smiled. "Tell ya what, Cletus. I don't think you're as tough as most folks make you out to be. You can beat on a woman, but what about a man?" With that, Axel laid the gun on the top of an old china cabinet next to the door. "Now, let's see how bad assed you really are!"

Cletus thought for a moment and then clenched both of his fists and moved slightly forward sizing Axel up. Axel stood his ground and didn't move a muscle. The smile on Cletus' face went away and was replaced with a look that indicated that he wanted to take a swing at Axel. He took another step forward and Brody reacted and brought the pointed end of his right cowboy boot up into Cletus' groin, the big man instantly doubling over in pain. Brody then gave him a savage upper cut sending him back over a chair onto the floor. Axel turned and picked the gun back up as he suggested, "I would strongly advise you to walk down that hall and get dressed or I can continue to use you as a human punchin' bag!"

Cletus slowly got to his feet as he complained, "This ain't right, it ain't fair!"

Brody aimed the gun directly at Cletus' head as he stated. "Yeah, well life ain't fair. Now, move your ass. The sooner you get dressed the sooner we can get this over with."

Violet huddled beneath the wool blanket in the front seat of Grant's cruiser. Grant, in the driver's seat noticed Lee making his way back down the road. Rolling down the window, Grant asked, "How did it go up at the house?"

"Piece of cake," said Lee. "Maude put up quite a fuss, but her ol' man, Otis was so drunk he doesn't know what's going on." Looking in the window at Violet, he asked, "Where's Axel...and Cletus?"

Nodding toward the trailer, Grant half smiled. "I think Cletus needed a little extra prodding to get him moving."

Just then the trailer door opened and Cletus dressed in jeans, tee shirt and an old ragged coat, stepped down from the cinderblocks and crossed the yard, Brody right behind him. Looking at Lee, Brody ordered, "Let's get Cletus into the other cruiser, then we'll drive up to the house and join Grimes."

Lee stared into Cletus' face at his bloody lower lip. "Did we have some trouble, Chief?"

"No, Cletus here tripped over a chair, that's all."

After Cletus was placed in Lee's cruiser, Brody ordered his two officers, "Drive up to the house and park behind Grimes. I'm gonna talk with Maude and Otis and see what I can find out."

Axel walked up the road and climbed in the front seat next to Grimes. Turning sideways he looked at Maude and Otis who were seated in the back. Maude's hair was going in every direction. She wore an old dress and a moth eaten dark green sweater. Otis, who wore the look of a drunken sailor, had apparently fallen to sleep in his clothes. Recognizing Brody, he slurred his words, "Chief...Brody. How about...a cold one!"

Maude backhanded her husband as she spoke sternly, "Shut up ya ol' drunk assed fool! I got me enough problems without yer damn jabberin'."

Axel, feeling he had the Stroud's right where he wanted them, remarked snidely, "Good mornin', Maude. Sorry to hear about Effy."

Maude snapped back, "Sorry, my ass! At least she ain't here ta see this injustice! Ya ain't got no right ta come onta my property and git us all out of bed. Where's my granddaughter? I swear ta God, if she gits injured in any way while yer out here, I'll have Merle Pittman sue yer ass off!"

Axel pointed at the back window as he answered, "She's in one of the cruisers where she can keep warm. She'll be fine. Besides that, you've got a lot more to worry about right now."

Pointing her fat finger at Axel, she demanded, "Grimes said ya had a search warrant. I ain't seen one yet!"

Brody reached inside his pocket and produced the folded paper as he displayed it to Maude. "Here it is in black and white." Laying the official document on the dashboard, he went on, "Now that that's settled, I've got a few questions to ask you and it would be to your benefit if you cooperate." Maude sat back in the seat and folded her arms across her chest in defiance as Otis mumbled something about wanting a beer.

Axel coughed, cleared his throat and then began his questioning, "First off, is there anyone else on the property. We heard that Harmon took Loretty and Rosemary and the kids down to North Carolina. That true?"

Maude glared back at Brody. "Ain't tellin' ya nothin'. Don't expect me ta make yer job easy. Far as I'm concerned ya can wipe yer ass with that search warrant, but seein' as how ya have one, yer gonna have ta put it ta good use. If ya want ta know there's anybody else on the property, then ya can just *look* fer 'em yerself!"

Grimes interrupted, "Well, if that's the way it's gonna be, I'm gonna get Lee so we can get started searching the other three trailers." Looking at Maude, Burt asked, "You have keys or do we kick in the doors?"

Maude reached into her sweater and pulled out a lighter and a pack of cigarettes. "Mind if I smoke in here?"

Brody rolled his eyes. "Be my guest."

Lighting what was to be her first smoke of the day, Maude answered Grime's previous question, "Like I said, I ain't gonna make yer job easy. I reckon I don't know what yer lookin' fer, but I ain't gonna help ya none!"

Getting out of the car, Grimes commented, "I'll just grab Lee and we'll start kickin' doors in!"

Axel rolled down his window as the smoke from Maude's cigarette started to invade the front seat. Smiling, he said, "I hear tell you have quite the interestin' garden on your property."

Maude puffed on her smoke as she fired back, "What the hell's that s'pose ta mean?"

Pulling out the crayon drawing, Axel held it up, "This was drawn by your granddaughter, Violet. Accordin' to her, she gave it to Russell Pearl. You told me you never met the man. Now, that wasn't exactly the truth was it?"

Otis, in his drunken stupor, spoke up loudly, "That damned Russell...he kilt Arliss and Dwayne!"

Reaching over, Maude took her husband by the collar of his wrinkled shirt and looked into his bleary eyes. "Otis Stroud! If ya don't shut yer mouth, I'll shut it fer ya!" She slapped him across his face and then threw him violently back against the seat. "Understand!"

Otis, with the fear of God across his face, pulled his feet up into a fetal position and mumbled, "Think I'll...take me...a nap."

Axel laughed. "You can beat on your poor husband all you want, Maude, but the cat's out of the bag. We know Russell stayed here for a spell." Holding up the drawing once again, he explained, "I believe this stick figure that's layin' down is Violet's momma...none other than Ruby Jean. I don't suppose you would be interested in tellin' me where this garden is?"

Taking the cigarette to her mouth, Maude looked out the side window. "Ain't got nothin' else ta say, Brody."

Axel looked at Otis and asked, "How about you, Otis?"

Maude glared at her husband, a signal that he needed to remain quiet.

Otis, receiving the message loud and clear, shook his head indicating he had nothing to add.

Brody opened the envelope and removed the photograph Grant had taken as he held it up for Maude to see. "This picture was taken somewhere on your farm. Notice the hangin' tire swing. It appears to be the same as the one Violet drew in her picture. All we have to do is locate that swing and I'm guessin' that's where we'll find this mysterious garden."

Maude let a low grunt as if she could have cared less and took a drag on her cigarette. Axel opened the door and was about to get out, but hesitated and then addressed Maude, "You hit your husband one more time and I'm gonna pull your ass out of this car and give you some of the same!"

Otis smiled and curled up in the seat.

Thirty-five minutes passed when Grimes and Lee came back down the road and met with Brody who was standing outside the car. Grimes nodded back up the road as he spoke, "Looks like there is no one else around at the moment."

As Grant joined them, Axel asked him, "Do you know where this garden is located?"

"Not exactly," said Grant, "but when I was out here yesterday, I saw an old metal shed at the end of a dirt road where the garden is. Maybe if we follow this road up to that shed up ahead we'll get lucky. When I was here yesterday, I came in from the back of the property. It can't be that far from here."

Axel looked up the road as he nodded. "Alright then. Let's drive up there and see what we can find. If we strike out, we've got all day to look around."

Grant followed the first two vehicles up the dirt road as he gazed up into the gloomy gray sky. The snow had all but stopped, the sun struggling to fight its way through the cloudy sky. The dirt road became forked, the road on the left continuing on into the trees, the one of the right circling around the side of the large shed. Grimes took a right and the other two vehicles followed. Driving as far as they could, they stopped when the road dead ended on the opposite side of the metal building.

Grimes was the first to spot the hanging tire swing. "This looks like the spot in the photo."

"Sure does," said Axel. "I'm gonna get everybody out of the cars."

Two minutes later, Maude, Otis, and Cletus stood with their backs up against the side of the shed. Violet stood next to Maude as she clutched at the blanket. Brody, who wasn't the highest ranking officer on the scene, but the one who was ramrodding the situation ordered, "Burt, why don't you keep an eye on our audience while me and the boys have a look see around the area."

Grant immediately went to the barbed wire fence where he pointed at the old tomato cages. Bending down, he shined the flashlight on a six by three foot area where there didn't seem to be as many weeds as the rest of the garden. "This is the approximate area where Violet said her momma was."

Burt knelt down in front of Violet and asked, "That right, Honey...is that the spot?"

Violet took a bite of licorice and looked up into Maude's eyes, but remained silent.

Burt stood back up as he spoke. "I don't think she's going to say anything with Maude being present."

"That's alright," said Brody "We'll start diggin' right here and see what turns up, if anythin'." Walking to the cruiser he opened the trunk and removed the tools he had brought along.

Looking at Maude for her reaction, he handed a shovel to both Lee and Grant and ordered, "Start diggin' boys!"

Maude lit up another cigarette, but aside from that she displayed no emotion. Otis, who could barely stand, slid down the side of the shed, folded his arms around his skinny frame and closed his eyes. Cletus, on the other hand began to fidget as he rubbed his hands together and looked nervously from side to side.

Grant slipped on a pair of work gloves and jammed the shovel down into the hard earth. On the opposite side of the plot, Lee did the same. Following three successive attempts with little results, Grant commented hopelessly, "The ground is really hard. This could take awhile."

"Stand back," said Lee as he grabbed the pick axe. Following a number of blows with the heavy duty, pointed tool, Lee motioned to Grant. "There, give that a try."

Grant scooped up the loose dirt easily, then stepped back so

Lee could attack the hard earth once again. The process continued for the next fifteen minutes, Lee and Grant taking turns with the axe.

The temperature was turning colder as Grimes looked at the Stroud's who resembled a group of refugees standing up against the shed, their warm breath escaping their lungs into the cold air. Looking up into the falling snow he suggested to Brody. "Why don't you put Violet back in my car where it's warm. I think we need to put the old man in Lee's car. He doesn't look too good."

Axel agreed as he walked over and shook Otis. "Come on, Otis, we're puttin' you in the car where it's warm." Otis, shivering, stood slowly and spoke, "Thank you." It appeared to Brody that the cold was starting to have a sobering effect on the old man.

Grimes walked over to Maude and gently took Violet by her arm, "Come on, darlin', let's get you in the car where it's warm. Now, you go along with Chief Brody."

Violet looked up at Maude for approval. "You go on child," said Maude. "It'd be best if ya git out of this cold."

Grant, out of breath, stopped shoveling and leaned up against a nearby tree. "We've only gone down about a foot and a half. At this rate, we could be another hour or so before we dig down far enough and that's even if this is the right spot."

Looking around, Lee suggested, "What about that backhoe sitting over there on the side of the shed? Can we use that?"

Brody, now back from placing Violet and Otis in the first two cars, answered, "Don't know why not. That would speed things up some."

Throwing down the axe, Lee walked over to the one-man machine and asked, "Do we have keys?"

Grimes turned to Maude. "You heard the man. Do we have keys?"

"Yeah, *we* have keys. The problem is *you don't,* and I ain't about ta tell ya where they are!"

Grimes spoke to Cletus, "Do you know the whereabouts of the keys?"

"No, and if I did, I wouldn't tell ya!"

"Don't make a difference," said Brody. "I'm gonna call Marge and have her call the mayor to get some city equipment up here.

Meanwhile, you boys need to keep diggin'.""

Grant picked up the axe and drove it into the hard earth as he stated, "This looks like one of those days when we really earn our money!"

After making the call, Axel walked over and stood in front of Cletus, "Your daughter, Violet, told officer Denlinger that you and Ruby Jean had quite a fight, the end result bein' that you killed her. I told you if I had to come back up here over your fightin' I'd put your ass in jail. The thing is, I always felt your wife was just as violent as you. Maybe you didn't mean to kill her. Maybe it was self defense."

Axel could tell by Cletus' reaction that he had hit a cord. "If it turns out that it was self defense, maybe things won't turn out so bad for you after all. Violet told Officer Denlinger that it was Maude and Effy who wanted to bury Ruby Jean here on the property. Why should you take the fall for what they wanted to do?"

Cletus glanced down at the scars on his fingers where Ruby Jean had cut him and was about to say something when he was stopped by Maude who scolded him, "Cletus! Ya keep yer mouth shut! Listen ta me! I'm yer Ma! Brody, he's jest messin' with ya!"

Cletus looked down at his feet and remained quiet.

Otis, sobering up, sat up in the backseat of Lee's car and looked out the front windshield and watched as Grant and Lee continued with the digging. It was just a matter of time before they discovered Ruby Jean's body and if they started to sniff around maybe even that tractor salesman. *He couldn't allow that to happen!* Maude never thought much of him. She never gave him credit for anything. If he could just get out of the car somehow then maybe he could rescue his family. He tried the back door but it was locked. Climbing over to the front seat, he tried the driver's side door. He grabbed the handle and pushed down. The door opened. Apparently, they hadn't locked the door as they no doubt felt he was too drunk to be a problem.

Outside of the car, he took a deep breath, the cold night air bringing him around. He crept alongside the car then cut in between two of the cars and made his way around to the front of the shed. Opening the door slowly, he got up and stumbled across the dirt floor to an old cabinet where they kept three rifles and some ammunition. Grabbing a 22 caliber rifle and a box of ammo, he sat on the floor and loaded the gun. Going to a rear window that was covered with cobwebs, he wiped away the webs and peered out. He could see Grant and Lee busy working on the grave, Brody standing off to the side. Sitting down against the wall he made his plan. He loaded the remaining two rifles and took them with him as he stepped back outside. He'd shoot Brody and then Grimes. It would take Lee and Grant a few seconds to react. If he was lucky he could take out all four. *I might be an ol' drunk,* he thought, *but I'm a good shot!*

Keeping close to the shed, he stayed down as he made his way past the last two cars, stopping at the passenger door of Grimes' cruiser. Going down on one knee he laid the two extra rifles against the side of the shed. Then, he heard a knocking on the car window. Looking up, he saw Violet looking through the window down at him. He placed his index finger over his lips; a signal for her to be quiet. She waved and took a bite of licorice.

Picking up the rifle, he noticed that his fingers were quickly growing numb from the cold air. The snow was just starting to pick up again as he brought the gun up and leveled it in Brody's direction. He got an odd feeling from the pit of his stomach as he placed the cross hairs on Brody who was standing sideways. The only vital shot Otis had at the moment was a head shot. The pain in his stomach caused him to wince as he brought the rifle up in line with the side of Brody's head. He took one last deep breath and then let it out slowly as he drew back his trigger finger. Just as he squeezed off the shot his body jerked. The shot was off. The bullet sliced through Axel's right shoulder and knocked him forward. Losing his balance, he stepped down in the two foot deep hole. Brody tried to control the fall, but stumbled and went down, half in, half out of the hole.

Everyone reacted at the same time; Grant and Lee ducking down, Grimes reaching for his revolver, Maude and Cletus dropped to their knees. They put their hands over their heads to try to shield themselves.

Otis' heaving stomach prevented him firing again as he doubled over, vomit spewing out his mouth and down the front of his shirt.

Grimes took three strides forward and raised his revolver to fire, but then he saw Violet at the window as she was screaming. Brody pulled his gun and fired twice, the first shot pinging off the side of the shed the second one finding its mark in Otis' left lower leg. Yelling in pain, Otis limped to the rear of the car and started to run awkwardly toward the trees.

Maude, with her cane, ran as best she could around the far side of the shed and headed for the dirt road.

Cletus tackled Grimes as he ran toward the spot where Otis had been. As Burt hit the ground the air was temporarily knocked out of him, rendering him helpless.

Brody tried to stand, but his foot slipped on the side of the hole and he went back down hard landing on his wounded shoulder.

Grant withdrew his gun and took aim at the fleeing Otis, the first shot breaking off a tree limb, the second one hitting Otis in his right leg, which caused him to stumble forward.

Cletus got up quickly and ran to the car scooping up one of the two remaining rifles. He fired five quick shots toward Brody, Lee and Grant.

Brody tried to take cover in the hole as Lee ran after Maude.

Grant took cover behind a tree as he watched Cletus run behind the first car and head for the woods.

Grant, concerned, ran to where Brody was laying and asked, "Chief, you alright?"

Pointing with his revolver, he ordered, "Don't let Maude get away. Grant! Go with Grimes and stop Cletus."

Running to help Burt to his feet, Grant pointed toward the woods. "Come on, Sheriff, we've got to go after Cletus!"

Grimes swore as he got to his feet. "Damn, what happened to Otis?"

"I think he got shot twice. He's laying on the other side of the cars."

Approaching the cars carefully, they spotted Otis on the ground, the rifle out of his reach. Grimes, still winded, bent over trying to get his breath back. Grant tapped him on the shoulder. "Listen! Stay here with Otis and check on Violet. Lee went after Maude." Looking at the woods, he popped two more shells in the chamber of his gun as he stated firmly, "I'm going in after Cletus." Running toward the tree line he yelled back, "You might want to check on Brody. He got hit, he's down. Call Kenny Jacks to get up here! We need an ambulance!"

The light coating of snow on the ground indicated that Cletus had run into the woods. Hesitating just after he entered the tree line, Grant knelt down and looked at the ground. The trees had prevented the snow from falling to the floor of the forest, so any idea of it being an easy thing to track Cletus vanished. Walking ten yards into the trees, he knelt down and thought about what direction would be the most logical for a man on the run to take. The woods at this point were only about twenty yards wide, the dirt road on the left, the adjacent field, bordered by the barbed wire fence on the right. Getting up, he continued straight on, as he shielded his body with tree after tree. It seemed logical that Cletus would run deeper into the trees, at least for awhile. Grant tried to recall all of the things Chief Blue had taught him about tracking. Looking down at the pinecone covered ground, he noticed where a number of cones had been smashed down by a heavy weight. He moved on, discovering that every two to three feet that the cones were disturbed. He remembered what Blue had told him about a wounded man on the run. About how they would continue on until they were too tired to go any further. Cletus wasn't wounded, but he had to be scared and that very fact made him dangerous. He might take a stance and wait for a clear and fatal shot.

Resting for a moment, he realized that Cletus was headed in a straight direction; probably with the thought in mind of getting as far away from the shed as possible. Crouching down Grant thought, *Will Cletus leave the property or just hide? Cletus knew every inch of the one hundred forty-three acre property He had the advantage. He had a rifle and he had fired it five times. How many shells did he have left? Did he have any extra ammunition?*

He stood up and started around a tree, when he heard a shot ring out followed by a sliver of bark flying from the tree just above his head. Ducking behind the tree, he realized, *Cletus had stopped running and was waiting for him. This changed things! Cletus knew where he was but he couldn't be sure exactly where Cletus was positioned.* Somehow, he was going to have to outsmart him.

Picking up a softball size rock, he took a deep breath, then tossed it a few yards to his left. As soon as the rock made contact with the dry pinecones, he sprinted to the right keeping as low as possible. A shot rang out as he slid into the loose cones next to a large pine tree. Waiting for a few seconds, he carefully peered around the side of the large tree. To his surprise, fifteen yards ahead and to his right, he saw the end of a rifle barrel sticking out from behind a tree. He now knew where Cletus was.

Sitting with his back against the tree, he saw something that sent a shiver through him; an animal trap, set to snap shut when some unfortunate animal stepped into the rusted jagged teeth. Then, he saw yet another trap, a few yards in the direction that he had just run from. He had come inches from stepping into it. *Damn,* he thought. *The woods might be full of traps and Cletus probably knew where everyone of them was located. He had to get out the woods!*

He could see the dirt road at the edge of the trees just ten yards away. Checking to make sure he had a full load, he stood up with his back against the tree, took a breath, then stepped out and fired four shots at the tree Cletus was behind. Sprinting toward the road he fired his last two shots toward the tree at the same time watching for any other traps. Sliding to the ground at the edge of the road, he turned just in time to see Cletus fleeing further back into the trees. Getting up he ran down the road as he reloaded, all the while keeping his eyes on Cletus. Loaded, he knelt down and took careful aim and pulled off six shots in the direction Cletus was running. Cletus let out a yell and stumbled forward. Grant reloaded as he watched for Cletus to get back up, all the while Cletus screaming wildly. Grant heard the sound of a car coming down the road.

Sheriff Grimes pulled up and rolled down the window and asked, "A lot of shooting going on back in here. Did you nail Cletus?"

Grant pointed into the trees as he answered with doubt, "I'm not sure. I think I might have. That's him screaming!"

Burt got out of the car and pulled his revolver from his holster. "With all that screaming you must have hit him good!"

Grant nodded toward the trees. "I'll circle around to the left, you take the right...and be careful! There are set animal traps scattered around the woods."

Following the screams, Grimes was the first to discover Cletus laying face down on the ground, his right hand clutching at his upper left leg, his left hand caught in one of the traps. He squirmed wildly, both his leg and wrist bleeding as he continued to scream, "Got damn! Git me free! I give up!"

Grant emerged from the trees from the left as he took in the scene; Cletus thrashing around, the rifle lying three feet beyond the trap.

Burt holstered his revolver as he placed his hand on Cletus' back. "Just hold on. We'll get you out of this thing." Looking up at Grant, he asked, "You know anything about these traps? Do you know how to open one?"

Grant knelt down and having little compassion for Cletus answered, "Not a clue."

Cletus continued to scream. "Son of a bitch! Get me out of this thing!"

"Calm down," ordered Burt. "If you don't stop moving around you're going to rip your hand off!"

Cletus was becoming hysterical as he yelled again, "I can't stand the pain! Git it off me!"

Grimes had enough. He rolled Cletus over onto his back, lifted his head and gave him a solid punch to his jaw, knocking him out. The forest was suddenly silent as Grant knelt next to Cletus and examined the rusted trap. I think there is supposed to be a release on the side of these things. After we get it open, we can try jamming a piece of wood in the teeth and then we can remove his hand."

Looking for the release, he asked Burt, "How'd things wind up back there at the shed?"

Picking up a nearby three inch branch, Grimes answered, "Everything's under control. We called an ambulance for Brody and Otis. Looks like ol' Cletus will be making the trip to the hospital with them. We also called the coroner and the city for some digging equipment. Oh yeah, Child Services is driving over to take custody of the child."

"What about Maude? Don't tell me she escaped?"

"Funny you should mention her," laughed Grimes. "Apparently, Officer Griner is quite the shot. He caught up with her as she tried to run down the road. He ordered her to stop. She turned around and gave him the finger. Griner goes down on one knee, takes careful aim and shoots her cane in half. I guess she went down like a sack of potatoes."

Grant motioned to Burt. "I think I found the release. When I get it open, jam that wood in there."

It was one-fifteen in the morning when Grant pulled into the driveway of Dalton's farm. Sitting back in the seat, he yawned and thought about the events that had unfolded during the long day. Placing his revolver inside his coat pocket, he felt a strand of licorice that he had forgotten to give to Violet. He smiled as he thought about her innocence, then frowned as he contemplated the horrible environment she had been raised in. She witnessed her own father kill her mother, then was forced by her elders to lie about what really happened. She had watched Cletus bury Ruby Jean, not at a funeral that all human beings deserved, but a secret and illegal burial. She had been in the middle of the shoot out at the Stroud's place and was now in the custody of the Blount County Child Services. He wondered what the future held for her.

Entering the kitchen, he was met with the wonderful smell of a fresh baked apple pie. Dalton sat at the table, working on a model ship he had received as a recent birthday gift and Greta was busy removing the pie from the oven. Leaning in the doorway, Grant looked at his mother and grandfather in amazement. "Do you people have any idea what time it is?"

Dalton laid the delicate balsa wood ship mast he had in his hand carefully down on the table as he looked at the kitchen clock. "Do you realize that it's been almost twenty hours since you left this house yesterday morning? You told me you'd be back later last night to tell us what happened. You said that by the end of the day, there was going to be some big news." Gesturing at the clock, he remarked, "Well, that day has come and gone. Your mother and I have been watching the news all day for any information and we don't know any more now than when you left hours ago."

Grant hung up his coat and sat down opposite Dalton. "You won't hear any news about what happened until the morning news. We just got things wrapped up about twenty five minutes ago over at the hospital. Brody got wounded in the shoulder, Otis and Cletus Stroud also got shot during an exchange of gunfire out at their place."

Setting the pie on the table, Greta looked directly at her son and asked, "Are you alright?"

Grant shrugged, "I'm fine...tired as hell, but otherwise...fine."

"What the hell happened at the Stroud's?" demanded Dalton.

"We had a lead that Ruby Jean Stroud really hadn't run off and left town like we were all led to believe, but that she was in fact buried up there on their property. So, we took a team up there armed with a search warrant. When we started to dig in the area where we suspected her body to be things went awry and that's when the shooting started to take place. Much later at the hospital, Cletus fessed up and told us what really happened to his wife. Turned out, he had a knock down drag out fight with her and she accidentally hit her head and died on the spot. Cletus said it was self defense as she had cut him with a steak knife and hit him with a frying pan, which is what he wanted to tell the police. According to him, Effy and Maude Stroud had different ideas. That's when they decided to bury her on their property and let everyone in town believe that she had run off. We still have some investigating to do but it looks like everyone in the family knew about it, so it might wind up that the whole lot will be sent off to jail. And, if that's not enough, when the city was digging up Ruby Jean they discovered another body that, also according to Cletus, was a tractor salesman that Ambrose killed a few years back."

Screwing the cap back onto a tube of construction cement, Dalton gave Grant a strange look. "You've completely lost me! Yesterday, right here in this kitchen you said you had a few loose ends to tie up in regard to Russell Pearl. Now, I'll admit, Ruby Jean's body and this tractor salesman being discovered up there on their property is newsworthy, but what does any of that have to do with the Russell Pearl case?"

Grant got up, walked to the counter and poured himself a cup of coffee as he answered, "It doesn't have anything to do with the Pearl case." Dumping some creamer into the cup, he explained, "We had another lead we were also following. We had reason to suspect that Russell Pearl was at the Stroud's place after he went over the Cumberland Gorge. Turns out, we were right. While Sheriff Grimes and I were interviewing Cletus, he told us that he knew everything about what happened to Russell Pearl after he went over the gorge, but that he wasn't going to say anything else unless we gave him a deal. Grimes agreed and Cletus spilled the beans on the rest of the family. He told us that Arliss and Dwayne found Pearl up near the gorge the day after he disappeared. They threw him in the back of their pickup truck and hauled him back down here to Townsend to their farm, thinking they could get a reward for Pearl. That's where things took a weird twist. Maude Stroud is the sister of Etta Pender, Russell's mother, who was shot to death over forty year ago. Maude and Effy agreed that since Russell was kin to them that they needed to nurse him back to health. According to Cletus, Russell was living right there on the farm right under our noses for close to four months."

Sitting back down at the table, Grant finished the story, "Cletus said Russell never got along with Arliss and Dwayne. Then, one night the three of them disappear in his truck. As we know, a couple of days later, Arliss and Dwayne are found murdered up near Jellico. Cletus said everyone in the family figured that Russell killed them. And that's not all! Cletus also told us that Ambrose was the one who was giving the Eland's all the trouble they've been having. So, that pretty well winds things up. Looks like the entire Stroud clan could be spending an extended amount of time behind bars, except for Cletus. Depending on how things work out, he'll have to serve time, but it won't be nearly as long as the rest of his relatives."

"Sounds like this whole mess is over," said Dalton, "but the one thing that's still hanging out there is who killed Luke Pardee?"

"I know," commented Grant sadly. "It just seems like that particular murder keeps getting shoved on the back burner when you consider everything else that's happened. I told you that I had suspicions about Zeb Gilling and Buddie Knapp being somehow involved, but I think that ship may have sailed. Buddie's getting ready to move out of state and I really don't have anything solid to go on in regard to either Buddie or Zeb. To tell you the truth, I think everyone would just as soon be done with it and move on. I'm tired of investigating murders. I'm ready for Townsend to get back to normal and I'm going to start right now by going upstairs to bed."

Getting up from the table, Grant walked down the hall but then hesitated as he addressed Dalton, "I know how you are when it comes to pie. I'm planning on sleeping in. There better be a slice of that pie waiting for me when I get up."

CHAPTER TWENTY

ZEB PUT DOWN HIS FORK AND GOT UP FROM THE CHAIR.
"Why is it that the damn phone rings every time we sit down to eat?"

"I'll get it, you just eat," said Betty as she made her way across the kitchen to answer the phone. "And anyway, how would the person calling know that we're eating?"

"It's noon, isn't it!" bellowed Zeb.

Picking up the phone, Betty spoke softly, "Gilling residence!"

After listening for a few seconds, she placed her hand over her mouth. "Oh, I'm so sorry to hear that! I'll tell Zeb. Thank you so much for calling."

"What's going on now?" grumbled Zeb as he stuffed a forkful of salad into his mouth.

"Sad news! Buddie Knapp is in Blount Memorial. He had a serious heart attack. That was Jeanette Steel. You know her. She lives next door to the Knapp's. You should go see him as soon as possible. She said his condition is serious."

Irritated, Zeb answered, *"No,* I don't know who Jeanette Steel is and, *yes,* I will go see him!"

Walking to the table, Betty demanded, "When? After all, he just happens to be one of your best friends! I would think that you'd be more concerned...show some compassion!"

"Dammit! Can't a man eat his lunch in peace! I'll go as soon as I finish eating and get cleaned up some."

"Well, aren't we crabby today! You look fine. Just go like you are. I'm sure Buddie won't care how you look."

Zeb threw his fork down and shoved the chair back. "Alright already. I'll go! I'll go just the way I am. Anything else?"

"You might want to change your attitude on the way over there. Tell Mary how sorry I am. Please tell her to call me if there's anything I can do..." She barely finished the sentence when Zeb was out the front door, slamming it behind him.

Backing out of the garage, Zeb stopped for a moment and contemplated going back into the house and apologizing to Betty.

It wasn't her fault that his current stage of life was such a mess. Besides that, Buddie was supposed to be leaving for Alabama in a day or two. It would have been a lot easier with him out of town. Why couldn't he have waited a few more days to have a heart attack? Reaching down, he rubbed his hand over the front of his shirt. He hated going anywhere without at least washing his face, combing his hair and having on clean clothes. It was a habit he had been used to all his life. Growing up, even though his parents were of moderate means, his mother always insisted that he look respectable when he left the house. Today, was the first time in quite awhile that he had broken that rule.

He remembered that not too long ago, and for many years, he had met with the guys for coffee at the Parkway Grocery. Luke always wore the same old blue jacket with the holes in the sleeves, Charley was usually unshaven and in need of a haircut. Buddie was pretty presentable, but Asa usually waltzed in looking and smelling like he had just tangled with a wildcat. Asa and the others always teased him that he didn't need to get all gussied up just to have coffee with them. He recalled times in high school when they referred to him as "pretty boy!" It always made him mad and more times than not he wound up rolling around on the ground, punching at the laughing Asa, who had always been stronger than him.

Shaking his head, he tried to clear away his thoughts. Those memories had been buried deep inside of him for years. It wasn't until Asa was murdered that a lot of the past has been dredged up. The five of them had been the best of friends. They laughed and joked with one another until that fateful morning at the Pender farm when four of them made the worst mistake of their lives. Charley had been fortunate enough not to be with them on that horrible day. It took a couple of years following the Pender murders for them to return to their old ways. They always wondered when the day would arrive when they'd hear the words, "You're under arrest!" They made a pact. The Iron Mountain incident, as they called it, was never to be mentioned again. For over forty years they had kept that terrible day a secret, but now he and Buddie were running right on the edge of the cliff. Grant Denlinger was starting to ask questions and was getting close to the truth. Now, Zeb felt like his life was just a series of one bad day following the next. Times didn't seem so good to him anymore. His life had become a dull routine that was beginning to grind on his nerves.

At the hospital, Zeb didn't need directions to the ICU. He had been to the hospital many times over the course of his own lifetime, both as a patient and a visitor. As he pushed open the large stainless steel double doors, he was greeted by the sounds of the medical machinery that was the life support for those lying in the small cubicles behind the long glass wall. At the end of the hall he entered the crowded family lounge and looked for any familiar face he could find. He excused himself as he passed a group of men, and then in the corner, he saw Mary seated on a leather couch. When she saw Zeb approaching her eyes filled with tears. Reaching out to him, she sobbed, "I'm so glad you could make it Zeb. It doesn't look good for Buddie. They've got him stabilized right now, but they said that the heart attack took a lot out of him. They're keeping a close watch on him."

Seating himself next to her, Zeb held her hand and asked, "What happened?"

"He complained about being so tired the last few days. I thought it was just from all the work he had been doing to get ready for the move. He was in the study packing up some books when I heard him call out my name. When I got back to the study, there he was lying on the floor."

A middle-aged man that Zeb did not recognize approached and placed his hand on Mary's shoulder as he spoke to Zeb, "I'm sure you don't remember me. I'm Buddie's son, Don."

Zeb shook his hand and answered, "I remember you vaguely. I haven't seen you since you left Townsend. That must be at least twenty years ago."

Don nodded. "That's about right. My wife and I were so excited about Buddie and Mary moving down to Alabama. Now, instead of my father coming down to us, we're back here with him." Reaching down, he took his mother's hand. "Mom, the doctor said you can visit with dad for a few minutes."

Zeb stood. "Look, I think I'll head on back home. I know they won't let me in to see him. I just wanted to let him know that I was thinking about him."

Mary reached up and touched him on the cheek. "I'll make sure he knows you were here to see him. You've always been such a good friend. When this is all over, you'll have to come visit us in Alabama."

Mary's idea of Zeb visiting them down in Alabama would never play out. Later that night, Betty received a call from Mary, telling her that Buddie passed away at three o'clock in the afternoon. Buddie was to be cremated. He was going to be traveling to Alabama in a brass urn with his name engraved on its side. Since their house was already sold and all the furniture packed up, Mary decided it would be for the best to have the service as soon as possible, so she could head down south with her son and daughter-in-law. A memorial service was to be held in two days.

Betty baked two pies and a chocolate cake for the luncheon that was to be held in the church basement following the service. She pressed Zeb's blue suit and shined his black dress shoes. After her shower, she put her hair up in curlers and made sure she had a pair of nylons minus any runs. All the while she was busy, Zeb sat in his La-Z-Boy and watched television. Betty imagined that he was experiencing a great deal of grief, so rather than nagging him about getting ready, she just let him be.

Zeb wasn't in mourning. Beneath his, what seemed like sadness, he was reveling in his thoughts: he was the last man standing! He was completely in control of his future. He now didn't have to worry about whether Buddie would cave in and run to Axel Brody and reveal what happened forty years ago over in the Iron Mountains. The secret was all his now. It was like a giant weight had been lifted from his shoulders. Smiling to himself, he thought, *I might even shed a tear today!*

The church was three-quarters full by the time Zeb and Betty arrived. They took seats in the second from the last row as the pastor walked to the podium. Grant, also arriving late, slid into the pew next to Betty. Leaning over, she spoke in a low voice, "Good to see you, Grant. How is Dana Beth and that lovely daughter of yours?"

Zeb gave her a harsh look and said, "Shh, be quiet!" He gave Grant a slight nod and wondered why he was there. Maybe Axel had sent him to the service to spy on him. He didn't care. Now that

Buddie was dead there was no one that Grant, Brody or anyone for that matter, could talk to about the Pender murders. He was free and clear!

The service was over in less than an hour. Betty cried along with most of the congregation when the organist played *Amazing Grace*. A few people, including Mary's son, stood at the podium and eulogized Buddie's life. Betty asked Zeb if he wanted to speak, but he begged off, saying that it would just be too difficult for him.

After the congregation stood and sang a final song, everyone left and began filing down to the basement. Zeb was glad. He was hungry and the smell from all the food that had been brought in wafted up from the basement. Zeb said hello and nodded to some of the people he knew as he patiently waited in line to fill his plate. Betty was talking to a group of women and he knew if he waited for her, the food would be gone.

Ten minutes later, when he got up to go to the dessert table she was still busy talking. Just as he reached for a slice of chocolate pie, someone called his name. Turning, he saw Mary coming toward him. Motioning toward an empty table, she spoke, "There is something I need to tell you, Zeb. I almost forgot about it, but when you walked by me earlier, I remembered. Please sit with me for a minute." Following her to the table, he sat across from her.

"I am so tired," she said. "I didn't sleep at all last night. This is the only time in our marriage that we haven't been together. I miss him so much already. What I wanted to tell you is that about two months ago, or maybe it was three, I discovered Buddie sitting at his desk in the basement. He spent the better part of two hours down there writing something. That struck me as quite strange. Buddie wasn't much on writing. I mean, it was all I could do to get him to sign a birthday card or initial something that we needed to mail off. When he was finished later that day, he asked me for two envelopes and stamps."

Zeb folded his hands on top of the table and tried to act like he was interested in one of her long stories that she had a habit of telling. *Get to the point,* he thought. *Buddie always said you were one of the most long winded people he knew!*

Rambling on, Mary continued, "Well anyway, I didn't have any business envelopes, but I did have a few square envelopes left over from some extra greeting cards. I gave them to him and he folded two different sheets of paper and put then inside the envelopes. When he took out our address book and started to address the envelopes, I asked him how did he know who the letters were for. He told me that they were identical. Then, he did something that was very odd. He told me to file the envelopes with our important papers and to make sure that I mailed them off in the event of his death. Needless to say, I was quite concerned. Buddie just laughed and told me that he wasn't planning on dying for a long time and that the two letters were just some things that needed to be said. I still wasn't satisfied with his answer but then he asked me to respect his privacy, so I didn't think anything more about it; that is until the other day, when it popped back into my mind. I was looking for Buddie's birth certificate and some insurance papers when I found the two letters. One is addressed to you and the other to Chief Brody."

Zeb could feel the color draining from his face, Suddenly, he felt sick to his stomach. Mary was still talking but he wasn't listening. Interrupting her, he asked nervously, "Do you have my letter with you?"

"Actually, I was going to bring both of them with me, but my son found them lying on the table in the foyer yesterday, so he mailed them for me. I just didn't want you to be shocked about getting a letter from your friend Buddie after he had passed on. I would think that you should get it in the mail today." Placing her hand on top of his, she began to tear up, "I just want to thank you for all the years you've been such a good friend to my husband. I'm sure the letter is nothing more than him saying just that. Buddie always did have a hard time expressing his feelings."

Zeb stood. "I have to go Mary. I'm not feeling very well." Searching for Betty, he finally spotted her eating at a table with some other ladies. Approaching, he apologized, "Excuse me, ladies. I need to go home, Betty. Suddenly, I have a headache. Do you think you could get a ride home with someone?"

Betty was surprised, "Well, for heaven's sake! If you can wait for just a few minutes, I'll be ready to go home myself."

Buddie objected, "No, I need to go home now!"

Betty, annoyed at his outburst, feigned a smile at the other ladies as she remarked, "Well, go ahead then, Zeb. I'll see you at home. I'll grab a lift with someone."

Buddie realized that his emotions were getting the best of him and that it was showing. He apologized to Betty and her friends, "I'm sorry! I didn't mean to go off like that. It's just that my head is really hurting." Kissing his wife on her cheek, he commented, "I'll be fine. I just need to go home and lay down for awhile."

Outside in the car, Zeb fumbled with his keys. His hands shook as he put the key in the ignition. *What in the hell has Buddie done? That son of a bitch! Even after he's dead, he can't leave well enough alone! Maybe it's not as bad as I think. Who am I kidding? It's probably worse! Especially, since he sent the same letter to both Axel and me!*

Zeb stopped the car at the end of the driveway and walked over to the mailbox. Inside, he found a grocery ad from the IGA, a bill from the electric company and an ominous white envelope with no return address. He removed the envelope and stuck it in his pocket and headed for the garage.

Turning on the light above the workbench, he sat down on a high stool and ripped open the envelope. Reading the first two lines gave him a glimmer of hope as Buddie apologized for anyone who had been hurt by what he had done. Zeb's head sank as he read the next few sentences where Buddie explained in detail what happened at the Pender farm over forty years ago. The one good thing was that Buddie never mentioned that Zeb had shot the Pender's or any of their animals. It was the next paragraph when Zeb realized that the situation was now hopeless. Buddie wrote about Luke Pardee's murder. Buddie talked about how he, Zeb and Luke had discussed the Pender murders and how Luke had decided to turn himself in. Buddie wrote further that he really wasn't sure that Luke would do it, but Zeb was convinced he was going to tell Chief Brody the next day and that they should kill Luke.

Zeb stopped reading for a moment as he thought, *That's a damn lie! I never once said that we should kill Luke. I remember the conversation that day. I said that I was going over to Luke's to talk some sense into him. I got my rifle and went over to Luke's house. All I really wanted to do was scare him enough so that he wouldn't go to Brody. Luke said he didn't care if I killed him. He felt like he was dead inside anyway and by the next afternoon he would be sitting in a jail cell with me and Buddie. I can't remember pulling the trigger, but then I saw the look of utter surprise in his eyes as he was blasted back into the foyer. I just turned and ran!*

It was all there in Buddie's handwriting. He had gone to Luke's house the night before Luke was found murdered. Buddie had gone there to reason with Luke and beg him not to go to Brody. He went on to explain in writing that he had parked his car down a block from Luke's house and walked up the street in the shadows. When he arrived at the corner of the property, he heard the shotgun blast and then saw Zeb running down the driveway.

He went on to say that if they hadn't committed the Pender murders years in the past, Russell Pearl would have never killed all those people. He felt that he, Zeb, Asa and Luke were responsible for their deaths. He hated the idea that he was so weak and scared about going to jail and ruining his family's life, but now that his life had come to an end, he hoped his family could find some way to forgive him. Zeb killed one of his best friends and now he should have to pay for what he had done. He killed Luke to protect himself, and now, he had to answer for that. Buddie ended the letter by stating that he was sending an exact copy of the letter to Chief Brody.

Zeb laid the letter down on the workbench. If only he would have known that when he told himself jokingly in the house earlier that *he might* shed a tear at Buddie's funeral that the tears would come later. He began to sob, softly at first but then the crying became an uncontrollable emotion of the reality of what was going to happen to him now. Burying his head in his hands he mumbled, "Why me, Buddie? All of you are dead now: Asa, Charley, Luke and now Buddie. Why do I have to be the one who pays? I only did what Buddie couldn't do to protect the two of us. No one would have ever found out the truth! Now, it's too late! When Brody reads his letter, he'll come for me! I can't let that happen!"

Kenny Jacks pulled into the lot of the Townsend Police Department, parked his car, got out and ran around to the passenger side door. Axel grunted as he scooted across the seat, while trying to keep from hitting his right arm that was secured by a medical sling. Kenny smiled and asked, "How do you like having your own personal chauffer, Chief?"

Getting awkwardly out of the car, Brody growled, "I don't! Just get over there and open the damn office door for me!"

Axel was no sooner in the doorway when Marge stood and spoke up in an upbeat manner, "Well, look who's back! What are you doing back here so soon?"

"Where the hell else would I go?" barked Axel. "I didn't get shot in the ass, ya know! I can still sit at my desk. Two days off is long enough!"

Marge realized that Brody was in one of his normal grumpy moods and apparently getting shot in the arm wasn't making his general demeanor any more pleasant. There didn't seem to be much sense in trying to make small talk with him, so she picked up the mail and followed Axel down the hall. In his office, she watched as Axel struggled out of his jacket. Placing the stack of mail on the corner of his desk, she commented, "Here's the mail. It's all official business. I sorted through it and pitched all the junk mail." Holding up the square envelope, she remarked, "I guess this must be a get well card from one of your many fans."

Axel eased himself down into his chair as he replied, "Very funny, Marge! If it's from anyone who knows me, it's probably a card wishin' me dead! Throw it out."

"You don't even want to open it! How can you throw away mail when you're not even sure what's inside?"

Axel reached across the desk. "Gimme that damn card!" Grabbing it out of Marge's hand, he flipped on the paper shredder and ran it through.

Marge rolled her eyes and turned to walk back out front, but was stopped as Axel asked, "Where's Denlinger?"

"He called earlier and said he'd be in around nine. I expect him any minute. If there's nothing else I have to get back to the phone, plus I've got some filing to do."

"Well, got damn!" said Axel loudly, "He's makin' his own hours now? Soon as he gets here, I want him and Kenny back here in the office!" Opening the morning paper, he spoke to himself as Marge gladly escaped down the hall. "Let's see if these newspaper clowns have anythin' else new to add to the way we cleared up that mess at the Stroud's."

It wasn't even a minute later when Axel forced himself out of his chair, tucked the newspaper under his left arm and started down the hall to his *other* office. Axel closed the bathroom door and Marge knew she had at least ten minutes of peace until he came back out.

The phone rang and she turned from the row of filing cabinets and picked up. "Townsend Police Department." She listened for a few seconds and then said, "I'll have someone over there right away!"

Running down the hall to the deputy's office, she leaned in the doorway and spoke to Kenny, "Kenny, call Grant and tell him to go straight to Zeb Gilling's house. The fire department is on the way. I'll call the coroner and see if he wants to meet Grant out there."

Axel, overhearing what Marge said, yelled through the door, "What's goin' on out there? Is there a fire? Somebody have an accident? Can anybody hear me? What the hell's goin' on?"

Marge yelled back, "It's Zeb Gilling! Looks like he committed suicide! He hung himself in his garage. Grant's on the way over there right now."

Brody yelled back, "Send Kenny also. I'll be right out!"

When Grant received the call he pulled to the side of the road and asked Kenny to repeat what he had said. He then pulled out, turned on his flashing lights and the siren which he seldom used. Making a U-turn on the Parkway he sped toward Zeb's house. *What in the world happened,* he thought. *I just saw him an hour ago eating in the church basement. He didn't seem that upset about Buddie. I hope this isn't about what I think it is!*

Minutes later, Grant arrived at the front of the Gilling residence. It always amazed him how people reacted to fire trucks, ambulances and police cars. Their emotions always seemed to change: first, it was a sense of dread, hoping that the emergency vehicle was not going to their home. Then their curiosity set in and the irresistible urge to find out what was happening took over. The scene in front of Zeb's house was no different. A fire truck and an ambulance were positioned next to the garage, a number of neighbors were gathered on the front sidewalk. Grant parked behind the ambulance, got out and entered the side door of the garage.

Randy Hooks, one of the local firemen was standing over a dark green body bag laying in the middle of the concrete floor. "Have any details yet? What have we got?" asked Grant.

"Not much," replied Randy, pointing at a stool tipped over on its side. "Looks like he stood on that and then kicked it out from beneath him. I've been in contact with the coroner. He said that since there weren't any signs of a struggle or forced entry he told us to cut the body down, but leave the rope around his neck. One of the EMTs filled out an approximate time of death form. We're getting ready to take the body over to the hospital. We're just about done here, so it looks like you're on the bubble. The man, who is one of his neighbors who found him is outside if you want to ask him any questions. His name is Frank Howard. He called Betty's daughter and she's in the house with her mother now. If you wouldn't mind I'd appreciate it if you'd direct traffic so we can back out of here."

Once the driveway was clear, Grant asked Mr. Howard a few questions then walked back into the garage. Nothing seemed out of place. There were the usual standard garage shelves lined with half used paint cans and cleaning supplies. On the back wall there a long workbench. The light over top of the bench was still on. Reaching up to turn it off, Grant noticed a folded piece of paper half hidden under some work gloves next to a torn envelope. He opened the letter and began to read.

CHAPTER TWENTY-ONE

GRANT SAT IN THE CRUISER FOR A MOMENT WONDERING what he was really doing here. He had been on the Townsend Police Force close to two years now and he thought that he had done a good job. Looking at the station, he knew Chief Brody was inside the building, just like any other day, but it was getting harder and harder to deal with him. He was getting tired of being put down by Axel and being referred to as Wonder Boy. It had to stop and *today was the day!*

Entering the office, Grant nodded at Marge and sat down in the chair next to her desk. He was about to speak, but was interrupted by Axel's booming voice that cut the air, "Is that Kenny!"

Grant rolled his eyes and Marge whispered, "The damn old fool! Why doesn't he get off his lazy ass and come out here and see for himself?"

Grant yelled back down the hall, "No, it's me, Grant! Kenny went after some guy going about ninety down the Parkway. If you're interested in what happened over at the Gillings' I can tell you. I was there too, in case you forgot!"

Axel's voice echoed back down the hall, "Well get your butt back here and fill me in on what happened!"

Grant winked at Marge, got up and ambled down the hall to Brody's office. He sat down in front of Axel's desk without waiting to be told to do so. Reaching into his pocket, he pulled out the letter Buddie wrote. Taking it out of the torn envelope, he tossed it on the desk.

"What's this?" Brody asked smartly.

Leaning forward, Grant demanded, "Just read it!"

Axel picked up the folded piece of paper, smoothed out the edges and began to read. Grant watched Axel's facial expressions change as he read each line. Between the "hmm's" and "I'll be damn's," Axel shook his head and slammed his hand down on the desk. "Can you believe this? Zeb killed Luke! Those four ol' coots lived right here in town all those years and we never even suspected they killed the Pender's!" Pitching the letter back down on the desk, he threw his hands into the air. "Talk about a stroke of luck! Looks like we get to close two murder cases in one day!"

Reaching out, Grant tapped the letter with his index finger. "Did you receive a copy of this letter today?"

Axel shot Grant a look of dismay, "Hell no, I never got no letter!"

Grant held up the ripped envelope. "Are you sure? It would have come in a plain white envelope just like this one."

"I said no! You callin' me a liar?"

"I'll just go ask Marge. She may have forgotten to give it to you." Grant started to get up from the chair, but was stopped by Marge who was standing in the doorway of Axel's office.

Leaning against the doorjamb, she politely defended herself, "Have you ever known me to forget to give Axel his mail, Grant?"

"No, not that I can ever recall."

Walking over to the desk, Marge picked up the envelope and pointed it at Axel. "I gave the Chief here an envelope that was identical to this one. I told him it was probably a get well card and that he needed to at least open it and read what it said." Tossing the empty envelope toward Axel, she explained, "He ran it through the shredder!"

"Marge!" demanded Brody. "I think we've heard enough from you. Now, why don't you go back out to your office and answer the phone like you're paid to do!"

Marge shot Axel and icy stare, then turned and walked out of the office.

Blowing off her comments, Axel waved his hand. "Maybe I did get the letter...maybe I didn't! Either way, it doesn't matter now."

"Doesn't matter!" exclaimed Grant. "Are you kidding me, Chief? If I hadn't found that letter or if Zeb had tossed it before he hung himself, there'd still be two unsolved murder cases on the books; one current and the other over forty years old! Do you even realize Axel, that if you would have taken the time to read the letter Buddie sent you, then you might have had enough time to get over to Zeb's before he took his own life! And, another thing, by running that letter through the damn shredder, you destroyed pertinent evidence. So, either way, I think it does make a difference...a big difference!"

Axel slammed his fist down loudly on his desk as Kenny walked in the outer office door. Hearing the disturbance down the hall, he asked Marge, "What's going on back there?"

Marge put her finger to her lips as she whispered, "Shh, those two are really going at it! Grant is giving the Chief some well-deserved criticism."

Axel was livid as he pointed his finger at Grant. "If I didn't have my arm in this sling, I'd punch you right on your damn nose! This matter is over...done...closed! I'll take care of the details, because that's what I'm paid to do. Understand, Denlinger! I'm the Chief of Police...you're one of *my* deputies! Don't tell me how to do my job. When you're sittin' in this chair, then you can make all the decisions about what you think is right, but until then, I'd suggest very strongly that you just concentrate on bein' just what you are; a deputy! Now, get the hell out of my office and finish up your report. After that, I want you to hit the streets. Furthermore, when the news about Gilling hits, I'm puttin' you in charge of crowd control. You got it?"

Grant stood and fired back at Axel, "No, I don't think you get it!" He unpinned the badge from his shirt, unbuckled his holster and threw them both on the desk. "I quit! As of this moment I am no longer an officer on the Townsend Police Force! *You got it?*"

Brody, temporarily set back on his heels, was speechless, but he recovered quickly. "You can't quit just like that. You are required to give me a month's notice. That's protocol! You quit without givin' me proper notice and you'll never serve as an officer in this state again!"

"That makes it even better!" said Grant as he turned, left the office and started down the hall where he was greeted by the stunned faces of Kenny and Marge. Grant reached for Kenny's hand. "Thanks for all your work. I've enjoyed serving with you." He hesitated, then spoke to Marge, "What can I say? This has been a long time coming. You're one of my favorite people." Bending over, he kissed her on the cheek. "Take care of that old bastard back there in that office. You're the only one who can keep him in line. Maybe I'll see you guys around town."

Dalton met Grant at the front door. "Heard you pull up. What are you doing home so early?"

"Long story, Dalton," said Grant, "but let's just say for right now, I have good news and bad news! Which do you want to hear first?"

"I'd rather hear the bad news first, so then I can enjoy the good. Let's sit. I just put a pot of coffee on."

While Dalton was pouring coffee into two cups, Grant broke the bad news. "Zeb Gilling hung himself in his garage earlier today..." For the next few minutes Grant continued with the details. "...and so, it looks like there is finally some closure on not only Luke Pardee's murder, but after all these years, the Pender murders as well."

Placing a cup in front of Grant, Dalton sat and remarked, "Wow, that's quite a shocker! It's going to take a little while for the bad news to sink in, so give me the good news."

Grant smiled. It was the first time he smiled since Dana Beth left. "I quit the force today. I turned in my badge and gun and just walked out. Before you say anything, I know leaving that abruptly wasn't right, but I was afraid if I stayed much longer, I was going to wind up on the wrong side of the law."

Dalton gave Grant a strange look as if he didn't understand.

Grant cleared up the confusion as he explained, "I would have been arrested for assault and battery after I beat the hell out of Axel!"

Dalton took a drink then added, "I had an inkling that might be part of the news. Axel called a few minutes just before you got here and said that if you came back to the office by noon, he would forget what happened. He didn't elaborate, but from the tone of his voice I figured you two must have gotten into it."

"Hope he doesn't hold his breath," said Grant. "I've got to get my priorities straight. I've been so miserable without Dana Beth and Crystal Ann that I don't want to experience another day without them. After we finish talking, I'm going to get out of the this monkey suit of a uniform, get cleaned up, drive up to Knoxville and book a flight down to Ft. Meyers." He stood, walked around the table and put his hand on Dalton's shoulder. "I hope I didn't insult you by calling my police uniform a monkey suit. I know that you were the chief of police here in town for a long time. I know how much you loved and were dedicated to your job. I guess it was just different for you than being an officer of the law has been for me."

Dalton reached up and patted Grant's hand. "Look, your career on the Townsend Police Force was much shorter than mine, but the two years you did manage to pack in from what I've seen has been a lot more stressful than the two decades I spent wearing the badge. I never even shot my gun; you on the other hand had to kill a man. We never had one murder; you've had to deal with a number of killings. You got shot in the line of duty; I never got shot. Don't worry about what I or anyone thinks. You've got to do what you think is best for you and your family. Now, go and get your wife and daughter."

"Thanks, Dalton." Walking to the sink to rinse out his cup, Grant made the mental list of things he needed to do out loud: "I've got to give Doug Eland a call and let him know that he and Max can relax. The Stroud's are out of their lives for good. I need to pack, go to the bank. I better get moving."

Eight hundred miles away, Dana Beth grabbed a bottle of water out of the fridge and headed for the beach for her morning run. It had become a ritual that she had started from the first day she arrived in Ft. Meyers. It gave her time alone to think about the recent events that were going on in her life. Each day, she had become closer to accepting what had happened. Ruth had been a saint; holding her when she cried and reassuring her that everything was going to be alright. Ruth also took care of Crystal Ann when, on occasion, Dana Beth had a meltdown and just wanted to be alone.

Trotting along next to the water's edge, she gazed out into the early morning tide when suddenly she felt a sharp pain in her left foot. As she hopped on one foot, she let out a string of "Ow, ow, ow's!" Sitting down on the wet sand, she examined the bottom of her tennis shoe and discovered a sharp broken piece of shell that had pierced the rubber sole and went into her foot.

As she carefully removed the shell, then the tennis shoe, she heard a woman's voice, "Are you okay?"

Dana Beth looked up into field of bright yellow, red and orange flowers covering an oversized beach robe. A large, floppy straw hat sat on the woman's head and her eyes were shielded from view by a pair of dark sunglasses. "Yeah, I think so," said Dana Beth. "I just stepped on a broken shell."

The woman squatted down and opened a straw tote as she

stated, "I come to the beach prepared." She pulled out a small first-aid kit as she went on, "Here's a sterile pad and a band-aid. I've seen you on the beach every day. You live around here?"

Dana Beth took the pad and the band-aid and answered, "No, just visiting. My name is Dana Beth Denlinger. Thanks for the bandage."

"Not a problem! My name is Billie Westfield. I live right there!" She pointed to a huge white beach house sitting just behind them. Plopping down next to Dana Beth, she retrieved a small travel cup from the tote along with a cold thermos. "Want a drink? Strawberry margarita. I just made it up before I came down here."

"No thank you. It's a wee bit too early for me." Looking directly at the woman's dark sunglasses, Dana Beth asked, "Are you allergic to the sun?"

Pulling back her shock of long red hair, Billie motioned toward the early morning sun. "Honey, if I let the sun get at this body, I would be one big freckle with a blister on it." Changing the subject, she asked, "So, you have a baby right? The other woman I've seen you with on the beach must be your mother. Don't get me wrong. I haven't been spying on you. It's just that I don't have much to do, so I sit out on my deck and watch people on the beach."

Dana Beth looked at the house Billie had pointed out. "That's an awfully big house for one person."

"I know. I thought that's what I wanted but now it doesn't mean a thing to me. I had a husband but he died last year."

"Oh, I'm so sorry," said Dana Beth compassionately.

"That's alright. I'm pretty much over that now. He was a good man, my Harold. But me, well, I'm trying really hard to get over it. He was doing the best he could, but I wanted more! We were living in a mobile home and I wanted a house that wasn't attached to wheels. He wanted to please me so he took on a second job driving a delivery truck. A few months later, a semi ran him off the road and he was killed. I bought the beach house with the money from the settlement. To tell you the truth, I'd live in a tent if I could just have him back. Like I said; he was a good husband and I never gave him a break. How about you? Are you married?"

"I am. My husband is back in Tennessee."

"Can I ask why he's not here with you or is that too personal?"

"It's really a long story. I just needed some time to figure out what I want to do next. I..." The tears began to well up in her eyes. Wiping away the tears, she apologized, "I'm sorry. I haven't talked much about it since I got here. I think about it all the time, but I've never tried to explain it out loud."

Billie shifted in the sand, making herself comfortable. "I'm a good listener."

Dana Beth was amazed that a total stranger had walked into her life and here she was about to share the intimate details about the last two years. "My father was a serial killer and so was my uncle. My husband is a police officer, but he kept the information about my father a secret from me. I was kidnapped by my uncle and that's when I found out the truth about my father. That was right before my husband killed my uncle..."

Billie sat up and put up her hands, "Whoa, whoa, whoa, that's some heavy baggage! You better back up and start over." She unscrewed the top off her cup and took a large swallow. Leaning back on one elbow, she let out a satisfying sigh and said, "Okay, I'm ready."

Nearly a half hour later, her cup was empty and she had listened to each and every word Dana Beth said without interrupting her again.

"So you see, Billie, it really hurt me that Grant didn't think I was strong enough to handle the truth. I love him and we never keep secrets from each other. This has really been hard to take. I love him so much and after what you told me about what happened to your husband, I wonder if I can ever live without him. I think I shifted the blame to him because I'm so ashamed to think about the horrible things my father and uncle did along with the other crazy family I'm related to. If Grant would have known all of this before we got married, I'm sure I'd still be single. I just keep thinking that if I stay away a while it'll give him time to think about if he wants to stay with me the rest of his life. Now, I find out that I'm going to inherit a ton of money and that's hard to accept, considering where it came from."

"If you want my two cents," said Billie, "I think you've got this all wrong. I think your husband loves you so much, he didn't want you to suffer one second with the horrible truth about your father. If he didn't want to be with you, he didn't have to risk his life to save you from uncle what's his name. Besides, we all have one or two nutcases in our families. Maybe they're not serial killers, but they can still drive you up a wall. What your father and uncle did has nothing to do with you. You haven't committed a crime. If I had someone who loved me, I sure wouldn't be sitting here on this beach. I'd be on the next flight out of here. Don't make the same mistakes I've made. You'll regret it the rest of your life!"

Dana Beth reached over and gave Billie a hug. Falling back on the sand, they both laughed as Billie remarked, "Look at us; lying on the sand like we don't have a care in the world. I think I'm going to put my house on the market this week and then head back to the Midwest where I belong." Sitting up, she emphasized, "I think you need to go make that plane reservation."

Dana Beth stood up and brushed the sand from her body. "Thanks so much, Billie. I want to give you my home number before I leave. Let's stay in touch."

Billie stood and made her way across the sand. "See ya around kiddo!"

Opening the sliding door at the condo, Dana Beth called out to Ruth, "Mom, where are you? I'm going to call the airlines. I want to go home."

Ruth's answer came from upstairs, "I'm up here with the baby. There's someone in the kitchen who would like to see you."

Turning around, Dana Beth's eyes widened when she saw Grant leaning against the kitchen counter, eating a sandwich. At a loss for words, she finally exclaimed, "I can't believe this! How long have you been here?" Rushing across the room she jumped into his arms almost knocking him over. He covered her face with kisses and traces of mayonnaise.

"Well, hello to you too," Grant said. "I've been here for about an hour, I guess. I've been playing with Crystal Ann. I was just about ready to come look for you." Holding her at arm's length, he complimented her, "You really look great! You're so tan."

"Never mind me. What are you doing here in the middle of the week? Aren't you supposed to be at work?"

"Nope! As of yesterday, I'm unemployed. I quit the

department. I couldn't take another minute away from you and besides that, Axel and I were at the end of our rope with each other." Grant pulled her close and put his face close to her hair. "You smell like the beach. I love you more than I can ever explain. I hope you know that. Whatever problems we have I know we can work them out."

"Let's go sit out on the patio. I'll grab us a couple of beers. We've got so much to talk about."

Coming down the stairs with the baby, Ruth suggested, "How does burgers sound for lunch later on?"

Just prior to the noon hour, Dana Beth bit into her burger. She wasn't interested in hearing any bad news, but Grant insisted on telling both her and Ruth about what happened with Zeb and the Stroud's. "It's all behind us now," said Grant. "Over and done with!"

"It's been two crazy years," commented Ruth, "I wish Conrad was here with us now. I'm sure he would have been just as upset as the rest of us about what has happened in Townsend."

Dana Beth gave Grant a furtive look as if to say, *I'll tell you later!*

Lunch over, Ruth motioned toward the beach. "Why don't you two go for a walk. I'll take care of the dishes. Crystal Ann is just about ready for a nap anyway. You two need some time alone."

Taking his mother-in-law up on her offer, Grant stood and took Dana Beth's hand as they started for the beach. "Excellent idea. Let's go, the ocean looks nice. It's really beautiful here." Crossing a small sand dune, the ocean spread out before them, Grant took in a deep breath of salt air. "I can see why people want to settle on the coast." He watched a group of seagulls swoop down over the water, the sun shining off their wings.

"I suppose," said Dana Beth, "but without you here, it was just a place to escape. I've been pretty miserable most of the time." She looked into Grant's eyes. "I hope you can forgive me for running away. While I was here I had quite a few long talks with myself. I was ashamed. Ashamed of my family, ashamed of what I put you through and I was afraid that you wouldn't want me back!"

Giving her a hug, Grant ran is fingers through her hair. "Just try and get rid of me! It won't be that easy. You're my wife, my high school sweetheart. We have a beautiful child. I love you way too much to ever let you go."

They spent the entire day walking on the beach, taking an occasional swim and looking at the shells scattered along the shoreline, until the sun finally started to disappear below the horizon.

Sitting on a log that had washed up on the beach sometime in the past, Dana Beth finally told Grant what she had been putting off saying. "I never told my mother the truth about Conrad. I just couldn't do it, Grant. I couldn't destroy the image she had of him, even though it's all a lie. I've finally figured out why you didn't want to tell me. I feel the same way about mom. He was *her* Conrad! Not the one we knew. I'm going to let her keep her memories." Changing the subject, she smiled. "I've been thinking a lot about all that money we're going to inherit. I think we should donate the cabin and the land up in Jellico to the Boy Scouts. It would be great place for a summer camp. We could even donate it in Conrad's name. I think that would make my mother feel good. I would also like to give some money to charity and the rest...well, I guess that belongs to us!"

"That's a good idea," agreed Grant. "Listen, there's something I want to talk with you about that I've had on my mind recently. Cletus Stroud has a daughter named Violet. She's a sweet little girl. Currently, she's in the custody of Child Protective Services. Since her mother is dead and her father will be in prison for quite some time to come she needs a foster home. Maybe being foster parents wouldn't be so bad...you know, an older sister for Crystal Ann."

Dana Beth squeezed his arm. "Well, look at you, you old softie! I would love to meet her." Standing, she walked a few feet toward the water, bent down, picked up a shell and tossed it toward the ocean. Turning back, she raised her hands as if she were displaying the beauty of where they were. "Now that you are no longer employed, we really have no reason to remain in Townsend. I've been thinking about giving Ruth the house back. I think she would like that. Maybe we could spend some time traveling, settle down in a small beach community along the east coast. We have a lifetime ahead of us."

Grant stood and walked to her. Taking both her hands in his, he smiled. "Hey, we can go anywhere we want. After all, we're millionaires!"

About the Authors

Originally from St. Louis, Marlene makes her home in Louisville, Kentucky. A wife, mother, grandmother and great grandmother, Marlene has a wide range of interests including watercolor and oil painting, yet writing has always been her passion. That comes through loud and clear in her wonderful novels!

These novels reflect a genuine sincerity with very strong characters to which her readers can relate. To quote Marlene: "It took me a long time to start writing, but now I can't stop. The stories just keep on coming."

Gary Yeagle was born and raised in Williamsport, PA, the birthplace of Little League Baseball. He grew up living just down the street from the site of the very first Little League game, played in 1939. He currently resides in St. Louis, Missouri, with his wife and four cats. He is the proud grandparent of three and is an active member of the New Hope United Methodist Church.

Gary is a Civil War buff, and enjoys swimming, spending time at the beach, model railroading, reading, and writing.

CIRCLE OF PREY

Ambition. Wealth. Greed. Power.
Truths turning to lies, father against son, friends becoming enemies, predator turning into prey and the circle continues.
Pitting man against the largest and one of the smartest animals on the planet makes for an interesting turn of events as you follow the journey of Jakuta, a bull elephant who is the ultimate prey.
[Modern Thriller, ages 14+]

Made in the USA
Columbia, SC
04 March 2020